CRASH INTO ME

"Sorenson's sleek sensuality and fresh new voice are sure to score big with readers."
—CINDY GERARD, *New York Times* bestselling author

"Beautiful characters, true-to-life emotions, heart-stopping action, and a bona fide bad guy—it doesn't get any better than this." —*RT Book Reviews*

"It was definitely hot. Sooo hot. Jill Sorenson is my new favorite romantic suspense author!"
—VICTORIA DAHL, author of *Start Me Up, Talk Me Down*

"*Crash Into Me* has so many unexpected events and twists that readers will be hooked all the way to the final page. Jill Sorenson is an author to watch!"
—*The Romance Reader Connection*

"Get comfy, because once you start reading *Crash Into Me,* you will not want to move for anything. It is like devouring decadent chocolate, you savor every bite, and cannot put it down until it is finished. Jill Sorenson does not miss a beat in this magnificent read with great pacing, intense emotions, and unexpected twists and turns that kept this reader guessing." —*Coffee Time Romance*

The Edge of Night

A Novel

JILL SORENSON

Bantam Books
New York

The Edge of Night is a work of fiction. Names, characters, places, and incidents are either the products of the author's imagination or are used fictitiously. Any resemblance to actual events, locales, or persons, living or dead, is entirely coincidental.

A Bantam Books Mass Market Original

Copyright © 2011 by Jill Sorenson

Excerpt from forthcoming novel copyright © 2011 by Jill Sorenson

Published in the United States by Bantam Books, an imprint of The Random House Publishing Group, a division of Random House, Inc., New York.

BANTAM BOOKS and colophon are registered trademarks of Random House, Inc.

This book contains an excerpt from a forthcoming novel by Jill Sorenson. This excerpt has been set for this edition only and may not reflect the final content of the forthcoming novel.

ISBN 978-0-553-59263-4
eBook ISBN 978-0-553-90737-7

Cover image: © Ryan McVay/Getty Images (man); © Digital Vision/ Getty Images (cityscape)

Printed in the United States of America

www.ballantinebooks.com

2 4 6 8 9 7 5 3 1

Bantam Books mass market edition: April 2011

Mom, you're the best.
I love you.

Acknowledgments

Thanks to the Chula Vista Police Department for granting me the incredible opportunity to ride along with the Gang Suppression Unit/Street Team. Sergeant Richard Powers was generous enough to sit down with me and answer every question I could think of. Officer Isabel Chavez drove me around all night, offering keen insights about her job and cruising by local graffiti hot spots so I could take pictures. It was a one-of-a-kind experience.

Special thanks to Anthony Ceja, project coordinator of the San Diego County Office of Education's Gang Prevention and Intervention Program. We met several years ago when I was working with at-risk youth in Oceanside, so I knew whom to call for information on local gangs. He does a great service for the community and doesn't talk down to kids.

Additional thanks to:

Jessica Sebor, my editor at Bantam Dell, for loving this story and helping me make it shine.

Joanna Clark, my fantastic new critique partner. Your input was invaluable.

Laurie McLean, my agent, for always believing in me.

My husband, Chris, who doubles as a Spanish-language consultant. He knows all of the good words and most of the bad ones.

My husband's family, for accepting me with open arms. Mama Lola, Rosaura, Anna, Maria, and the girls—*gracias!*

Jennifer, my great friend. You made being a young, single mom look easy. Now that I have kids of my own, I know it wasn't.

The Edge
of Night

1

In the city of Chula Vista, freshly tagged walls were a common sight.

The densely populated area, sandwiched between downtown San Diego and uptown Tijuana, was so close to the border it was practically in Mexico. Half of the billboard ads that sprawled above the crowded streets were in Spanish. Although the city's name translated literally as "beautiful view," most of its neighborhoods boasted quite the opposite. On a sweltering Saturday afternoon, the air shimmered with heat and exhaust fumes. A thin layer of grime coated every road sign.

From where Officer Noah Young sat, in the passenger side of a patrol car, the only view was of bumper-to-bumper traffic.

And wall-to-wall graffiti.

Noah deciphered the newly painted messages with an almost subconscious ease, drumming his fingertips against his thigh. It was only his second year on the gang unit and his fifth as a patrol officer, but already he understood the symbols better than his partner, Senior

Officer Patrick Shanley, did. Patrick had spent almost three decades on the Chula Vista Police Department and still hadn't bothered to learn Spanish, either.

While they waited for the light to change, Noah moved his gaze to the sidewalk, scanning pedestrians for illegal activity.

About a hundred feet ahead, two dark-haired boys climbed over the top of a chain-link fence and dropped down to the pavement below. The fence surrounded an old elementary school, long closed. It was now an active gang hideout.

The boys noticed the patrol car at the same time. Exchanging a worried glance, they started to walk in the opposite direction, shoulders together, heads down.

Noah guessed they were about eight or nine. Too young to be unsupervised, old enough to get in trouble. "Pull over."

Patrick shot him an impatient look. "For a couple of taggers?"

"They aren't taggers." It wouldn't have surprised him if they were, because he'd seen kindergartners with spray cans, but neither of these boys had a backpack. Their attitudes didn't necessarily imply guilt, either. There were plenty of other reasons to be wary of cops in this area. Legal status, cultural attitudes, general distrust.

"Just give me a minute," he said anyway.

With a show of reluctance, Patrick sounded the siren and jerked the car to a halt at the curb. Noah expected the kids to bolt, so he didn't waste time. He hopped out and caught up with them in three long strides, giving them no opportunity to run.

"*Esperanse, por favor,*" he said, holding his palm up.

The boys stopped and looked at him, feet shuffling on the hot sidewalk. Twin sets of brown eyes darted toward the squad car, the busy street, the chain-link fence. Their features were so similar, they had to be brothers.

"*Adónde van?*" Noah asked.

"To the market," the older boy said, his tone full of pride and contempt. *I speak English, asshole.*

Noah smiled in understanding. His Spanish was good and getting better every day, but it would never be perfect. He preferred to do interviews in English. "Why did you cut through the old schoolyard?"

"To save time."

He directed his next question to the younger boy, because he looked more frightened and less inclined to lie. "What did you see back there?"

The boy didn't answer.

"Nothing," his brother prompted, elbowing him in the ribs.

"*Nada,*" he mumbled, shifting from one foot to the other.

At six foot two, Noah was too tall to look this little kid in the eye. So he braced his hands on his knees and crouched down, level with him. The boy's gaze was filled with trepidation. "What did you see?"

"A woman," he whispered.

A chill traveled along Noah's spine. "Was she pretty?"

The kid's face paled. He made a gurgling sound, low in his throat. Noah jumped back in just enough time to avoid having his shoes splattered by what appeared to be a regurgitated orange Popsicle.

"Where is she?" Noah asked the older brother, feeling his own stomach lurch.

"By the stairs."

Patrick must have decided the impromptu shakedown had merit, because he left the comfort of the air-conditioned cruiser. Noah didn't agree with all of his partner's personal philosophies, but he appreciated his professional support.

On the street, they had each other's back.

Noah gestured for Patrick to keep an eye on the boys as he passed by. He climbed the fence quickly, taking care not to snag his gun belt on the chain link, and dropped down to the other side. He'd patrolled the area before, so he was familiar with its basic layout. The classrooms were housed in individual one-story buildings, low to the ground and evenly spaced. This kind of design was typical for schools in Southern California.

Right now, in early August, it was a blazing ninety-five degrees. Sweat trickled between Noah's shoulder blades, dampening his undershirt. His CVPD uniform was dark blue, and the heavy fabric seemed to suck up sun and hold in heat.

A slight breeze ruffled the short hair at the nape of his neck as he stepped into the shaded walkway and waited a few seconds for his eyes to adjust to the light.

The stairs were at the end of the walkway, between two administrative buildings. A fenced-in parking lot on the other side of the buildings was most likely the juveniles' point of entry. His rubber-soled shoes made very little sound as he advanced.

Every wall he passed was covered with graffiti. Because the area was so private and the artists had all the time in the world, many of the images were painstakingly detailed. Noah recognized some of the work by style alone. One prolific tagger, who signed all of his pieces with a cryptic lowercase *e*, could have made a decent living by painting murals or designing graphics for T-shirts.

Instead, he used his talent to destroy county property.

Noah ignored the colorful designs and focused on the shadowed walkway, making steady progress. The uneasy feeling he'd had since catching a glimpse of those scared-eyed juveniles dogged his every step.

What was waiting for him at the end of the staircase?

Noah unsnapped his gun holster and flexed his fingers, letting his right hand hover above his Glock. Judging by the kids' reactions and the vomit on the sidewalk, he was about to encounter a dead body.

As he reached the top of the stairs, a pair of shoes came into view. Black canvas flats. Size six or seven, women's.

Noah's gut twisted at the sight. His little sister wore shoes like that.

The rest of the body was blocked by the side of the building, but he could tell she was lying on her back, motionless.

He kept his hand near his gun. "Ma'am?"

No response. Not even a twitch.

Noah descended the steps, his pulse racing. After taking a quick survey of the surroundings to make sure he was alone, he returned his gaze to the fallen woman. And sucked in a sharp, painful breath.

Her legs were bare, her denim skirt shoved up to her

waist. She was brutally exposed. A torn flannel shirt hung from her slim torso, and strands of long black hair snaked across her neck. A clear plastic bag, the implement of her death, covered her face. Her mouth was open, frozen in a silent scream.

The killer had watched her suffocate while he raped her.

Noah turned away from the gruesome sight, swallowing hard. His eyes watered and his hands clenched into fists.

Most of the dead bodies he'd seen weren't homicide victims. He'd stumbled across a few homeless guys lying in their own waste. Drunk drivers sandwiched inside wrecked vehicles. He'd encountered bloated corpses and burned flesh.

As a gang unit cop, he'd also assisted in a number of murder investigations, of course. Gang members killed other gang members on a regular basis. It was tragic but not unexpected. Violent men met violent ends.

This was different. More twisted, more disturbing.

Killing a rival gang member was wrong. Raping and strangling an innocent young woman was . . . evil.

The radio at Noah's waist signaled, startling him. "Officer Young, Code Four," Patrick said. It was a basic status inquiry.

"Code Five," he replied, his voice hoarse with emotion. He glanced at the victim and cleared his throat, trying to toughen up. "We have a DB, Hispanic female, teens or twenties." There was a small purse lying on the concrete beside her, but Noah didn't touch it. "This one is for Santiago; over."

Victor Santiago was the lead homicide detective in

the department. Patrick's former partner and current nemesis.

"We've got a 187?" Patrick asked.

"And 261," Noah replied.

Patrick was silent for a moment. There was no more heinous crime than rape/murder, unless it also involved a child. Noah wasn't sure it didn't, in this case. The plastic bag partially obscured the girl's face, and he could only guess her age.

"Copy that," Patrick said, signing off to call dispatch.

For an indeterminable period, Noah stood guard over the body. He knew he should try to analyze clues and search for motives, but his mind was reeling. He also felt unsteady on his feet. The best he could manage was to stay put and not compromise the scene.

After a couple of slow, deep breaths, he pulled himself together enough to study his surroundings. The abandoned buildings were a perfect meeting place for petty criminals, and Noah knew that gang members frequented the location. There were several easy lookouts and even more dark corners to hide in.

A crouching assailant could wait in the shadows, unseen.

The wall behind the victim was marked *CVL #1,* a common tag in this neighborhood. The Chula Vista Locos had claimed the schoolyard, and many nearby locations, as their turf. They were the most prominent gang in the city.

Noah returned his gaze to the body, forcing himself to evaluate any visible evidence. Her face was contorted, her hair tangled and dark. She was slim but not undeveloped. Her frame was slender, like a teenager's. Her clothes looked cheap.

Poorly made, easily torn.

She didn't have any defensive wounds, from what he could tell, but her arms and legs were riddled with tiny red sores. They appeared to be self-inflicted, possibly from compulsive scratching. It was an ugly side effect of several different street narcotics, including rock cocaine and crystal meth.

The signs of addiction—and adulthood—didn't ease the tension in Noah's stomach. Drug abuse was a risky behavior, like prostitution, and perhaps it had made this particular victim vulnerable to attack. But there was nothing she could have done to justify her killing. No one deserved to die like this.

Within moments, a county medical examiner, a crime scene photographer, and evidence technicians descended on the scene. The rest of the afternoon passed in a blur. Noah continued to stand watch, partly because he was like a sponge, absorbing different procedures and techniques, but also because he felt protective of the victim. Through no fault of her own, she'd been violated and left like trash, her young life taken too soon.

He wanted her to be treated with the utmost respect.

When one of the homicide detectives zipped up the body bag carefully, Noah felt his shoulders relax. Detective Victor Santiago appeared before him. "A couple of juveniles reported her?"

"Not exactly, sir," Noah said, giving Santiago his full attention. "I saw them climbing over the fence and pursued."

Santiago was about Patrick's age—and his polar opposite. Patrick's blond hair was so short and sparse it looked white. Of sturdy Irish stock, Shanley was florid, heavyset, and outspoken. A big man with a big mouth.

In contrast, Santiago had a quiet strength that Noah admired more. He was dark-haired and olive-skinned. Although his clunky glasses made him look like an academic and he stood several inches shorter than Noah, he exuded a strong presence. He didn't use words or gestures to excess, nor did he carry an extra ounce of weight.

He also ran a crack team, and Noah wanted to be on it.

Patrick, who had assisted in securing the scene, eased up beside Noah.

Santiago looked back and forth between them. "Is that what you do on GU these days? Chase down little boys?"

"At least we chase down somebody," Patrick replied, tugging on his gun belt. With his considerable bulk, he couldn't catch a toddler. "Hard to do that from behind a desk."

Santiago ignored the gibe. Homicide detectives spent a lot of time in the office, but they also held the most demanding, most prestigious positions in the department. "Why'd you stop them?" he asked Noah.

Noah frowned, trying to pinpoint a particular reason. "I don't know," he said, shrugging. "They just looked scared."

Santiago's dark eyes were cool, assessing. Noah wished he'd thought of something more specific to say. "Victim is Lola Sanchez, age twenty-three," Santiago said, handing him a driver's license in a plastic bag. "Seen her around?"

Noah studied the pretty face in the photo. "No," he said, passing it to Patrick.

"She had some paraphernalia in her purse," Santiago continued. "You know a dealer who hangs out here?"

"No one comes here but CVL," Patrick asserted, returning the license to Santiago. "And kids too stupid to know better."

"I'm going to need your unit to assist," Santiago said. "We found a card in her wallet for Club Suave. The manager says she worked there. Had a shift last night."

Noah blinked a few times in surprise. He couldn't believe Santiago would let them in on such a high-profile investigation. This was, by far, the most vicious crime he'd ever seen. His pulse quickened at the thought of catching the sick bastard who did it. He'd never been more eager to be a part of a case.

Patrick merely waited for instructions, unmoved.

"Interview her coworkers. Get surveillance tapes. I want to know what her gang connections are, who she was dating, and if she left with someone last night."

"Yes, sir," Noah said, his shoulders straight.

Santiago waved them away.

After a final glance at the small figure in the zippered bag, Noah walked toward the chain-link fence with Patrick. It had been clipped for easier access. They passed through the opening, made their way down the street, and climbed into the patrol car.

"Do you have to kiss his ass?" Patrick asked.

"Do you have to piss him off?" Noah shot back.

They lapsed into an uncomfortable silence. Noah

understood that Patrick felt threatened by Santiago and chalked it up to professional rivalry. Patrick's career had stalled, while Santiago had moved up—way up—in the ranks.

Noah wanted to take the same direction in the department, and he wasn't going to let Patrick, or anything else, get in his way. The gang unit saw a lot of action, and he was in good shape. Unlike Patrick, he could win a footrace with any criminal on the street. He also enjoyed interacting with juveniles, having a visible presence in the community, and keeping the neighborhoods safe.

But what Noah loved most was solving puzzles. He'd excelled in Spanish and deciphering tag signs, perhaps because both languages had a discrete set of rules and symbols, pieces that fit together to create meaning.

He hoped these strengths would translate well to homicide. Noah planned to apply to that unit in a few short months, after completing the required five years on patrol.

And Patrick knew it.

"Well," his disgruntled partner said at last, "I guess it's no hardship to interview the girls at Suave."

Noah smiled wryly. Club Suave used to be a strip joint. Now, due to licensing issues and zoning laws, it was just a popular singles bar. From what he'd heard, the music was loud, the drinks were cheap, and the waitresses wore very little.

"No hardship at all," he murmured, staring out the passenger window. During the past few minutes, darkness had settled over the city.

2

🌿 April Ortiz hated Saturday nights.

Fridays were busier, but they were also lively and fun. Attractive, interesting people came to the club on Friday. The tables were packed with flirty single women and rowdy young men. Everyone wanted to enjoy a few cocktails, hit the dance floor, and leave their troubles from the workweek behind.

By Saturday, some of the lightheartedness wore off. The men who hadn't gotten lucky the night before came back with a vengeance. They were the hard drinkers, the bitter unemployed, the recent divorcés. An air of desperation soured the crowd.

It was a night of glittering eyes and groping hands.

And it had just started. Although it was early, still shy of 8:00 P.M., the joker at table seven had already tried to pull April into his lap. As soon as she was finished cleaning the women's restroom, she had to go out and wait on him again.

"*Perro*," she said under her breath, scrubbing at the crude message on the bathroom door. Last night, apparently, one of the patrons had used it as ad space.

"Guess who's late again?"

April glanced at her coworker Carmen, who was standing in the open doorway. "Did she call in?"

The other waitress propped one hand on her hip. The Club Suave uniform, a thin white tank top and short black skirt, did great things for her figure. "Of course not. She'll waltz in whenever she feels like it. I don't know why Rico keeps her on."

Carmen called their boss Rico Suave, after the cheesy Latin heartthrob from the nineties. His real name was Eddie, and they both knew why he kept Lola on. Every time the girl was late, he took her to his office for an "evaluation."

"I'm never going to be late," April said with a small shudder, and resumed scrubbing. The idea of servicing their boss made her gag.

"Me, either," Carmen agreed.

Eddie chose that moment to duck his head into the restroom, his face stern. He didn't approve of employee chitchat behind the scenes. "Company meeting," he announced. "I want to talk to everyone in back."

Carmen gave him an annoyed look. "This is the ladies' room, Rico. Can't you read?"

"Now," he said, pointing a thick finger at her before he continued down the hall.

April stashed the cleaning supplies in a locked cabinet and hurried after him. They were already operating on a skeleton crew, so she hoped he wasn't planning more layoffs. She needed this job. Unlike Carmen, she had a daughter to take care of.

She couldn't afford to get fired.

Carmen fell in beside her as she walked down the

hallway. The sound of house music, with its thumping bass line, grew louder as they approached the main room. April kept her gaze trained on the back of Eddie's head. He was a short, muscular man with a lot of body hair.

As soon as they passed through the double doors to the kitchen, the lights brightened and the noise dimmed. The other waitresses were already there, wearing identical expressions of impatience on their pretty faces.

They wanted to be out on the floor, making money.

"I already talked to the guys," Eddie said. In addition to a half dozen waitresses, the club employed two bouncers, a bartender, and a dishwasher who doubled as a cook when a customer was brave enough to order from the *botanas* menu. "I got a call from the police department. They said Lola's been in an accident."

"What kind of accident?" April asked.

"I don't know, but a couple of cops are coming over here to interview the staff. So I guess it's pretty serious."

Carmen frowned. "Is she okay?"

Eddie didn't answer. He picked up a kitchen towel and wiped the sweat from his forehead. It was a gesture they'd seen many times. "I'd like for everyone to cooperate with the police. You don't have to say anything, but be polite. We don't want cops making a scene, scaring off customers. Do you understand?"

The other girls nodded automatically, murmuring words of assent. He did a slow sweep of the room, his gaze zeroing in on April.

Her heart started to thump in her chest. She knew he was asking them to stay quiet about his relationship with Lola. And although Carmen was the most outspoken waitress on staff, April was the least likely to lie.

"I understand," she said. She needed this job. God help her, she did.

Eddie looked relieved. She wondered if he felt guilty about the affair. He had a wife and three kids. "Go on, then," he ordered halfheartedly, and walked over to the industrial-size fridge for a cold Corona.

April said a quick prayer for Lola in Spanish, and the waitresses hustled back out to the main floor, a united front. The room was packed with customers, some of whom were still waiting to have drink orders taken.

But every female head turned toward the front entrance.

The police officers had already arrived.

April recognized the older of the two, Officer Shanley. He'd worked on the neighborhood gang unit since the beginning of time. Her eyes skipped past him immediately, for his partner was the showstopper. He was tall and lean, with a strong, angular face. His midnight-blue uniform fit well, accenting broad shoulders and a trim waist.

While she watched, the young officer scanned the clientele, his stance relaxed, one hand resting on his gun belt. Strobe lights danced across his close-cropped hair, disguising the color. In the sun, it would probably be dark blond.

Even from across the room, she felt a jolt of awareness.

Handsome men came into Club Suave all the time, and they were often the biggest jerks, so good looks never impressed April. Maybe it was the combination of intimidating uniform and compelling presence that had her mesmerized.

"*Ay, papi,*" Carmen said, touching her fingertips to her décolletage. "If I'm naughty, will he handcuff me?"

"I've seen him jogging past my house," Nikki said dreamily. "He looks even better without a shirt."

At that moment, Shanley's partner glanced their way, his focus landing on April. Her breath caught in her throat. Keeping his eyes on her face, he murmured something to his partner. She tore her attention away, instantly flustered.

Carmen arched a brow. "I didn't know you could blush."

"It's just makeup," she muttered, nudging Nikki forward. "Customers are waiting, you guys. *Vamonos.*"

The other waitresses dispersed into the crowd, and Eddie came out to greet the officers. April ducked behind a mirrored pillar with Carmen, tugging her by the wrist. "Are you going to say anything?"

Her brows slanted downward. "Hell, no. And not just because of Rico. You know who she was running with."

Tension unfurled in April's stomach. "Yeah."

"Besides, I don't owe her anything. She stole from me, *chica.*"

"I know." April cast a miserable glance toward the officers at the front door. "What do you think happened to her?"

Carmen followed her gaze. "Something bad. And we don't want it to happen to us, *verdad?*"

April nodded mutely, letting her wrist go. Carmen dissolved into the strobe lights, her hips swaying seductively, hair a dark, curly halo.

Over the next hour, April slung drinks with her usual precision, tray balanced, head high. Meek girls got chewed up and spit out in this business; she'd learned that the hard way. Places like Club Suave attracted a lot of men who didn't respect women. The jerk from table seven, for instance. He'd taken his grabbing act to the dance floor.

After five years in fishnets and high heels, April had cocktail waitressing down to an art. She always maintained a polite distance but pasted on an inviting smile. She knew how to expose a tasteful hint of cleavage as she bent forward and when to avert her eyes so she wouldn't catch them looking.

She could walk ten miles, lift a hundred heavy trays, and laugh off a dozen come-ons. Every single night.

Some of the girls thought they would get better tips if they let the customers touch them. They were wrong. In April's experience, the gropers tipped less, not more. They were the type of men who felt entitled to a free sample of any wares on display.

With Lola gone, and the five remaining waitresses rotating in and out of Eddie's office for questioning, April had to hustle to keep the drink orders filled. For a busy Saturday night, it wasn't too bad. The crowd was mellow.

By the time it was her turn for an interview, she was juggling six tables, most of which were running tabs.

"You're on," Nikki said, taking the tray off her hands.

April grabbed her order pad and added a few totals in her head, scribbling them down before tearing off the sheets. As she slipped the tabs into Nikki's waist apron, she did a quick survey of the room. Mr. Grabby had struck out on the dance floor. "Watch the hands at seven," she said. "And tell Maya to cut off the tie at ten. He's wasted."

"Got it," Nikki said.

Another surge of anxiety coursed through April. "Here goes nothing," she muttered, squaring her shoulders as she walked toward the office. It was strategically located at the back of the club, and raised up a level. A large, tinted glass window offered views of the dance floor but didn't allow the clientele to see inside.

Taking a deep breath, she ascended the short staircase that led up to the room. The door was slightly ajar. She stepped inside.

Both officers were sitting at the round table Eddie used on poker night. They watched her cross the room. Away from the flashing lights and loud music, she felt more self-conscious about the way she was dressed. She wouldn't be caught dead in an outfit this revealing outside the club, and she wished she didn't have to do a formal interview in it.

The younger officer rose to greet her. His eyes were a startling blue, cutting through her like a knife. She couldn't detect a hint of softness in his form or features. From his straight nose and chiseled jaw to his corded forearms and suntanned hands, he was strong.

"Miss Ortiz? I'm Officer Young, and this is my partner, Officer Shanley."

April accepted his handshake warily. There was power in his grip, of course, but it was hardly crushing. His hand was large and warm and rough-textured, his manner respectful. Her skin tingled where his palm met hers.

Feeling color rise to her cheeks, she lifted her gaze to his and imagined a flash of heat in his eyes. Flustered, she pulled her hand away quickly and glanced at Officer Shanley, whose weathered countenance was much less unsettling.

Shanley didn't attempt a handshake. Nor did he bother to stand. "Have a seat, honey," he said, gesturing at the chair across from them.

April sat down, her posture stiff. With her back to the tinted window, she felt closed in. Which was surely what they intended. Too nervous to look directly at either of them, she stared at their drinks. Black coffee for Shanley. Clear soda for Officer Young.

"Would you like something?" Officer Young asked. "Water?"

How novel. A man offering *her* a drink. "No, thanks," she said, stifling the urge to cross her arms over her chest. Under bright lighting, her Club Suave tank top was almost transparent. "I'm fine."

Officer Shanley leveled with her. "Lola Sanchez was found dead this afternoon."

April felt her stomach drop. "Dead?"

"Murdered."

Logically, she'd known they were investigating a serious crime. But she hadn't been prepared to hear this. "By who?"

"That's what we're trying to find out." He gave her a moment to process the information, a too-brief pause. "When did you see Miss Sanchez last?"

"Yesterday. Last night."

"Did she leave with someone?"

April tried to remember. "I don't know."

"How did she get to and from work?"

She frowned. "I think she had a friend drop her off last night. But sometimes she took the bus or caught a ride with one of the other girls."

"Do you know her friend's name?"

"No."

"What about her current address?"

April's throat went dry. "She was couch-hopping. Staying with anyone who would put her up. Carmen, one of the other waitresses, let her crash at her apartment for a while. But that was several weeks ago."

"Did she ever sleep on your couch, Ms. Ortiz?"

"No. I have a five-year-old daughter, and I . . . don't bring home strangers."

Shanley's brows rose. "She worked here for six months."

"I guess I never got to know her."

"You're the head waitress, right?"

She nodded.

"How was her work performance lately?"

April struggled for a diplomatic answer. "It was . . . okay."

"Had she been acting odd?"

She hesitated, worried about revealing too much. Lola was a decent waitress when she wasn't high. The rest of the time, she was easily distracted and unpredictable. April had often suspected her of doing lines in the bathroom.

"Miss Ortiz, you're the most experienced waitress on staff. Part of your job is to evaluate sobriety, right?"

"I'm familiar with the effects of alcohol, yes."

Shanley glanced at her employee file. "Your address

is 551 South Orange. Are you telling me you don't know what a meth head acts like?"

April flushed. She lived in a rough neighborhood, but it was the best she could afford. "I knew Lola was using," she admitted. "Some nights she seemed really spun out. I probably should have sent her home or written her up. But I didn't."

"Her murder might be drug-related."

She closed her eyes, feeling tears gather in the corners. Taking a slow breath, she willed them away. Reporting Lola's behavior to Eddie wouldn't have done any good. Maybe April should have tried to help her, but she had her own problems to deal with. She was a part-time waitress, part-time student, and full-time single mother.

"Do you know who she was dating?"

Eyes still wet with tears, she shook her head.

"Did men come to see her here?"

"Not that I recall."

"Any favorite customers?"

"I don't think so."

Officer Shanley glanced at Officer Young, giving him the floor.

"We'll watch the surveillance footage," Officer Young said, taking over the interview, "but if you can give us names or descriptions of any of last night's customers, that would be very helpful."

April relaxed a little. Young was the kinder of the two officers, and she felt more comfortable with his line of questioning. "I remember my own customers, but I don't pay as much attention to the other girls' tables."

He smiled encouragingly. "Anything you can tell us will be fine."

She pictured the first group she'd waited on last night, their laughing faces and flashy clothes. After she described them, she moved on to the next table, and the next, and the next. When she was finished listing details about the customers at her own tables, she visualized the rest of the room. Several times a night she did a thorough sweep of the floor, making sure her girls were working hard, checking for trouble.

She described as many patrons as she could.

"That's all I can remember," she said finally.

Both of the officers were staring at her as though she'd grown two heads. There were several sheets of paper in front of Officer Young, filled with his slanted handwriting. "You have a photographic memory."

"Not really," she protested. "I just do these . . . mental tricks to keep track of who ordered what. I try to focus on a few specific details, like the color of tie or type of dress. I teach the other girls to do the same."

"You described about a hundred people."

"Well, we must have had three hundred customers last night. I can't even remember half of them."

He seemed amused. "Can you tell us the makes and models of the cars in the lot? Their license plate numbers?"

She let out a nervous laugh. "I don't even know my own plate number."

Officer Young glanced at his partner before asking the next question. "Did Miss Sanchez associate with any gang members, specifically the Chula Vista Locos?

Did she have a drug dealer or boyfriend who might fit that description?"

April felt the color drain from her cheeks. If she hadn't spent countless hours at the club, honing a cool façade, she might have faltered. Instead, she held her chin up and kept her gaze steady. "I don't know."

They must have believed her, because Officer Shanley ended the interview and Officer Young thanked her for her time.

She rose from the chair carefully, smoothing down her short skirt.

"Call us if you remember anything else," Officer Young said, handing her his card. Her fingertips brushed against his as she accepted it.

His eyes really were amazing.

Again she glanced at Shanley, needing a reality check. His craggy features offered no comfort, however. He gave her a brief, insincere smile, the kind used to dismiss a person of little importance. Because his attitude struck her as insulting, she lingered a second longer, memorizing the lines of his face.

He seemed to disapprove of the way his partner had treated her. Maybe he hated cocktail waitresses. Or business cards.

Disconcerted, she slipped the card into the front pocket of her apron and left, feeling two sets of eyes follow her all the way to the door. Without glancing back, she made her way down the staircase, weak-kneed with relief, racked by guilt.

As soon as she was out on the floor, she took the card from her pocket and read it. *Officer Noah Young, Gang Suppression and Investigations Unit.*

Committing the information to memory, she tucked the card into her apron again and resumed waitressing. Carmen was called into the office next and came out a few moments later, appearing much less conflicted about the meeting.

"What did you say?" April asked.

Carmen shrugged. "Nothing."

"Did he give you a card?"

"No. Why?"

Together, they watched the officers exit the club. Officer Young nodded at April as he passed by, wading through gyrating patrons.

"I think he likes you," Carmen said.

April tore her gaze away from the handsome cop. "Why?"

"He was staring at you. The whole time I was in there, his eyes kept straying out the window. Following you across the floor."

"He knew I was lying."

"Not saying anything isn't the same as lying."

"Sins of omission," April murmured.

"Sins of my ass," Carmen retorted. "You should give him your number."

April shook her head. Even if she wanted to give the man her number—which she didn't—this wasn't the appropriate time or place. What kind of unfeeling slut would use a murder investigation as a dating opportunity?

Besides, the waitresses at Suave weren't allowed to give out personal information, and April had always approved of the rule. Unlike the other girls, she'd never been tempted to leave her phone number on the check.

Then an idea occurred to her. "Maybe I will," she said, tearing a ticket off her order pad.

Carmen's brows rose with surprise. "Really? I was joking."

"I'll give him a number. Maybe even an *address*."

Her eyes rounded in understanding. "Hurry up," she said, glancing around to make sure no one was watching.

April quickly scribbled out a first and last name. Numbers weren't as easy for her to remember, so she wrote down a simple description. Then she folded the paper into a neat square and cupped it in the palm of her hand.

"Do you want me to pass it to him?" Carmen asked.

"No. I'll do it." Feeling a jolt of apprehension, April strode toward the front entrance. Outside, the sultry night air enveloped her like a lover. A short line of customers waited to pay the cover price. Omar, the bouncer, was checking IDs at the door.

Eddie had walked out to say goodbye to both officers.

She took her place beside him, directly across from Officer Young. "Please let us know if we can do anything more to help," she said, extending her right hand with a cool smile. Time slowed down to a trickle. A rapid pulse thudded at the base of her throat.

The moment his palm touched hers, she felt the same tingle of awareness as before.

Ignoring it, she wrapped her left hand over his knuckles, giving him the extra-warm hand hug, praying the paper wouldn't slip out. If he failed to notice the concealed message, she'd have a lot of explaining to do.

April knew the instant he felt the square against his palm, and she read the immediate understanding in his eyes.

"Thank you, Miss Ortiz," he said, squeezing her hand before he released it. He transferred the note to his pants pocket, as smooth as silk, and turned his attention back to Eddie. "You have the prettiest waitresses in town."

Eddie put his heavy arm around her shoulders. The gesture was part pride, part ownership. "Come back anytime."

April forced a smile.

Officer Young glanced at the place where Eddie's hand touched her bare skin, his gaze darkening. "I sure will," he promised.

3

Noah knew there were security cameras monitoring the parking lot, so he didn't take the note out of his pocket right away.

Eddie Estes had given them copies of last night's footage to review at the station. Although Eddie had denied its existence, Noah suspected there was another hidden camera in his office. It may have inhibited the waitresses' responses.

"We should ask those girls to come down to the station for a formal interview," Patrick mused, reading his thoughts. "They weren't exactly forthright."

Noah settled into the passenger side, studying the neon sign in front of the building. Glowing pink lights depicted the curvy outline of a woman's body, a leftover from the club's topless dancer days.

"Speaking of which, you shouldn't go so easy on the female interviewees. Not all women and children are innocent bystanders."

"Most are."

Patrick started the engine and turned on his radio.

"When some babyface pulls a gat, you'll change your mind."

Noah drummed his fingertips against his thigh, where the note was burning a hole in his pocket.

"You're also going to have to learn to school your reactions better. You can't get dazzled by the T&A in a place like that. I'm not saying I wouldn't have been tempted by a sweet-looking piece like April Ortiz when I was your age—"

"Come on," he said, although he knew he'd been staring. "I wasn't dazzled."

"Right. I practically heard the table thump when she started rattling off descriptions. Only you would get turned on by a woman's brain."

Noah didn't bother to argue; he *had* been attracted to her. All of the waitresses were hot, with tight little bodies in barely there outfits, but he'd hardly noticed the others. For whatever reason, he'd zeroed in on April.

She wasn't what he'd expected.

On the surface, she resembled any experienced working girl. Pretty but guarded, with sharp eyes and a fake smile. Her dramatic makeup and overstyled hair were like sexy armor. Beneath the façade, she was untouchable. Mysterious.

He wanted to know her secrets.

It wasn't the first time he'd seen a girl at a club and heard his libido whisper, *That one.* But he was usually more circumspect, even when he was off duty. He'd never stopped dead in his tracks or approached a woman without perusing the rest of the room. One glimpse of April was all he needed. *That one.*

If he'd been free to act on impulse, he would have approached her straightaway, without taking his eyes off her.

During the interview, her composure set her apart from the other girls. She was alert, self-assured, and cautious. Her responses were carefully constructed, her manner polished. She wasn't the friendliest intervie-wee, but she was the most intriguing.

By the end of the interview, he was fascinated. He'd made a sketch of the club's layout, using her table-by-table descriptions. Very few people noticed so many details and could keep them all straight. Noah's memory was good, especially for names and numbers, but he didn't have the same facility as April.

He'd never met anyone like her.

Although she was beautiful and obviously intelligent, there was another, softer quality that drew him in: compassion. She seemed distressed about what happened to Lola and protective of the other girls.

"You won't last two weeks on homicide if you let every honey who bats her eyelashes off the hook," Patrick said, maneuvering into light traffic. At midnight, the only gridlock was on the Mexico side of the Tijuana border. "Women know how to exploit a man's weaknesses. An officer with a soft spot for the ladies can be a liability."

"Or an asset," Noah said, digging into his pocket.

"What's that?"

He opened the folded note and scanned its contents. "Just something one of those wicked harlots slipped me. I feel so exploited."

Patrick's gaze sharpened. "A tip?"

Noah read the note aloud:

Tony Castillo
gray stucco w/ dark-blue shutters
large cactus out front
400? Fairfax

"If I'm not mistaken, April Ortiz gave us the name and location of Lola Sanchez's gang connection."

Patrick glanced in his rearview mirror, making sure the road was clear before executing a quick U-turn and heading back toward Fairfax Avenue. "What was I saying about female interviewees?"

"A bunch of bullshit," Noah said, smiling.

Patrick smiled back at him. "Okay, smart-ass. I'll give you this one."

Noah logged on to his computer, entering Tony Castillo's name in the system. He had two priors, both for drug possession. The mug shot featured a sleepy-eyed Hispanic man with a tattooed neck and shaved head.

"There's a warrant out for his arrest," Noah said. "Failure to appear."

Patrick grunted his approval. "Last known address?"

"City Heights." He did a quick search of residents on Fairfax. "Arturo Castillo is listed as the owner of a rental property in that area. Number 413."

Patrick touched the receiver at his shoulder, calling it in.

"Proceed with caution," Detective Santiago said. He sounded pleased.

Noah's pulse began to pound with excitement. In a homicide investigation, the first twenty-four hours were critical. A lead like this could provide the break they needed. And Santiago was letting them follow it.

A thought occurred to him. "Did you tell him I'm applying to his division?"

"I didn't offer the information," Patrick hedged.

"He asked?"

"Yes. Said he heard you had promise."

Noah's face warmed with a pleasant sort of discomfort. It was the same way he'd felt when April Ortiz came out to say goodbye. For a second he'd thought she was interested in him as a man, not as an officer. Then he'd read her expression, which held no hint of sexual suggestion, and understood her intention.

"You think the club manager's got something to hide?" Patrick asked.

"I wouldn't be surprised," he replied. Didn't everyone?

Number 413 Fairfax was just as April described it. A giant prickly pear cactus lined the sidewalk, partially obscuring the front of the house. Mexican women used the tender new shoots to make nopales, and this one had been picked clean, leaving only the largest, thickest ears. It was as tall and wide as their squad car, a hulking beast with a dozen arms. Streetlights cast its creeping shadow across the barren front yard.

At midnight, most of the neighborhood was dark. There were a few hot spots at the end of the block, with groups of young men and clusters of parked cars. Fairfax was a poor area, known for drug sales and gang activity, but it was also home to honest, hardworking people. Nice families struggling to make a better life.

Noah wished dirtbags like Castillo would stay in designated areas, where kids wouldn't get caught in the crossfire. Then again, most criminals had children of their own. The future generation of gang members.

Patrick and Noah approached the front door together, their eyes and ears peeled. There was no particular reason for stealth—this was a drop-in interview, not a drug bust—but they didn't immediately advertise their presence.

Outside the door, Noah paused to listen for voices inside the residence, noting the closed curtains and dim interior lights. He heard shuffling motions, followed by a moment of taut silence. They'd been made.

Patrick rapped his knuckles against the door. "Chula Vista Police Department," he said. "We'd like to speak with Tony Castillo."

The person inside exploded into motion. Heavy footsteps scattered in the opposite direction, toward the back of the house.

"He's running," Noah said, poised for action.

Patrick muttered a curse, fumbling for the radio at his shoulder. "Go!"

Noah took off in a flash, slamming around the corner of the house and high-jumping a crooked picket fence without missing a beat. The suspect flew out the back door and kept going, his white T-shirt gleaming in the dark.

"Chula Vista Police," Noah shouted at him. "Get down on the ground!"

Ignoring him, Tony Castillo sailed over the back fence, into a neighbor's yard.

"Fuck," Noah said under his breath, following him

over. The instant his feet hit the grass, he was running again. A pair of snarling pit bulls tore across the lawn, barking and nipping at his heels.

Luckily, none of the teeth caught hold.

Castillo made a quick left, climbing a block wall that separated the housing tract from a business area.

On the other side, he'd have more room to run.

Noah hit the wall hard and heaved himself over it, hurtling into the unknown, throwing caution to the wind. He landed in a copse of eucalyptus trees, almost losing his footing before he took off again. The steep slope angled down toward a mega-mart parking lot. Castillo was already streaking across the asphalt, making a break for it. Noah scrambled after him, his shoes seeking purchase among the fallen leaves and rock-strewn dirt.

As soon as he was on stable ground, Noah started to gain on him. Castillo was fast, but Noah was faster. Noah felt confident that he had greater endurance, as well.

Aware that he was losing the race, Castillo made another evasive maneuver, darting between buildings.

Noah struggled with the same decision he'd faced earlier: follow blindly or wait and listen. This time there were no snapping pit bulls to consider, and visibility was an issue. The rest of the parking lot was well lit, but the alleyway was cloaked in shadow.

Cursing silently, he paused at the corner of the building, flattening his back against the rough concrete wall.

He listened for running footsteps. The only sound he heard was blood rushing in his ears and his heart pounding in his chest. Touching the radio receiver at his shoulder, he gave Patrick a quick status report.

Then he heard the familiar rattle of a body hitting chain link.

"Continuing pursuit," he said, entering the dark passageway. Castillo's white T-shirt shone like a beacon at the end of the alley, which was barricaded by a sizable fence. Noah ran hard, knowing he'd lost several precious seconds in hesitation.

Castillo started to climb.

Noah thought about drawing his weapon but had the suspect pegged as a noncompliant, the kind of criminal who wouldn't respond to threats. And Noah didn't have cause to shoot him. If Castillo hadn't been several feet off the ground, Noah would have used his Taser. A hundred volts of electricity usually made the most resistant arrestee docile.

Instead, Noah employed a bit of old-fashioned brute force. When he caught up to Castillo, he grabbed him by the ankle and dragged him backward, anticipating a satisfying physical confrontation. He didn't expect the suspect to cooperate. Noah was hoping he wouldn't, in fact. He was juiced from the chase and spoiling for a fight.

He got a little something extra.

Castillo clung to the fence with his left hand and reached into the waistband of his pants with his right.

In the next second, Noah was staring down the barrel of a .22.

His entire world ground to a halt. The moment seemed magnified somehow, sharpened by his senses, every detail in extreme focus.

He could smell Castillo's sweat. His own sweat. The dim haze from the parking-lot security lights bathed them both in a pale orange haze. Castillo's eyes appeared black within black, feral, inhuman.

Castillo pulled the trigger. The gun clicked. And then, nothing.

It took Noah a second to realize that Castillo hadn't disengaged the safety. As Castillo remedied that mistake, Noah brought his right arm up, knocking the weapon aside. It discharged in an earsplitting blast.

The bullet ricocheted off the block walls all around them.

Noah jerked Castillo away from the fence and slammed him to the ground, facedown. Hard enough to stun him. "Put your hands behind your back!"

This time, he cooperated.

Noah wrenched his arms back and cuffed him, searching the pockets of his baggy pants. His hands were shaking from the near miss, his mind racing in a dozen different directions. Both he and Castillo were breathing hard.

There was a small bag of white powder in Castillo's front pocket. The sight of it filled Noah with fury. "This is why you pulled a gun on me?" he said, tossing the bag on the asphalt. The tattoo on Castillo's neck stood out in harsh relief, his pulse throbbing beneath it. "For an eight ball of coke?"

Noah didn't mention Lola Sanchez, but he wanted to. He wanted to give Castillo another hard shove. Slam him into the asphalt a few more times. If he'd raped and murdered a defenseless young woman, he'd earned the rough treatment.

Instead of lashing out at Castillo, Noah took a calming breath. Getting physical with a suspect after he'd been restrained was never a good idea. Noah was a conscientious police officer, and he liked his arrests to stick.

Patrick appeared at the end of the alleyway a moment later, his gun drawn. Noah imagined the scene through Patrick's eyes, and it didn't look pretty. The suspect was facedown beneath him, shirt torn, nose bloody.

"Officer Young, stand down."

Noah climbed off Castillo, feeling woozy.

"He fired at you?"

"Yeah."

"Have a seat."

Noah slumped against the wall, closing his eyes. He was still breathing heavily, his heart pumping with adrenaline. His lungs were burning and his knuckles felt raw. Patrick called in their location, and backup arrived within moments.

Several officers patted Noah on the shoulder, praising him for a job well done. He didn't deserve it. Officers were trained to consider every suspect armed and dangerous, but Castillo had caught him off guard. Noah should have expected a documented gang member, convicted drug dealer, and possible murderer to have a gun.

He'd been careless. And if Castillo had been quicker on the trigger, he'd be dead.

Castillo started to grumble about police brutality. The blood on his face had dried into a macabre black caul. With his huge pupils and shaved head, he looked like a fucking ghetto vampire.

They cleaned him up and took him away.

The crime scene photographer took a photo of Noah's hands. They had blood on them, his and Castillo's. He cringed at the sight, hoping he wouldn't be accused of excessive force. He'd been close to losing control for a minute.

"I scraped my knuckles on the side of the wall," he said, remembering a flash of pain as he took Castillo to the ground.

"I don't care if you scraped them on that asshole's face," Patrick replied, giving him some foam hand wash. "A guy who resists arrest, carries a concealed weapon, and takes a shot at you? He's lucky you didn't beat him senseless."

"He was fast."

"On his feet?"

"With the gun, too. One second I was yanking him away from the fence, the next he'd drawn on me."

"Good thing he missed."

"The safety was on."

Another patrol officer, who'd been listening in, let out a low whistle. "You must have an angel on your shoulder, man. That is some crazy shit."

Noah's eyes met Patrick's. The warning his partner had given him earlier, about a young criminal pulling a gun, hung in the air between them. Patrick had been right. Noah's tendency to throw caution to the wind was a dangerous thing.

A more experienced cop wouldn't have made the same mistake.

After giving a brief statement, they headed back to the station. Santiago would question Castillo in the morning, after he'd been processed. Noah didn't get a chance to look at the surveillance footage from Club Suave, because it took him a couple of hours to complete the arrest sheet. He was meticulous with every detail.

Maybe Castillo would confess to Lola Sanchez's murder and the case would wrap.

By the time Noah got home, it was almost 3:00 A.M. His house in Imperial Beach was cool, quiet, empty. Although he was exhausted, he didn't go up to bed. Grabbing a cold beer, he sat down in the dark living room, trying not to replay the ugliest scenes of the day.

Touching the sweating bottle to his forehead, he closed his eyes and pictured something beautiful: April Ortiz.

4

April was certain Eddie hadn't seen her give the note to Officer Young, but she still worried about the repercussions.

Tony Castillo was a violent man with dangerous connections. He'd had a rocky relationship with Lola, and he was a longtime member of CVL. She also suspected Tony of supplying her boss with drugs.

Eddie had a lot to lose if the truth came out. His marriage, his business, and even his life were on the line.

Her stomach was tied in knots for the remainder of the evening. Maybe Tony had killed Lola in a jealous rage and planned to target Eddie next. If Tony found out about the note she'd written, he could very well come after April.

Hands shaking, she called home to check on Jenny.

No one answered.

Her mother, Jenny's babysitter, was a night owl. On the weekends, she often went out in the wee hours of the morning, after April got home. It was possible that Josefa had already gone to sleep, but not likely.

April scrambled to fill the final drink orders, in a hurry to finish her shift. Tonight she had no patience for stragglers. When the guy at table seven loitered, trying to put his hand on the back of her thigh, she "accidentally" spilled water all over his lap.

"*Ay, Dios mío,*" she said, whipping some napkins out of the pocket of her waist apron. "I'm *so* sorry."

He left without tipping. Jerk.

At closing time, she turned in her totals and rushed off. The other girls were already gossiping about Lola, and Carmen probably wanted to grill her about Officer Young, but April couldn't indulge them.

"Where's the fire?" Eddie asked.

"At my house. Mom isn't answering the phone."

He nodded absently. "See you next week."

Everyone at the club knew about her home situation. They just didn't appreciate the severity of the problem.

Her mother had injured her wrist about a year ago, and she'd been on pain medication ever since. April wasn't convinced that Josefa still needed the drugs. Recently, her dependency had skyrocketed. April suspected she was abusing the medication by taking more than the prescribed dose and mixing the pills with alcohol.

Last week, April had found her passed out on the front step, unresponsive. She'd almost called an ambulance.

Josefa had always been a little unpredictable, but she was a kind person and a wonderful grandmother. April had agreed to let her watch Jenny under two conditions: no men, and no drinking. Until recently, Josefa had complied. She was an exemplary caregiver—with Jenny. That hadn't been the case when April was a child.

The situation had become unmanageable in a very short time, and April didn't know how to deal with it. She loved her mother and depended on her in many ways.

And it wasn't as if she could leave Jenny with her father.

April drove too fast on the way home, checking her rearview mirror for flashing lights. The distance was only a few miles, and the roads were deserted. At this time of night, even the mean streets of South Orange were quiet.

She pulled in to the one-car garage and engaged the vehicle alarm as soon as she got out. In this neighborhood, it was necessary to take every precaution against theft.

The door to the kitchen was unlocked, which was typical. April locked it behind her and stashed her purse in the cabinet above the fridge. Even inside the house, she had to be careful. Josefa would borrow cash from her purse.

"Mamá?" she called, walking through the pint-size kitchen and past the small dining area, into the living room. The television was on, volume turned down low. April picked up the remote and clicked it off.

Her mother's bedroom door was open.

She peeked inside. The room was empty, the bed neatly made. Her unease grew. Frantic, she jogged down the hall, checking the room she shared with Jenny. Again, the bed was unoccupied. The striped blankets lay askew.

April whirled around, looking in the tiny bathroom. "Jenny?"

"Mommy?"

The voice was muffled, hesitant. April crossed the bedroom in two horrified strides, wrenching open the closet door. Her five-year-old daughter was huddled in the corner, hugging her favorite stuffed animal, Lalo, the one-eared dog.

Tears of relief filled April's eyes. She knelt down and held out her arms. Jenny launched herself into them.

For a moment, April was so overwhelmed she couldn't speak. She hugged her daughter tight, savoring the feel of her slight body, the smell of her hair, her soft pajamas.

Jenny was everything to her. She was her reason for living.

"What happened, *pepa*?" she asked, pulling back to study her daughter's pretty face. Jenny was a miniature version of April, black-haired and brown-eyed.

The only hint of Raul was in her stubborn little chin.

"I woke up and Abuelita was gone," she said, her mouth trembling. "I thought a stranger might come, so I hid in the closet. Like we did that one time."

Pain squeezed inside her chest. "Has a stranger ever come before?"

"No, Mommy. I was just worried."

"I'm here now," April said, hugging her again. "Everything's fine."

Jenny sniffed back her tears. "Is Abuelita okay?"

"Of course. She probably had to get some more medicine."

"Is she still sick?"

"Yes," April said, whispering. "She's very sick, and we have to help her get better. Can you do that with me?"

Jenny nodded, her eyes solemn. She was a thoughtful, tenderhearted child. And April loved her so much it hurt.

"Let's go back to sleep now, *pepita*."

Nodding, Jenny picked up Lalo, who had fallen to the closet floor, and climbed into bed. April lay down beside her, smoothing the hair away from her tear-streaked face, crooning softly in her ear. Soon, her breathing came deep and even.

April was tired but too hungry to drift off. She was also worried about Josefa, though she knew better than to try to hunt her down. Josefa's cell-phone service had been canceled months ago, and when she was out partying, she didn't want to be found.

Easing away from Jenny, April removed her shoes and left the room. She closed the door behind her and padded into the kitchen, her fishnet stockings making no sound on the linoleum floor.

Josefa had made chicken enchiladas for dinner, so there were leftovers in the fridge. Stomach rumbling, April served herself a plate and stuck it in the microwave, watching it rotate. When it was finished heating, she went to the only table. The small dining area had a window that overlooked the backyard.

April had chosen this place because of the yard. It wasn't lush or spacious, but it had a vegetable garden and room for Jenny to play.

As soon as she sat down, a man's face appeared at the window.

Raul.

April leapt to her feet, drawing a breath to scream.

"It's just me," he mouthed, holding up both hands.

Not Raul. *Eric.*

She exhaled in a rush, her heart pounding. Embarrassed by her own skittishness, she went to let him in. "You scared the hell out of me."

"Sorry. I didn't want to wake Jenny." He leaned in to kiss her cheek, his attention straying to the food on the table. "What's that?"

"Enchiladas. *Lo quieres?*"

"Did you make it?"

She stuck out her tongue. "No."

He laughed. "Then, yes, I would love some."

After warming up a plate with about twice as much food as she would eat, she grabbed drinks from the fridge for both of them and came back to the table.

"Thanks," he said, digging in.

They ate in companionable silence, as they'd done many times before, in the stillest hours of the night.

"This is awesome. Your mom is a great cook."

April made a murmur of agreement. Josefa didn't prepare meals as much as she used to, so the enchiladas were a rare treat. During the past year, April had assumed almost all of the responsibilities around the house, including cooking, but she couldn't hold a candle to her mother in the kitchen.

The tension she'd experienced earlier this evening shrank her appetite, and she couldn't finish all of her dinner.

Eric ate the rest for her.

"So, what's up?" she said, taking the empty plates away.

"Nothing. I was just checking in. I meant to drop by earlier, but I got tied up."

"Hmm."

His eyes narrowed, cruising over her face. "How are you?"

After a moment's hesitation, April gestured for him to follow her into the living room, where they could talk more comfortably. He sat down on the couch, his lean body taking up a lot of space. She settled in on the other side, keeping an arm's length of distance between them. "When I came home tonight, *Mamá* was gone. I found Jenny hiding in the closet. She woke up alone and got scared."

Eric rubbed a hand over his mouth, as if he wanted to say something unflattering about Josefa but was restraining himself. "I'll come over more often," he promised. "Every night you're at the club."

April shook her head. Eric already did too much. He worked during the day, his grandmother was ailing, and he had other responsibilities. She appreciated his offer, but he wasn't an appropriate choice for a babysitter.

"I can't leave Jenny with my mom anymore." Her throat closed up. "I'm going to have to ask her to move out."

Eric's eyes softened with sympathy. He knew that physical contact made her uncomfortable, so he didn't put his arm around her. At one time, she'd have been grateful for his restraint. Tonight, she felt empty and alone, aching for human touch.

She studied Jenny's uncle from beneath lowered lashes, considering him in a way she never had before. He was younger than she was, but not boyish. He had the dark good looks of their culture, paired with above-average height and an athletic physique. His black hair was cropped short, his white T-shirt immaculate.

She knew he was popular with the girls in the neighborhood, but he didn't create drama. He was a player *and* a gentleman.

On the downside, he looked exactly like Raul. And she loved him like a brother.

"I have another problem," she murmured.

His eyes sparked with interest. "Yeah?"

"Did you hear about Lola Sanchez?"

"No. I just got back from TJ."

Taking a deep breath, she told Eric about her visit with the officers at the club. "I gave them Tony's name."

He straightened abruptly. "How?"

"In a secret note. I don't think anyone saw me."

Relaxing a little, he said, "Okay."

"Do you think he did it?"

"He'll be sorry if he did."

April felt a cold sensation, like an icy hand on her spine. "What if someone figures out I mentioned his name?"

Eric's expression turned fierce. "No one will ever touch you."

His conviction was reassuring, and she believed he would protect her. She also couldn't help but consider the literal interpretation of his words. It had been years since she'd been touched by a man. Not that she didn't have urges, but usually those were vague needs, easily ignored or self-assuaged.

Tonight she wanted to feel close to someone else.

And her desire had a specific reason, an identifiable source: Officer Young. She didn't just want a man to touch her, she wanted *him* to touch her. She thought about his strong hands and intense blue eyes and shivered.

Eric gave her an odd look, as if he could sense her thoughts.

Flushing, she crossed her arms over her chest. It occurred to her that Eric might offer to help her out in that arena. Maybe he saw her as a woman, not a sister. From what she'd heard, he liked to make a girl feel good. Repeatedly.

His eyes traveled down her body, from her ultra-thin tank top to her fishnet tights. "I hate that outfit," he muttered.

It was such a brotherly thing to say, she laughed.

"Call me tomorrow," he said, rising to his feet. "Let me know if you need anything."

"I will."

He reached into his pocket for a stack of bills.

She put a hand up in protest. "Eric—"

"For Jenny," he said. "For a new babysitter."

While she wavered, trying to decide what was best, he pressed the twenties into her palm, refusing to take no for an answer. After another quick buss on the cheek, he left.

For a long time, she stared at the wad of cash, wishing she didn't need it, wishing she didn't ache for a man's touch. Tears filled her eyes, spilling down her face and splashing on the surface of the drug money.

Like her, it would never be clean.

Someone's in the house.

A faint noise startled Noah, jerking him out of his reverie. The beer he was holding, half full and still cold, sloshed over his knuckles. He set it aside, wiping his hand on his jeans, and listened harder.

The sound came again, a vague whisper of movement.

Frowning, he rose to his feet and went to the front window. After a quick glance at the dark, deserted street, he checked both doors, making sure they were locked, and looked out at the minuscule backyard. He didn't see anything unusual.

Maybe it was just the house settling, but he couldn't shake the feeling that he wasn't alone.

Earlier this evening, with Tony Castillo, he'd been too pumped up on adrenaline, too mindlessly aggressive. He hadn't proceeded with caution. He wouldn't make that mistake again.

Moving stealthily, he ascended the steps and walked down the hall, pausing outside the door of the guest room.

The bedsprings creaked.

Every nerve in his body went taut.

With quick, silent steps, he continued to his room, ducking inside. This time, he wasn't rushing in unprepared. He headed to the closet and reached for the locked box that held his personal revolver. In less than a minute, he had the loaded gun in his hand.

It felt good there.

More comfortable now that he was armed, he strode

down the hall and stood outside the guest bedroom once again, listening.

There was only the soft sound of deep, even breathing.

Motherfucker.

Flipping on the hall light, he opened the door. "Chula Vista Police," he shouted, aiming his revolver at the lump on the bed. "Put your hands where I can see them!"

The sleeping figure sat forward, her eyes springing open. Screaming loud enough to wake the dead, she cradled her arms around her head and assumed the fetal position, as if that would protect her from a bullet.

Meghan.

He put his left hand over his heart, which was galloping beneath his palm, and pointed his gun down at the floor.

She quieted, peeking out from underneath the shelter of her arms. "Noah?"

"Yeah."

"I came to visit."

He let out a slow breath, almost a laugh. "I can see that. Let me just . . . put this away."

"Okay."

Meghan had a key to his house, but her presence here was unexpected, to say the least. She lived in Cedar Glen, with their parents, and she'd already spent two weeks with him this summer. She was supposed to start her sophomore year of college soon.

Noah returned to his room, removing the bullets from the gun with shaking hands. Focusing on that task gave him a minute to regroup. The entire night had been surreal. He could have been shot. He could have shot his sister.

What the hell was wrong with him?

Maybe Patrick was right. He wouldn't last long on homicide if he couldn't tell the difference between friends and enemies or lies from truth.

He took a few deep breaths, trying to slow his pounding heart. When he felt calm again, he went back to Meghan, wondering what she was doing here. She hadn't shown up unannounced before.

His sister was sitting up in bed, her knees hugged to her chest. She'd turned on the lamp. A pale blue blanket covered her from the waist down. She was using one of his old T-shirts as a nightgown.

Not sure where to begin, he sat at the end of the bed.

"That was pretty cool," she said with a nervous little smile. "I've never seen you in action before."

"I could have killed you."

Her throat worked as she swallowed. "I'm sorry. I should have called first."

"It's okay," he said easily. He was glad to see her, under any circumstances. "I didn't mean to freak you out. Something weird happened earlier, and I was on edge."

She frowned. "Something weird?"

"A guy pulled a gun on me. But it didn't go off."

Her face paled. "Holy shit, Noah."

"I'm fine now," he said, pushing away the disturbing images of the past twenty-four hours. He couldn't talk about the murder investigation. "Just kind of shaken up. Don't tell Mom."

She nodded automatically and glanced down, her

bangs falling into her eyes. It occurred to him that she looked different. "About Mom—"

"What the fuck did you do to your hair?"

She lifted a hand to her head, self-conscious. "You don't like it?"

Her hair was honey blond, a shade lighter than his, and it had always been beautiful. A month ago it had been almost waist length. Now it was cropped short and asymmetrical, with long bangs on one side.

She looked like one of the homeless teens on 4th and B.

Without all that long hair, her face stood out more. Her eyes seemed bluer, her features finer. The style was offbeat, not unflattering. What really disturbed him was her demeanor. He sensed a new maturity about her, along with a hint of sadness.

He much preferred her in pigtails and braces.

"Mom didn't like it, either," she said, falling back against the pillows. "She asked if I got run over by a lawn mower."

Noah smiled, imagining their mother's reaction to the haircut. As a former beauty queen and current preacher's wife, she had very conservative tastes. Both of their parents were stern, strict, traditional.

"We had a fight," she continued.

"About your hair?"

"Among other things. I dropped out of Chapel."

Chapel College was in central California, several hours north of their hometown. It was small and unremarkable, a quiet Christian university. Noah had attended it for two years before transferring to San Diego State. "Why?"

"I hate it there. Everyone is so fake. Bible study and choir practice, then beer kegs and puke parties."

He knew she wasn't exaggerating, because he'd encountered some of the same hypocrisy when he was a student. There were plenty of girls at Chapel who looked real sweet on Sunday but didn't mind acting sinful on Saturday night. Noah had considered that a plus. "Those aren't required courses, Meg."

"They may as well be. I'll never fit in there. I'm different."

His gaze narrowed on her jacked-up hair. "Different?"

"The students at Chapel aren't like me. I want to expand my horizons, meet new people, explore the world."

He arched a brow. "You went to Paris last summer."

"With the youth group," she said, rolling her eyes. "How am I supposed to find myself in such an insulated situation?"

Noah hid another smile, trying to remember what it was like to be nineteen. He'd always known he wanted to be a cop, so he was lucky in that sense. He'd never felt a burning need to find himself. But he was no choirboy, and he'd had his share of conflicts with their parents. They couldn't believe he was more comfortable on the mean streets of Chula Vista than in the quiet village of Cedar Glen.

"We don't have to solve the mysteries of the universe tonight," he said gruffly. "I don't know about you, but I could use some sleep."

She moistened her lips. "I have to ask you something first."

"What?"

"Can I stay here?"

"Of course. You think I'd throw you out?"

"For a while, I mean. I want to live with you."

Noah was taken aback by the question. His first instinct was to say no, and not only because he valued his privacy. Meghan usually came to visit when he was on vacation and had time to spend with her. Right now his work schedule was very demanding. He was gone almost every evening, and the neighborhood was rough. A local girl had just been murdered. His sister would be safer at Chapel.

"I'm not going back there, Noah. And Mom won't pay for a secular school."

"Neither will I! I can't afford to put you through college."

"I'll get a job."

"You have no experience, no money, and no car." He paused for a moment. "How did you get here, anyway?"

"I took the bus," she said, sounding very pleased with herself. "And I'm perfectly capable of doing it again. Southwest College is only two miles down the road. I can work and go to classes, like you did."

"Fuck," he said, rubbing a hand over his face. "Let me think about it."

She made a squealing sound and bounced up and down a few times, as if he'd said yes. "I won't be any trouble," she promised. "I'll hide if you bring a date home. You won't even know I'm here."

"I said I'd think about it."

She threw her arms around his neck. "I love you, Noah."

And the last vestiges of his resistance slipped away.

5

April awoke to the sound of seabirds and naval flutes.

"Who lives in a pineapple under the sea?
SpongeBob SquarePants!"

With a low groan, she rolled onto her stomach and cradled the pillow around her head, trying to muffle the annoying theme song. Then the events from the previous evening came rushing back to her, jolting her from half sleep.

She opened her eyes.

The digital clock on the nightstand said 9:01 A.M. She'd gone to bed at around 4:00. Beyond the bedroom door, which was slightly ajar, she could hear someone rifling through the refrigerator. "Jenny?"

Her daughter appeared in the doorway, a hopeful look on her face. She was still wearing her faded pink pajamas. "Are you awake now, Mama?"

April felt a familiar pang of guilt. Jenny wasn't always quiet in the mornings, but sometimes she let April sleep in for hours. "I'm awake," she sighed, rubbing her grainy eyes. "But I need help to get up."

Smiling, Jenny entered the room. As soon as the little girl held out her hand, April tugged her onto the bed, ravishing her with hugs and kisses. Jenny squealed with laughter, delighted by the game. It was part of their morning ritual.

April sat up and formed her hands into claws, doing her best zombie impression. "I'm so hungry I could eat . . . brains!" With a playful growl, she pounced, pretending to feast on Jenny's sweet tousled head. Then she tickled her until they were both out of breath. Side by side, they listened to SpongeBob's nasal twang coming from the television in the living room.

"Did Abuelita come home?" April asked.

"No."

She rose from the bed. "What do you want for breakfast?"

"Pancakes!"

Stretching her arms over her head, April walked into the kitchen, heading straight for the coffeemaker. While her coffee was brewing, she checked the contents of the fridge. "How about cinnamon tortillas?"

Jenny shrugged. "Okay."

April tossed a couple of tortillas on a flat pan on the stove. When the surface bubbled, she flipped them with her fingertips. As soon as they were done, she spread a small amount of butter on the surface, sprinkled them with cinnamon and sugar, and rolled them up.

"Here you go, madam," she said, delivering the quickie meal on a paper plate. "Milk or orange juice?"

Jenny scrunched up her face in concentration. "Milk."

"Good choice." She poured her daughter a glass of low-fat milk and took it to the table. While the pan was hot, she heated up another tortilla for herself. She hadn't eaten much yesterday, and she was hungry. "What do you want to do today?"

"Abuelita said she would take me to the beach."

April poured herself a cup of coffee. She was still furious with Josefa for leaving Jenny alone last night. But what if she hadn't taken off to buy drugs? Maybe she was hurt, or confused, or . . . dead.

Like Lola.

Shivering, April sat down across from Jenny.

"Do you think she forgot?"

"Forgot what, *m'ija*?"

"About the beach."

April sighed, raking a hand through her hair. Josefa didn't have a car, and she wasn't allowed to drive April's. There was no way she could take Jenny to the beach. "Remember how I said that your grandma was sick?"

"Uh-huh."

"Well, sometimes she forgets things and makes promises she can't keep. She isn't supposed to be driving."

"Oh," Jenny said, disappointed. Then she perked up. "Will you take me?"

On a day this hot, the beach would be packed with tourists and locals alike. Parking in Chula Vista was a nightmare in the summer. Sometimes, when April really needed to escape, she took Jenny to one of the quieter, cleaner beaches up north.

Right now they both could use a break. "All right."

After breakfast, April packed a light lunch and put it in an oversize mesh bag, along with a couple of ratty old towels. Jenny did her part, donning a turquoise swimsuit and collecting her beach toys from the backyard. They were sun-faded and dirty from frequent use, so Jenny washed them carefully under the spigot.

April retreated to the bedroom to get ready. In the top drawer, she had a dark-blue tankini and a newer, skimpier two-piece she'd never worn. Carmen had talked her into buying it on sale a few weeks ago.

She preferred modest attire during her time off work, so she chose the old suit. It was more appropriate for building castles with Jenny, anyway. No reason to ruin the new one, which was mostly white, with flecks of black sand.

Pairing the suit with a flowy cotton skirt, she slipped her feet into rubber flip-flops and tied back her hair. Jenny's hair was just like hers, thick and dark, with the tendency to tangle. April was trying to tame it when she heard the rumble of a motorcycle outside. Fashioning a quick ponytail, she set the hairbrush on the dresser.

"Don't forget to brush your teeth. And go potty."

"I already went."

"Go again."

While Jenny was in the bathroom, April raced into the kitchen, removing her purse from the upper cabinet and stashing Eric's money in her wallet. She'd have to stop at the ATM before they went to the beach.

Burying her purse among the towels in the beach bag, she approached the front window to look out at the street.

A leather-clad biker was dropping Josefa off at the curb. He was silver-haired and tall, about ten years older than her mother. April didn't like any of the men Josefa dated, but she preferred the more mature ones. It was humiliating to watch her mother hang all over guys April's age.

Which she did. Frequently. Josefa was only forty-one, and still beautiful. She had a great figure, a party-girl attitude, and an infectious smile. When Josefa and April went out in public together, strangers often assumed they were sisters.

"See you around, Josie," the man on the bike said, his eyes on Josefa's shapely backside as she walked to the front door.

"Anytime, big guy," she said, waving a jaunty *adiós*.

Inside the house, she breezed past April, too intoxicated to read the anger and disappointment on her face. "I could use a nap," she said, climbing into bed, fully dressed. "Will you turn the light off, honey?"

"It's the sun, Mom."

"Hmm?" A moment later, she was asleep.

Gritting her teeth, April picked up Josefa's faux-leather purse and upended it at the foot of the bed. There were cigarettes, condoms . . . and cocaine. April stared at the tiny plastic bag, unable to believe her eyes.

She'd known her mother drank to excess and used prescription drugs. But this level of self-destruction was unprecedented.

Or was it?

Maybe Josefa had been using street drugs all along. Snorting lines in the bathroom while Jenny watched

Disney movies. Inviting her boyfriends over as soon as Jenny fell asleep.

The sight of the plastic bag on the bed infuriated April. It represented everything she loathed. A slew of memories washed over her, infecting her like a sickness. She knew what that kind of high felt like. She could almost taste it, numbing the back of her throat.

Just this once, it whispered.

"Ugh!" she yelled, wanting to tear her hair out. Instead, she grabbed the bag of drugs and headed straight to the bathroom.

Jenny gave her a curious look. "What's that, Mama?"

"Poison."

Hands trembling, tears burning her eyes, she dumped the contents into the commode and flushed. Then she rinsed the bag, threw it in the wastebasket, and took the trash out, dumping it into the receptacle by the back door. When every hint of the stuff was gone, she went to the sink and washed her hands.

And washed them. And washed them.

"Are you okay, Mommy?"

April turned off the faucet, drying her hands on a dish towel. Taking a deep, calming breath, she sank to her knees and hugged Jenny tight. "Now I am," she said, finding solace in her daughter's small arms. "Now I am."

When Noah woke up, he smelled bacon. And remembered Meghan.

Groaning, he kicked off the sheets and swung his legs over the side of the bed, putting his feet on the floor. He should probably encourage his sister to go back to Chapel. If he let her stay, he'd be in the doghouse with their mother.

Noah could handle his mom's disapproval, but he didn't *want* to. She'd always been touchy about Meghan.

"Shit," he said, fumbling for his jeans on the floor.

Downstairs, Meghan was sitting on one of the bar stools at the kitchen counter, reading the newspaper. She'd made a carafe of fresh coffee, a heaping plate of scrambled eggs, and a half dozen slices of crispy bacon.

His stomach growled.

"Good morning," she said sweetly.

Mumbling the same, he poured himself a cup of coffee and dug in. As the caffeine and satisfying meal began to transform him into a functional human being, he noticed that she'd tidied up the kitchen.

The dishes were put away, the surfaces clean.

He'd been living away from home since he turned eighteen, so he knew how to fry bacon and wipe down counters, but he certainly didn't mind letting her do it. There were some positive points to having his sister around, he supposed.

Meghan flattened the newspaper on the countertop. She was wearing jeans that were snug around the ankles and a tank top with horizontal stripes. Her crazy bangs were held back by a slim headband.

She looked pretty. All grown up.

His eyes strayed to the framed photo of them in the hallway. It was taken at the top of Mount Whitney about five years ago. She had her hair in a cute ponytail;

they were both suntanned and smiling. He realized that his mental picture of Meghan hadn't matured.

"*Work at home in your spare time,*" she read. "*Easy job, excellent pay.*"

"Scam," he predicted, taking a bite of eggs.

"You're probably right. Ooh, here's an interesting one. *Upscale gentleman's club seeks dancers. Make thousands per day.*"

"Over my dead body," he muttered, though he knew she was joking.

"But it says *no experience necessary.*"

He squinted at her, conveying his lack of amusement.

"Jeez," she said. "You're so grumpy in the morning."

"A rude houseguest kept me up too late."

"Do you still have that bike in the garage?"

"The beach cruiser? Yeah."

"Can I borrow it?"

Shrugging, he ate more bacon. "Sure."

"I think I'll ride it down to the business area on Broadway. Pick up some applications."

He thought about the business district he'd run through last night. Picturing Castillo's eerie black eyes as he pulled the gun, Noah set his fork down. "You won't find any Starbucks or fashion outlets around here, Meghan."

"There's a pet shop. And a grocery store."

He rubbed the back of his neck, feeling a prickle of apprehension. Maybe he should try to talk her out of this arrangement. "I know you want to . . . spread your wings a bit, and I agree that Chapel isn't the most exciting place in the world. But the point of going to college is to get a quality education. Why give up an opportunity to have all expenses paid?"

Her blue eyes darkened, like the sky before a storm. "You don't understand, Noah. The rules have always been different for you because you're a *guy*. Mom and Dad don't care if you shoot people for a living, or never go to church, or sleep around."

His breakfast felt weird in his stomach. "I don't sleep around."

"Whatever. How's Cindy?"

A flush rose to his cheeks. "We broke up."

"Exactly."

He knew what she was implying, and it wasn't quite fair. He liked being single, but he'd also had his share of steady girlfriends. He wasn't afraid of commitment. If he hadn't settled down yet, it was only because he hadn't found the right woman.

A new idea occurred to him. "What about *your* boyfriend? Won't Michael be upset when he finds out you aren't going back to Chapel?"

Her mouth thinned. "I doubt it. We aren't seeing each other anymore."

"Ah."

"He's not the reason I dropped out." She folded the newspaper in half, avoiding his eyes. "Not the only reason, anyway."

Noah studied his sister closely, catching her troubled expression. His mind flashed back to the young victim at yesterday's murder scene, and his thoughts took a disturbing turn. "Did he do something to you?"

A line formed between her brows. "Like what?"

"Like . . . force himself on you," he said, uncomfortable. Although he had difficulty seeing Meghan as a woman, it hadn't escaped his attention that other men did. They'd been ogling her at the beach since she was sixteen.

Perverts.

Laughing unexpectedly, she shook her head. "No. He wanted to get married. I said I wasn't ready."

Noah shuddered, taking another sip of coffee. "Good," he said. And good riddance. Getting married too young was one of the unique dangers students faced at Chapel, where premarital sex was treated like a sin.

"I wouldn't mind having a live-in boyfriend," she said, thoughtful.

He almost sputtered a mouthful of coffee all over the countertop. "Oh, no," he said in a warning tone. "Don't be thinking you can invite boys over or stay out all night. The rules here will be the same as Mom and Dad's."

She smirked, crossing her arms over her chest. "Okay."

Noah worked the evening shift, of course, so he wouldn't be around to enforce any of those rules. "Mom's going to kill me," he groaned, taking his empty plate to the sink. "Do you really want Mom to kill me?"

She rose from the bar stool, looking very pleased with herself. "Mom will be mad at me," she countered. "Everything you do is golden."

"That's not true."

She changed the subject. "Are you working today?"

It was Sunday, his day off. But murder investigations

didn't keep regular hours. "Yeah. I have some stuff to finish up in the office."

"Will you check that bike before you go?"

He sighed, downing the rest of his coffee. "Fine, but the business district on Broadway isn't safe. Homeless people panhandle in the parking lot. The liquor store on Fifth Avenue gets robbed every other weekend. Junkies shoot up in the restroom at the burger joint. And the massage parlor . . . isn't known for massages."

She frowned. "Maybe I'll head toward the coast instead."

The beach areas were almost as shady as the inner city. "Don't go too far," he said, already disliking his new role as guardian. "I don't want you riding that bike at night, either. The neighborhood is too dangerous, and the bike doesn't have reflectors. Be aware of that when you list your available hours."

Her chin took on a stubborn tilt. "Is there anyplace you consider appropriate, big brother?"

"Not really," he said. Not in Chula Vista.

After Noah aired up the tires on his beach cruiser and gave Meghan the combination for the padlock, he went down to CVPD headquarters. Santiago had asked him to view the footage from Club Suave, and he intended to follow through. If Castillo confessed to the murder, the legwork would be unnecessary, but he wasn't counting on any easy solutions.

At the station, Deputy Williams was hunched over his computer, hand on the mouse, dark face just inches from the grainy images on the screen. Williams was a rookie on homicide. He was young, and smart, and very large.

"What up," he mumbled, not blinking.

Noah grabbed the chair next to Williams, hoping he had the scoop on the case. "Did they interview Castillo?"

"Yeah. Motherfucker has an alibi. Check it out."

Noah watched the screen, instantly intrigued. The footage showed Castillo's gold Camaro pulling up to a booth at one of the border checkpoints. "Is that San Ysidro?"

Williams nodded. "He crossed into Tijuana at one minute after midnight. Came back at six fifteen. Got clear footage both ways."

"Did the ME make an official ruling on the time of death?"

"Nah. But unofficially it's between two and four A.M."

According to the waitresses at Suave, Lola Sanchez didn't leave the club until 2:15, so that narrowed the window even further. She'd probably been killed between 3:00 and 4:00 A.M. There was no way Castillo could have done it from across the border.

"Shit," Noah said, raking a hand through his hair. He'd wanted Castillo to be guilty, and not just so he could say he'd collared a killer. Every officer in the department wanted the man who raped and murdered Lola Sanchez off the streets.

"DEA is investigating him for trafficking. Sounds like they're getting a warrant to search the house and impound the vehicle."

Noah wouldn't be surprised if the dope he'd found on Castillo had been smuggled across the border. "What did he say he was doing in TJ?"

"Cruising the red-light district. Alone."

Noah studied the freeze frames of the Camaro at the checkpoint. Castillo had lied. He was traveling with another man. The passenger kept his face averted, as if he knew exactly where the camera was. "Do you have another angle?"

"Nope."

Williams did a few techie tricks, magnifying the best shot. The passenger's head was turned away, but he looked young and fit. He had short dark hair, and he was wearing a plain white T-shirt, like Castillo. A bandanna encircled his left wrist.

"CVL," Noah guessed.

"Maybe Santiago can use it." Williams hefted his muscular bulk out of the chair. "You want to come to the viewing room?"

Noah leapt at the chance. "Sure."

The viewing room was right across the hall. There were several detectives seated at the control panel, watching the interrogation in progress. Santiago appeared cool and calm, as unruffled as ever in gray trousers and a blue shirt. In contrast, Castillo looked like a crashing addict: gaunt, sweaty, and exhausted.

Williams passed one of the detectives a printout of Castillo with his friend at the border. He communicated the news to Santiago via earpiece.

"We've got footage of you crossing into the United States with a passenger," Santiago said. "I'm sure the DEA will take special interest in your trip. Cooperating with the investigation could save you from doing some serious time."

Castillo was suffering from withdrawal, but he

wasn't stupid. He knew he would go to jail no matter what. "I told you everything I did Friday night. I went to TJ. None of the girls looked good. I came back. That's it."

"Who were you with?"

"Nobody."

"Is 'Nobody' affiliated with CVL?"

Castillo's eyes flashed with defiance. "You think I'm going to talk about CVL?"

"They won't have your back in prison, man."

That was definitely true. The California penal system was ruled by larger, more organized gangs. The Mexican Mafia made the Locos look like Boy Scouts.

"I want a lawyer," Castillo said, shutting off completely. "I didn't do anything to Lola. I'll fucking kill whoever did."

Santiago rose, gesturing for the guard to take Castillo back into custody. He would spend the night in lockdown and speak to a court-appointed attorney tomorrow. The show was over, so Noah left the viewing room with some of the other detectives.

"I heard you took him down hard last night," Williams said.

Noah grunted, flexing his right hand. A rash of scabs had formed across his knuckles. "Almost got shot in the head, too. Pretty stupid."

"Hey, at least you caught him. Once they get away from me on foot, it's over. I wish I could run like the wind."

"I wish I could hit like a Mack truck," Noah said reasonably. "So I guess we're even."

Williams smiled. "How were the girls at Suave?"

"Nice," he admitted.

"You need any help with that footage?"

Noah planned to make a log of any customer interactions with the victim. He would also try to match them up to the descriptions April Ortiz had given him. It would be a tedious job, but he'd rather do it alone. Just in case he took an unprofessional interest in the length and fit of April Ortiz's skirt.

"I think I can manage," he said, smiling back.

"Why don't I ever get to interview fine ladies?" Williams complained to his partner. "Haven't I been good?"

Meghan didn't have any luck along the coast.

Although there were specialty boutiques and ice cream shops, sports-equipment outlets and sandwich delis, none was hiring. At the end of summer, most small businesses were looking to drop a few employees, not gain new ones.

She thought about applying for a work program on campus, but classes didn't start for another three weeks, and she couldn't wait that long. Noah wouldn't understand how serious she was about staying if she didn't get a job.

With renewed determination, she pedaled east, toward the business district on Broadway that her brother had warned her about.

It was a busy area, and there were some raggedly clothed people hanging out around the bus stops, but Meghan didn't feel threatened. She felt . . . enlivened. Unlike her hometown, which was small and quaint and homogenous, Chula Vista was a sprawling urban center, a melting pot of different cultures. It was noisy, and foreign, and a little dirty.

She liked it.

Noah was right about the hiring prospects, however. Meghan didn't speak Spanish, so she was useless in this part of town. The Korean fish market wouldn't want her. And the burger joint looked *really* gross.

Despite her teasing exchange with Noah earlier, she had no intentions of dancing nude or performing "massages."

The sun was burning her bare shoulders, pelting down on the top of her head, and sweat trickled between her breasts. She started looking for a place to buy a cold drink rather than a possible work location.

There was a grocery store on the corner. She'd shopped there before. It was medium size, not one of the huge outlets. The front windows were clear, and the interior looked clean. She didn't see any drug-dealer types near the entrance.

Feeling hopeful, she continued around the building, searching for a bike rack. She spotted one near the back door. As she got off her bike, kneeling to lock it up, a young man sped around the corner, startling her.

He seemed surprised to see her, too. "Sorry," he said, hopping off his own bike. It was one of those freestyle types that could do tricks and maneuver through traffic. The rider was about her age, maybe a year or two older. With his short black hair and nondescript clothing, he resembled many of the other boys she'd seen today.

She watched his hands, so close to hers, as he threaded

a plastic-covered chain through the spokes of his front wheel. For some reason, her heart was racing.

"That's a good lock," he commented.

With trembling fingers, she secured it and looked up to meet his eyes. There was no hint of menace in his face, just mild curiosity. "My brother's a cop," she said, rising. "He says this type of lock is the best."

He stood also, nodding his agreement. "He's right."

Meghan's tank top was sticking to her damp skin, and she felt flushed from the heat. Her fellow bike rider also looked sweaty. He had a blue polo shirt slung over one shoulder, as if he meant to change it inside.

"Do you work here?" she asked.

"Yeah."

"How is it?"

He shrugged. "Could be worse."

"Are they hiring?"

"I think so. Two baggers quit last week."

She moistened her lips. "Who should I talk to?"

"Jack," he said in a derisive tone. "He'll probably hire you on the spot."

"You think so?"

"He likes pretty girls."

Meghan lifted a hand to her hair, embarrassed by the compliment. He seemed to want to say something else, but he didn't. "What's your name?" she asked.

He held out his hand. "Eric."

"I'm Meghan."

"*Mucho gusto.*"

He smiled as he shook her hand, and she felt an odd jump in her tummy. He had nice white teeth, and he smelled kind of good. Like he'd just showered.

"*Mucho gusto,*" she repeated lamely, releasing his hand.

He laughed. "No, you say, *El gusto es mío.* 'The pleasure is mine.' "

She couldn't possibly say that to him. In fact, she was ready to burst into flames at the mere mention of pleasure.

His amusement faded as he became aware of her discomfort. "Jack will be out front. Good luck."

"Thanks." She walked along the side of the building, chiding herself all the way. He hadn't even been trying to flirt with her. It was just that he was handsome, and everything sounded sexy in Spanish.

"*El gusto es mío,*" she practiced huskily, rolling her eyes.

Inside the market, the air-conditioning hit her overheated flesh like an arctic blast. She walked past the checkout aisles, looking for an office area.

There were two employees lounging at the electronics counter, both wearing identical blue shirts. The girl had black hair with ash-blond streaks. She was attractive, in a sultry kind of way. Her companion was tall and lanky, with shaggy brown hair and sleepy eyes.

"Hello there," he said, looking Meghan up and down.

This must be Jack.

"Hi," she said, feeling an attack of nerves. "I was wondering if I could pick up an application."

"Sure! I've got one around here somewhere."

While he riffled through a stack of papers underneath the counter, the girl leaning against it arched a critical brow. "Nice haircut."

Meghan gave her a similar inspection. "Nice high-lights."

"I'm Cristina," she said, dropping the attitude. "This is Jack."

Jack passed her an application. "Meghan Young," she murmured, introducing herself. "Do you mind if I fill it out here?"

"Be my guest."

"I have work to do," Cristina sighed.

Jack watched her walk away. His eyes were glazed and a bit bloodshot.

"Are you hiring?" Meghan asked.

He turned his attention back to her, drumming his fingertips against the counter. "Depends."

"On what?"

"Do you have any experience bagging?"

She didn't have any experience, period. "You put cold stuff with cold stuff," she said. "Heavy on bottom, light on top."

He smiled lazily. "What do you say to customers?"

" 'Need any help out with that, ma'am?' "

"How do you do a price check?"

Meghan shrugged. "Take the product back to its place on the shelves and read the tag."

"What's Brie?"

"Cheese."

"Where would you find falafel?"

She had no idea what that was. "Ethnic-foods aisle?"

"*Habla español?*"

"No. Sorry. I know some sign language."

"Okay," he said, coming out from behind the

counter. "You seem like a fast learner, and I have enough dipshits on staff. Come on back for a W-2."

She hadn't even filled out the application yet. "I'm hired?"

"Yep. Can you start right now? We're shorthanded."

She followed him through a set of double doors with flaps around the edges. "Okay," she said, looking around the storage area. It was chaotic. There were boxes of produce stacked up to the ceiling. Eric and another man were moving cartons of milk.

Perhaps because the workers had to come in and out from the unloading dock so often, there was no air-conditioning in the back room.

After spending time in the front of the store, Meghan felt comfortable and cool. Eric and his coworker weren't so lucky. She saw beads of sweat gathered at Eric's hairline. The muscles in his forearms flexed as he lifted two gallons.

"How many times do I have to talk to you guys about hygiene?" Jack said in a loud voice. "We sell antiperspirant in aisle five."

"Fuck off," Eric grunted, not breaking his stride.

Jack laughed, as if Eric was joking. Meghan didn't think he was. "Here's a shirt," he said, handing her a royal-blue polo. "We have large and extra-large."

"Large is fine," she said, accepting the garment. It wasn't new, but it looked clean.

"Bathroom's there." He pointed at a door with male and female symbols in a blue circle on the front. "Fill out all that stuff and clock in."

She hugged the shirt to her chest, swallowing drily.

"Cristina will train you."

"Great."

Eric and his coworker didn't slow down after Jack exited the storage area. They kept the same steady pace, stocking gallon after gallon. Meghan tried not to stare at them as she filled out the necessary forms, but her interest was piqued.

Eric was the taller of the two, and he had a strong, lean physique. There was a brown bandanna tied in a cuff around his wrist. An odd fashion accessory, but not unattractive. As he stocked the upper levels of the milk cooler, his short sleeve fell back a few inches, revealing a line of tattooed script curling around his biceps.

Meghan didn't find that glimpse of skin unattractive, either.

Flushing, she glanced away, studying her surroundings. The small table was flanked by three plastic chairs. There was a microwave and mini-fridge near the time clock. As employee lounges went, it was pretty dismal, but beggars couldn't be choosers. She completed the application, leaving the *desired pay* box empty.

This position had minimum wage written all over it.

It took her a few more minutes to fill out the W-2 and to figure out how to clock in with a time sheet. When that was done, she retreated to the bathroom to change her shirt. The energy-efficient lighting made her face look wan and her eyes hollow.

Shuddering, she rearranged her headband and walked out.

Eric was standing by the table, drinking bottled water. She watched his smooth brown throat work as he swallowed.

"Um . . . where can I put my stuff?"

Glancing at her canvas messenger bag, he opened a lower cabinet. "Here."

She tossed her bag inside, among others. "Thanks."

He nodded politely, but his demeanor seemed guarded. Maybe Jack's comment about hygiene had embarrassed him.

"*El gusto es mío,*" she said on impulse.

Laughing softly, he shook his head. "That phrase isn't really appropriate for this situation, but okay."

"I guess I need more practice."

His gaze dropped to her lips for a moment, and she got the impression that he wanted to offer his assistance.

"Well, um, see you later," she said, beating a hasty retreat.

"Later," he agreed.

The next few hours passed in a rush. Jack hadn't lied about being shorthanded, and his hands-off managerial style was inefficient. Some employees were more helpful than others. Meghan bagged double the amount of groceries as did Cristina, for example.

Before she knew it, darkness had fallen, and it was closing time.

"Come back tomorrow afternoon," Jack said.

When Meghan left the building, Eric was already outside, unlocking his bike. It was a dark, hot night. "Do you live far?" he asked, reading the trepidation on her face.

"A few miles. Imperial Beach."

He nodded. "I can ride with you."

"Where do you live?"

"Castle Park."

That neighborhood was in the opposite direction, which made his offer twice as sweet. "Is—is it safe around here this late?"

"Not always. Not for a girl alone."

"I'll be okay as long as I stay on my bike," she asserted.

"You have a cell phone?"

She shook her head. In a fit of pique, her mother had demanded that Meghan return it before she left home.

"Hold on a minute," he said, rummaging through his backpack. He found a metal whistle on a white string. "Try that."

Pursing her lips, she brought it to her mouth and blew. The sound it made was loud and shrill, piercing the night air. They both laughed in surprise.

"That'll attract attention," he said.

She looped the whistle around her neck. "I'll give it back tomorrow."

"Don't worry about it. My niece gave it to me. She thinks I like toys."

Meghan smiled. "Then it's extra-special."

They stared at each other for another moment. She wished she'd agreed to let him take her home. Flustered, she bent to unlock her bike from the rack. When they parted ways on the main drag, she felt a strange pull, as if an invisible thread connected them.

Touching the metal at her neck, still cool against her skin, she pedaled home.

6

🌿 April sprang awake at seven the next morning, her heart pounding.

She'd had a nightmare that Josefa took Jenny to the beach on the back of her boyfriend's motorcycle. April was chasing after them in her car. She thought she could hear Jenny screaming, but she couldn't get the windows rolled down. Her front windshield was dusty and the sun was too bright, obstructing her vision.

Traffic stopped suddenly. In a squeal of tires, she rear-ended another vehicle.

Shaking off the bad dream, she sat up, pushing the hair out of her eyes. Jenny was a soft, warm weight beside her. As usual, she'd drifted toward April in the middle of the night. Now her small body was on April's side of the queen-sized bed, leaving the other half empty.

April slid off the edge with a groan. Although she paid every penny of rent, she shared a room with Jenny. Until recently, she'd been satisfied with the arrangement. Jenny had never liked her crib, not even as a newborn, so April had brought the baby into her bed, where they were both comfortable. She'd been a nervous young mother, and keeping Jenny close felt reassuring. Being together at night had worked for them.

Over time, April began to wish for more personal space. Jenny didn't need to be snuggled as much or watched every moment. Like most little girls, she longed for her own room, filled with fun toys, decorated in her favorite colors.

April ached to give her those things. She hadn't planned to be a teen mother or a single parent, but she'd promised to do right by Jenny. She wanted more for her daughter than what she'd had: no father figure, no financial stability, no positive role models.

But here she was, struggling to make ends meet, going it alone. Like Josefa, April had a history of poor choices and bad men.

She knew her mother was sorry about leaving Jenny the other night. When they came back from the beach, Josefa had greeted them with a nice dinner. She'd even made Jenny's favorite desert, orange flan. April wasn't appeased by the gesture, but she hadn't said a word. After a tense evening, they all retired early.

April couldn't keep her silence any longer.

She used the bathroom and dressed quickly, splashing cool water on her face. Then she woke Jenny, giving her a light breakfast before ushering her out the door. Yesterday, she'd spoken to her neighbor about taking over for Josefa as Jenny's babysitter. Consuela had three daughters of her own, the youngest of whom was Jenny's age, and the girls were already playmates. Her husband worked a seasonal job up north, and Consuela said she could use the extra money. It was a relief to have the details settled.

Now she had to break the news to Josefa.

April took Jenny by the hand, looking both ways before they crossed the street. Filled with apprehension, she knocked on Consuela's front door. "Can Jenny play with Fabiana for a few minutes?" she asked in Spanish, after the woman answered. "I need to talk to my mother about our . . . situation."

"My *abuelita* is sick," Jenny said helpfully. "She takes too much medicine."

Consuela waved her inside. "Of course, *m'ija.* Take all the time you need."

"Gracias."

April wiped her sweaty palms on her shorts as she returned to her house. It was cool and overcast at this time of morning, but the sun would burn through the clouds soon enough. Inside the living room, Josefa was curled up on the couch, her slender hands wrapped around an oversize coffee mug.

April needed some caffeine herself. She'd tossed and turned most of the night, anticipating this conversation.

"Where's Jenny?"

"At Consuela's. From now on she's going to sleep over there on the evenings I work."

Her mother recoiled as if she'd been struck. Then she set her mug aside. "I'm sorry about the other night. I feel terrible about leaving Jenny. I meant to come right back, and—" She waved her hands in front of her face, erasing the memory of her transgression. "No excuses. It won't happen again."

April sank into an overstuffed chair, not bothering

with coffee. Her stomach was already churning. "Has it happened before?"

She blinked her pretty brown eyes. "No."

Hiding her unsteady hands, April crossed her arms over her chest. "Have you brought men over?"

"No," Josefa said, with more vehemence.

April thought she was telling the truth, but Josefa was a good liar. "If I find out you let a man so much as *look* at my daughter, I will never forgive you. Ever."

Josefa's eyes filled with tears. "I haven't."

April felt the same pressure behind her eyelids, so she took a deep breath. She pictured Jenny cowering in her closet, and it tore her apart inside. As a child, April had done the same, when one of Josefa's boyfriends had tried to break in to her room at night.

She'd rather die than allow that to happen to Jenny. "I'm sorry, *Mamá*. I can't live like this anymore. You have to get help—or leave."

Josefa stared at her in disbelief. "Because of one little mistake?"

"It was a big mistake, Mom. And hardly your first."

"It won't happen again," she swore.

"I found coke in your purse."

Her face paled. "That wasn't mine."

Although her throat felt raw, April made a scoffing sound. "What if Jenny found your stash? What if she decided to try one of your 'vitamins'?"

"I'll cut down," she said, making the sign of the cross. *"Te lo juro."*

She'd heard that promise before. "No."

"What do you mean?"

"I want you to quit. Join a program. Attend meetings. Whatever it takes."

Josefa stayed silent for a moment, wiping the tears from her cheeks. "My life has been damned hard, and I think I deserve to have some fun. When Jenny gets older, you'll want to let your hair down, too."

"You've been letting your hair down since before I was born, Mom."

"That's not true! I doted on you when you were a baby. I've always been devoted to you. And to Jenny. How many hours have I cared for her and never asked for a dime? This is the thanks I get? For taking you in when you were pregnant, your face bruised—"

April held up a hand, warding off the tirade. "You watched Jenny in exchange for reduced rent, which you haven't paid in months. You've also stolen money from my purse. We're more than square."

Her mother reached out to grab her wrist. "Don't take Jenny away from me. I love her so much. Please."

April pulled away from Josefa's clawlike grasp, pressing her lips together to keep them from trembling. "You're not welcome here anymore. I won't accept your calls or let you visit. Until you decide to get clean, I don't want you in my daughter's life." Her voice wavered, threatening to break. "I don't want you in my life."

"You're throwing me out on the streets," Josefa said, rising to her feet. "Where do you expect me to go?"

Her mother knew at least a dozen men who would take her out partying, but none who would support her on a long-term basis. Most of her friends were irresponsible drunks. She hadn't worked in almost a year, and she no longer received disability checks for the minor injury that had fueled her prescription-drug addiction.

She had no money, no resources, no opportunities. April was literally kicking her mother to the curb. "I'm sorry," she said, swallowing hard.

Josefa stormed out of the room, making her choice. "I can quit anytime I want to." Cursing in Spanish, she opened her dresser drawers and started throwing her clothes on the bed. "Just because you're *fría,* you think everyone should live like a nun."

April looked away, blinking the tears from her eyes. "I'm taking Jenny to the park for a few hours," she said, moving toward the front door before she could change her mind. "I don't want her to be traumatized by a big scene. If you love her as much as you say you do, you'll go quietly." She walked out, stifling a sob with the back of her hand.

Oh, God. She'd just sentenced her mother to a lifetime of turning tricks and sleeping under bridges.

What kind of a horrible person was she?

Hitching her purse up on one shoulder, she strode across the street to retrieve Jenny. Consuela looked concerned, and April couldn't think of a way to put her mind at ease. Giving her a wobbly smile, she took Jenny by the arm and pulled her along, needing to get away from the neighborhood before she broke down.

They walked to the nicer park, the one in the quiet neighborhood near Imperial Beach. Jenny bothered her with incessant questions the entire way. A tension headache began to throb at her temples, blurring the edges of her vision.

Most of the time, Jenny was a sweet, well-behaved child, but her boundless energy and quick intelligence made her difficult to care for. She was active, inquisitive, and chatty. When April was upset or distracted, Jenny often reacted by dialing up the wattage on her high-octane personality. Today there was no shushing her.

As soon as they arrived at the park, April bought a diet soda from the vending machine. After taking a long drink, she surrendered to the inevitable and let Jenny have a sip. "Just what you need," she muttered. "Caffeine."

"Can I go play now?"

She collapsed on the park bench. "Hang on a second. I want to talk to you about something."

Jenny sat down next to her, impatient. Her eyes darted across the grassy lawn, still wet with morning dew, toward the small playground.

April put her hand on Jenny's arm, holding her attention. "Your *abuelita* will be staying with some friends for a while. She's not going to live with us anymore."

Jenny frowned. "Why?"

A lump rose to her throat. "Because the medicine is making her sick," she managed, "and she needs to go away to get better."

Jenny's eyes filled with tears. "Will she be gone forever, like Daddy?"

April hadn't seen that question coming, and it hit her like a sucker punch. Raul had been gone only a few years, and he had several more left in his prison sentence. It probably seemed like forever to Jenny, who had very few memories of her father. To April, it wasn't long enough by half.

"I don't know," she said honestly. "I hope she'll come back. For now you'll go to Fabiana's house on the nights I have to work."

Jenny's face became animated. "Like . . . a sleepover?"

"Yes."

She thought about it for a moment. "Okay."

After a few more questions, about which toys she could take with her, Jenny leapt off the bench and ran toward the playground, happy.

April drank her Diet Coke in silence, relieved by the respite. She hadn't been sure how Jenny would take the news. More tears would probably come later, after she had time to process the information.

Hopefully, Josefa would leave with dignity rather than hysterics.

If Jenny had a father at home, things would be different. April had no one to turn to for emotional support. Other than work or class, she didn't go anywhere without Jenny. There were no days off from being a parent. She couldn't take a nap on the beach while Jenny splashed in the waves or doze on the park bench while she ran around the playground.

The constant vigilance was exhausting.

What she needed most—a break—she couldn't have. And yet, despite Jenny's company, she felt unbearably alone.

"Damn it," she said, wiping her eyes with the back of her hand. Even tears seemed like a luxury at this point. No matter how much she wanted to, she couldn't break down and bawl like a baby in a public park.

When she'd left Raul, she vowed to be a good mother. For years, she'd had no interest in dating. She hadn't wanted to be like Josefa, bringing strange men in and out of her daughter's life. Now she wondered if she'd made the right choice. Jenny adored Eric, and there were other nice guys out there. Maybe Jenny would have benefited from having another man around.

April could certainly use the help.

Her mother had called her *fría*—cold. She wasn't cold; she was afraid. Afraid that if she started dating again, she'd make bad choices. If she had a few drinks, she'd go back to her old ways. If she let down her guard, she'd get hurt, physically and emotionally, all over again.

She sighed, taking a small notebook out of her purse to crunch numbers. During the summer she always worked full-time, so they were in good shape. She'd planned to cut down her hours at the club when school started. Serving drinks until the wee hours of the morning made it difficult to stay alert in class.

Now that she had to pay for a babysitter, she'd have to work at least three nights a week or continue to rely on Eric for handouts. Frustrated, she shoved the notebook back into her purse, glancing toward the playground.

Jenny was gone.

Noah's running shoes pounded the pavement as he crossed 5th Avenue. He usually stayed in his own neighborhood, paying only cursory attention to his surroundings. Today he'd brought the case with him and been drawn to a different part of town.

The grainy footage from Club Suave had been almost worthless. The quality was so poor, he could barely tell the waitresses apart. Both Lola Sanchez and April Ortiz had long, dark hair and similar body types. On closer study, he recognized April by her brisk walk and confident posture. Lola delivered drinks in a more leisurely fashion, lingering at certain tables. From what he could tell, none of the customers behaved in a strange or inappropriate way.

Tony Castillo said he hadn't seen Lola at all that day. He'd admitted that Lola was his sometimes girlfriend but stuck to the story that he'd been cruising the red-light district alone. Even after a cache of narcotics was seized at his residence, Castillo refused to name his partner. He'd been charged with possession, intent to sell, and trafficking.

But was ruled out as a murder suspect.

It was obvious that Castillo had gone to Mexico for more drugs. Noah figured that Lola, like most addicts, hadn't wanted to wait for her fix. She went looking elsewhere and ran into serious trouble.

One of the other waitresses had dropped Lola off at a friend's house after work. The friend, who'd been letting Lola sleep on the couch, hadn't heard her come in. She'd probably walked down the street to score a hit.

Usually, women knew their killers on an intimate level. Husbands, boyfriends, and lovers were natural suspects.

But there was also a possibility that Lola had no connection to her killer. If he was a stranger to her, all bets were off. Lola might have been targeted simply because she was available or fit a certain type. This kind of perpetrator would be difficult to catch without witnesses or trace evidence.

He might strike again, choosing a similar victim.

Noah jogged past Lola's friend's house, giving it a cursory glance. In any murder investigation, regardless of motive, locations were important. The distance between Lola's last known address and the crime scene would be mapped in an attempt to retrace her steps. He'd wanted to visit these key points on foot and get a feel for the physical space.

April Ortiz lived nearby, according to her employee file. Alegría Park was less than a mile away. During the day, the park was frequented by children and families, but after sunset, drug dealers lurked in the shadows.

Maybe Lola had gone there for a buy.

Noah continued on to the park, trying to catch his stride over the next few blocks. Running was a great stress reliever for him, but today he felt off balance. The sun began to burn through the clouds, beating down on the top of his head, and the air thickened with humidity.

He slowed as he rounded the corner of the park, still thinking about the investigation. Santiago hadn't asked him to give the matter his complete attention, but Noah had. Someone in this neighborhood knew something.

He paused at the drinking fountain, his mind whirring with information. Time of death. Chula Vista Locos. April Ortiz.

A little girl in pigtails stood in front of him, struggling to get a drink. She couldn't quite reach the spout. Noah looked around for help, wondering if he should give her a boost. There was a slender dark-haired woman sitting on a park bench, her back to them. "Here," he said, planting his foot in front of the fountain. "Step up."

The child's eyes darted from the woman, to his face, to his size 12s. She looked thirsty.

"Go on."

She did, standing on the top of his shoe, watching him warily as she drank. When she was finished, she stepped down, wiped her mouth, and stared at him.

There was something familiar about her.

Noah glanced toward the woman on the bench. Now she was giving him a good profile, sitting up straight and frowning at the empty playground. He recognized her immediately. "That your mom?" he asked.

The little girl ran back to the playground.

April caught the movement and relaxed, spotting her quarry. Then, like any protective mother, she turned to look at him, assessing a possible threat. Her eyes widened and she whirled around, facing forward once again.

Noah's heart, still pumping hard from the run, surged in his chest. It was the same sensation he'd felt the first time he saw her. Lucky for him, he had a professional reason to approach. Tamping down his excitement, he bent his head and drank from the fountain, gulping a few swallows of tepid water before he walked across the grassy lawn.

The little girl ducked behind a play structure, watching him.

April was wearing a pearl-gray tank top and navy shorts with white ankle socks and ratty tennis shoes.

Her legs were long, smooth, honey brown. He wasn't sure how the modest outfit could look sexier than her skimpy work uniform, but damned if it didn't.

She kept her attention on the playground. She also appeared to be holding her breath. Maybe keeping her fingers crossed, too. When she finally stopped pretending he wasn't there and leveled her gaze at him, his breath quickened.

With her casual clothes and fresh-scrubbed face, she looked approachable. Touchable. Like she'd just rolled out of bed.

"Hi," he said.

Her cheeks colored, very slightly. "Hi."

"Did you not want to talk to me?"

"No, I . . ." She trailed off, giving up the pretense. Of course she hadn't wanted to talk to him. But she couldn't ignore him, either. "Have a seat."

"Your daughter?" he asked, nodding at Little April as he sat down.

"Yes."

"She looks just like you."

Noah could tell she wasn't any more relaxed with him here than she'd been at the club, so he cut to the chase. "Thanks for the tip the other night. I know you were taking a risk by giving me information. I appreciate it."

"You're welcome. Did it work out?"

"Maybe. He had an outstanding warrant. He's in custody." Noah hesitated, considering how much to reveal. "He, uh, pulled a gun on me."

Her eyes flew to his, her expression alarmed. She gave him a quick once-over.

"I wasn't hurt."

"Oh, my God," she whispered, covering her mouth with one hand.

"Does Eddie do business with Castillo? Is that why you wouldn't say anything at the club?"

She looked at her daughter, who was alternating between watching them and playing. There were two other children on the playground, and they'd begun a friendly game of chase. "Tony doesn't come to the club," she murmured, evasive. "I'd dropped Lola off at his house one night, so I assumed they were involved."

"Had they broken up recently?"

"I don't know. I wasn't lying when I said we weren't friends. Carmen told me their relationship was troubled. I think she went out with whoever had drugs."

"Including Eddie?"

She shrugged.

"He didn't mention a camera inside his office. Do you know what goes on in there? Does he meet with drug dealers, gang members?"

"I know he plays poker. There might be some gambling and stuff."

"According to your coworkers, Lola called in sick a lot and was frequently late. How did she keep her job?"

She gave him a sideways glance. "How do you think she kept it?"

He couldn't prevent his gaze from sliding down to her lips. She had the most sensuous mouth he'd ever seen. "Are you saying that she performed sexual favors?"

"I have to go," she said, tugging on the strap of her purse.

He put his hand on her arm. "Wait. I didn't mean to make you uncomfortable."

She stared out at the playground, refusing to meet his eyes.

Noah felt her skin against his fingertips and watched the rapid pulse at her neck. He swallowed hard, aware that he was losing his objectivity. She wasn't being totally honest with him, and he didn't blame her. With reluctance, he dropped his hand. "Do you know if Tony has a partner, someone connected to CVL?"

Her attention jerked back to him. "No," she said, shaking her head in overemphasis. "Why?"

"I'm just trying to collect information for the case," he said mildly.

"You aren't a homicide detective. Your card says gang unit."

He was flattered that she'd noticed. Most people tossed his card in the trash. "Lola's murder might be gang-related, and I hope to work on homicide someday. If I do well on this case, I'll have a better chance of making the team."

Her mouth softened, but she didn't relax her posture. "I've said more than I should have already. I can't afford to get fired. I have a daughter to take care of."

Noah glanced at the girl on the swing, considering April's dilemma. She was fiercely protective of her child, an admirable trait. He got the impression that she guarded herself with the same diligence. He'd studied her body language on video, noting the subtle distance she kept from male customers.

Someone had made her cautious.

"Are you still with her dad?" he asked.

It was an impulsive question, inappropriate and personal. Her eyes became shuttered. "What does that have to do with your investigation?"

"Nothing," he admitted.

She stared at him for a moment, silent. The air between them grew heavy, weighted with tension. Although she didn't respond verbally, the exchange felt intimate. Simply by holding his gaze, she shared more than she'd given in the secret note.

Noah knew he should disengage himself from this situation. Although he was off duty, he was acting in an official capacity. Police officers weren't supposed to put the moves on interviewees.

Even if she was available and interested, he wasn't free to pursue her.

A trickle of sweat ran down the line of his jaw, reminding him that he was damp and disheveled. Not very appealing. "Damn," he said, lifting the hem of his T-shirt to wipe his face. "This heat wave is killing me."

Her eyes wandered over to the exposed part of his torso. "It's the humidity," she said, her voice thin.

Great. Now they were talking about the weather.

"Mommy!" April's little girl ran toward the park bench, her cheeks flushed. "I don't want to play anymore." She slipped her arms around her mother's slim waist, giving Noah a look that was surely an invitation to buzz off.

"I'm Noah," he said, smiling.

She stuck out her tongue.

"Jenny!"

He laughed, taking no offense.

"That's not nice," April said. Jenny hid her face against her mother's hip.

"It's okay," he said easily. He'd needed the interruption.

April put her hand on Jenny's shoulder. "I'm sorry," she said, flashing him an embarrassed smile.

He rose to his feet, blinking the stars from his eyes. "Well. Thanks again for the tip."

"You're welcome. Noah."

After he left the park, he ran like the wind, feeling oddly lighthearted. This investigation was the most challenging of his career by far. And April Ortiz was the sexiest, most irresistible puzzle he'd ever met.

7

The heat didn't let up all week.

On Friday, the sun was out in full force as Eric rode his bike down Chula Vista's main drag, toward Bonita Market. He'd been keeping a low profile since Tony Castillo got arrested. Although he'd made some subtle inquiries about Lola Sanchez, no one in the neighborhood seemed to know anything.

Tony was a dopehead and a thug, but Eric knew he hadn't killed Lola. Pulling a gun on a cop or getting into an altercation over a drug deal—those were crimes he was capable of. Murdering a defenseless woman? Eric couldn't believe he'd stoop so low.

Then again, he'd seen Tony do some horrible things in the ten years they'd been acquainted. One memory continued to haunt him. Last night he'd dreamed he was helping his brother dig another hole.

Eric pushed aside those dark thoughts and pedaled faster, cutting through the heavy traffic on Broadway. He rolled into the parking lot at his usual time, five minutes before 3:00 P.M. He worked six hours, five days a week.

The job was neither difficult nor easy. Unloading and stocking grocery goods, no matter how tiresome and monotonous, was better than laying bricks, flipping burgers, or digging ditches. He knew because he'd done all three.

Bonita Market had its perks.

He locked up his bike and went inside, spotting one of the perks the instant he walked through the back door. Meghan Young was sitting at the break table with Cristina, sharing the earpieces from an iPod.

Her bangs swept down over her face, covering one eye.

The two girls had become fast friends, which surprised him. They didn't have much in common. Meghan was from some hick town up north; Cristina had been born here in the city. Cristina favored low-rise jeans, belly-baring tops, and flashy colors. Meghan had a quieter, more eclectic style.

Meghan glanced up at him and smiled, causing his pulse to accelerate.

Today she wore faded Levi's and a sleeveless checkered shirt. Her haircut was boyish. Kind of emo, he guessed. It didn't detract from her beauty. There was an artistic, intelligent quality about her that drew his attention.

Cristina, with her overt sex appeal and bad-girl attitude, was Eric's usual type. Self-centered and fun-loving, not particularly thoughtful or ambitious. She had a pierced tongue and low expectations. If he asked her out, she'd say yes. He could probably just fuck her, with or without a date.

But he wouldn't.

Cristina was his best friend's little sister, for one thing. He also wasn't that into her. Meghan was a lot more tempting but equally off-limits. She had a cop brother, which gave her an automatic fail in the hookup department.

Sighing, he stashed his backpack under the counter and tossed his work polo over his shoulder. Nodding at Meghan and Cristina, he headed to Jack's office. He had a special delivery to make, and the door was open.

Jack was inside, leaning back in his desk chair. Basically doing nothing.

"Don't you ever fucking knock, dude?"

Eric shut the door behind him and took the plastic bag from his pocket, tossing it on the surface of the desk.

Jack's annoyance disappeared. Sitting forward, he snatched up the bag and brought it to his nose, inhaling deeply. With his bony face and sparse goatee, he reminded Eric of a rat. "This is the good shit?"

Eric hadn't exactly tested it out. Jack wanted pot so strong he saw spaceships, and Eric preferred to stay on planet earth. "It's good enough for you."

After Jack grumbled a little, breaking Eric's balls about Mexicans and their no-good dirt weed, he reached into his wallet and pulled out a wad of cash. Eric didn't bother to count it. Jack was an asshole, but he didn't underpay.

"Thanks," Jack said. He knew he was getting a good deal.

"Anytime, man," Eric replied, pocketing the money and leaving the office. He didn't have high standards for the clients he sold to. As long as they were adults, and reasonably discreet, he didn't care what they thought of him.

At the break table, Cristina asked Meghan a question about the band they were listening to. When Meghan shook her head, the earpiece fell out of her ear. They both reached for it at the same time. Somehow, Cristina got her bracelet snagged on the front of Meghan's T-shirt. Meghan gasped and covered her breast with her hand, as if she'd been pinched, and they both dissolved into giggles.

It was a fleeting, innocent exchange, but Eric's mind went straight to the gutter. When two hot girls were sitting close together, laughing and touching each other, a guy couldn't prevent his thoughts from wandering.

"Get to work, slacker," Jack called out, ruining the fantasy.

Eric glanced back at him, clenching his hand into a fist. He hadn't even clocked in yet, and Jack knew it.

Jack also knew Eric wasn't a slacker. Slacking off, and pretending to manage the store, was Jack's job. As the owner's son, his behavior was above reproach, of course. He didn't appreciate the opportunity he'd been given, because he hadn't worked for it. Jack spent his afternoons daydreaming about waves and harassing female employees. Maybe one day his dad would get fed up and fire him. Until then, Jack was the boss, and Eric would have to refrain from punching him in his dope-smoking mouth.

Meghan rose from the table, afraid she would get reprimanded also, and Cristina put her iPod away, rolling her eyes.

Eric went to the bathroom to change his shirt, his

motions choppy with anger. Before Meghan got hired, Jack's attitude hadn't really bothered him. For some reason, being heckled in front of her was more humiliating.

When he walked out of the restroom, she was standing there. "What's up, Gusto?" she said in a breathy voice. For his ears only.

"Nothing much, Mía."

Smiling, she ducked inside to change her own shirt.

Since the day they met, she'd been teasing him with that pet name, a play on their first conversation. He'd picked it up immediately. She called him *Pleasure* and he called her *Mine*. With another girl, the game might have seemed sexual, but he wasn't sure she was aware of those undertones.

Eric certainly understood them, and he would have to keep his distance. She wasn't the kind of girl he could fool around with.

He clocked in and got to work, unloading the delivery truck with Hector at his side. For Eric, the repetitive physical labor was relaxing, and some of the stress of his everyday life ebbed away. When he was lifting cartons and carrying boxes, there was no police car following him. No gang politics, no mother in Mexico, no brother in jail.

Soon enough, it was quitting time. He paid for some groceries, using his employee discount, and put the items in his backpack. On his way out, he overheard Jack chatting up Meghan and Cristina, trying to talk them into something.

"There's a bonfire tonight in IB," Jack said, draping

an arm across Meghan's shoulders. "You girls should come out. It'll be off the hook."

"Where at?" Cristina asked.

"The south pier."

She shrugged. "Sounds cool."

Meghan glanced at Eric. "Are you going?"

Eric adjusted his backpack, considering. Jack hadn't invited him, and he had some other responsibilities to take care of tonight. But he felt a stronger, more pervasive urge to do whatever pleased her.

"I don't think Eric is allowed in that part of town," Jack said with a smirk. "Do homeboys go to the beach?"

Meghan frowned at Jack's language, taking offense. She had no idea.

"I can make it," Eric heard himself say.

Jack's brows rose in surprise, but he didn't protest. When push came to shove, he was kind of a pussy. Eric got the impression that Jack was secretly intimidated by him. Maybe that was why he acted like such a jerk.

"See you there," Eric said, cursing under his breath as he left the building. Why had he made such a stupid promise? He didn't want to hang out at the beach with a bunch of drunk, belligerent surfers.

Cristina followed him out the door, watching while he unlocked his bike. "You aren't going to tell Junior, are you?"

He laughed, shaking his head. "No."

"Good," she said, relieved that her big brother wouldn't be showing up to spoil her fun. Eric didn't want Junior there, either, for personal reasons. His best friend couldn't be trusted not to start a fight.

As soon as he straightened, Cristina leaned in and

kissed his cheek, letting her fingertips linger where her mouth had been. "*Al rato.*"

Meghan came through the back door just in time to witness the exchange.

That kind of kiss was no big deal, but Cristina had a suggestive way about her, and she'd put him in an awkward position. It would be rude not to return the gesture. "*Al rato,*" he said, brushing his lips over her cheek.

Meghan looked away, uncomfortable.

"Later," he said to her.

She gave him a tight smile. "Bye."

On the way home, he told himself it didn't matter what she thought. It was better not to get involved with her. In fact, he should skip the bonfire altogether.

He weaved through traffic, torn by indecision. The temperature had dropped at least ten degrees, and the humidity had eased off, making his ride more pleasant. A light breeze rippled through his white T-shirt, drying the sweat on his skin.

The city pulsed with heat and energy on Friday night. Traffic lights lit up the streets, radios were on full blast, and car horns blared. The neighborhood seemed like a living, breathing thing, a monster awakening from sleep.

Eric hadn't felt this alive in a long time.

Meghan had a strange effect on him. Her presence made him realize how unsatisfied he'd been lately. He did whatever it took to get by, and he wasn't ashamed of that, but he was more aware of the consequences of his actions now. If he had only himself to consider, he might leave Chula Vista.

Sometimes he wished he could just . . . run away.

At home, the volume on the TV was turned all the way up. He quieted the noise, greeting his grandmother with a kiss on the cheek. "Is your hearing aid on?"

Chuckling, she adjusted it. "*Se me olvidó.*"

"What do you want for dinner? Tomato soup?"

"*Sí, m'ijo. Gracias.*"

He put the groceries away and heated a bowl of soup for both of them, adding a quesadilla on the side. He devoured his meal in record time and went to take a shower, eager to get ready for the bonfire. Wiping away the condensation on the mirror, he checked his face for stubble.

After slapping on some deodorant and gargling mouthwash, he wrapped a towel around his waist and left the bathroom.

Junior was sitting on his bed, flipping through an old issue of *Lowrider*. "Damn," he said, studying a picture of a girl bent over a tricked-out El Camino. Her metallic silver bikini bottoms left nothing to the imagination.

"Do you mind?"

Junior waved his hand in the air. "Nah, bro. Go ahead."

Eric was the one who minded, of course, but not enough to argue about it. He grabbed a pair of boxer shorts from his top drawer and put them on, along with his newest pair of jeans. Tugging a sleeveless undershirt over his head, he opened his closet and stared at its contents. After a brief hesitation, he chose a dark-green polo.

"What the fuck are you doing?" Junior asked. Normally, they dressed alike. Tan pants, white T-shirt, brown bandanna. "I thought we had plans."

"Sorry. Something came up."

Junior narrowed his eyes. "You're trying to get on a chick."

Eric glanced at his reflection. "Nah."

"Yeah, you are."

He wasn't going to admit it. First of all, he didn't plan on hooking up with anyone. Second, he wouldn't tell Junior if he was. Third, he couldn't explain how he felt about Meghan. There was no shame in trying to get laid, but hanging out with a cop's sister because he liked her company—well, that was social suicide.

"Is it April?"

He frowned at Junior. "Hell, no."

"I'd try to get on her if I was you. Holy fuck, she is hot."

Eric had heard that before, so he didn't bother responding. April was his niece's mother, and he wouldn't disrespect Raul by hitting on her.

"This sucks, dude, because I stopped by the craft shop on my way here."

He watched while Junior pulled two black cans of spray paint from his backpack. They were professional quality, for graphic artists. A grin broke across Eric's face. "Hell, yeah. How much do I owe you?"

"*Nada, güey.* I ganked them."

Eric laughed, giving him a CVL handshake and a one-armed hug. "We'll go out tomorrow night and put these to good use."

As soon as his friend left, Eric stashed the cans in his closet. When he wasn't home to help his grandmother into bed, she often slept in the recliner in the living room. Before he said goodbye, he put her walker by the chair and placed a blanket within reach.

On his way out, he stopped by the garage, deliberating. His '72 Chevelle was a pretty sweet ride, but he drove her on special occasions only. Most of the time he could get around faster on a bike, and he preferred that anonymous method of transportation.

For a date, he'd take the car. But—this wasn't a date.

Running a loving hand along the side of the car, he whispered, *"Hasta la vista,"* locked the garage, and walked down to the bus stop.

"I'm not wearing that," Meghan said, pushing the shirt at Cristina.

"Just try it on."

"I can't. It's too . . ."

"Sexy?"

"Slutty."

Cristina squinted at her. "Do you want to look like a girl or a boy?"

Meghan grabbed the black tank top Cristina had brought for her and went back into the bathroom, slamming the door. She changed quickly.

The thin black top had a low, scooped neckline edged in lace. It wasn't as revealing as she thought it would be. Her boobs weren't falling out, and her bra didn't show. "Whatever," she said, rolling her eyes.

"Much better," Cristina said with a nod, finishing her makeup. She was wearing a red tube top and skintight jeans.

Meghan had to admit, her friend had a great figure.

Walking up beside Cristina, she scrutinized her own appearance in the mirror. With her smoky eyes and shimmery lip gloss, she hardly recognized herself.

"We look hot," Cristina declared.

Anticipating Eric's reaction, Meghan felt a flutter of excitement in the pit of her stomach. "Come on. I have to leave my brother a note." Downstairs at the kitchen counter, she paused, pen in hand. "When do you think we'll be back?"

"Just say you're spending the night at my house," Cristina suggested. "If I get too drunk to drive, we can sleep in my car."

Meghan smiled, scribbling a vague message about staying with a friend. She'd never done anything like this before. The idea of having no set plan for the evening, of doing whatever struck her fancy, was both frightening and delicious.

She indulged in a brief fantasy of walking down the beach with Eric, spreading out a blanket on the sand . . .

"Oh, my God. Is this your brother?"

Meghan glanced at Cristina, who was staring at a framed photo of her and Noah. "Yes."

"He's cute."

"Yeah, I guess," she said, her mind elsewhere. "Have you and Eric ever . . ."

"Hooked up?" Cristina turned away from the picture. "No. But it's not for lack of trying. Maybe tonight I'll get lucky."

Her heart sank. Earlier, when she'd seen Cristina kiss Eric on the cheek, she'd wondered how her friend felt about him.

"Watch out for Jack, by the way. He has a total boner for you."

"You think so?"

"Absolutely. But it's a small one, and he doesn't know what to do with it. Consider yourself warned."

Meghan laughed, shaking her head.

"From what I hear, Eric doesn't have that problem." They walked outside together, where Cristina's Ford Fiesta was waiting. As she drove to the beach, she continued to chatter about boyfriends and penis size, sharing a wealth of information.

Meghan found it all very fascinating.

Cristina glanced at her sideways, frowning. "You're not a virgin, are you?"

"No," she said, blushing. "My ex-boyfriend and I did it . . . once."

"Only once? Did he break up with you right after?"

"No. I broke up with him."

Cristina winced. "Was it that bad?"

"It wasn't good," Meghan admitted.

"Oh, honey. You need a real man. How long has it been?"

"Almost a year."

"Oh, my God. Don't you get tired of doing it alone?"

Meghan covered her face with her hands. She was going to die of embarrassment. "I can't breathe."

"Say no more," Cristina said, giggling. "We'll find you a cute guy. And one for me, too. Eric might not go for it because of my brother, but no worries. Jack has a bunch of good-looking friends, surfer types, so we'll have plenty of choices."

Meghan hoped Cristina would set her sights on any-one but Eric. Over the past week, she'd come to like him more and more. She watched him put produce away, his biceps flexing. The tattoo around his upper arm made her curious. She wondered what it said, what it meant . . . if he had others.

Every time he smiled at her, her tummy jumped.

Cristina parked in the pay lot at the south pier in Imperial Beach. It was full dark now, and a bonfire was already blazing. They brought a multicolored blanket with them, approaching the lively circle. About thirty young people were gathered around the fire, mostly guys in their early twenties.

Jack greeted them in his typical fashion, with a too-loud voice and a too-wide smile. Reggae music was blaring from a radio. His eyes were red, and he smelled like something sweet and a little acrid. Meghan scanned the crowd, realizing that they were smoking marijuana.

She'd never done that before.

"Get your drink on, ladies," Jack said, pointing to a blue cooler. Inside, there were a couple of jugs of fruity liquid.

"What is it?" Cristina asked.

"Jungle juice," he said, handing them both a cup.

Meghan accepted the drink easily. She might be inexperienced with pot, but she'd had alcohol before. Even Noah had given her a beer once.

It was no big deal.

"Whoa," she said, tasting the juice. It was like fruit punch—with a kick.

Cristina took a healthy swig. "Go slow, *amiga*. It's too early to get crazy."

While Jack wandered back to his equally loud friends, Meghan sat down on the blanket with Cristina, about ten feet away from the fire. A cool night breeze drifted in from the Pacific, ruffling through her hair. It was a refreshing respite from the day's heat.

None of the other girls at the party came over to say hello. The boys also continued to talk among themselves, having boisterous conversations that Meghan couldn't follow above the lilting music and crashing waves.

Although she felt self-conscious, the atmosphere wasn't unpleasant. The evening air seemed charged with energy, almost electric. Meghan sipped from her cup, stared at the licking flames, and waited for Eric.

It wasn't long before the space around the fire became crowded with revelers. Someone started to pass a joint around. When it came to Cristina, she took a quick drag and handed it to Meghan.

Meghan stared at the burning cigarette pinched between her fingers. A couple of lame excuses filtered through her mind, ways she'd been taught to "say nope to dope."

"Puff it or pass it," one of the boys said.

She passed it.

"I have to pee," Cristina said, tugging on her arm.

Meghan's cup was already empty, so she left it in the sand. She staggered sideways a few times on the way to the restroom, which struck them both as uproariously funny. She realized, with some chagrin, that she was already intoxicated.

It felt . . . great!

Still giggling, she used the facilities and trudged back

down the beach with Cristina. The trip took several minutes, and walking seemed like a chore. When they returned to the bonfire, Eric was standing near the cooler with Jack.

"Hello, Mío," she said, hugging him. The polo shirt he was wearing felt soft; the body underneath, anything but.

"I'm Gusto, remember?"

She laughed at her silly mistake. "Right."

He had an odd look on his face, as if he didn't quite recognize her. Then his gaze drifted south, settling on the lacy edge of her tank top. Rather than feeling embarrassed, she experienced a shiver of pleasure.

"Maybe you should sit down," he said.

"Good idea."

The four of them went back to the blanket, sitting boy–girl, boy–girl. Jack brought a half full jug with him. "Need a refill?"

Meghan lifted her empty cup. "Sure."

Cristina also partook in the spirits, but Eric declined. He cracked open a can of beer instead, taking a long drink.

Meghan stared at his throat, mesmerized.

"Are you having fun?" he asked.

"Yes," she said dreamily, wishing the crowd around them would fade away.

It didn't.

Cristina put her arm around Eric, stealing his attention, and Jack lit up another joint. After taking a quick puff, he passed it to Meghan. "Thanks again, man," he said to Eric. "This stuff is awesome."

She took the joint from Jack, frowning. "You gave him this?"

Eric shrugged, neither admitting nor denying it.

Meghan had been tempted to take a hit the first time around. Knowing Eric had supplied the pot made her feel safer about trying it. Bringing the joint to her lips, she inhaled deeply and held her breath, wanting to do it right. Coughing a little, because the smoke burned her throat, she exhaled and passed it on.

Eric didn't look impressed. In fact, he seemed irritated. He handed the joint to Cristina without smoking any.

Meghan started to feel very odd after that. Her skin tingled all over, and the rising flames warped her vision, making the faces around her appear distorted. It seemed like everyone was talking at the same time. She couldn't distinguish individual voices.

Her heartbeat felt too heavy, her cheeks too hot. And her throat was so dry. She drank from her cup, trying to regain the contentment she'd experienced before.

Jack began to stroke the back of her neck, and his touch confused her further. She wanted male attention—but not his. Instead of protesting, she closed her eyes, struggling to overcome her disorientation.

When she opened them again, the world tilted on its axis. She straightened, trying to right herself. Beside her, Cristina had climbed on top of Eric, straddling his waist. Laughing, she pushed him down on the blanket, pinning him with a kiss.

Meghan turned away from the sight, nauseous. "I need some air," she whispered in Jack's ear.

He rose immediately, helping her stumble toward

the shore. "Keep walking," he said, putting his arm around her waist. "It'll clear your head."

She nodded and leaned against him, focusing on the task of putting one foot in front of the other. Her legs didn't seem to work properly. Her mind was as sluggish as her steps. A few minutes ago she'd felt sexy and confident.

Now she felt like crying.

The pier loomed before them, monstrous stilts of treated wood jutting up toward the night sky. When the sand beneath her feet shifted, she sank to a sitting position.

Jack sat down beside her. "Drink this."

It was bottled water. She gulped it eagerly.

"Go slow."

After another, smaller sip, she handed it back. "Thanks."

"Better now?"

"Yeah."

They were silent for a few minutes. Meghan couldn't get the awful image of Cristina kissing Eric out of her head. Despite her current state of inebriation, which was considerable, she knew she didn't want Jack. She didn't like him—not even as a friend.

But he was being nice to her, and she was hurt and angry and confused. So when he leaned over and pressed his lips to hers, very gently, she allowed it.

He slanted his mouth over hers, trying to deepen the kiss. She lifted her hand to his chest, hesitant. She meant to stop him, but her balance was off. Before she knew it, she was flat on her back in the sand, and he was stretched out on top of her.

At that moment, Meghan felt totally disconnected from reality. The only thing she could think about, while he skimmed his hands over her breasts and thrust his tongue into her mouth, was what Cristina had said about his small boner.

Instead of pushing him away, she turned her head to the side and laughed.

He froze at the sound.

"I'm sorry," she gasped, still laughing. "I just . . . thought of something funny."

"Shut up and lay still," he said in a strained voice, fisting his hand in the lace between her breasts. His knuckles dug into her cleavage, hurting her, while his other hand fumbled with the waistband of her jeans.

Meghan stopped laughing and started to struggle. As she twisted beneath him, her shirt ripped down the front, exposing her all the way to the belly button. He grunted his approval and lifted up, allowing her to enough freedom to roll over.

She tried to crawl away from him on her hands and knees, her head spinning. Was this really happening?

When he jerked down the back of her pants, tearing her underwear in the process, she clutched at the sand and screamed.

8

The mood at Club Suave was tense.

Lola's murder remained unsolved, and all of the waitresses were on edge. As far as April knew, Tony Castillo hadn't been charged with the crime, though he remained in jail. The police hadn't named another suspect.

Her funeral had been this morning. April took Jenny along, avoiding eye contact with Tony's friends while Lola's mother wept. Again, she regretted never reaching out to Lola and tried not to imagine a similar demise for Josefa.

Eddie and most of the Club Suave staff had also attended. Her boss looked stiff and formal in an ill-fitting black suit, the cuffs a half inch too short, buttons straining over his midsection. The waitresses clung together, pretty and sedate with their pulled-back hair and minimal makeup. April read the expressions of fear and sorrow on their faces, feeling hollow. Lola had caused a lot of friction at the club. She'd been high maintenance, high drama. But no one had wished her this sad end.

The entire neighborhood was in mourning. Lola had been a daughter, a sister, a girlfriend, a coworker. Chula Vista had lost too many residents to drugs, violence, and gangs. Everyone who lived here had been touched by death.

The same tragedies that rocked the city made it stronger. The community members came together through similar experiences and a shared heritage. Many were survivors who'd endured hard times before.

Like the funeral service, Josefa's departure had been a quiet, heartrending affair. Jenny had cried for hours, finally falling into a fitful sleep late that evening. She liked the lively atmosphere at Consuela's house and seemed to be adjusting well to the change of caretakers, but she asked about her grandmother often.

April hadn't heard from Josefa since she left.

Jenny also had questions about Officer Young— Noah. *Who was that man, Mommy? Why was he talking to you?*

Besides Eric, there were no men in their lives. Even before Raul went to prison, he hadn't taken much of an interest in parenting.

April hadn't had a father when she was growing up, either. Her dad lived fast and died young; her parents never married. It had always been just the two of them, April and Josefa. Then, after Jenny came along, just the three of them.

The house seemed so empty without her mother there.

Now that the extra bedroom was available and every vestige of her mother was scrubbed away, April had a queen-sized bed to herself. The additional space felt odd. She'd tossed and turned every night this week, plagued with concerns about finances, neighborhood troubles, and Josefa's well-being.

There was another, more embarrassing problem. Seeing Noah at the park had thrown her hormones into overdrive, and being alone in that big bed amplified her discomfort. She couldn't stop imagining his strong hands all over her body, stroking her to completion.

Sleep had been elusive, and she was exhausted.

Although she felt like slumping in the nearest chair, April held her head high, delivering the bill to a table of raucous college boys. Only one more hour until closing time. She couldn't wait to shower and crawl into bed.

The loudest guy at the table reached out as she passed by, detaining her. "It's my friend's twenty-first birthday," he shouted. "How about a lap dance?"

April stared at the hand on her hip. No one would ever grab a waitress this way in a restaurant, let alone ask her to put on a sleazy show. It was insulting and idiotic. "Sure," she said anyway, smothering a yawn. "Who's the birthday boy?"

With a lopsided grin, the customer pointed at the ruddy-faced guy on her left. He looked harmless and a little reluctant.

She held out her hand, inviting him to come with her. When he stood, she did a quick, graceful maneuver, taking his seat. Once there, she smiled up at him expectantly, waiting for him to start dancing.

The guy glanced around the table in surprise, realizing he'd been duped. His friends burst out laughing.

April pantomimed opening a shirt, encouraging him to take it off.

He was a good sport, and his friends were egging him on, so he unbuttoned his shirt for her, swaying his hips to the music. April applauded his efforts, enjoying the role reversal. His physique was less than svelte, which made the striptease even funnier.

Laughing, she patted his backside when he turned around.

When she'd first started waitressing, she was afraid of her customers. Over the years she'd gained enough confidence to joke around. She was still careful about letting them get too close, but she didn't suspect every man she waited on of wanting to hurt her.

Before she left the table—with a great tip—she kissed the birthday boy on the cheek to thank him.

On her way back to the cash register, she noticed a man standing at the bar, watching her. His stance was casual; shoulders relaxed, hands in his pants pockets. He was wearing a simple white dress shirt and tan trousers.

It was Noah.

She'd seen him this morning at Lola's funeral. He'd paid his respects and left, never having approached her. She wondered if he had a girlfriend. A man like him wouldn't have any trouble attracting beautiful, willing women.

There were a couple of hungry-eyed young ladies checking him out right now.

Although he couldn't have been oblivious to the attention, his gaze didn't linger on any particular female as he surveyed the room. Rather, he nodded at the group of college boys she'd just waited on.

Realizing he'd witnessed the spectacle, she felt a flush rise to her cheeks.

"Is spanking one of your regular job duties?" he asked, a smile tugging at his lips.

"Only on birthdays."

"I'll remember that."

She couldn't resist smiling back at him. Out of uniform, he was even more handsome. His shirt fit nicely, accenting his broad shoulders. With the sleeves rolled up and the tails not tucked in, he looked comfortable. He wasn't trying too hard to be cool, and she liked that. She'd never been impressed by the guys with bulging biceps, designer T-shirts, and gelled hair.

Mirror-kissers, the waitresses called them. They didn't tip well.

"I'd offer you a drink," she said, leaning her hip against the bar, "but last call was five minutes ago."

"I didn't come to drink."

She wanted to ask why he came. The idea that he'd made a special trip for her made her throat go dry. She swallowed, staring at the open collar of his shirt. The other day she'd caught a glimpse of his bare stomach. It was taut with muscle, slick with sweat.

The sight had played a major role in her fantasies all week.

"I'm working, actually. Scoping out the clientele."

She blinked away an image of her sprawled over him, her cheek resting on his flat belly. Concentrating on the clothed Noah, she lifted her gaze from his torso. This morning he'd been wearing a tie and jacket. "Were you working at Lola's funeral?"

"I would have gone anyway."

"Why?"

He paused, considering the question. "Because I feel connected to her. I was the first on the scene." His blue eyes met hers, intense and earnest. "Her death . . . the case . . . it's very important to me."

The lights overhead clicked on, a rude glare that signaled closing time. Grumbling patrons began to shuffle out the front entrance. April crossed her arms over her chest, self-conscious in her cheap outfit and heavy makeup.

Noah was so clean-cut, so handsome and sincere. In contrast, she felt soiled, as if the grit of the club coated her skin. Her hair probably smelled like booze and cheap cologne. "What about Tony?" she asked, keeping her voice low.

"He has an alibi."

"You don't think he's responsible?"

"No. But he's involved in some other crimes, so it was good to get him off the streets. You did the right thing."

She glanced toward Eddie's office. He hadn't said a word about Lola, but he'd donated some funds for the funeral. Perhaps his conscience was bothering him. "I have to clear tables."

"When do you get off?"

"A little after two."

"Can we talk?"

She felt a twinge of unease. Or maybe it was just excitement. At the park, when he'd asked about Raul, she'd been convinced that his interest was personal. He wanted to know if she was available. For him.

April was an expert in letting men down easy. She received offers from customers almost every night. Some requested her phone number or tried to give her a friendly hug. Others invited her to wild after-parties, hot-tub socials, and hotel-room trysts.

None had tempted her half as much as Noah.

"I'll wait for you in the parking lot," he said, studying her face.

Although a polite demurral was second nature to her, her mouth refused to form the words. "Okay."

He turned his attention back to the crowd, his lips curving with satisfaction. The expression was another hint that he wanted more than information from her.

Heart pounding, she went behind the bar and filled a glass tumbler with ice and lemon-lime soda. Any amount of interaction with him was a risk. Eddie would assume she was turning against the neighborhood, telling secrets.

Hand steady from years of practice, she passed Noah the tumbler, watching while he took a measured sip. He didn't seem surprised that she remembered his preference.

She stared at his mouth, wondering how it would taste.

Blushing, she blinked out of her stupor, grabbing an empty tray from the bar as she walked away. Feeling his eyes on her backside, she added a little extra swing to her hips. Then she glanced over her shoulder, catching him looking.

He smiled, guilty as charged. And lifted his drink, saluting her efforts.

Laughing breathlessly, she set her tray down and started to clear off tables.

Noah watched the Club Suave parking lot from a distance, drumming his hands against the steering wheel.

Over the past week, the trail had grown cold. Santiago seemed convinced that the murder was a random act of violence, but Noah couldn't shake the feeling that the killer would strike again. He'd driven by the club several times this week, scanning the parking lot.

Although Eddie Estes, the club's manager, had been investigated, he'd been working late the night of the murder. Security cameras showed him leaving the club at 5:00 A.M., well after the estimated time of death.

Estes might not be a murderer, but he was a shady character, and Noah didn't like him.

He was also disappointed with the lack of progress in the investigation. Most homicide cases that weren't wrapped in the first forty-eight hours went unsolved, so he knew the clock was ticking. Failure would be devastating, and it wasn't even his case.

Noah had been burning the candle at both ends all week, performing his regular duties on the gang unit and volunteering on homicide. He hadn't been home much, and he suspected that Meghan was enjoying his absence. She had a job he couldn't find fault with, and she'd enrolled at Southwest College. The other day she'd brought home a bag of groceries and some decorations for "her" room.

She was definitely staying. And their mom was *pissed*.

As the parking lot emptied of patrons, he kept his eyes peeled for suspicious characters. He saw a very drunk young woman, slumped against her friend's shoulder, and a couple of possible DUI candidates. None of the drivers violated any traffic laws or showed obvious signs of impairment.

After most of the customers had cleared the area, April came out of the back entrance, chatting with another waitress, Carmen.

Trying to remain objective, he analyzed the similarities between April and Lola. They had the same hair and eye color, the same basic height. They were both slender, although April was a little curvier. From a distance, it would have been difficult to tell them apart.

April waved goodbye to Carmen, yawning behind her hand. The streetlamps overhead cast shadows under her eyes, accentuating her fatigue. Inside the club, she hid it well, keeping her smile bright and her posture straight. If the sexy spike heels she wore made her feet ache, she didn't show it.

Noah felt a strange tug in the middle of his chest. He was familiar with physical desire, and he'd even been in love before. But he couldn't remember having an overwhelming urge to give a woman sleep.

He got out of his truck, letting her know he was there.

She stopped near a ten-year-old beige Taurus, waiting for him with her arms crossed over her chest and a sardonic expression on her face. "I'm not going out with you."

Noah was surprised by the declaration. He hadn't said anything about a date. And he wasn't used to getting shot down in advance. "Fair enough," he said anyway, clearing his throat. "Is this your car?"

She followed his gaze, frowning. "Yes."

"Did you drive it to work last week?"

"Actually, it was in the shop until Wednesday."

"For what?"

"The air conditioner wasn't working."

"Did you get it fixed?"

"No," she muttered. "I couldn't afford the repair."

He nodded. "How did you get home on those nights?"

"Carmen."

Noah rubbed a hand over his jaw, feeling the scrape of new stubble. Carmen had given Lola a ride the night she was murdered. Friday night. One week ago, exactly. "Did you have any trouble with customers last week? Or see any strange men in the neighborhood?"

"Not that I recall. Why?"

"You and Lola look kind of similar from a distance. It's probably nothing."

April shivered, glancing around the deserted parking lot.

"Do you mind if I follow you home? Just to make sure you get in safe."

"Okay," she said, then, after a short pause, "but you're not coming inside."

He agreed easily, though he found her boundaries a bit odd. In the club, she'd felt secure enough to flirt with him. Now that they were alone, she seemed stiff and uncomfortable, as if he'd made untoward advances.

Shrugging, he got into his truck and turned on the engine.

He knew he shouldn't act on his attraction to her. Apparently she didn't want him to, so crossing the line wouldn't be a problem. No matter how intense their physical chemistry was, or how come-hither her eyes looked, he had to listen to what her mouth said.

If a lady wasn't available, she wasn't available.

He waited for April to exit the parking lot before he pulled away from the curb. Her resemblance to the victim might be coincidental, but he had a hunch that it wasn't. He wanted to stick close to her. Protect her.

April's house was a small bungalow with a composite roof and stucco exterior. The front yard had a single fruit tree and a simple sidewalk. While she parked in the narrow garage, Noah idled by the curb, feeling frustrated on many different levels.

Just as he was about to drive forward and call it a night, he noticed an open window. The screen lay propped against the side of the house, its frame bent. A white eyelet curtain fluttered in the breeze.

There was no way April would leave the house unsecured like that. Not in this neighborhood.

"Fuck," he said, reaching into the glove compartment for his service revolver. As soon as the gun was in his hand, he jumped out of the truck, rushing toward the front door.

It was ajar.

He nudged the door open with his shoulder, holding the gun straight out in front of him, doing a quick survey of the living room. It was clear.

April walked in from the garage, via the kitchen. When she saw him, her eyes widened with shock.

Noah shook his head, imploring her to stay quiet. Pointing his gun toward the bedroom on his right, he gestured for her to go back out the way she came. She nodded once, disappearing.

Relieved that she'd reacted sensibly, he strode forward, flipping on the light switch. The room was empty. Someone had gone through the dresser drawers, and there were items of clothing strewn across the hardwood floor.

Other than that, the space was uncluttered, the bed neatly made.

Noah found another empty room down the hall. It was Jenny's, judging by the décor. The blanket on the bed featured a little cartoon girl with brown hair and brown eyes. He moved on, checking the rest of the house, the garage, and the backyard. There was no one.

Tucking his gun in the back of his pants, he went outside. April was standing near the curb, her arms crossed over her chest. She appeared annoyed rather than concerned.

"It looks like you had a break-in," he said. "Where's Jenny?"

"At the sitter's. She stays overnight."

She walked through the front door and into the bedroom, staring at the clothing scattered on the floor. It was mostly bras and panties, he realized. A mix of serviceable white cotton and basic black.

"Is anything missing?"

Shaking her head, she knelt to scoop up the demure lingerie.

"That's evidence."

"Of what, my nonexistent sex life?"

He raked a hand through his hair. "April, some rapists collect women's underwear. They collect *victims'* underwear."

She shoved the panties back in the drawer. "It's not what you think. I kicked my mother out earlier this week. This room used to be hers, and she has a drug problem. I found pills taped to the underside of these drawers, so I flushed them down the toilet. She probably broke in, looking for her stash."

Noah was silent for a moment, absorbing the information. Her conclusion was more reasonable than the one he'd jumped to.

He closed his eyes, cursing himself silently. "I'm sorry if I startled you."

She finished putting away her things and brushed by him, taking a seat on the living-room couch. "I appreciate your investigative fervor, Officer Young, but there's nothing to see here. It's just your regular, everyday family dysfunction."

He studied her face, wishing he could help her. No wonder she looked exhausted. He also figured she was embarrassed about revealing her problems—and her underwear—to a stranger.

"What's she on?" he asked, sitting across from her.

"OxyContin, mostly."

"There's a methadone clinic on E Street."

"Is it free?"

"Of course."

She rubbed her temples. "I don't think she'd go there. She doesn't want help from anyone. She dates a lot of losers, but she doesn't rely on them. I'm the only real family she has, and I haven't heard from her since she left." Her voice broke on the last sentence, and her shoulders slumped forward, shaking with emotion.

Noah couldn't stand to watch a woman cry without comforting her, but something about April's body language suggested she'd flinch away from his touch. He curled his hands into fists, wanting to do it anyway. "Addicts with no enablers are more likely to get sober," he said. "You're doing the best thing for her."

She grabbed a tissue from the coffee table, casting him a questioning glance. "How do you know that?"

"I deal with drug users every day."

"Sounds . . . horrible."

He smiled. "No. It might be if I didn't believe I could help anyone."

She didn't smile back at him. Crushing the tissue in her hands, she studied his mouth for a moment, her expression curious and a little confused. When she dragged her gaze back up to his, heat simmered between them.

He thought of another way to comfort her.

She moistened her lips, drawing his attention to how soft they looked, bare of lipstick and somehow vulnerable. He leaned in slowly, giving her time to pull back. She didn't. When he touched his lips to hers, she lifted her right hand to his shoulder, steadying herself. It seemed like a blatant invitation to deepen the kiss.

Noah was happy to oblige.

She opened her mouth for him, and he delved inside, stroking his tongue over hers. The kiss went from sweet and tentative to down and dirty in record time.

Her fingernails dug into the fabric of his shirt, and he slid his arm around her waist, bringing her body closer. Her breasts flattened against his chest. She moaned against his mouth, clutching at his shoulders, exploring the muscles in his back.

When she felt his gun, they both went still.

Noah broke the kiss, breathing hard against her parted lips. "I can put it away if it bothers you."

She eased back. "No. I'm sorry."

"For what?"

"I'm just not comfortable with . . . casual relationships."

He rested his elbows on his knees, trying to quash his arousal. Unless he'd misread her, he wouldn't be getting lucky tonight. Which was best, as they hardly knew each other. "It doesn't have to be casual."

"What do you mean?"

"We can go out," he said, thinking fast.

"Why?" she asked, suspicious.

"I like you."

"You like the way I look, you mean."

He stared at her lips, which were a natural pinkish-brown, full and moist and very sexy. Her chest was rising and falling with each breath, her breasts straining against the Club Suave tank top. He could see the outline of her nipples. His erection throbbed in response, so he averted his gaze. "I like the way you think, too."

She crossed her arms over her breasts, sighing.

"I also have a feeling we might . . . click."

Her eyes darkened. "I don't click."

He laughed at her deadpan delivery, realizing that he liked her sense of humor, as well. She was irresistibly contrary, and he was more eager than ever to figure her out. "You don't *want* to click."

"I don't have the time to click. Or the money," she explained. "I'm not going to pay for an extra night's babysitting to go out with you."

He thought of a way around that. "Bring your daughter along."

"What?"

"You have days off, right? We can go to the zoo, or . . . Wave City. My sister's been bugging me to take her there. I'll invite her, too."

"She lives here?"

"She just moved in with me," Noah admitted, hoping it would score him some nice-guy bonus points.

She narrowed her eyes at him, still wary. "If I offered you one night with me—one night only—or one friendly date, no kiss, no follow-up, which would you take?"

"Is this a trick question?"

"Which would you take?" she repeated.

"Neither. I've never slept with a woman I wasn't dating. And, no offense, but I don't want to be 'just friends.' "

Maybe that was too blunt, because she fell silent.

"I'm not asking for a relationship or a major commitment. I only want you to give me a chance. This may not go anywhere. We could be all wrong for each other. I might find out that you hate baseball. Or drown kittens."

She didn't seem to think that was funny. "You play baseball?"

"I used to. Now I coach. Little League."

"You like kids?"

He smiled. "Yes."

"Do you want some of your own?"

"Sure, eventually."

"How many?"

He'd never really thought about it. "One or two, I guess. How about you?"

She shook her head. "Maybe after I finish school. Eventually, like you said. I was an only child, and it was lonely sometimes. I think Jenny feels the same way."

He pictured Jenny's cute little face, scrunched up as she stuck her tongue out at him. "You're going to school?"

"I start SDSU this fall."

"What are you studying?"

"Social service."

Noah didn't need to hear any more. She was nice, and smart, and wanted to help others. Plus, she was so fucking *hot,* he couldn't stand it. "One date," he said. "Wave City. Jenny will have fun. If it doesn't work out between us, no big deal."

She nibbled on her lower lip, considering.

"When's your next day off?"

"Sunday."

"I have Sunday off, too. I'll pick you up at ten."

"Okay," she said finally.

Noah was flattered by her capitulation. He'd seen the way she interacted with the men at the club, so he believed her when she said she didn't date. She was polite but inaccessible. She probably shot down customers all the time. The fact that she was tempted by *him,* when no one else could get close to her, gave him a surge of male pride.

He said goodbye with a brief kiss, barely touching his

lips to hers. As he strode down the sidewalk, he felt like pumping his fist in the air.

Now he just had to find a break in the case, and he'd be on top of the world.

Of course, he knew that getting involved with her was against the rules. But it seemed like a minor infraction, a matter of discretion. He wasn't the lead investigator, and she wasn't a suspect. Even so, he'd have to tread carefully.

He didn't stop thinking about April, replaying their kiss, weighing the consequences, until he got home. And saw the note from Meghan.

9

Eric was aware that Meghan and Jack had left the bonfire, but he couldn't do anything about it with Cristina on his lap. Dumping her off would humiliate her in front of everyone, so he held still and hoped she'd get the hint that he wasn't interested.

Meghan was wasted. He'd known the instant she stumbled toward him, her smile crooked, eyes half lidded. She'd been too drunk to walk before she'd taken that hit of chronic. Now she was probably spinning.

Thanks to Jack.

Although Eric wasn't responding to Cristina's overtures, she continued to undulate on top of him, nipping at his lower lip. She had a light touch, and he didn't dislike it. Frowning, he put his hands on her hips to move her aside. Unfortunately, his fingertips found the exposed skin above her jeans, and she drew in an excited breath.

"I have to check on Meghan," he said.

She stopped kissing him. "Why?"

"She's messed up."

"Jack's with her."

"That's what I'm worried about. Get off me."

Her eyes narrowed. Not ready to unstake her claim, she switched tactics. "You really like her, don't you? I think she likes you, too." She put her lips close to his ear. "Let's ditch Jack and go back to your place, just the three of us."

Eric tried not to picture that scenario. He really did. But his mind was open to her suggestion, and his body wasn't immune to her touch. He could feel the heat of her *concha* rubbing against his fly. If his hands drifted any lower, he'd be cupping her ass.

"I could talk her into it," she murmured, licking his earlobe.

"Wait here," he said, scrambling out from underneath her. "I'll go get her."

As soon as he was thinking clearly again, his blood cooled by the breeze coming off the Pacific, he discarded the idea. Even if Meghan agreed to Cristina's . . . experiment, she was in no condition to participate.

The only thing she'd be caressing tonight was a toilet bowl.

"*Baboso,*" he muttered, kicking himself. He'd wasted several minutes letting Cristina cock-tease him, and now he wasn't sure which direction Jack had gone. The pier offered would-be lovers a modicum of privacy, so he headed that way.

As lights from the bonfire faded, his concern for Meghan grew. Jack wouldn't have gone this far to let Meghan puke.

He started to jog, then sprint, down the beach.

There were two figures beneath the pier, locked in

struggle. Eric could hear Meghan screaming. Although the area was steeped in shadow, and the moon had slipped behind the clouds, he knew exactly what was happening.

Jack was holding her down. Raping her.

Eric felt a cold, dark fury overcome him. He'd witnessed this kind of scene before, and he'd been frozen, unable to stop it. Never again. Now he was strong enough to take action. He raced toward them, clenching his hand into a fist. The first punch he threw carried ten years of pent-up rage with it.

Jack hadn't seen him coming, so he wasn't braced for the blow. He fell off Meghan, slumping to his side in the sand. He appeared dumbfounded.

His fly was undone, and his dick was out.

"You motherfucker," Eric said from between clenched teeth, grabbing the top of Jack's scraggly hair. He drew back his fist and sent it flying, wailing on him hard. He struck again and again, smashing flesh, breaking bones.

"It's not what you think!" Jack screamed, gripping Eric's wrists. His eyes were swollen and his lips bloody.

Eric glanced at Meghan, who was fastening her jeans. Her panties lay on the sand, torn from her body. Tears streaked her pretty face.

"You're going to wish you were dead," Eric said, ramming his knee into Jack's nose. His efforts were rewarded by a satisfying crunch. Jack shrieked in pain and curled into the fetal position, covering his head with his arms.

Disgusted by his cowardice, Eric kicked him while he was down.

Jack groaned and stayed put.

"*Puto*," Eric spat. "If I ever see you again, I'll fucking kill you."

One beating, however severe, wasn't punishment enough, in his opinion. But a voice in the back of his head whispered a warning to move on. He picked up Meghan's underwear and put them in his pocket, leaving Jack semiconscious on the sand.

When he offered her his hand, she flinched, shrinking away from him.

"Let's go," he said gently. "His friends might come."

After a brief hesitation, she took his hand and he helped her to her feet. When her knees buckled, he hooked her arm around his neck and encircled her waist, practically carrying her down the beach.

He kept moving forward, urging her along. He was worried that Jack's surfer buddies would catch up to him and misunderstand the situation. If they did, he wouldn't be able to protect Meghan. Eric was a good fighter, but he couldn't take on a group.

"I'm going to be sick," she moaned.

He set her down immediately, and she hunched forward, retching. The sickly sweet smell of fruit punch made his own stomach queasy. He glanced away, grimacing. When she was finished, her eyes were watery and her mouth wet.

"Take this," he said, offering her his bandanna.

"Thanks."

"Better now?"

"Yes. Much."

He led her away from the mess, pulling her head against his shoulder. She pressed her face against his shirt. "I'm sorry," she said, hot tears spilling out her eyes.

"For what?"

"Getting so wasted. Acting like a slut."

He hugged her closer, comforting her. "You didn't do anything wrong."

"Y-yes I did," she sobbed.

"We should call the police."

She clung to the front of his shirt, terrified. "No."

"Your brother, then."

"No, I can't. He'll make me go back to my parents."

"Meghan—"

"Nothing happened!"

"You were screaming. Your clothes are torn."

She followed his gaze down her chest. Her top was gaping open, exposing her bra. Clutching the fabric together, she sank to a sitting position in the sand.

"Did he hit you?"

"No," she whispered.

"Did he rape you?"

She shook her head. "He kissed me once . . . and I let him. I don't remember much else. The police would arrest you, not him."

He was quiet for a moment. "I think you should report it."

"In the morning," she said. "When I'm sober."

Eric didn't like that idea, and he wasn't sure he believed her about the attack. He knew Jack hadn't finished. Maybe Eric had arrived in time, and he hadn't really started yet.

Then again, it was just as likely that Meghan was telling him what he wanted to hear. She was reluctant to talk to the police, afraid of disappointing her brother and her parents. April had never reported Raul's abuse, either.

Eric understood a lot about guilt and shame and silence.

If she decided not to turn Jack in, that was her business. Eric had already exacted a bit of vigilante justice, the kind he preferred. He also wasn't keen on getting arrested for assault. The police would take the word of a middle-class white kid over his any day.

"Come on," he said. "There's a public restroom up ahead."

At the entrance to the restrooms, he paused, taking off his shirt. He thought about giving her the polo, but the sleeveless undershirt exposed his upper arms, and he was in enemy territory. It wasn't wise for him to strut around, flashing CVL tats in Imperial Beach.

He removed the undershirt, handing it to her.

She stared at his inked-up torso, her eyes flat. Most of the script was in Spanish and the symbols identifiable only to other gang members, so she wouldn't understand it. But she did seem to realize that he wasn't the person she thought he was.

"Thanks," she said stiffly, taking his shirt.

While she went into the ladies' room, he walked around to the men's, washing Jack's blood off his hands. His knuckles were raw and swollen but not broken. Letting them drip dry, he sat down at the picnic tables, waiting for Meghan.

She came out a few minutes later, wearing his undershirt. It was too big for her, so it gaped at the sides, revealing her bra. She appeared to have washed her face, but her eye makeup was still smudged.

There was something sexy about the sight of her in his shirt, and he wished he was responsible for her disarray. He would much rather have ended this evening the way Cristina had suggested.

Uncomfortable with the direction of his thoughts, he took out his phone and sent Cristina a quick text message, letting her know he was leaving with Meghan.

Sitting down across from him, Meghan said, "Give me your hand." She must have used his bandanna to wash up, because it was damp. Now she wrapped his knuckles in the cool cloth, tying a knot to secure it. "Why do you carry this?"

"Why do you think?"

"Are you a gangster?"

He shook his head. Not denying it. Just amazed at her naïveté. "Is your brother's house far from here?"

She looked around, as if she had no clue where they were. "It's on Verde Avenue."

"We can walk."

They started off in that direction, heading east, traveling through a cross section of backstreets. She leaned on him heavily, but he didn't mind holding her up. "Do you think Jack drugged me?"

"No."

"Why not?"

"Because you're conscious."

"I'm really out of it."

"Have you ever mixed pot and hard alcohol before?"

"I've never tried either."

He grunted, shifting her weight to the other side. "That explains it."

After they'd walked several miles, Eric turned right, away from the quiet neighborhoods. Soon they were in sight of an all-night restaurant, garishly painted with green and yellow stripes. *Taco Tico, open 24 hours,* the sign read.

He'd been here before, and the food was okay. They both needed to rest, and she'd feel better if she ate. "Are you hungry?"

She shuddered. "No."

"You should eat something."

"I want to sit down."

"After we order."

Nodding her agreement, she straightened her shoulders, trying to look more alert. He put his hand at the small of her back, ushering her into the restaurant. It was really just a taco stand, with some red tables and an order window.

As soon as they came through the door, he realized his mistake. This was a neutral area, but it was still Imperial Beach. He should have paid attention to who was inside. There were a couple of Eastside guys sitting near the entrance.

Eric's heart sank. Beating a hasty retreat was out of the question. But he didn't know any of them by name, so maybe they didn't know him, either. Keeping his left hand on Meghan's waist, he slipped his right into his pocket, hiding the bandanna around his knuckles.

They didn't make eye contact.

While Eric ordered a few items from the menu, Meghan leaned against the counter, squinting under the artificial lighting. Taking money out of his wallet without revealing his colors was tricky, but he managed. After paying for the food, he put his arm around Meghan, leading her back outside.

Luckily, the *chavalas* ignored him in favor of ogling her. When a pretty girl walked into a dive like this, she got stared at. The time of night and her obvious inebriation made her fair game for lewd comments.

"*Cuanto cuesta?*" one of the guys asked.

"*Un burrito,*" another answered, and they all laughed.

Eric ignored them.

There was a round table out front with two plastic chairs. He offered one to Meghan and grabbed another for himself.

"What did they say?" she whispered.

"Nothing."

"I want to know."

"The first guy asked how much you charged. The other guy said, 'One burrito.' "

She groaned, rubbing her eyes. "Do I look like a drugged-out prostitute?"

"No," he said, studying her face. Even with mussed hair and streaked mascara, she was cute. Most of the crack whores he'd seen were older women who had bad skin and worse teeth. "You're young and beautiful. It was a stupid joke."

The Eastside boys left the restaurant without saying anything else, and soon their food was ready. He set the tray down on the table. There was a burrito wrapped in yellow paper for him and a Styrofoam cup for her.

She opened the lid. "What's this?"

"Tortilla soup. It's good."

After taking a tentative spoonful, she made a murmur of approval. Her stomach couldn't have handled a rich meal, but the soup was mild, with bits of chicken and vegetables and softened strips of tortilla.

Eric popped the top of his soda can, and they ate for a few moments in silence. Meghan's cheeks took on a healthier color. The effects of the marijuana had worn off, he suspected, and she was beginning to come out of the alcohol-induced fog.

She studied the bandanna over his hand, frowning. "Did you give that pot to Jack?"

"No."

"Did you *sell* it to him?"

He took another bite of his burrito, not answering.

"Do you do drugs?"

"Sometimes," he admitted.

"Why not tonight?"

"I can't let my guard down at a party like that."

"Why did you go?"

"I don't know," he said honestly. If he'd gone to protect her, he'd done a piss-poor job. Given half a chance, he might have taken advantage of her himself. So he changed the subject. "Why don't you want to go back to your parents' house?"

"They're mad at me for dropping out of college."

"Which college?"

"Chapel. It's a Christian school."

"They teach about God?"

She sipped her soda. "They offer all of the regular courses. You don't have to study religion. But it felt . . . oppressive."

Eric was surprised by her description. He couldn't imagine having no job and no responsibilities. Going away to school sounded like freedom rather than oppression. "Some people would kill for that opportunity."

She sighed, conceding his point. "Do you go to college?"

"I didn't even finish high school."

"Why not?"

"My brother went to prison during my senior year. He'd been taking care of me, so I had to get a job to support myself."

"Where are your parents?"

"My dad is dead. My mom went back to Mexico ten years ago."

"Do you ever see her?"

"All the time. She lives in TJ."

She stared at him with wide eyes, bewildered by his nonchalance. He supposed she'd led a sheltered existence, if she found his situation unusual. Around here, there were many kids with absent mothers and relatives in jail.

"You're lucky your parents can afford to send you to college," he added.

"I can go without their help. I just enrolled at Southwest and applied for financial aid."

"Hmm."

"You could go, too."

Eric shrugged. Between taking care of his grandmother, working at the store, and fulfilling his obligations to CVL, he didn't have a lot of spare time for classes. Besides, his crew members would frown on any attempt at higher learning.

They'd think he was trying to get out of the gang, overreaching his step.

By the time Meghan finished her soup, she looked as if she was starting to feel human again. He didn't envy her the sobriety. Once the fuzziness faded, she'd have a lot of unpleasant things to think about.

The soup stayed down, to his relief. After a brief rest, they rose from the table and continued on their way. Her brother's house was about a mile from the restaurant. As they arrived, dawn was edging over the horizon.

"This is me," she said, toeing the sidewalk.

He glanced at the numbers on the mailbox, committing them to memory.

"Do you want your shirt back?"

"No."

She took a step toward him, resting her hand on his shoulder. He tensed at her touch. "Thank you," she said, kissing his cheek. "I don't know what I'd have done if you hadn't come along."

Although he accepted the gesture, he didn't react to it. His eyes were shuttered, his body language closed off.

"I guess I'll see you later."

"Go on," he said.

Taking out her key, she approached the front door, her hands trembling. With one last glance back, she slipped into the house and locked herself inside. Moving quietly, she disappeared into the downstairs bathroom, avoiding her reflection as she removed her clothes. Feeling numb, she stepped into the shower stall and turned on the faucet.

She stayed there a long time.

When the pounding hot water failed to soothe, she tried a cooler temperature, letting it flow over her and over her. Her hand drifted down her belly, and she touched herself tentatively, wanting to make sure she was still . . . normal.

The experience hadn't robbed her of sensation or taken away her ability to respond. But it had changed how she felt about herself.

Tears sprang into her eyes, and she shut the water off. Wrapping a towel around her body, she crept upstairs, holding the pile of discarded clothes. Rather than shoving the items in her laundry basket, she hid them in her closet.

She put on a clean T-shirt and panties and climbed into bed, pulling the covers over her head. Shutting out the world.

In a few moments, she was asleep.

10

Noah's cell phone rang, vibrating across the nightstand, tugging him back to reality.

The cold shower he'd taken the night before didn't ease his desire for April. Sleep hadn't come easy, and he'd only just drifted off. He caught his phone as it fell over the edge of the nightstand. The screen read 6:22 A.M.

It was Detective Santiago.

"What's up?" he said, his voice like gravel.

"We have another vic. Sexual assault, asphyxiation. Possibly gang related."

He sat up in bed, alert. "Where?"

"South pier."

The tension in his chest lessened a bit. The victim wasn't April. She was home, asleep. "I'll be there as soon as I can."

Dressing quickly, he went down to the kitchen and put on a pot of coffee, glancing at the note his sister had left. He hadn't heard her come in, but he got the impression she was here. Frowning, he walked past the guest bathroom. Someone had just showered. "Meghan?" he called out, jogging upstairs.

Her door was closed. He rapped his knuckles against it. "Meg?"

No answer.

When he opened the door, she groaned and rolled over in bed, burying her face in the pillows. "Go away."

"I thought you were staying with a friend."

Her response was muffled, unintelligible.

"We'll talk later. I got called in to work."

She pulled the covers over her head.

Noah shut the door and went back downstairs, glad she was home. He didn't need any additional worries right now. There was a killer on the loose.

He didn't have time to go to the station for his uniform, so he arrived on the scene in plain clothes. It was already a clusterfuck of media, civilians, and police officers. Lola Sanchez's death hadn't caused a huge stir. This one would. A second sexually motivated killing in as many weeks suggested serial murder, maybe even a spree.

At almost 7:00 A.M., the beach was cool and overcast. The sand was damp. In a few more hours, the sun would burn through the clouds.

There were dividers around the body, and police tape squared off a large area underneath the pier. Noah stepped inside, joining Detective Santiago. The scene was disturbing, and gruesome, and difficult to look at.

Another Hispanic girl, late teens or early twenties. Like Lola Sanchez and April Ortiz, she had dark hair and a slim build. She was lying on her stomach, her head turned to one side. Her jeans were tangled around her ankles, her red top pulled down to her waist. Noah walked around the perimeter, trying to catch sight of her face.

She'd been suffocated by a thin plastic bag.

Her eyes were wide open, her mouth gagged with a black bandanna. He could see the design on the cloth through the cloudy plastic.

"Cristina Lopez," Santiago said. "Sister of Junior Lopez."

"I know him," Noah said. Lopez was a tax collector of sorts. He took a portion of the illegal earnings from every gangster who worked on CVL turf and gave it to the top crew members. Those who didn't pay earned a beating.

"You heard anything on the street?"

"Nothing new."

The Chula Vista Locos were longtime rivals with Eastside Imperial Beach. Although colors weren't as important to them as to some of the L.A. gangs, CVL was associated with white and brown, and Eastside wore black.

This could be an Eastside hit.

Gang violence usually involved men and boys, but not always. For women to be targeted, there had to be some serious shit going down.

Santiago took off his glasses, wiping them with a white handkerchief. He looked flustered, and Noah had never seen him that way before. "This is going to cause a fucking war," he muttered. "You and Shanley go interview Junior Lopez. Don't tell him about the bandanna, but find out if he has a beef with Eastside."

"Yes, sir."

Noah called Patrick on his way to the station. Shanley sounded groggy and irritated, reluctant to come in. They rarely worked this early in the morning. "I'll be there in thirty minutes," he said, hanging up.

Patrick's attitude had been bothering Noah all week. He was a good cop, an experienced cop, but he'd lost his objectivity. He seemed to think every kid was a punk, every person of color an illegal immigrant, and every criminal a recidivist.

He'd crossed the line between pragmatism and pessimism at least a year ago.

Noah knew that Patrick had some personal issues and that he disliked working with the homicide division. But he wished Patrick would put those prejudices aside for now and help Noah with the investigation. Young innocent women were being murdered—and Patrick didn't seem to care.

After Noah suited up, he went to his desk and logged on to the network, checking the details of the case. With no official report filed, there wasn't much information available. Preliminary time of death was between midnight and 3:00 A.M. Possible cause of death, asphyxiation. She'd been sighted by a jogger at 5:25.

A cell phone recovered from her back pocket showed some recent activity. A couple of numbers had been entered in the system. One text message, from a caller identified only as *E*, read: *Leaving w/ M.*

Noah printed it out, along with a recent arrest sheet for Junior Lopez, and drank some more coffee. Patrick came in a few minutes later, fresh from the shower, his eyes bloodshot. He'd probably been at Mulligan's last night, getting hammered. Noah couldn't bring himself to feel any sympathy for Patrick's condition. Over the past few months, his drinking, like his attitude, had become steadily worse.

They walked down to the parking garage in silence.

"Where to?" Patrick asked, climbing behind the wheel of the cruiser.

Using the keyboard on the console, Noah entered Lopez's last known address. The screen lit up with mug shots from prior arrests and directions to the location. "Junior Lopez, age twenty-four, height five foot ten, weight 205."

Patrick grunted with interest. He liked a scuffle.

"It's an interview, not an arrest," Noah explained.

"Shit."

They used the drive time to discuss the similarities between the two murders. The victims resembled each other. There was no doubt in Noah's mind that the crimes had been perpetrated by the same killer. Even Patrick, who had feigned disinterest in the previous case, understood the implications. Santiago was entrusting them with a delicate situation.

"How'd it go at Club Suave last night?" Patrick asked.

Noah shrugged. "Average shot-in-the-dark surveillance."

"Did you see that waitress you like?"

"I might have."

He didn't elaborate, so Patrick dropped the subject. "I was thinking about taking the boat out tomorrow morning. You and Meg want to come along?"

Noah was surprised by the offer. He couldn't remember the last time he'd hung out with Patrick after hours. "Thanks, but I can't," he said, feeling a little guilty. They arrived at Lopez's residence, an avocado green apartment building called Cholla Terrace. "I have a date."

Patrick glanced at him, squinting in suspicion. "With April Ortiz?"

After a brief hesitation, he nodded.

"You sneaky son of a bitch," Patrick said, sounding impressed.

Noah got out of the squad car, shaking his head. It was impossible to hide anything from his partner. And there was no reason to, because Patrick didn't give a damn about rules. If Noah screwed the prime suspect, Patrick would probably ask for details.

Neither spoke as they ascended the stairs. Lopez lived on an upper level, and they were in luck. He was already outside, smoking a cigarette.

Patrick and Noah had arrested him several times, on multiple charges, so Lopez knew who they were. His face showed no emotion upon seeing them. He took another drag of his cigarette, leaning his forearms on the terrace railing.

He was shirtless, barefoot, puffy-eyed.

Noah had done calls like this before, and it was his least favorite part of the job. He'd notified mothers that their sons were dead. Breaking the news to Lopez wouldn't be any easier because he was a gang member.

"You might want to sit down," Patrick said.

Lopez looked back and forth between them. The hard expression he'd been wearing changed. His eyes registered shock, and fear, and then denial. "No."

"Can we talk inside?"

"Fuck no."

"It's your sister," Noah said. "She's been killed."

Lopez didn't react for a few seconds. He stood there, staring at Noah with his lips curled back, like he might throw a punch. Then his eyes filled with tears and he let out a hoarse yell, slamming his fist into the apartment siding.

He repeated the action several times, with less force, and pressed his forehead to the door, praying in Spanish. There was a large tattoo on his back, a brilliantly detailed Virgin of Guadalupe. Blood dripped down his knuckles.

"You're sure?" he asked finally.

Noah nodded. "She had her cell phone on her, and picture ID."

He squeezed his eyes shut, trying to stanch the tears. "How?"

Patrick fielded the question. "We're investigating that right now. Maybe you can answer a few questions, help us out."

After a brief hesitation, Junior opened the door to his apartment, waving them inside. Beer cans were stacked on the coffee table, and take-out boxes littered the floor. Lopez disappeared into the bedroom, causing both Noah and Patrick to put their hands on their revolvers.

"*Despiértate*," he growled. The bedsprings rattled. "*Sácate, ya!*"

A sleepy young woman stumbled out of the bedroom, carrying a pile of clothes. Her dark hair was mussed, her makeup smudged. When Lopez shoved a purse at her, she retreated into the bathroom, cursing him in Spanish.

Noah and Patrick exchanged a glance. There was no question as to what Lopez had been doing last night. A moment later the woman came out of the bathroom, fully dressed, her eyes flashing with anger.

"I'll call you," Lopez said, wrapping a T-shirt around his bloody knuckles.

Giving him a look of disgust, she left.

As soon as she was gone, Lopez turned and kicked over the coffee table, sending its contents crashing to the floor. Noah knew he was acting out of grief, but he also got the impression that Lopez felt ashamed of the way he lived. He didn't seem to respect his apartment or his woman. Maybe his tough-guy front had slipped away for a moment and he was seeing himself through their eyes.

Visibly upset, he sat down on the couch, gesturing for them to join him.

"We'll stand," Patrick said.

Junior Lopez was a big boy. Stocky rather than muscular. His head was shaved, almost to the skin. The kids in the neighborhood respected him, and women liked him. Although he was a hardened criminal and a troubled young man, he had a charismatic personality.

"Do you know where your sister was last night?" Patrick asked.

"No. I texted her, but she didn't text back."

"She have a boyfriend?"

Junior shook his head. He looked . . . lost. "I don't know."

"Can I see your cell phone?" Noah asked.

He took it from the pocket of his jeans, glancing at the screen before handing it over. Noah scrolled through the list of contacts. "Who's Eric?" he asked, comparing the number to the printout. It matched.

"A friend of mine."

Noah knew who Lopez ran with; it was his job. "Eric Hernandez?"

"Yeah. Why?"

"Any reason he would call or text her?"

"They work together."

"Where?"

"Bonita Market."

A chill ran down Noah's spine. That was where Meghan worked. "Did she have a shift last night?"

"I think so."

"Until what time?"

"They close at nine."

He checked the time of the text. "A message from him was sent to her phone at one seventeen A.M."

Lopez's eyes narrowed. "What did it say?"

"I can't give out that information. Do you know anyone named M?"

"I know some motherfuckers whose names *start* with *M*."

"Did you see Eric last night?"

"Yeah. I was at his house for a few minutes before he left."

"Where did he go?"

Lopez shrugged. "He wouldn't tell me, but he was dressed up kinda nice."

"You think he was meeting your sister?"

He clenched his hand into a fist. His knuckles were

still seeping blood, spotting the cotton fabric. "I think he's got a lot of explaining to do."

"We'll handle that," Noah warned. "Don't call him and tip him off."

"Maybe some Eastside boys saw your homie with Cristina," Patrick broke in. "Decided to rough her up."

"They might mess with him. Why would they hurt her?"

"She was CVL."

Lopez gave Patrick a fierce look. "No. She wasn't."

"Your sister was raped and suffocated because of your gang connections, *ese*," Patrick said. "They found a black bandanna shoved in her mouth."

Lopez jumped to his feet, ready to fight.

Noah got between them, bracing his hand on Lopez's heaving chest. "Officer Shanley is only speculating," he said, protecting Patrick from Junior's wrath. "She had some kind of cloth in her mouth. It hasn't been identified yet."

"I'm going to kill all those Eastside bastards!"

"Let us talk to Eric and build a case. If word gets out about that bandanna—true or not—the investigation could be jeopardized." He glared at Patrick, who knew better than to let that detail slip. "The man who killed Cristina might go free. Do you want that?"

"Fuck," Lopez said, relaxing his stance.

"Some officers are heading over to your mom's house to notify her. Maybe you should go there now. Be with your family."

"Fuck," he repeated, his eyes swimming with tears again.

Noah was so angry he couldn't speak. He'd made a point of telling Patrick not to say anything about the bandanna.

He couldn't help but suspect that his partner had shared the information on purpose, in a deliberate attempt to cause trouble for Santiago. Patrick didn't care if he incited gang violence. If a few crew members shot one another, he'd call it a good start.

Noah was also worried about Meghan. Her coworker had been murdered last night. He left a message at the house, asking her to stay put. He thought about sending a patrol car over but decided against it.

Instead, he called Santiago.

"How'd it go?"

"All right," Noah answered. "We found out that E is Eric Hernandez. He worked with the victim at Bonita Market. Like Junior Lopez, he's documented CVL." He paused, not sure if he should reveal Patrick's mistake. "Do you want us to follow up?"

"Yeah. Go question him."

After Noah ended the call, he entered Hernandez into the system. Eric had never been arrested, but he had some violent associates. His brother, Raul, was once a major player with CVL. Now Raul was doing hard time for armed robbery.

Hernandez lived in the Castle Park area, in a rundown fourplex on Lime Street. Before Noah knocked on the door, he heard a cranked-up TV broadcasting telenovelas. Maybe Hernandez liked the Spanish-language soap operas.

He answered the door about sixty seconds later.

Behind him, there was a gray-haired woman in glasses, sitting on the couch.

"Eric Hernandez?"

"Yeah."

"We have a few questions for you."

Instead of inviting them in, he came out. Like Junior Lopez, he appeared to have just woken up. Noah had seen him around the neighborhood before. He wasn't as big as Junior or as tough-looking. His hair was very short rather than shaved. He was wearing a white T-shirt, dark-blue jeans, and black socks.

Eric was a quieter kind of gang member. On the surface, he looked like a nice Hispanic boy, handsome and well groomed. But that didn't mean he wasn't weaving in and out of shadows at night, selling drugs or tagging walls. Noah thought about the more elaborate artwork at the old schoolyard, signed by *e*.

Eric stared at Noah's uniformed shirt, waiting for him to speak.

"Were you with Cristina Lopez last night?"

He blinked a few times, as if he'd been expecting questions about something else. "Yeah, for a little while."

"What time?"

"Around midnight, I guess."

"You saw her at midnight?"

"Yeah."

"Where?"

"A bonfire near the south pier."

Noah found his demeanor very strange. Eric seemed to be monitoring their reactions. Usually, it was the other way around.

Visibly nervous, he fidgeted with a brown handkerchief on his right hand.

If Noah hadn't just seen Junior's bloody knuckles, he might not have suspected Eric of hiding an injury. "Were you in a fight recently?"

Eric gave him an odd look. "Have you talked to Meghan?"

Noah's blood went cold. "Meghan Young?"

"Your sister."

"No, I haven't talked to her this morning. Why?"

Eric hesitated again.

"Just spit it out, son," Patrick ordered. "And when you're speaking about an officer's sister, you better watch your language."

Eric's mouth twisted at the warning, but he accepted it without complaint. "Our boss, Jack, had a party at the beach last night. He invited Meghan and Cristina, and they asked me to come along. I met them there. Cristina started wrestling around with me—"

"What do you mean?" Noah interrupted. "Wrestling how?"

"Trying to kiss me, getting on top of me."

"And you weren't interested?"

"Not really, sir. Then Jack walked away with Meghan, so I told Cristina to wait there, and I followed them."

"Why would you do that?"

"Because Meghan was too drunk to stand up. And Jack is kind of a bad guy."

"You thought he'd take advantage?"

"Yes."

"And did he?"

"I think so," he said, his voice flat. "I found them

under the pier, and she was screaming. Her shirt was torn, almost in half."

Noah felt a wave of shock and rage pass over him, followed by an icy, unnatural calm. Even when Tony Castillo had tried to shoot his face off, he hadn't been this primed to retaliate. "I'll kill him."

Patrick put a hand on Noah's shoulder, forcing him to take a step back. "What did you do when you saw them?"

Eric massaged his cloth-covered knuckles. "I helped her."

"You struck him?"

"Yes."

"How many times?"

"I don't know. At least five. Maybe ten."

"Did he fight back?"

"No."

"Why did you stop?"

"Because he wasn't defending himself."

"Then what?"

"I helped her to the restrooms on Second Street. I think she washed her face or something. We ate at Taco Tico, and I walked her home."

"Did you call the police?"

"No. She said nothing happened."

"And you believed her?"

"Not really. But she said she wanted to sober up first, so I let it go. I think she was too scared to report it."

"Scared of Jack?"

"No." He glanced at Noah. "Scared of you. Afraid you'd send her home."

Noah's eyes burned and watered. Caught between

guilt and anger and absolute misery, he cleared his throat, looking away.

"What about Jack? What if he'd gone on to the next girl?" Patrick pressed.

"I doubt if he went looking for anything but an ice pack. Maybe some painkillers."

"You worked him over that good?"

"Yes, sir."

"Let's see your hand."

Eric took off the bandanna. His knuckles were raw and swollen, as if he'd been sparring with a cinder block.

"The text message you sent to Cristina," Noah said, finding his voice. "You told her you were leaving with Meghan?"

"Yeah. They came to the party together. I didn't want her to worry." He frowned, covering his knuckles again. "How do you know about that?"

"A jogger found Cristina Lopez under the pier this morning. Raped and murdered."

Eric's face went pale. He sat down on the top step, burying his head in his hands as the horrible ramifications of the previous night sank in. He'd left Junior's sister, drunk and alone, at a bonfire. She'd probably wandered off, looking for him.

And found her killer.

11

Noah found Meghan at home, still in bed, the covers pulled over her head.

"Hey," he said, nudging her shoulder.

She startled, sitting up too fast. Then she winced, touching her temple.

"I need you to come to the station."

Everything he'd expected to see, if Eric had told them the truth, was written on her face. Fear, nausea, fatigue. "Why?"

"You know why."

"H-how did you find out?"

"Cristina Lopez was murdered last night."

Meghan's reaction was similar to Eric's, but her stomach wasn't as strong. She scrambled out of bed and ran down the hall, locking herself in the bathroom. He could hear her throwing up, then dry-heaving. Tears burned his eyes again, because he hated to see his sister this way. He wanted to protect her from life's ugliness.

Instead, he was rubbing her face in it.

He followed her, rapping his knuckles against the

bathroom door. "Get dressed, okay? I'll wait for you downstairs."

While he waited, he called dispatch again. Detective Santiago had sent a patrol car to pick up Jack Bishop on suspicion of murder. What were the odds that two different rapists were hanging out under the pier last night?

"They have the suspect in custody," the operator said.

"Thanks," Noah replied.

Meghan came down a few minutes later. Her skin was pale, and there were dark circles under her eyes. She was wearing jeans and a loose-fitting blouse. A slim black headband kept her hair out of her face.

He took a deep breath, trying to pull himself together. "Do you want to eat something before we leave?"

She shuddered. "No."

"I won't be the one questioning you."

"Good."

"I can't investigate the case, either. But if you want me to stay with you at the station, for support—"

"No."

"Maybe we can talk about it later."

She brushed by him. "I don't even want to talk about it now."

He wrapped his hand around her upper arm. "Whatever happened . . . it wasn't your fault, Meghan."

She jerked away from him. "Let's just go."

Noah couldn't remember the last time he'd felt so lost, so ill at ease. She must be going through hell. He followed her outside, wishing he knew how to make it better.

When she saw Eric sitting in the back of the squad car, she paused. "What's he doing here?"

"He has to make a statement."

Looking like she might die from embarrassment, she continued down the front walk and climbed into the backseat beside him.

"I'm sorry," he said quietly.

She gave Eric a wobbly smile, her eyes shining with tears. Something passed between them, an intimacy Noah didn't understand or approve of. Then she turned her head and stared out the window, wiping her cheeks with one hand.

His sister had *feelings* for Eric Hernandez.

Meghan would have known to steer clear of an obvious thug like Junior Lopez, but she wasn't savvy enough to realize that Eric was equally dangerous. He had the same bad-boy appeal, along with an angel-faced exterior.

And he'd beaten the crap out of her attacker.

Noah got into the passenger side, his stomach tied in knots. He didn't know whether to thank Eric or warn him off.

At the station, they parted ways. Patrick escorted Meghan to one interview room, and Noah took Eric to another. She glanced over her shoulder as they rounded the corner, her face full of anxiety—and hero worship.

As soon as she was out of sight, Noah turned to her rescuer, clearing his throat to speak. Meghan was damned lucky she hadn't ended up like Cristina Lopez. Eric may have thwarted more than a rape.

Odd as it sounded, Noah owed this gang member a debt of gratitude. "Thank you for stepping in."

Eric's eyes registered surprise, then a grudging respect. "It was nothing."

"It means a lot to me."

He just shrugged, uncomfortable with the exchange.

Noah felt the same way, so he moved on, opening the door to the interview room. "Someone will be with you in a few minutes."

Eric went inside and sat down, looking as if he'd rather be anywhere else in the world. Noah continued down the hall, toward the viewing room. Minerva Watts, the SVU captain, was inside, chatting with Detective Santiago. She would probably interview Meghan. "You can't be a part of this, Officer Young."

"I know," he said. "But I . . . want to see his face."

She exchanged a glance with Santiago, who gave a slight nod. Watts waved Noah in, pointing at one of the screens.

Jack Bishop was sitting alone in the interrogation room. He was tall and lean, with longish brown hair. Eric Hernandez wasn't small, but he wasn't as big as this guy. Despite his greater size, Bishop had a black eye, a busted lip, and a taped nose.

"Okay," Noah said, stepping away from the screen. Seeing his sister's attacker bruised and beaten wasn't as satisfying as giving him the bruises, but it would have to do. Noah walked out of the room, his hands clenched into fists.

He sat down at his desk, drumming his fingertips against the surface. Last night, instead of chasing after April Ortiz, he should have checked up on Meghan. He felt as though he'd failed his sister, failed the investigation.

And now he couldn't do anything but wait.

Meghan had never felt so sick in her entire life.

She was fuzzy-headed from the hangover, numb with shock. Last night, the drugs and alcohol had worked like an anesthetic, insulating her from the reality of what had happened. Now the high had worn off, leaving her flat.

She was so low, she was scraping asphalt.

Every few seconds she flashed back to the events at the bonfire, and her stomach lurched with nausea.

And, oh, God—Cristina.

Meghan had left her there, alone. She hadn't given a second thought to her friend's welfare. Obviously, Cristina had worried about Meghan. When Meghan didn't come back to the party, Cristina must have wandered down the dark beach, searching for her.

This was all Meghan's fault.

She moaned, thinking about all of the stupid things she'd said and done to attract Eric's attention. Flaunting her body in that low-cut top, smoking pot. If Meghan hadn't acted like such an idiot, Cristina would still be alive.

After a considerable wait, in which she changed her mind about what she was going to say a dozen times, a redheaded woman came into the interview room. She was wearing nice slacks and a pale-pink blouse. "Meghan? I'm Captain Watts."

Meghan shook her slender hand. She'd expected a

stodgy old officer, like her brother's partner, Patrick. This woman was slim and pretty.

"I work with the Special Victims Unit, and I'll be interviewing you. Our conversation will be recorded. After we're finished talking, you can decide whether to file a crime report. You can do so anonymously, if you like." She gave Meghan a brief smile. "Of course, you don't have to speak with me at all."

"I don't?"

"No."

"And I don't have to press charges?"

"Not if you don't want to."

Meghan shifted in her seat. "Okay."

"If you'd like to continue, I would ask that you tell me everything you remember about yesterday evening, in your own words. Any details related to Cristina may be especially important."

"Will my brother be listening?"

"No."

She swallowed back another wave of nausea, her heart pounding in her chest. Knowing she had some choices made her feel a little better, and Captain Watts's calm persona helped put her at ease. Even so, she wanted to get this over with. "It was a normal afternoon at work," she began. "Around closing time, Jack asked Cristina and me if we wanted to go to a party. She said yes, but I hesitated."

"Why?"

"Jack always makes me uncomfortable. He stands too close to me and stares at me in a weird way. When Eric said he would come along, I felt . . . safer."

Captain Watts scribbled on notebook paper. "Go on."

"We went to my house to get ready. Cristina let me borrow a tank top."

"How was her mood?"

"Upbeat, I guess. She was excited about the bonfire."

"What did she say about it?"

"She mentioned wanting to hook up with Eric or one of Jack's friends. And she made some comments about Jack."

"What kind of comments?"

Meghan felt heat suffuse her cheeks. "That he liked me . . . and that he was, um, small. Down there."

"She said he had a small penis?"

"Yes."

"Had they dated before?"

"I guess so. Maybe only . . . once."

Watts made a note of it. "What else?"

"Well, we got to the party. Everyone was drinking and having a good time. We had some kind of punch."

"Who gave it to you?"

"Jack. He also, um, had a joint."

"Did he offer that to you, as well?"

"Yes," she admitted, her head spinning with the memory. "We both smoked some. Eric showed up, and he sat down with us. Cristina climbed on his lap. I started to feel really weird, like I was going to pass out or something, so I told Jack I needed some air."

Watts waited for her to continue, a tranquil expression on her face.

"We walked down the beach and sat under the pier.

He gave me some water, I think. I was . . . really confused. He kissed me. I didn't . . . resist, at first. He pushed me down on the sand, and I was just . . . so drunk. Instead of being afraid, I thought about what Cristina said about him, and I—I started laughing."

"Laughter is often a sign of distress or high anxiety," Watts said. "It's totally normal, even in this kind of situation."

"He didn't react to it well."

"How so?"

"He told me to shut up and hold still. I thought he was being too rough. Getting aggressive. So I tried to twist away, and my shirt ripped."

"He ripped your shirt?"

"Yes. I rolled over, crawling through the sand." Tears welled in her eyes, but she forced herself to continue. "He yanked down my jeans and tore off my underwear. I screamed and tried to get away, but he had me pinned. He started touching me. When he unzipped his pants, and I realized what he was going to do, I think I . . . froze." She closed her eyes and took a deep breath. "The next thing I remember is Eric hitting him."

"Did he penetrate you? With his penis, fingers, any foreign object?"

"No."

"You said he touched you."

"Yes."

"Where, specifically?"

"My breasts, my butt, my . . . vulva." She blushed again, wallowing in shame and embarrassment.

"Did he ejaculate?"

"I don't think so."

"Did you say no?"

"I don't remember."

Captain Watts tilted her head to the side. "Did you communicate your unwillingness in another way?"

"Well, I was struggling. Screaming."

"Do you think he understood that you were not giving consent?"

"Yes," she said, with complete conviction.

Captain Watts smiled. "Thank you, Meghan. I know how difficult it is to discuss an attack like this, and I commend you for coming forward. Every time a woman speaks out against sexual violence, she encourages others to do the same."

Meghan didn't feel brave, but she felt better. "I wasn't even raped."

"You *were* sexually assaulted. Attempted rape is a very serious crime."

"What should I do?"

"I always recommend a physical exam and sexual-assault counseling. Some victims block out memories of the attack or show symptoms of post-traumatic stress disorder. It's important to speak with a professional."

"Isn't that what you are?"

"I'm a police officer, not a doctor or a psychologist. My job is to take your statement and collect any available evidence. Your case is strong because we have a witness—a rarity in these situations. Even if you don't press charges, we can move forward. And the suspect is already in custody."

Meghan felt a shiver of apprehension. "Do you think he killed Cristina?"

"He's a person of interest in the murder investigation."

"Okay," she said, touching her aching forehead. "I'll cooperate any way I can."

Noah had been sitting at his cubicle for hours, trying to distract himself with paperwork, when Patrick approached him. "Let's go."

He jumped up from his desk, following his partner down the hall.

"Santiago cleared you to come back," Patrick said. "Meghan's done, and they're about to start interrogating the suspect. Official charge, according to Watts, is attempted rape. Looks like Eric Hernandez arrived just in time."

Noah's relief was immense. He paused in the hallway, closing his eyes. Patrick laid a hand on his shoulder, giving him a comforting squeeze. Then Noah's anger came seeping back. "That mother*fucker*—"

"Stop," Patrick warned. "You know I'd love to hold that guy down while you beat him. And I'd take a turn myself. But right now we have to act like 'peace' officers or you're going to get kicked out of the viewing room again."

Noah took a deep breath, pushing his rage into a dark, ugly place inside himself. For a moment he felt like . . . Patrick. Mad and mean and ready to brawl. Their eyes met, and they understood each other perfectly. In some situations, civility was overrated. But Noah had to maintain his composure if he wanted to assist the investigation.

"Can I see Meghan?"

"Not yet. She's speaking with a counselor."

He nodded. "Okay."

They continued on to the viewing room and took seats in the back. Santiago's interview with Jack Bishop was in progress.

"Who gave her the alcohol?" Santiago asked.

"I did," Jack replied.

"What else?"

"We smoked some pot."

"Yours?"

"Yeah."

"How drunk was she?"

Jack's expression was belligerent. "She stumbled a little, but she could walk. She knew what she was doing."

"What was she doing?"

"Hanging all over me! Whispering in my ear. She asked me to take her away from the party so we could be alone."

"Where did you go?"

"Near the pier."

"Any reason you went there?"

Jack shrugged. "It's kind of private, I guess. There are a lot of shadows."

"What did you have in mind?"

"Well, I'm not going to lie. She's a cute girl, and I wanted to hook up with her."

"You wanted to have sex with her?"

"Yeah."

"And was she interested in the same thing?"

"I think so. She was kissing me, touching me. Then

her crazy boyfriend came and attacked me for no reason."

"Her boyfriend?"

"Eric Hernandez."

"Why do you think he hit you?"

"Because he was jealous. He caught me by surprise, too. The first punch stunned me, and I was so disoriented, I didn't fight back. He even kicked me." Jack stood and lifted his shirt, showing dark bruises along his rib cage. "He's a fucking maniac!"

"After the altercation, did you go back to the party?"

He sat back down. "No, I went to my car and passed out for a while. I didn't want anyone to know Eric beat me up."

"Did you see Cristina Lopez again that night?"

"I didn't see anyone. In the morning, when I felt well enough, I drove home."

Santiago leaned back in his chair. He wasn't buying any of Jack's bullshit. "Are you aware that Meghan's brother is a police officer?"

Jack paled beneath his surfer tan. "No."

"Well, he is. He brought her in this morning, and she has a very different story."

"She's lying."

Santiago took a photo out of his briefcase and slid it across the table. "Do you know who that is?"

Jack grimaced when he saw it. "It's . . . Cristina," he whispered, looking away. For the first time in the duration of the interview, he appeared contrite. He pushed the picture back to Santiago, his eyes watery.

"We found her under the pier this morning, dead. She'd been raped."

Jack shook his head, wordless.

"It's time for you to get real. Meghan Young said you were holding her down and tearing off her clothes. We have a witness who corroborates her version of the story, not yours. And we have a second victim in the same place."

"No," Jack said.

"Things are not looking good for you, Jack. Are you ready to tell me the truth, or should I go ahead and book you on murder charges?"

Jack stared up at the ceiling, pressing his lips together.

Santiago gathered his paperwork, preparing to leave.

"Okay," Jack said, his voice hoarse. "I got a little rough with Meghan. But I swear to God, I didn't do anything to Cristina. I'm not a killer."

"Just a rapist?"

"No!"

"Why don't you tell me what really happened under the pier?"

Jack crossed his arms over his chest, sullen. "After I kissed her, Meghan started laughing."

"Why?"

"I don't know."

"How did that make you feel?"

"Angry. I wanted her to stop, so I grabbed the front of her shirt. She twisted away, and it tore down the front."

"You tore her shirt?"

"It was an accident."

"Did she stop laughing?"

"Yeah."

"Then what?"

"I let her roll over, because I didn't want her to . . . see me."

"Why not?"

A dark flush crept up his face, reddening his cheeks. "The last girl I was with said I was . . . small. Since then I've been self-conscious about it."

"Did you want to punish her for laughing? Make her pay?"

"No," he said, shaking his head. "That wasn't it at all."

"Come on, Jack."

"I wasn't going to hurt her!"

"You turned her over and yanked down her pants," Santiago said in an even tone. "Then you ripped her underwear off her body. Are you seriously trying to tell me that your intention wasn't rape?"

He appeared nauseous. "I only wanted to look at her."

"Right," Santiago scoffed.

"I just wanted to look at her . . . and use my hand, okay?" His voice rose, almost breaking, and his eyes filled with tears. "I figured she wouldn't mind that much. She was so drunk, she might not even remember."

Santiago was silent, weighing Jack's words.

"I was drunk, too, and . . . I wasn't thinking clearly. It was stupid. But it wasn't rape."

"What happened after Hernandez came?"

"Like I said—he beat the shit out of me, and I went back to my car. I didn't see anyone. I could hardly walk."

The interrogation continued for another hour, but Jack didn't change his story. Although he admitted to sleeping with Cristina Lopez—the girl who'd made fun of his penis—he was vehement in his claim that he hadn't seen her after the altercation. And he insisted that his intention with Meghan had never been rape.

The mood in the viewing room was subdued. Everyone in the police department wanted to catch the killer. The SVU team would have liked to book Jack Bishop on a serious sexual-assault charge, but he'd probably end up with a slap on the wrist for lewd conduct.

Noah had barely managed to contain himself during the interview. He tried not to entertain thoughts of violent retribution.

For the first time in his life, it sucked to be a cop.

Santiago didn't take him off the case, but he did send him home early. Eric Hernandez had mentioned seeing some Eastside guys at the taco stand, so Patrick and another gang-unit officer would be following up on that.

In the meantime, the homicide investigators were searching for a connection between the two murders.

Noah wanted to stay and help, but Meghan needed him, too. He spoke with her sexual-assault counselor, who recommended that he let his sister recover at her own pace. He should be available and supportive, not smothering. To his surprise, the psychologist had recommended that Noah as well as Meghan should attend counseling. Family members of sexual-assault victims often dealt with feelings of rage, helplessness, and guilt.

He admitted that he was struggling with those same emotions and promised to keep himself healthy, for Meghan's sake.

When he saw his sister again, she looked exhausted. Respecting her boundaries, he didn't touch her as they left the station, and they barely spoke on the way home. There was an old-fashioned burger joint near his house that reminded him of the soda fountain in Cedar Glen, so he stopped there.

She picked at her meal, but drank most of a vanilla milk shake. Some of the color returned to her cheeks. A good night's sleep would diminish the circles under her eyes.

Noah could use some rest himself.

"Do you want to talk about it?"

She dragged a French fry through ketchup, drawing a slick red line across her plate. "No. Do you want to talk about your sex life?"

"It wasn't sex, Meghan."

"Are you going to tell Mom?"

"No. Are you?"

She shrugged, abandoning the mutilated French fry. "She'll want me to come home."

Noah didn't dispute that, but he wasn't going to send her back like an unwanted gift. As uncomfortable as he was admitting it, Meghan was an adult now. He couldn't decide what was best for her. "I have some time off tomorrow—"

"No," she interrupted.

"You don't even know what I was going to ask."

"An outing, to cheer me up?"

He sighed, raking a hand through his hair. "I have a date," he admitted. "And she has a daughter. I told her about you."

There was a flicker of interest in her eyes. "How old is she?"

He knew that Meghan liked kids. She used to earn

pocket money babysitting and had been a favorite among the parents in their hometown. "She's five. I said I'd take them to Wave City and bring you along. I think you're the reason she agreed."

She snorted. "You must be losing your touch."

"You could be right."

"So you want me to babysit the little girl, keep her out of your way?"

"No," he said, frowning. "It was supposed to be a family thing."

She studied his face for a moment. "You like her."

"Yes."

"She's divorced?"

"I think she never got married."

"Hmm. As much as I approve of you dating some-one who doesn't sound like your usual type, I don't think I'm up for an amusement-park adventure right now. Besides, that wouldn't work out as well for you."

"What do you mean?"

"It would end up with me instead of you playing with the kid. And that wouldn't impress her mommy."

Noah smiled. "Good point. But I can always cancel."

"Why?"

He just stared at her.

"You don't need to stay home with me, Noah," she said, throwing her napkin down. "I'm fine."

He paid the check and followed her outside, wishing he didn't feel so fucking ineffectual. She wasn't fine. And he couldn't do a damned thing about it.

12

April didn't sleep well. Again.

Last night at Club Suave, she'd heard the news about the latest murder. All of the waitresses were terrified. The police hadn't made any definitive arrests, but they were investigating a link between the two crimes. According to Carmen, the second victim had worked with Eric at Bonita Market.

April was worried for him, and for Josefa, who was still MIA.

Noah's kiss had also dominated her thoughts. She'd been afraid that her memories of Raul would interfere with her enjoyment, but she hadn't thought of Jenny's father at all when Noah put his hands on her. She'd been too busy kissing him back, moaning into his mouth. If she hadn't felt the cool metal of his gun tucked into the waistband of his pants, she might have completely forgotten herself.

Flushing with heat, she opened the top drawer of her dresser and took out her new bikini. It looked even skimpier than she remembered. Nibbling on her lower lip, she grabbed her other suit, comparing the two. The demure tankini showed a lot of wear and tear. The message it sent was *unavailable*.

The bikini, on the other hand, said *hot for it*.

Reminding herself that this was a date and that it was okay to look sexy, she tugged on the new bikini. It was mostly white, with flashy gold geometric shapes. Black strings held the top together, securing at the nape of her neck and the middle of her back.

There were two more ties at each hip.

Brevity was an issue, but the fabric covered all of the essential parts. She turned, checking out her backside in the mirror. There was nothing indecent about the fit. Some of her low-rise jeans revealed more.

She called Jenny in for a second opinion. "What do you think?"

Her eyes lit up with approval. "Your boobs look pretty."

April laughed, adjusting the triangle top. She was more concerned about the bikini bottoms, which exposed her hips and tummy, but Jenny had been fixated on breasts lately. April blamed the anatomically correct Bratz doll that Josefa had bought her. Underneath her hoochie outfit, the doll had sparkly underwear and plush boobies. "Thanks."

Jenny frowned at her own flat chest. "When will I get them?"

"When you're sixteen," she said, hoping that was true. April had developed early and remembered feeling self-conscious about it. She hugged Jenny close, dropping a kiss on top of her head. "Don't grow up too soon, okay?"

Jenny squirmed away. "Why can't Eric come?"

She sighed, choosing a green sundress from her closet. "Eric's not invited. But you'll have lots of fun. Don't worry."

Jenny often picked up on April's nervousness and then mirrored it. Today was no exception. Changes in their routine also caused her energy level to skyrocket. She'd been bouncing off the walls all morning.

While Jenny did somersaults on the living-room couch, April fussed over her appearance. Should she put her hair in a practical ponytail, or leave it soft and loose at her shoulders? Would wearing makeup to a water park look too high maintenance? Were rubber flip-flops too casual for a first date?

In the end, she left her hair down and wore the flip-flops. After applying some waterproof mascara and a touch of lip gloss, she walked out into the living room. Jenny had just spilled orange juice all over the coffee table. She was trying to mop it up—with the nice beach towels April had set aside for Wave City.

"Why did you do that?"

She blinked her big brown eyes. "It spilled itself."

April groaned, taking the towels to the laundry basket. In Spanish, saying "the cup spilled itself" was perfectly acceptable, but the phrase didn't translate the same way in English. April knew Jenny understood the difference.

"You spilled it," she corrected, pointing her finger.

The only other large towels she owned were frayed and faded. She grabbed them out of the bathroom cabinet and repacked her beach bag. Then she fixed Jenny's askew pigtails. "Go put your sandals on," she said, swatting her bottom.

The doorbell rang a moment later.

"Oh, my God," she breathed, holding a hand over he[r] stomach. She was so nervous, she felt like throwing up.

What if her swimsuit was too skanky? What if Jenn[y] did something embarrassing?

She took a deep breath, pushing aside her fears as sh[e] walked toward the front door. If Noah didn't like he[r] bikini, he needed to get his testosterone checked, and i[f] bratty kids scared him off, it wasn't meant to be.

Her heart skipped a beat when she saw him. In a ta[n] T-shirt and navy shorts, he appeared relaxed, casua[l] and achingly handsome. She could feel his gaze, eve[n] through the lenses of his sunglasses, skimming dow[n] her dress.

And—he brought flowers.

"You look beautiful," he said, smiling. After a quic[k] kiss on the cheek, he handed her the bouquet of Gerbe[r] daisies.

She tried not to goggle at them. "Thank you."

"They're for you and Jenny," he explained.

It took her a second to realize that Jenny was stand[-]ing beside her. "Come in," she said. "I'll put these i[n] water."

"Where's your sister?" Jenny asked.

"She couldn't come. I hope that's okay."

"Of course," April said, grabbing a vase from unde[r] the sink. Actually, she was relieved. Navigating th[e] course between Noah and Jenny would be difficul[t] enough without throwing another personality into th[e] mix.

"I told her about you," he continued, taking a piec[e]

of paper out of his pocket for Jenny. "And she wrote you a note."

Jenny accepted it shyly. "What does it say?"

"Open it and see."

April arranged the flowers in the vase, watching as Jenny unfolded the note. "It says my name!"

Noah laughed at her enthusiasm. "Yes."

Jenny brought the note to April. "What else does it say, Mommy?"

Noah's sister had drawn a stick figure of a little girl on a surfboard, catching a wave. April read the message. "It says, *Have fun at Wave City! Love, Meghan.*"

"Is Meghan your sister's name?" Jenny asked.

He nodded.

"How old is she?"

"Nineteen."

"What grade is that, Mom?"

"That's college, *pepita.*"

She ran off, excited. "I'm going to put it in my room, with Daddy's letters!"

April dried her hands on a dish towel, realizing that she shouldn't have worried about Jenny misbehaving in front of Noah. The bigger concern, by far, was that her daughter would get instantly attached.

She stared at the daisies, feeling her throat close up. Like the note, they were more thoughtful than grand.

"Is something wrong?" he asked.

"No," she said, swallowing. "They're lovely."

"You're lovely."

"Stop."

He stuck his hands in his pockets, perusing her living room. When Jenny rejoined them, April picked up her tote bag, trying to stay calm. It was just a date. He wasn't perfect. There was no reason to freak out.

"Ready?"

April wondered if he thought he was driving. "We have to take my car."

"Why?"

"Jenny's car seat is in there."

"My truck has an extra cab. I'm sure it will fit."

April hesitated. She'd never allowed Jenny to ride with a stranger before. On the other hand, his truck looked brand-new, and it probably had a working air conditioner. "Okay," she said, heading into the garage. He watched her remove the seat, and then he carried it outside for her, his biceps flexing.

She secured it in his backseat, and Jenny hopped in, smiling at the novelty. "I like your truck. It's clean!"

"Thanks," Noah said.

April flushed, climbing into the passenger side. She couldn't remember the last time a man had driven her around. This was a big deal for her. It was kind of silly how infrequently she relinquished control.

He drove out of her neighborhood, merging onto the freeway a few minutes later. His truck *was* nice. Nothing fancy or oversize, but it was relatively new and smelled like interior polish. He didn't turn on the radio.

Although he seemed at ease behind the wheel, April felt uncomfortable. The silence stretched between them.

"My sister said you might like Dora the Explorer," Noah ventured, glancing at Jenny in his rearview mirror.

Shy again, Jenny didn't answer.

"That's her favorite," April murmured.

"I'm a SpongeBob man myself."

Jenny shifted in her seat. "Mom thinks that show is dumb."

"Well, we know better, don't we?"

She giggled, delighted to have a partner in bad-television crime. April gave him a chiding glance, but she couldn't fault his strategy. Winning over Jenny would always be the way to April's heart.

He paid for parking at Wave City, and they walked toward the front entrance. When Jenny saw the tops of the waterslides, she squeezed April's hand, excited. "Can we go on all the rides, Mommy?"

"I don't know if you're tall enough for the big ones, *pepa*."

"Have you been here before?" Noah asked.

"No," April said. For the same price, she could take Jenny on a dozen other outings. By necessity, she was a budget mom. As they approached the line to pay, she reached for her purse, noting the exorbitant entrance fee.

"I bought our tickets online," he explained.

She stopped digging around in her bag. "Why?"

"Why not?"

"I'll reimburse you."

"Don't even think about it," he warned.

"I'm not some charity case."

He lowered his voice. "No, you're my *date*. This is a date, and I pay on dates. I pay for admission, and lunch, and ice cream, and whatever else I feel like buying."

April had never seen him annoyed before. He also

looked a little tired, as if he'd been working late. She felt a pang of sympathy for him.

"Ice cream?" Jenny said, hopeful.

He stared at April, demanding her compliance.

She knew she was being prickly, even unreasonable. Paying her way kept a safe distance between them, and he wanted her to let go of her inhibitions. "All right," she said, holding up her empty hands.

It felt kind of good to . . . surrender.

He gave the tickets to a park attendant, and they proceeded inside. The day was already warm, getting hotter by the minute. Jenny's hand felt sticky in hers, and a bead of sweat trickled between her breasts.

"I guess we need a locker," he said, buying a key on a spiral wristband. After he opened the locker, he gave the key to Jenny.

"Cool," she said, admiring it on her wrist.

He took off his shirt and tossed it inside the locker. April tried not to gape at his muscles. His board shorts rode low on his hips, and his flat belly was dusted with golden-brown hair. Although he was lean and well toned, he didn't have the waxed-and-sculpted look that was popular with young men these days.

He put the pretty gym boys to shame.

"Are you going to wear that all day?"

She blinked out of her stupor. Jenny had already added her outfit to the pile of clothes in the locker. Blushing, April pulled the dress over her head and folded it neatly. Noah inspected her bikini in detail, his mouth going slack. Maybe he felt that complimenting her in front of Jenny would be inappropriate, because he didn't say anything.

She thought about covering up with a towel.

"Can I go, Mommy?"

April glanced toward a large play area for younger children. Jenny definitely fit the height requirement, and it seemed a logical place to start. She shot Noah a questioning look.

"Whatever you want," he said, clearing his throat.

They put their towels on a couple of lounge chairs near the kid zone, and Jenny ran off, squealing with joy. It was ideal, really. April could talk to Noah while Jenny romped in the shallow water, splashing around with about a dozen other preschoolers.

April sat down in the chair, holding herself stiffly. Her bikini seemed to shrink under his appreciative gaze. Without Jenny there to chaperone, the air between them felt heated, sizzling with sexual tension.

"I like your suit," he said.

"Um . . . I like your shorts."

As soon as she said it, she wanted to cover her face with her hands and groan. The level of awkwardness was off the charts. Noah was charming and obviously polite. But she could guess that he was better at relating to women at a club or over dinner. He probably hadn't gone on a first date with a mother and child before.

"We should talk about something cold," he decided. "Have you ever been to Antarctica?"

She laughed. "I've never even seen snow."

He took off his sunglasses. "Are you serious?"

"Yes."

"Not even at Mount Laguna or Palomar?"

"No."

"It snows in Cedar Glen, where I'm from. Sometimes it melts as soon as it hits the ground, but every once in a while it snows a couple of inches. When it's really cold, this silvery crust forms on the top. It sparkles in the moonlight."

"Sounds pretty," she said wistfully, watching Jenny frolic.

"It is."

She glanced at Noah. "Why'd you leave?"

"Well, there isn't much crime there. And I like it here, too. I like the energy, the heat." His blue eyes met hers. "How about you?"

"I like it most of the time." Chula Vista had a lot of culture and vibrancy. Someday she would move into one of the less volatile neighborhoods and be able to appreciate the city's finer qualities. "The crime isn't a plus for me, though."

"I'm working on that."

She smiled. "It does create a social need, and that will help me get a job when I graduate, so I shouldn't complain."

He leaned back in his chair. "Why are you interested in social work?"

"Someone helped me once, when I was pregnant with Jenny. She really made a difference in my life."

Contemplative, he looked from April to Jenny. "Is her dad around at all?"

"He's in prison."

His brows rose at her blunt admission. "Does she know?"

"Yes."

"And . . . when he gets out?"

She shook her head. "I don't want to see him, if that's

what you're asking. I don't want her to see him, either. Thankfully, he's never taken much interest. I've tried not to say bad things about him in front of her, but . . . he's a bad man."

"I'm sorry."

"I'm sorry, too." Not a day went by that she didn't regret her involvement with Raul and its repercussions for Jenny. But she couldn't change the past, and she was doing her best to make a better future.

"How old are you?"

"Twenty-three."

"You were just a kid when you had her."

"I grew up fast."

"How's your mom, by the way?"

"I haven't heard from her." She was distracted for a moment, because Jenny had slipped on the stairs of the pirate ship. When she got up, unhurt, April relaxed. "What about you? Are you involved with the latest murder investigation?"

"Yes."

"I don't suppose you can talk about it."

"No. But I do have to work tonight."

She searched his face, concerned. "You should've told me."

"It's no big deal. We have plenty of time."

"Do you want to reschedule?"

"No way. Even the lead investigators aren't allowed to work around the clock. Everyone puts in extra hours during a high-profile case, but we're also encouraged to take breaks. De-stressing, they call it."

"You wouldn't rather be home, resting?"

His gaze skimmed down her body. "There's nowhere I'd rather be."

They were silent for a few minutes, but the mood was comfortable rather than awkward or sexually charged. When an older boy squirted Jenny with one of the pirate ship's water guns, Noah rose from his lounge chair.

"That kid is going *down*," he said, stepping onto the course.

April watched, laughing, while he pelted the offending child with staccato blasts from the water gun. Then he went ahead and attacked Jenny for good measure. She screamed in delight and retaliated. April, of course, had to join the battle.

They all ended up soaked.

The next few hours passed in a pleasant, dreamlike idyll. They drifted down the lazy river on clear plastic inner tubes, drinking in the sun. Jenny wasn't tall enough for the big waterslides, and April wouldn't dare try them, but Noah talked them into a log ride. Later, they braved the raging rapids and visited the wave pool.

As promised, Noah paid for lunch—and ice cream.

And, as April had feared, Jenny loved him. It wasn't the ice cream, or the trip, or anything he'd paid out of pocket. It was just him. He gave her his complete attention, and he actually listened to what she said but didn't cater to her every whim. His easygoing attitude suited Jenny's energetic personality quite well.

He was great with her. That was it.

In the early afternoon, he offered to give Jenny a swimming lesson. She'd never had one before, and she was a little uncertain in the deep water. "I was a lifeguard at the lake every summer in Cedar Glen," he boasted.

April imagined that he'd been popular. "I'll bet there were a few girls who pretended to drown to get your attention."

He grinned at her. "Actually, no. The only mouth-to-mouth I performed was on an eighty-year-old man."

Jenny giggled, picturing the scene.

"He recovered fully, I'll have you know. So, how about it?"

"Fine with me," April said. "I'd love for her to learn the basics. But I think you both need some sunscreen first."

Jenny rarely burned, but she wasn't usually out in the sun this long. April sprayed her with SPF 15, carefully rubbing it over her face. "There you go, *pepa*." She turned to Noah, whose shoulders already looked ruddy. Admiring his sleek muscles and golden tan, she applied the spray sunscreen to his back.

He had the kind of physique that attracted attention. She'd noticed female eyes following him all day. There were some beautiful women here, in bikinis even smaller than hers, but she hadn't caught him returning any stares.

"What about you?" he asked.

Although she probably didn't need it, she lifted her hair, letting him spray the lotion over her back.

"Stupid invention," he said in a low voice, annoyed that no touching was required.

Laughing, she stretched out on a nearby lounge chair, watching the lesson rather than participating. Jenny kicked and blew bubbles and tried to float. Soon she was jumping off the side of the pool into Noah's arms.

April couldn't remember the last time she'd felt so . . . languid. In the shade, the temperature was perfect, warm and breezy. There was nothing pressing to do, no one demanding her attention. It was positively decadent.

She closed her eyes and sighed, savoring the feeling. A moment later, she was asleep.

13

Noah should have taken them to the zoo. They were having a great time at Wave City, but April's bikini was driving him crazy. Dry, it was sexy. Wet, it was spectacular.

Although the fabric wasn't see-through—thank God—it was clingy. The suit molded to the curves of her body, leaving very little to the imagination. With Jenny right there, it wasn't appropriate for Noah to check out April's luscious ass, or her perfect breasts, or the sweet triangle between her legs. So he tried not to stare.

It was too easy to picture her naked.

He was mildly ashamed of himself but not surprised. It wasn't unusual for his senses to be heightened when he was working on a tough case. Close calls and dangerous situations brought out the physical side of many men. Dealing with death made Noah want to reaffirm life in the basest, most basic way.

He'd never been so tempted by a woman.

Thankfully, Jenny provided a convenient distraction. For sanity's sake, he focused most of his attention on her. She was a cute kid, easy to get along with. She also had her mother's quick intelligence. After twenty minutes of swimming lessons, she'd learned how to glide, kick, and float.

"I have to go potty," she said suddenly.

Noah glanced at April. She'd fallen asleep on the lounge chair, and she looked adorable. "Okay," he said, boosting Jenny out of the pool. "I'll take you."

The bathrooms were close by, so Noah didn't bother to wake up April. After delivering Jenny to the ladies' room, he ducked into the men's. When he came out, Jenny was standing there, shifting back and forth on her bare feet.

"Did you go?" he asked.

"I can't get out of my swimsuit."

Noah eyed the crossover straps, frowning. This was not his area of expertise. He looked around for female assistance, and a pretty brunette caught his eye.

She assessed the situation in an instant, offering Jenny a warm smile. "Need some help, honey? I'll take you."

Jenny nodded, accepting her hand.

"Thanks," Noah said.

The brunette winked at him. "No problem."

About two minutes later, Jenny walked out of the ladies' room with her helper. The brunette flashed Noah a flirtatious smile. "She's a cutie," the woman said, looking back and forth between them.

Noah read the question in her eyes. With her dark coloring, Jenny was obviously not his. "Thanks. She's my girlfriend's daughter."

"Ah. Too bad."

He watched her saunter away, more as a male reflex than with any genuine interest. She had a nice figure, he noted absently.

"My mommy is your girlfriend?" Jenny asked.

"No," he said. "I was just—"

"Jenny!"

Noah turned to see April rushing toward them. She looked frantic. And . . . pissed off. When she put her arm around Jenny's shoulders and glanced in the direction of the saucy brunette, he knew he was in trouble.

"Why didn't you wake me?" she asked.

He massaged the back of his neck, not sure what to say. Her reaction seemed a bit extreme. "Uh—"

"You have no right to take my daughter anywhere without my permission."

Noah didn't feel compelled to defend himself. He also knew better than to argue with a woman in public.

"I think we should go home."

He nodded curtly. Now *he* was pissed off. "Whatever you like."

They went back to the lockers and got ready to leave. Jenny didn't want to go, unsurprisingly. For the first time that day, she turned on the drama, crying and pulling away from her mother, refusing to put on her shoes.

April looked near tears herself.

Noah didn't have a lot of experience with little girls and temper tantrums. There was no crying in baseball, as the saying went. But he remembered something he used to do when his sister was upset.

"Come on," he said, kneeling beside her. "I'll give you a piggyback ride."

Sniffling, Jenny climbed aboard.

April tossed her daughter's shoes in the tote bag and followed them out to the parking lot, her mouth thin. Maybe she didn't appreciate the interference. He got the impression that she wasn't used to letting anyone help her.

Jenny slumped against his back, exhausted from too much fun in the sun. By the time Noah pulled onto the freeway, she was asleep in her car seat.

He glanced at April, wishing the date hadn't ended this way. If he didn't say something to smooth things over, he knew he wouldn't get another chance to go out with her. But—why apologize when he hadn't done anything wrong?

"I'm sorry," she said quietly.

And those two simple words changed everything. "Don't be," he said, feeling like a jerk. "I shouldn't have left with her."

"No. I overreacted."

"You looked so peaceful, and I didn't want to bother you . . ."

"It's okay," she said, giving him a wobbly smile. "When I woke up, and she wasn't there, I . . . panicked."

"Of course you did. It was stupid of me."

"She's never been around a man before, other than her uncle. I know I'm overprotective, because of some . . . issues in my past. It took years before I'd leave her alone with anyone, even family members."

He wanted to kill whoever had hurt her. "I'm sorry," he said, wishing the world wasn't full of abusive assholes. "I don't expect you to take my word for it, but I'd rather die than touch your daughter. And I'd cut off my own hand before I used it to harm a woman."

She nodded, acknowledging his statement. "This is why I was hesitant to go out with you, Noah. You seem too good to be true, and I don't let my guard down easily. If you're just looking for sex—"

Jenny made a noise in her sleep, her head lolling to one side.

"I'm not," he said, lowering his voice.

April looked out the window. He wasn't sure she believed him. It was difficult to be convincing when sex was at the forefront of his mind. The hungry looks he'd been giving her all day didn't help.

For the remainder of the drive, he questioned his own motives. He was taking a professional risk by dating her, and he'd never done anything like that before. Beginning a "complicated" relationship—with April *and* Jenny, for they were a package deal—wasn't the wisest course of action.

He shouldn't have asked her out.

The more time he spent with her, the more attached he became. Maybe he should walk away now, before things got . . . sticky.

At her house, Noah carried Jenny inside. While April put her down for a nap, he took the car seat out of his truck and placed it on her doorstep. Then he waited for her in the living room, his hands in his pockets.

Any minute now she was going to come back and say she was sorry but she couldn't see him anymore.

And he was going to let her.

April tiptoed out of Jenny's room, shutting the door behind her. She paused in the hallway, turning on the air conditioner full blast. The mechanical whir would drown out their voices, should Jenny awaken.

She usually didn't take naps, but the day had been long and eventful. April assumed she would sleep for another hour, at least.

Noah was waiting for her in the living room. She felt a pang of regret for the way she'd acted. He'd been wonderful with Jenny today, and she'd repaid his kindness by freaking out, scolding him, and demanding to go home. When Jenny started to throw a tantrum, April had almost broken down in tears, too.

He probably never wanted to see her again. And yet he was still here. Too polite to leave without saying goodbye.

"Would you like a drink?" she asked tentatively, fisting her sweaty hands in her skirt. The cotton fabric inched up her thighs, drawing his attention.

"Sure," he said, clearing his throat. "Water's fine."

She filled two glasses with ice and purified water. As soon as she sat down, he took the space next to her on the couch, draining half his glass in long swallows.

"Thanks."

They were silent for another moment.

"To pick up where we left off," she began, feeling self-conscious. "I was talking about my trust issues?"

He nodded, listening.

"I'll probably always be overprotective of Jenny, and I might never get completely comfortable around you. When we're alone, I mean." She hazarded another glance at him. This was so embarrassing. "My behavior the other night was kind of strange. You see, I'm usually a little more . . . reserved with men."

His gaze dropped to her mouth, as if he was remembering their kiss. She couldn't help but replay the scene herself. He was so close she could smell him, a heady mix of male skin and summer heat.

She moistened her lips, wanting his mouth on hers so badly she could taste it. "Anyway, this is all irrelevant, I'm sure. I just wanted to finish explaining why I reacted that way. Thank you for a lovely day, and I'm sorry for—everything."

His eyes met hers. "So this is goodbye?"

"Yes."

He didn't argue with her, but he made no move to leave. She sensed his reluctance, and his disappointment, and his desire. They stared at each other for a long beat, poised at the edge of an unknown precipice.

Her chest rose and fell with every breath, and she was aware of the still-damp swimsuit against her pebbled nipples.

His hands flexed against his thighs, and she felt an answering tug between her own. She wanted him to touch her. Everywhere.

April wasn't sure if he leaned in or if she did. One moment they were agreeing it wasn't going to work out. The next he was kissing her senseless. His mouth was hot, agile, hungry. She moaned, touching her tongue to his, twisting her fingers in his hair. His hands spanned her waist and squeezed, burning through the fabric of her dress.

He kissed her over and over again, as if he couldn't get enough of her mouth. She arched her back, wanting to feel more of his body. He complied on instinct, pressing her down on the couch, crushing her breasts to his chest. When the ridge of his erection settled into the apex of her thighs, he groaned.

She wrapped her legs around his waist and dug her fingernails into his shoulders, gasping against his mouth.

His fingertips danced over the tie at her back, tugging it loose. She felt her bikini top fall away and her dress inch down. He broke off the kiss to stare at her exposed breasts. The skin beneath her bikini top was a shade paler than the rest. Her nipples were small, tight beads. She'd never experienced anything more erotic than watching his eyes darken with lust for her.

Before his head descended, she braced her hands on his shoulders. "Wait," she said. "I can't . . . do this . . . here. Not with my daughter home."

"Let's go to your room. I'll be quiet."

"The bedsprings squeak."

"Who needs a bed?"

She tried not to picture him lifting her up against the wall, pinning her with slow thrusts. "No bedroom. No sex."

"Okay," he whispered, his fingertips trailing down her throat. He bent his head to moisten one nipple, then the other, sucking gently. Surveying his work, he blew on the wet, puckered tips, wrenching a gasp from her.

"Noah—"

"This isn't sex. It's just . . . touching." Repositioning himself, he slid his hand underneath her skirt. With a quick tug, he untied her bikini bottoms and brushed his mouth over hers again, drinking her protests. His fingertips found her, hot and wet.

He let out a hissing breath.

"That feels like sex," she panted. When he dipped one finger inside her, she moaned, spreading her thighs a little wider.

"How about this?" He moved his slippery finger up to her clitoris, circling it lazily.

"That feels . . . better than sex."

"What if I did it with my mouth?"

She thrashed her head back and forth. "I've never—oh, my God." He pushed her skirt out of the way so he could get a good look at what he was doing, but he didn't go down on his knees. He flicked his tongue over her nipples and continued to caress her heated flesh, tracing her opening with his fingertip, strumming the taut pink nub.

"Oh, my God," she moaned again, biting down on her lip. She was going to come.

The surprising part wasn't the orgasm itself. She'd had those before. Even Raul, who'd been a selfish lover, had managed to bring her off a few times. But he'd labored over the task, treating it like a nuisance on the rare occasions that he bothered.

And he'd never put his mouth on her.

Noah showed more tenderness and more aptitude in a few languid strokes than Raul had offered in their entire relationship. His attention was rapt, attuned to her responses, and his fingers were so well placed . . .

"Oh, God," she gasped, gripping his forearm. She blurted out something in Spanish. *Right there, don't move, don't stop.*

When she started to shudder, he covered her mouth with his, swallowing her cries of pleasure.

April came back down to earth in slow increments, realizing that her dress was bunched around her waist, exposing everything above and below. Noah removed his hand slowly, his fingers slick. His eyes were half lidded, hungry with arousal.

Lifting his fingertips to his mouth, he tasted her.

Shocked by his behavior and appalled by her own, she scrambled into a sitting position, tugging her dress into place. Her heart was throbbing dully, her brain sluggish. "You—I—that was a bad idea."

He leaned back against the couch and closed his eyes, seeming pleased if unsatisfied. His erection was clearly visible, straining at the fly of his shorts. He pressed the heel of his palm against it, as if encouraging it to go down. "Maybe."

She raked a hand through her hair, darting a glance toward Jenny's door. "That was depraved."

He chuckled weakly. "Not really."

"You should go now."

His brow arched. "Can I see you again?"

Her lips parted in surprise. "Yes."

"Then I'll call you tomorrow," he said, kissing her once more before he left.

14

🔥 Eric showed up to work on Sunday afternoon, not sure what to expect. As far as he
knew, Jack was still in jail. Jack's dad, the owner, was
there with bags under his eyes.

No one talked about Cristina.

Although Eric had known her most of his life, and
he grieved for the loss, he hadn't gone to the Lopez
house to pay his respects. He wasn't sure he'd be welcome there, and he didn't want to intrude on the family
at such a difficult time.

He was waiting for Junior to come to him.

By talking to the gang-unit officers, Eric had broken
a major neighborhood code. The streets had ears and
eyes. People knew he'd gone down to the station of his
own free will. Cooperating with the police wasn't cool.

There was only one honorable way to leave the 'hood
in a squad car—handcuffed.

If the gang thought he was turning his back on them,
he was in serious trouble. Members had been killed for
similar transgressions.

Eric hoped his life wasn't in danger. His brother was

the liaison between the Locos and the Mexican Mafia. Raul's involvement with the prison gang had cast a dark shadow over Eric's life, but right now it afforded him a modicum of protection.

Of course, Junior was a loose cannon. Eric had been friends with him long enough to know he did whatever he felt like doing and to hell with the consequences. Junior might blame Eric for Cristina's death.

He anticipated a beating, at the very least.

Instead of dwelling on those fears, he continued to stock shelves in an orderly fashion, his thoughts drifting to Meghan. He'd dreamed about her the night before. Strange, sexual dreams. In the first, he'd been the one holding her down under the pier, taking what he wanted from her. In the second, he'd been watching Junior do it.

Both scenarios turned his stomach, but his dick was less particular. When it refused to stop throbbing, he gripped himself firmly and closed his eyes, picturing Meghan's pretty mouth and soft tits. For a few seconds afterward, he was ashamed of the fantasy.

Then he fell asleep.

When his shift ended, he was reluctant to head home. He'd rather go see Meghan or visit Jenny and April. But he had some deliveries to make, and his grandmother was waiting. With a sigh, he pedaled his bike toward the grim streets of Castle Park, whizzing past rusted cars and run-down apartments, into the belly of the beast.

He wasn't surprised to see Junior's charcoal-colored Malibu idling under the streetlight in front of his grandma's house.

Eric rolled up to the driver's side, feeling a hard jolt of apprehension. This wasn't a friendly visit. Junior's eyes were guarded, and he didn't offer his usual handshake. He had a brown quart bottle of beer in his lap.

"*Qué hubo?*" Eric murmured, moistening his lips.

"Get ready to come out."

Eric didn't consider saying no. At this point, he had no options. This was the hand he'd been dealt, the life he'd made for himself. If he'd wanted out, he should have graduated high school, applied for a scholarship, or joined the army.

He'd chosen *this*.

Eric went inside the house, putting away his bike and grabbing a brown hooded sweatshirt. His grandma was dozing on the couch. She said she wasn't hungry, but he made her a quick meal anyway.

"*No sales esta noche,*" she said, clutching his sleeve. "*Por favor.*"

Eric disregarded the request. No one had been able to tell him what to do since he'd been ten years old. Even though this was her house, Eric paid all of the expenses, and he'd earned the right to come and go as he pleased.

"Don't worry," he said, gently removing her hand. "I'll be back."

"*No sales.*" Don't go.

"*Salgo.*" I'm going.

She shook her birdlike fist at him. "*Que vete al diablo, ya!*"

"I'm already there," he muttered, stepping out into the thick night. Junior looked a bit like the devil, with his dark eyes and gleaming head. Eric walked around to the passenger side, which was already occupied by a guy they called Conejo, or Rabbit.

Conejo was barely out of high school, skinny as hell, and crazy as fuck. He couldn't sit still to save his life. Right now, however, he was staying put. Although Eric's status dictated that Conejo move to the backseat, he didn't budge. His challenging attitude solidified Eric's suspicions: Junior had it in for him.

Eric could handle a beating. But if they thought he was going to lie down and take it like a bitch, they were wrong.

"Get in the back," he said to Conejo, showing him his fist. His knuckles were scabbed over, healing well, and his adrenaline was pumping. Although he didn't want to brawl in front of his house, he would if he had to.

Conejo glanced at Junior, who nodded his permission. Beady eyes flashing, he scurried to the backseat.

They drove to an overlook near Telegraph Canyon, where Junior parked among a row of cypress trees. The branches jutted toward the night sky like the edges of a serrated blade, sharp and jagged and precise. Below them, the city lights sparkled.

It was a common hangout to drink or just kick back and listen to music, but the mood tonight wasn't jovial. Junior's CD player was thumping a hard and heavy baseline, Columbian gangster rap.

Eric could feel Junior's cold gaze assessing him. He wondered if his best friend had brought him here to kill him.

"The cops told me you texted Cristina on Friday night."

He let out a slow breath. Talking was better than dying. "Yeah."

"You were with her?"

"I went to a bonfire. She was there."

"You went to meet her?"

"No."

Junior took a swig from his bottle. "Don't fucking lie to me, *cabrón*. You were acting all secretive. I know you were trying to get with her."

Eric couldn't tell Junior that Cristina hadn't wanted her big brother ruining her fun at the party. So he told him about Meghan. "I wasn't trying to get with your sister. I was trying to get with her friend."

"Then why did you keep it from me?"

"Come on, *güey*. You know how it is. It's hard enough to talk to a girl without your friends hanging around."

Junior drank some more, wiping his mouth with the back of his hand. He'd never appreciated the concept of privacy. Eric knew from experience that Junior would fuck whoever, wherever, whenever. He seemed to take a perverse pleasure in performing in front of others. Or perhaps he got off on exhibiting whichever female he was with.

Eric suspected that an incident from their youth was the reason for Junior's proclivities. The experience had affected Eric, as well. When he saw Jack on top of Meghan, the memory had resurfaced, infuriating him further.

He'd watched men mistreat women his entire life. He'd stood by, helpless, while his father beat his mother. He'd tried to stop Raul from hitting April.

But the worst act he'd ever witnessed, by far, was one Junior had participated in. Eric considered him a victim *and* a perpetrator. They were ten and fourteen, respectively, and the attack had made an indelible impression on them both.

They never discussed it.

"Did you see any *chavalas* at the party?" Junior asked.

"No. There were some guys at the taco stand later, though."

"Describe them."

He did.

"*Pinche chavalas* killed my sister," Junior said, his voice catching.

Eric froze, remembering the questions he'd been asked at the police station. "Why do you think that?"

"The cops said she had a gag in her mouth. A black bandanna."

Disturbed by the news, Eric told Junior everything he remembered about Friday night, omitting Cristina's flirtatious behavior.

"You think your boss did it? I'll fucking rape *his* ass."

Eric hesitated. He didn't believe Junior meant that literally, but he knew his friend was out for blood. "No, man. I don't think he did it. I beat him up pretty bad. He could hardly walk when I was done."

"That's why you talked to the police?"

"Well, yeah. Because I wanted to help Cristina, too."

"Fucking cops," Junior muttered, throwing his empty bottle out the window. It bounced off a tree stump, remaining intact. "Fucking Eastside!"

Revving the engine, he turned the car around, sending a spray of gravel down the hillside. He almost lost control on the first turn. Eric braced himself for the inevitable accident, but Junior managed to stay on the road.

He drove downtown, navigating the city streets with the same reckless imprecision. He was drunk and upset, and he'd probably been up all night. His foot was too heavy on the gas, his hands too light on the wheel. He turned the music up too loud.

Conejo, that stupid ass, howled an encouragement, drumming his hands on the back of Eric's headrest.

Finally—*finally*—they slowed to a stop in a quiet neighborhood. Meghan didn't live far from here, Eric realized, reading the street signs. Now that he'd told Junior the truth about Friday night, maybe his friend would let him get out and walk.

But Junior obviously had other plans. He reached under his seat, taking out a 9mm semiautomatic pistol.

"Oh, fuck," Eric breathed, pressing his shoulder blades against the passenger door. Trying to distance himself from the situation.

"This is where the Eastside leader lives. Oscar Reyes. He's one of the *chavalas* you saw that night. I went to school with him."

Eric glanced toward a dark house. "No."

"Yeah."

Conejo started bouncing up and down in the back. "Let's do him."

"No," Eric repeated. Hands trembling, he reached out, touching Junior's shoulder. "*Dos Emes* will flip out, man. We can't do this without permission."

Dos Emes was another name for the Mexican Mafia, the prison gang CVL paid dues to. The Locos were a big deal in Chula Vista, but they were a small group in the grand scheme of things. Impromptu drive-by shootings were absolutely not allowed.

"Fuck *Dos Emes*," Junior said, shrugging him off.

Swallowing his fear, Eric looked toward the front of the house. It had been recently painted. There was a shiny black El Camino in the driveway. "What about his family? You could hit anyone in there!"

Junior disengaged the safety. "I don't give a fuck about his family. Do you think he gave a fuck about my family when he was raping my baby sister? When he was choking the life out of her? Motherfucker!"

Again, Eric was assaulted by memories from ten years ago. Images swirled through his head, making him nauseous. The girl, begging for help, her hands tied with a bandanna. The masked man handing Raul money, paying for his turn.

"What if it wasn't him?" Eric said, grabbing Junior by the front of the shirt. "What if it was . . . *el hombre mascado*?"

They'd never mentioned him. Neither of them knew his real name. But, even drunk on booze and sorrow and rage, Junior understood exactly whom Eric was talking about. His eyes filled with tears and he turned the gun on Eric. "Don't talk about that," he whispered, his voice shaking. "*Never* talk about that!"

Eric released Junior's shirt and shrank back slowly. It wasn't the first time a gun had been pointed at his head. It wasn't the first time someone he *loved* had put a gun to his head. Raul had done this once.

It was intensely terrifying. Soul-wrecking.

Despair swelled over him, and he could only close his eyes, waiting for the blast. He was aware of blood rushing in his ears, his heartbeat thudding against his chest.

When Junior pulled the trigger, Eric flinched.

The report was deafening, a series of staccato blasts. Glass popped and shattered, raining down on the street. As they left the scene in a squeal of tires, Eric opened his eyes. He was still alive. Junior had shot up Oscar's tricked-out El Camino.

Not the house. Not Eric.

He put a hand over his heart, amazed to feel it beating.

His relief didn't last long. Junior swerved all over the road, narrowly missing a parked car on the passenger side. A second later, the unmistakable peal of a police siren pierced the night air. They were being pursued.

"Fuck!" Junior righted the wheel, glancing in his rearview mirror.

Eric braced his hand on the dash and looked back. The police car must have been driving down one of the cross streets. Or, even more likely, it had been parked near Oscar's house, doing surveillance.

Maybe the cops had anticipated this kind of retaliation.

Eric's stomach dropped. They were all going to jail. It didn't matter that Junior had been the only one who pulled the trigger. This was a drive-by shooting, and the city had a zero-tolerance policy on gang violence.

Junior leaned back in his seat and stepped on the gas, punching it down the deserted street. He squealed around the corner and kept going, accelerating to a dizzying degree. If they didn't crash, they were going to kill someone. The black-on-black squad car followed at a safe distance, sirens blaring.

"Pull over," Eric said. "Let's take our chances on foot."

"Fuck no," Junior replied, downshifting. His jaw was set with determination, the 9mm lying ready in his lap. Eric knew then that Junior wasn't going to surrender. If they didn't get away in the vehicle—and they surely wouldn't—Junior would open fire.

Powerless to stop him, Eric could only cling to his seat, tensed for the impact, watching the blur of trees and parked cars go by.

Suddenly a pair of headlights swam before them. Junior jerked the wheel to the right, jumping the curb, and that was it. There was a feeling of weightlessness as the car caught air. Then it came down in a sickening crunch, flipping sideways.

Eric couldn't count the number of times the car rolled over. His seat belt caught and held, blazing a painful strip across his chest. Something slammed down on the top of his head. Vaguely, he realized it was the roof.

When the car shuddered to a stop, he was disoriented. A wet trickle dripped down his neck. The engine was still roaring, wheels spinning uselessly against the thick underbrush. They were stuck in a ravine, surrounded by eucalyptus trees. Junior was slumped against the driver-side door, blood on his face.

With a groan, Eric released his seat belt and reached out, turning off the gas. Junior's head lolled forward. He appeared unconscious rather than dead.

A glance at the backseat revealed that Conejo was also hurt but alive. He moaned, insensible. Eric squinted out the window, seeing flashing red lights through the trees. The road they'd driven off was only a couple of hundred feet away. In moments the police would descend upon them.

He fumbled with his door handle, trying to get out. It wouldn't budge.

The back window had shattered, creating an alternate exit. Eric crawled past Conejo, who was crumpled in the corner. Dragging himself over the glass-covered backseat, using his elbows, he scrambled out, sliding across the trunk. As soon as his feet hit the ground, his knees buckled, threatening to give way.

He took a deep breath, praying for strength. After a few seconds the vertigo passed. His head was throbbing, his neck wet. Brushing the pebbled safety glass from his clothes, he fled, forcing his way through the thick brush, hopping tree trunks.

Soon he was stumbling onto a dark sidewalk.

Instead of running, he flipped up the hood of his sweatshirt and strolled at a leisurely pace, his heart thumping against his ribs. He had no idea where he was, so he concentrated on putting one foot in front of the other, distancing himself from the scene.

Now he was a block away. Then another. And another.

Finally, when he felt sure that stopping wouldn't result in his immediate arrest, he collapsed on a bus bench on a deserted street. Although the cut on his scalp still hurt, it was no longer bleeding. A deeper laceration on his calf probably needed stitches, but he didn't dare go to the emergency room.

Fighting back tears of pain and exhaustion, he leaned against the bench and closed his eyes. He couldn't believe he was alive. Alive, and relatively unharmed, and *free*. He'd walked away from the accident.

He wasn't in jail.

It occurred to him that he didn't want to live this way. He didn't want to *die* this way. He was lucky to have escaped and grateful for this second chance. For the first time ever, he felt as if his life was worth something.

He took the crucifix out from beneath his T-shirt. "*Gracias a Dios,*" he whispered, touching it to his lips. Tears streaming down his face, he looked up at the night sky, seeing an endless expanse of stars.

15

On Monday afternoon, Noah reported for work.

He'd tried to spend some time with Meghan this morning, but she'd insisted that she wanted to be alone. She didn't need him "breathing down her neck," as she put it. She been holed up in her room all weekend.

When he came home from April's yesterday afternoon, in need of another cold shower, he'd looked in on her. She pretended to be asleep.

The counselor had told him to expect extreme behavior. Sluggish fatigue or hyperawareness. Overeating or rejecting food. A victim might be needy one day, standoffish the next. She could speak of the incident constantly or refuse to say a word.

Noah wanted to help Meghan, but she was shutting him out. Maybe because he was a man. For the hundredth time he considered calling their mother. Was he making a mistake by keeping her secret?

Rolling the tension from his shoulders, he walked through the station, heading toward his cubicle. Patrick was already there, a surly expression on his face. "Sarge wants to talk to us."

"What about?"

Patrick shrugged.

Noah had a pretty good idea. He'd heard about the car chase last night. He and Patrick had been on the other side of town, so they'd missed the action. Apparently, Junior Lopez and another gang member, Carl "Conejo" Arroyo, had fled the scene of a drive-by. Arroyo broke his collarbone in the resulting crash, and Lopez suffered a moderate concussion. They were awaiting charges.

Oscar Reyes, the intended target, hadn't been home. His girlfriend and their two-year-old daughter were sleeping inside. One of the bullets had ricocheted, hitting the side of the house, but they'd been spared.

Noah wondered how the Lopez family was dealing with Junior's arrest. Daughter dead, son headed to jail. Unfortunately, these kinds of trigger incidents were all too common. Traumatized people led traumatic lives.

He followed Patrick into Sergeant Briggs's office. Detective Santiago had pulled up a chair next to Briggs, presenting a united front. Behind his black-framed glasses, Santiago's eyes were flat. Briggs's expression also revealed nothing.

Each man had a distinct presence; together, they were formidable.

"Have a seat," Briggs said, indicating the two unoccupied chairs across from his desk. He was a former military man with rigid posture and a streamlined physique. His job took him into the realm of city politics and away from the nitty-gritty of police work, so they didn't see him very often.

Patrick slumped in one chair, his body language defensive, and Noah grabbed the other. This wasn't going to be a pleasant chat.

"I assume you know about the 318 last night."

"Yes," Noah said, and Patrick nodded.

"Junior Lopez demanded a lawyer as soon as he regained consciousness, but he won't escape charges. Officers witnessed him opening fire. Luckily, they were patrolling the area." He looked back and forth between them. "Is there any reason Lopez would think the Eastside leader was responsible for his sister's murder?"

Noah glanced at Patrick, who maintained his stony silence.

"Officer Cruz told me you asked her to keep an eye on the situation, Officer Young."

Now Patrick was looking at Noah. Feeling his ears heat, he said, "Yes, sir. I thought Lopez might try to retaliate."

"Why?"

He massaged the back of his neck. "When we were interviewing him, some information about the case . . . slipped."

Santiago leaned forward. "What information?"

"He knew about the bandanna, sir."

"Officer Young, I told you specifically not to mention that detail. Do you remember my exact words?"

"Yes, sir."

The lead detective glanced at Patrick. "Did your partner convey that message to you, Officer Shanley?"

"What does it matter?" Patrick shot back, his expression hostile. "The only progress in the investigation has been made by our unit. We've delivered two viable suspects, and homicide hasn't done shit. This is the thanks we get for busting our asses on your case?"

"Officer Shanley, did you tell Junior Lopez about the physical evidence?"

"Yes," he said, lifting his chin. Daring Santiago to make something of it.

Santiago turned to Noah, a muscle in his jaw twitching. "Officer Young, do you think your partner leaked the information on purpose?"

Noah struggled for an honest answer. He didn't want to believe Patrick was capable of gross negligence or outright malice, but he suspected him of making a deliberate attempt to jeopardize the investigation. Patrick had a troubled history with Santiago, and his animosity had spiraled out of control.

"Fuck you," Patrick said, lurching to his feet. His chair toppled over. Instead of righting it, he glared at Noah. "And fuck *you*."

Noah avoided his gaze, hating the position he'd been put in. What could he say after stabbing his partner in the back?

Sergeant Briggs stepped in. "Officer Shanley, you're on administrative leave, starting now. Please turn in your weaponry and follow proper sign-out procedures. I'll let you know the duration when I make my decision. Until then, you're dismissed."

Patrick kicked his chair aside on his way out. It hit the far wall, knocking one of Briggs's plaques to the ground.

They all stared at it for a few seconds.

Briggs turned his attention back to Noah, folding his hands on top of the desk. "Officer Young, when an interviewee is given confidential information by a member of your unit, you need to tell the lead investigator immediately. I know Shanley is your superior, but I hold you responsible for failing to notify Detective Santiago of the slip."

Noah had never been reprimanded by Sergeant Briggs or any other high-ranking official. Receiving the criticism in front of Detective Santiago, a man he'd hoped to impress, was twice as humiliating. Worse, he knew he deserved the set-down. "Yes, sir," he said, clearing his throat. "I'm sorry, sir."

Briggs grunted in response. "I'll let it slide this time, because of the . . . family incident you were dealing with. How is your sister doing?"

"She says she's fine, sir."

"Good." Visibly uncomfortable, Briggs glanced at Santiago. "You'll ride solo while Shanley is on leave, and continue to assist in the homicide investigation as needed."

Santiago picked up where Briggs left off, riffling through a stack of papers on the top of the desk. "Witnesses place Oscar Reyes at the Taco Tico restaurant early Saturday morning. He'd been at a house party the entire night. According to our contacts, most of the Eastside crew attended, and there were no altercations with CVL. We don't have a reason to suspect him of either murder."

Noah was disappointed but not surprised by the news. Raping and killing of women by hard-core prison gangs wasn't unheard of, but it just didn't match the local boys' m.o. Besides, neither victim had been a documented member.

Maybe the bandanna was planted as a diversionary tactic.

"My unit has interviewed Jack Bishop's friends and acquaintances from the bonfire," Santiago continued. "Several remember seeing the victim walk away from the crowd by herself. No one stands out as a likely candidate, but we're looking into it."

"Is there anything you want me to do?"

"Yes," Briggs said. "Watch out for a payback effort on CVL by Eastside. Monitor activity at the Lopez household—maybe the killer is in their circle of friends. And ask around about the car chase. We know there was a third passenger."

"Did Lopez say who?"

"Lopez won't say anything. Carl Arroyo claims he was the only rider, but officers at the scene spotted three men in the car."

Noah nodded his understanding. "I'll get right on it."

As soon as he was excused, however, he went looking for Patrick. Noah found him in the parking lot, about to climb into his white Ford Ranger. His face was red, suffused with anger.

"I'm sorry," Noah said, raking a hand through his hair. "I didn't know what to say."

Patrick nodded. "You did what you had to."

Noah knew Patrick felt betrayed by his actions. A partner was supposed to have your back, no matter what. But Patrick had gone too far this time. Noah couldn't believe he would screw up just to annoy Santiago and then expect Noah to cover for him. Patrick's actions had been dangerous, irrational, and *wrong*.

Noah wasn't a patsy, or a liar. He had his entire career ahead of him, and Patrick was near retirement. There was no way he'd sacrifice his shot at working homicide to spare his partner's feelings.

Patrick gave him a weighted stare. His gray-blue eyes looked like dirty ice, and sweat dotted his ruddy forehead. "How was your date?"

The question was so accusatory, Noah flinched. "None of your business."

Patrick snorted his derision. "That's what I thought," he said, unlocking his truck. "You're fucking some crew member's baby mama, but I'm the one who gets sent home for inappropriate conduct."

Although it was at least ninety degrees on the blacktop where they were standing, Noah felt a chill run down his spine. "What do you mean?"

"Your sexy little girlfriend has some serious gang connections. She didn't tell you? Maybe her mouth was too busy."

Noah stifled the urge to grab Patrick by the front of the shirt and busy *his* mouth—by knocking a few teeth loose. "Who?"

"Raul Hernandez."

The name hit him like a ton of bricks. April had told him Jenny's father was in jail, but she'd failed to mention any specific details about her ex. Noah couldn't believe she was capable of getting involved with a man like Hernandez. The guy was scum.

Noah had been on the gang unit for only two years,

so he'd never met "Ruthless" Hernandez in person, but he'd heard about him. The former leader of CVL was currently in a maximum-security penitentiary, doing hard time for armed robbery. He wasn't just a thief and drug dealer anymore, either.

Now he was a member of the Mexican Mafia.

"No," he said, refusing to acknowledge the truth. April couldn't have been mixed up with a guy like that. And she wouldn't have kept it a secret.

Would she?

Patrick made a sympathetic face. "I hope you didn't buy that sweet and innocent act. What did I tell you about women?"

"You're so fucking bitter since your wife left you," Noah said in a low voice. "Not all women are lying whores."

Hurt flared in Patrick's eyes. They'd discussed his home situation only once, when Patrick had been too drunk to self-edit. Noah's partner had always put his job ahead of his family, and now he was paying the price. He'd be spending his mandatory vacation in an empty house. "Not all women," he agreed. "Some men are, too."

"I didn't lie."

"You sold me out."

"Did you expect me to take the fall for you? My career is just starting, and yours is—"

"Over?"

Noah looked away, uncomfortable.

"I'd rather be bitter—and alive—than green and dead. We'll see how fucking honest you are after twenty years on the force. If you make it that long." Mouth twisting, he got into his truck and slammed the door.

Noah didn't stand around in the parking lot after Patrick left. He went back to his cubicle and looked up Raul Hernandez. His rap sheet wasn't that impressive. The charges ranged from drug possession to domestic violence—the typical top two.

Hernandez's mug shot looked familiar. He resembled his brother, Eric, but with jailhouse muscles and a harder edge.

Raul's gang-affiliation profile included pictures of his tattoos. A large bold *13* covered the side of his neck. The Mexican Mafia had adopted the tag, *M* being the thirteenth letter of the alphabet. He also had *R-U-T-H* spelled across the knuckles of his right hand and *L-E-S-S* written across his left.

Noah's gut clenched at the thought of him putting those hands on April. Had he abused her? Maybe this was why she never dated and was so "reserved" with men.

The rest of Hernandez's tattoos were basic gangster fare, an ironic mix of religious symbols, violent images, and sexy ladies. On the side of his rib cage, there was a tribute to Jenny. Her name was written in cursive, over a tiny heart.

Noah closed the screen, covering his eyes with one hand. His own heart was aching, beating hard in his chest.

This was fucked up on so many levels. He was a gang-unit officer, dating Raul Hernandez's ex, and he didn't even know it. If word got out in the department, he'd be a laughingstock. He might even face administrative action.

Their relationship was a major conflict of interest.

Even if dating her wasn't inappropriate, it was still unwise. Did he want to get hung up on someone with this much . . . baggage? April had mentioned some trouble with her mother, and she'd just had a break-in. Hernandez would get out of prison in a few years, and he might ask for visitation rights.

Noah had never dealt well with girlfriend drama. He tended to choose fun, easygoing women who didn't cause him any aggravation. There hadn't been anyone who'd made a lasting impression on him, either, which was probably why he'd found it so easy to move on. With April, everything was different. More challenging, more complicated.

He was so *drawn* to her.

Could he really walk away?

"Fuck," he muttered, dragging a hand down his face.

Putting April out of his mind, he began to search through the digital files on his computer, uploading the footage of Junior Lopez's wreck. The pursuing squad car had recorded the accident from a distance, but it was impossible to identify the occupants.

The passenger in the front seat, however, had a bandanna on his wrist.

Although the sight was common, Noah straightened in his chair. He pulled up the older footage of Tony Castillo crossing the border, studying the unidentified occupant. The man was too lean to be Junior Lopez, and his hair was short rather than shaved.

Noah had a pretty good idea who Castillo's trafficking partner was. He was also a likely candidate for having fled the scene of the accident last night. And he was the last person Noah wanted to arrest.

Eric Hernandez.

Meghan checked all of the locks on the windows and doors—twice.

She'd never felt unsafe in Noah's house before. The neighborhood was quiet, several blocks from the closest business district. Car break-ins happened often, but more serious crimes were rare. A few nights ago she'd pedaled her bike down the darkened streets, enjoying the city's mystique.

Tonight she was cowering inside, peeping through the blinds for intruders.

Logically, she knew her fears were unfounded. Jack's parents hadn't posted bail, so he was still incarcerated. No one was creeping up the sidewalk, crouching behind the bushes, or plotting a sneak attack.

"Stupid," she muttered, moving away from the front window.

Noah had encouraged her to get out and exercise. She'd had breakfast with him this morning, but they hadn't spoken much. He was disappointed in her, she knew. She'd promised not to be any trouble.

Maybe she should have gone back to work. Noah didn't want her to, because of what happened to Cristina. She also wasn't sure how Jack's dad, the owner, would react. Although she didn't necessarily want to deal with conflicts right now, being cooped up was driving her crazy. And she longed to see Eric.

Noah had some exercise equipment in the garage, so she put on her workout clothes and went to investigate. The weight-lifting bench didn't interest her. Bypassing it, she found some ten-pound barbells and a jump rope.

Her arms were burning after less than five minutes with the barbells. She frowned, flexing her scrawny biceps. Maybe she should toughen up, in case some asshole like Jack decided to target her as a victim again.

The jump rope was more her style. After fifteen minutes, she was sweating. She realized that she felt better. Not good, but better. For the past two days she'd been wandering around like a zombie, sleeping all the time, groggy when awake. Now her heart was pumping again, making her feel strong. Alive.

Noah's punching bag beckoned. She'd watched him hit it before, laughing at the sounds he made. Now she studied the piece of equipment more seriously, not sure how to use it. Her hand made a knobby fist. She punched once, in an awkward jab.

Not satisfying.

The bag looked soft and cushiony when Noah hit it. For her, it felt impenetrable. The stuffing didn't have any give.

Kicking it, she almost landed on her butt.

Narrowing her eyes, as if the punching bag were her mortal enemy, she continued to attack, hitting it repeatedly, fists flying. A few minutes later she sagged against the bag and rested her cheek on the firm surface, panting.

When she realized someone was knocking on the door, she froze.

The garage was right beside the front walk, but it had no windows. Trapped, she considered her options. Escaping to the backyard seemed appropriate. Or she could run inside and call Noah.

"Meghan?"

The voice was masculine, hesitant. Nonthreatening.

"It's me, Eric."

Relieved, she went to answer the door. He was standing there on the front step, wearing a dark-gray T-shirt and faded jeans, his forehead wrinkled with concern.

She was so happy to see him, tears sprang to her eyes. "Hi," she said, breathless.

The corner of his mouth tipped up. "Hi."

She'd been worried that he wouldn't want to talk to her anymore. If she hadn't acted like such an idiot on Friday night, Cristina might still be alive. Eric couldn't have enjoyed hearing the news or suffering through the subsequent police interrogation.

He didn't seem angry, however. His gaze swept down her sports top and jogging pants before returning to her face.

"I was just . . . exercising," she said lamely.

"I can see that."

She tucked a strand of hair behind her ear. "Do you want to come in?"

"Okay."

Once he was inside, she wasn't sure what to say or where to go. Inviting him up to her bedroom seemed silly. Giving him a tour of the downstairs would take about thirty seconds. Maybe she should offer him a drink or a place to sit.

"How are you?" he asked.

"I'm fine." She crossed her arms in front of her chest, suddenly aware of how sweaty and unkempt she was. "My brother has a punching bag in the garage, and I was trying to learn how to, um, hit."

He nodded, assessing her words. "You want to be able to protect yourself?"

She didn't have a plan, other than working out some aggressions. But what he said sounded reasonable. "Yes. I guess I do."

"I can give you some pointers."

"Really?"

"Sure."

He followed her into the garage, whistling at Noah's equipment. It was nothing new or expensive, but Eric looked impressed. "What does he bench?"

"I have no idea."

"Is he home?"

"No."

"Good."

Meghan smiled, watching him take a few jabs at the punching bag. His strikes made more of an impact than hers. "Who taught you how to fight?"

"My brother."

"Are you close?"

"We used to be."

"Do you still see him?"

"Yeah."

If she remembered correctly, he'd said his brother was in prison. She was curious about how Eric visited him, but he seemed uncomfortable with the subject, so she didn't pursue it. "Will you show me how you hit Jack?"

He gave her slender arms a dubious glance. "I could, but it wouldn't do you much good. You don't have the upper-body strength to trade punches with a man."

"What if I bulked up?"

He didn't laugh at her question. Instead, he walked over to stand next to her, extending his left arm. Motioning for her to do the same, he compared the two. "I'm not that tall, but my reach is much longer than yours. That means you have to come closer to hit me and move farther away to get out of my range. You also have a small frame. No matter how much muscle you put on, you'll be at a major disadvantage with most men."

She studied his arm, admiring his excellent muscle tone and dark complexion. Her skin looked very pale next to his. When he made a fist, she followed suit, noting the discrepancy in size. His knuckles took up a lot more space than hers did. They were also covered with marks, fresh scabs and old scars.

"The best thing for you to do is try to get away."

"How?"

"Any way you can. Hit the eyes, nose, throat, knees. Kick, bite, scream. Pick up a rock. Use your elbows."

Assaulted by memories of the attack, Meghan dropped her fist. She remembered feeling utterly powerless, clutching the sand. She should have thrown it in Jack's eyes. Or elbowed him in the mouth. And kneed him in the groin.

With grim determination, she turned her back to Eric, practicing an elbow jab.

"Good," he said. "You can do that if someone grabs you from behind."

"Jack . . . let me roll over."

"It was easier for him that way. Restricted your movement."

She nodded, recognizing the truth when he spoke it. "How do you know?"

"From experience."

Over the next hour, Eric showed her a few dirty fighting techniques and some simple self-defense methods. Then he went ahead and taught her the proper way to throw a punch. Although he recommended that she run away rather than hold her ground, he said it was good for strength training.

When he noticed her slowing down, he cut the lesson short. "Why don't you rest now and practice your moves again tomorrow?"

"Okay," she said, stretching her arms. Her muscles burned pleasantly and her head buzzed with fatigue. "Let's get a drink."

He followed her into the kitchen, grabbing a chair at the table while she raided the fridge. "Noah has beer."

"And the ability to arrest us for underage drinking."

"How old are you?"

"Twenty."

Smiling, she took out two bottles of water. As she handed him one, she noticed an inch-long gash on the top of his head. "What happened to you?"

He touched the spot absently, smoothing a hand over it. "Nothing."

She set aside her water and put her fingertips on his jaw, tilting his head toward the light. The wound was recent but not serious. "Did you get knocked out?"

"No."

"You're lucky."

When his eyes drifted south, she realized that she was practically cradling his head against her breasts. Although he wasn't complaining, she let him go and sat down, taking a few gulps of water to cool her embarrassment. They fell silent for a moment.

"I'm sorry," she said.

"For what?"

"Cristina."

His gaze held hers. "It wasn't your fault."

"Yes, it was. I wore that skimpy top to get your attention."

"It worked."

She warmed at the implication but tried not to let it distract her. "When I saw Cristina hanging all over you, I got jealous. That's why I left with Jack. If I hadn't been so drunk and desperate and stupid, Cristina would still be alive."

"You don't know that."

"She went looking for us, Eric."

"Maybe," he acknowledged. "But, knowing Cristina, she could just as easily have gone looking for one of those surfers or ditched the party in a huff."

"Are you saying that to make me feel better?"

"No."

"She wanted you."

"I didn't want her."

She looked across the table at him, wishing she knew

what he was thinking. Even if he'd been attracted to her before the bonfire, he wouldn't act on it now. Meghan's hopeless infatuation with Eric had caused a terrible chain reaction of events. Jack's attack, Cristina's murder. She should have been drowning in guilt and shame. Instead, she was staring at Eric's hands, wishing he would touch her.

"I better go," he said.

"Why?"

He rose from the table. "Just because."

She walked him to the door, her heart sinking with every step. She felt raw and broken, like damaged goods. "Do I disgust you?"

He stopped and stared at her, wide-eyed. For a moment he seemed shocked into silence. Then he said, "You could never disgust me. I disgust myself."

She moistened her lips, nervous. "What do you mean?"

He dragged his gaze from her mouth, clenching his hands into fists at his sides. "Do you know what I was thinking about, the entire time in the garage? Fucking you."

A thrill raced through her. She studied the dark flush over his cheekbones, marveling at his taut expression. "Really?"

His eyes met hers, stark with need. "On the floor, against the punching bag, over the weight bench."

"Oh," she breathed, trying to picture it. "I had no idea—"

"Well, get a clue. You know what I am."

"A good person?"

He shook his head, impatient. "Maybe I'm no better than Jack."

"I don't believe that."

"You shouldn't have let me in."

"I trust you."

"I don't trust *myself.*"

"You just spent an hour teaching me self-defense."

His fist thumped against his chest. "Partly to protect you from me!"

Meghan couldn't stand to see Eric beat himself up like this. He hadn't done anything wrong. She stepped forward, closing the distance between them. "I don't need anyone telling me who to trust or what to believe," she said, touching his face. "I can make those decisions on my own."

His jaw tightened beneath her fingertips. "You don't even know me."

Moving slowly, she lifted her chin until her lips were almost brushing his. "Describe what you wanted to do to me in the weight room. That was . . . interesting."

He held himself rigid, as if struggling to remain aloof. She could feel the tension in his body, smell the heat on his skin. She had the urge to rub against him like a cat. All of her senses were alive, purring with desire.

Mouth hard, he splayed his hand over her bare stomach, pushing her back until her shoulders touched the wall. Once he had her where he wanted her, he just looked at her. Her skin tingled with anticipation, and her sports bra felt too tight.

After what seemed like an eternity, he braced his

other hand against the wall beside her head and lowered his mouth to hers. The first kiss was gentle, tentative. His hand was a hot brand on her belly, and she quivered at his touch. She parted her lips, tasting him.

He kissed her again with an open mouth, using his tongue.

Murmuring her approval, she wrapped her arms around his neck and returned his kiss in hungry bites, nipping at his bottom lip. His hand moved from her waist to her backside, cupping her to him. When his lower body met hers, she gasped in surprise, and he speared his tongue into her mouth possessively. She made an urgent sound and crushed herself against him, wanting his hands on her breasts.

Maybe she was a little too aggressive, because he stumbled sideways, and the wall at her back fell away. They landed on the carpeted stairwell in a clumsy sprawl. When his weight settled on top of her, she experienced a moment of panic.

"Stop," she said, shoving at his chest.

He rolled away from her immediately. "What's wrong?"

The way he responded laid most of her fears to rest. She smiled at him, touching his lips. "You see? You're much better than Jack."

His eyes darkened, and she leaned toward him, replacing her fingertips with her mouth. After a moment's hesitation, he kissed her back, going slower this time, smoothing his hand down her hip. Rather than getting on top of her, he shifted his jeans-clad thigh between her legs, bumping a very sweet spot.

She melted against him, lost.

16

Eric knew he should stop.

But her mouth tasted so good, and her body was . . . *por Dios*. Every time he kissed her, her skin felt a little hotter. He couldn't resist the temptation to press his thigh higher, rocking her against him.

He didn't *have* to stop. He was pretty sure she would let him continue. If he took her to her bedroom, he could make them both happy.

He wanted it. She wanted it.

But when her hands drifted down to his waistband, tugging on his belt, he had an attack of conscience. "No," he said, tearing his mouth from hers.

Her lips were swollen from his kisses, her eyes half lidded. "Why not?"

With all of his blood rushing south, he couldn't think of a good reason. But he knew there was one, so he moved his thigh from between her legs. She moaned a drowsy protest, confused by his reticence. To take the sting away from the rejection, he bent his head to her bare stomach, placing an openmouthed kiss on her flat belly.

She trembled beneath his lips.

He stared at the wet mark his mouth had made, tortured by the impulse to drag down the front of her pants and keep going. He wasn't sure he could do that without losing control or asking her to return the favor. His *palo* throbbed at the thought of her tongue on him.

He groaned, resting his cheek against her stomach. "I can't."

"You don't want to?"

"Please. I'm about to explode."

She stroked the back of his neck, acquiescent, and even that innocent touch drove him up the wall. He couldn't remember being this primed before. His balls were going to ache *como loco* tonight.

Despite his discomfort, he couldn't bring himself to pull away from her. There were so many things he wanted to tell her, about his fucked-up childhood and dead-end future. Deterrents, he realized. An explanation for his reluctance to get involved with her. No matter how badly he wanted her as his girl, it wasn't going to happen right now.

The close call with Junior had changed his life. He'd tossed and turned most of the night, wondering what to do next. He still didn't know. Until he figured out how to disentangle himself from the mess he was in, he had no business hooking up with Meghan. His situation was too precarious.

He couldn't drag her down with him.

When he lifted his head to speak, he heard someone open the front door. Sensing trouble, he braced his arms around her, looking over his shoulder.

The "intruder" was her brother, in uniform.

"I'm okay," she said hurriedly.

Eric appreciated the clarification; Officer Young had his right hand on his gun holster. "Get out," he said, narrowing his eyes.

"Yes, sir."

Meghan held him back. "You don't have to leave, Eric."

"The fuck he doesn't!"

"I'm going," Eric said, standing up. At least he no longer had a hard-on. That would have made the situation even more awkward.

Meghan glared at her brother, her lips quivering. "Why are you doing this? I'm not a baby anymore. You're such an asshole!" Tears filling her eyes, she turned and fled, stumbling on the stairs in her haste to get away.

Officer Young watched her go, a muscle in his jaw flexing. Eric remembered how he'd reacted to the news that she'd been assaulted—like any protective older brother. Although Eric respected his intensity, he didn't want to be on the receiving end of it.

"Let's go," he said, motioning for Eric to precede him.

Eric walked out the door and down the sidewalk, growing more uneasy with each step. Now that the sexual haze had lifted, he realized the interruption wasn't accidental. Officer Young had been looking for him.

"You carrying any drugs, weapons, paraphernalia?"

"No," he said, tensing a little as he was patted down. Other than his wallet and keys, he was clean.

"Have a seat."

Eric sat on the curb, his heart sinking.

"Is that your Chevelle?"

Although he told everyone the car was his grandmother's, it was registered to him. "Yeah. It's mine."

"I've seen you on a bike."

"I use that more."

"Easier to do drug deals?"

It was, sometimes. Eric also enjoyed the freedom and anonymity of riding his bike. Because his friends didn't know he had a car, they never asked him to take them anywhere or to transport illegal substances.

He stared up at Officer Young, mute.

"I'm investigating the drive-by shooting that happened last night. You know anything about it?"

"No, sir."

"If I lifted some fingerprints from the passenger door and compared them to the ones you just left in my house, they wouldn't match?"

He shrugged. "I've been in a lot of cars."

"Do you bleed in a lot of cars?"

Eric resisted the urge to smooth a hand over his scalp. He knew the cut on his head was a dead giveaway, but he doubted the police would run DNA tests.

"Junior thought you were fooling around with his sister."

"I wasn't."

"You think he'll cover for you?"

Eric couldn't predict Junior's next move. But even if his friend didn't give him up, Conejo probably would. That mouthy little shit.

"I also have some footage of a guy who looks like you crossing the border with Tony Castillo," he continued. "Drug trafficking is a very serious charge."

Eric put his head in his hands, stifling a groan of dismay. He was so fucked! How could he talk his way out of this?

"Give me one good reason not to arrest you."

"I can get information," he blurted.

"What kind of information?" Officer Young sounded interested.

He moistened his lips, not sure how much to reveal. If he mentioned the recent murders, he'd be taken down to the station immediately. "It's about a crime that happened ten years ago. An unsolved case."

"A murder?"

Eric nodded, half convinced that the cases were related. According to Junior, Cristina had been found with a bandanna in her mouth. The girl from their past had been tied up, and then strangled, with one. It was an odd similarity.

"You saw it happen?"

Eric hesitated. "Not exactly. I need to talk to someone before I can say anything more. Give me a few days."

"You might not have a few days," Officer Young said. "If I can put two and two together, placing you at the scene of the drive-by, so can Eastside. Don't you think they'll come after you?"

Eric stared at his shoes, miserable. He'd already thought of that.

"Have you ever considered getting out?"

He gave Officer Young an impatient look. Of course he'd considered it. Over the past twenty-four hours, he'd done nothing but consider it. "It's not that easy.

People count on me. My grandma, my mom, my brother . . . my niece."

"Your niece?"

"My brother's daughter," he said absently. "Jenny."

For some reason, Officer Young flinched at the name. He stared across the street, pensive. "You can't help anyone from a jail cell."

Eric let out a harsh laugh. "People can do a lot of things from jail cells, but the difference is that I wouldn't be walking away voluntarily. In my *barrio*, getting locked up is more acceptable than abandoning your responsibilities by choice."

"Do you really want to end up like your brother? Shanking homeboys in prison, a puppet for *Dos Emes*?"

His throat closed up, and he could only shake his head.

Officer Young didn't appear sympathetic. "You seem like a smart kid. If I hadn't just found you with my sister, I might feel bad for you. Do you think she owed you something for helping her the other night?"

Eric glanced at the upper-floor window, wondering if Meghan was watching them. He wasn't sorry he'd touched her. But he regretted very much having been caught. "It wasn't like that. I was checking up on her."

"Why?"

"I don't know. I feel protective of her."

"You think you're good for her?"

"No. I'm not good for anyone."

Officer Young rubbed a hand over his face, sighing. "I'll give you two days," he said. "In the meantime, try to keep a low profile. Don't be out on the streets after dark, and don't come here. If I see you in this neighborhood, I'll arrest you on the spot."

"Yes, sir."

"And if you ever fucking touch my sister again, you'll wish Eastside got you before me. *Entiendes?*"

Eric understood perfectly. He was no stranger to harsh threats, and he appreciated Officer Young's no-bullshit attitude. Meghan's brother was okay—for a cop. "*Entiendo,*" he replied, shaking Noah's hand, *cholo*-style. "I will stay out of your *barrio*."

He left in a hurry, knowing he'd dodged another bullet. For now.

There was no way he could continue selling drugs. Without the extra income, his grandmother would have to go back to Mexico, where she had limited access to her diabetes medication. He had no solution for that problem, but April and Jenny could manage without his help, and his mom would be okay.

Maybe he could join one of those work programs and start sending money to his family again once he got settled.

First he had to stay alive, and stay out of jail.

Unfortunately, he also had to talk to Raul.

Noah watched Eric drive away, wishing he was convinced he'd done the right thing. He didn't know who to trust anymore or what to believe.

He'd been bluffing about arresting him, fishing for a promise that Eric wouldn't come sniffing around Meghan again. CVL had a code against talking to the police, so Eric had a pretty good chance of escaping charges. This time.

The bigger threat to Eric by far was a retaliatory strike by Eastside.

He didn't know if Eric was lying about the unsolved murder, either. Police officers made shady deals with criminals all the time, looking the other way in exchange for information, but that wasn't Noah's style.

He felt disconnected from himself, a stranger in his own uniform.

With a heavy heart, he went back inside to check on Meghan. Attending to personal business while on duty was another rarity for him. Soon he'd be taking bribes, eating lunch at the strip club, and napping in his squad car.

The door to her room was closed. He knocked lightly.

"Go away."

He went in.

Meghan was sitting on her bed, pretending to listen to her iPod. Her eyes were swollen and her nose was red.

He pulled a ladder-back chair away from a small desk. It occurred to him that he'd never seen either piece of furniture before. "Where did this stuff come from?"

"I bought it at a garage sale."

The desk was old, its wood surface lightly scarred. She'd placed it facing the room's only window, which overlooked the front yard. He imagined her studying there and felt a sudden pressure behind his eyes. "Meggie—"

"Don't call me that."

He massaged the bridge of his nose, wishing he could tell her how he felt, rather than what he knew. She was the emotional center of the family, the one most likely to share her feelings, initiate a hug, or say I love you. He couldn't bear to see her so withdrawn.

"He's a gang member."

Her brows rose. "So?"

"He was involved in a shooting attempt last night."

She tugged the earpieces of her iPod out. "I don't believe you."

"Did you notice the cut on his head? After a high-speed pursuit, the car he was in flipped three or four times."

"Was he driving?"

"No."

"Was he the shooter?"

Noah hesitated. "I don't think so, but he can still be prosecuted for participating. And his rivals don't care if he pulled the trigger."

She nibbled on her lower lip, concerned for Eric.

"He put you in danger by coming here. I told him I'd arrest him if he touched you again."

Her face fell. "You can't do that."

"Yes, I can. And it's for your own good. You were sexually assaulted, Meg. If you don't think your behavior is a cry for help, you're kidding yourself."

"Oh, my God," she wailed, fisting her hands in her hair. "You are so melodramatic! I wasn't even raped. I'm *fine*."

"Promiscuity is common in victims—"

"I'm *not* promiscuous."

"What do you know about Eric?" he pressed. "Besides the fact that he's a gang member who likes to fight at parties?"

"That's not fair," she said, crossing her arms over her chest. "What do you know about your new girlfriend, the single mom? Let me guess—she's hot."

Noah felt a flush rise up his neck. Meghan had a good point. He didn't know April very well, apparently. Their attraction was based on physical chemistry, and perhaps he'd overlooked some red flags, in a haze of lust.

Patrick was right, too. Noah had always been a sucker for the sweet-and-innocent act.

"Eric's brother, Raul, is in prison," he said quietly. "He's a member of the Mexican Mafia, a hard-core criminal organization. And he's Jenny's father."

Her lips parted in surprise. "He's . . . what?"

"Jenny's father."

"April told you that?"

"No. Patrick did."

"Oh," she said, the layers of it sinking in. "Oh."

"Yeah," Noah said, raking a hand through his hair. This certainly put a damper on his lecture about dating the wrong person.

"Have you talked to her about it?"

"Not yet."

"You think she's playing you?"

He shook his head. Every conversation they'd had seemed so real. He hated the idea that she'd been feigning interest in him, leading him on. "She almost said no the first time I asked her out. If she has an agenda, I don't see how avoiding me fits into it."

"Right," Meghan said, her shoulders relaxing. "You know, some women don't even tell a guy they have kids on a first date."

"Where did you hear that?"

"I read it in *Cosmo*."

That figured.

She gave him a hopeful look. "Did it go well yesterday?"

"It wasn't perfect," he admitted, thinking about April's reluctance to let him pay and their argument at the end of the day. "The things that went wrong went really wrong. But the things that were good . . ."

"Were really good?"

"Phenomenal." The time spent on her couch was a highlight, of course, but even without it, the date had been special.

"Do you want to see her again?"

"Yes," he said, amazed at his knee-jerk reaction. He was still desperate to be with her. God. He was already whipped.

Meghan jumped up from the bed. "Come on. I have something to show you."

Intrigued, he followed her down to the garage, watching while she hit the punching bag. She'd obviously had some boxing lessons. "Who taught you that?"

"Eric."

"Tonight?"

"Yep."

Noah didn't want to revise his opinion about Eric. There was no doubt in his mind that the kid wasn't good enough for his sister. He was a petty criminal, at best.

But—he'd fought for Meghan. And encouraged her to fight for herself.

"When he stopped by, I was out here, trying to learn on my own. He offered to show me some moves."

He'd shown her some moves, all right. On the stairwell.

"Maybe I do feel a little . . . scared. And I know you want me to talk about what happened. But I don't want to talk about it. I want to just go on." She hit the punching bag again. "Being with Eric is one of the ways I'm dealing with it. He makes me feel safe."

Noah pressed his fingertips to his eye sockets, taking a moment to collect himself. "I'm your big brother. *I* want to make you feel safe."

She steadied the bag, leveling with him. "You can't."

17

🌿 April arrived at Club Suave a few minutes early on Tuesday. Since her car's air-conditioning quit, she'd been getting ready at work.

Sailing into the bathroom stall with an oversize bag, she took off her sundress and stepped into her fishnet stockings. She was still tugging them into place when another waitress came in, heels clicking.

Carmen popped her head over the divider. "*Te lo cogiste?*"

April straightened, holding her tank top to her chest. "No," she said in a furious whisper, glaring at her friend. Carmen knew she'd had a date with Noah on Sunday and they hadn't spoken about it yet. "I did not 'fuck' him."

Carmen disappeared behind the stall. "What did you do, visit the library? Play golf?"

"Don't make fun of me."

"Let me give you some advice, *m'ija*. White boys like the same things as our *paisanos*. Women with curves. Blow jobs."

"That's your advice?" she said, wriggling into her skirt. "Blow him?"

"Definitely."

April finished dressing and left the stall, shaking her head. When she leaned over the sink to finish her makeup, Carmen came up beside her. April's hand trembled as she applied mascara.

"You look guilty," her friend accused. "You did *something*."

April hid a smile, dusting her face with powder. Today she didn't need blush.

"Was he good?"

"Stop," she chided, snapping her compact shut. "We had a nice date at the water park. He was great with Jenny. It was fun."

"You took Jenny? *Estás loca?*"

"She fell asleep on the way home, and he kissed me goodbye."

"What kind of kiss?"

She bent forward, painting her lips crimson. "A sexy kiss," she admitted, shivering at the memory.

"Are you going out again?"

"I think so."

Carmen did a bump and grind, offering her interpretation of their next date.

April struggled not to laugh. "Let me give *you* some advice—*m'ija*. Sometimes it's better to leave a little mystery."

"Oh, really?"

"Mmm-hmm." She studied her reflection in the mirror, twirling a lock of hair around her finger. Maybe it wasn't smart to get involved with Noah, but she didn't care. Her cautious side warned that he would hurt her. Another, secret part of her was starved for his touch and yearning for more.

Carmen smirked, skeptical. "We'll see how long you hold out."

The evening passed quickly. For a Tuesday night, it was busy. After a few slow days, business had picked up again. In two weeks, when college classes started, the San Diego bar scene would explode.

Although the recent victim had no ties to the club, most of the waitresses were still jumping at shadows. They gossiped incessantly about the murders, sharing stories of creepy men and dark nights.

Nikki swore that she'd had a Peeping Tom once. Maya said she'd almost gone home with a customer a few weeks ago but had changed her mind because his car smelled like death. Lupita recited a bone-chilling tale from her hometown in Mexico, about a demon that preyed on prostitutes.

The streets of Chula Vista were quieter than usual. Women were urged not to be out alone at night. People went home earlier, and voices were less raucous. The club's bouncers had been escorting female customers to their cars, as a precaution.

April thought about her mother often. Last night someone had called, but not spoken. She listened to the taut silence, convinced it was Josefa. She'd finally said, *"Mamá?"* but the connection ended.

It broke her heart to imagine her mother struggling and alone. She'd second-guessed her decision a thousand times. Maybe she should have taken Josefa to the methadone clinic or tried to find a low-cost rehab. Her mother's drug and alcohol addiction had cast a pall over April's life. At least now Josefa's behavior didn't directly affect Jenny.

April had to move forward.

She was pleased with the new babysitting arrangements, excited to see Noah again, and anxious to start her upper-division classes at San Diego State. It felt good to step out of her comfort zone and to imagine a brighter future.

When her shift was over, she said good night to Eddie and walked outside with Carmen. As they crossed the parking lot, April's cell phone rang—a rare occurrence.

It was Noah. "Can I see you?"

"When?"

"Right now."

"Um . . ."

"I'll meet you at your house."

Her heart skipped a beat. "Okay," she said, moistening her lips. After he hung up, she darted a glance at Carmen.

So much for leaving a little mystery.

"Booty call," Carmen sang, getting into her car.

"It is not."

Her friend waved goodbye, laughing.

April drove home at a snail's pace, growing more nervous with each mile. Noah hadn't mentioned what he wanted, but he'd sounded tense. Maybe he wasn't as friendly on the phone as he was in person.

Would he expect sex?

When she arrived, he was already waiting outside. April parked in the garage and walked through the kitchen, setting her purse on the countertop. Thankfully, the house was tidy. She grabbed Jenny's stuffed dog off the floor and tossed it into her bedroom.

They wouldn't be going in there, anyway.

She walked toward the front door, wishing he'd given her time to wash the stink of the club out of her hair.

He was wearing jeans and a T-shirt, casual clothes that fit him well. His shoulders seemed to span the width of the doorway, perhaps because his stance was so rigid. Tonight, there were no flowers, no relaxed attitude, no lazy smile.

His gaze cruised over her thin tank top and short skirt. His mouth twisted wryly, as if he both appreciated her outfit and resented her wearing it.

She felt a flutter of unease. "Would you like to come in?"

He nodded, brushing by her. Once inside, he appeared uncomfortable. His hands were clenched at his sides.

She didn't offer him a seat.

"Is there anything you want to tell me?" he asked finally.

"About what?"

"Jenny's father. Your gang connections."

Her throat tightened. "Raul and I have no contact. There's nothing between us. I told you that."

"What about Eric Hernandez? Do you have 'contact' with him?"

"Yes. He visits Jenny."

"Not you?"

She swallowed, nodding. "We're friends."

"Does he give you money?"

"Yes," she said, lifting her chin. "He helps me out here and there. Not that it's any of your business."

His brows rose. "He's documented CVL. He's also a coworker of Cristina Lopez, victim number two. And I have reason to believe he fled the scene of another recent crime."

She'd heard about Junior's accident but not a whisper from Eric. He hadn't visited since the night Noah had interviewed her at the club. Feeling her knees weaken, she collapsed on the couch, stunned.

"Does he sell drugs?"

"He has a job at the market," she murmured.

"A part-time gig, at minimum wage, wouldn't even cover his rent."

"He—he lives with his grandmother."

"An elderly undocumented immigrant with no job. She's not eligible for public assistance."

She already knew Eric took care of his grandmother. And Noah could tell that she knew. His questions felt like a setup, a rope to hang herself with. "What do you expect me to say?" she asked, throwing her hands up. "What do you want from me?"

"The truth."

Tears pricked her eyes. "I told you Jenny's father was in prison. I said I had a hard time trusting men because of some issues from my past. Do you think it was easy for me, opening up like that?"

He looked away, his jaw clenched. When his gaze met hers again, it was cold. "You're accepting money from a kid who slings dope to fund gang violence. Your ex is a member of the Mexican Mafia. I'm a gang-unit officer.

It didn't occur to you that the department would frown on our relationship?"

She shook her head, tears spilling down her cheeks. "No. I've had a lot of other things on my mind. As far as my 'gang connections' go, everyone in this neighborhood has them. You can't grow up Mexican in Chula Vista and never have associated with a gang member. Surely you understand that."

He made a scoffing sound, infuriating her.

"It doesn't make *me* a criminal," she said, placing a hand on her chest.

"You don't think it's wrong to benefit from drug sales? Your own mother is an addict!"

Furious, she rose from the couch, walking to the kitchen for a drink of water. He followed, watching her pour the glass with trembling hands. After she slaked her thirst, she said, "Don't you dare talk to me about money. You don't know anything about my life! You came to this city to clean up the streets—you don't know what it's like to live on them. You've never had to apply for Medi-Cal, or wait in line at the clinic, or buy groceries with food stamps. You don't know how it feels to be poor, Noah." She slammed her cup down. "I'm sure your childhood was like a Norman Rockefeller painting."

"Rockwell," he said.

"What?"

"Norman Rockwell. He did the Americana paintings."

"Oh, fuck you," she said, pushing past him. She could field his criticism and match his anger, but she'd be damned if she'd put up with his *condescension*. "Why don't you go back to your summers at the lake and your sparkly snow and leave me alone."

When he wrapped his hand around her left wrist, preventing her from walking away from the argument, she reacted without thinking. Drawing back her right arm, she slapped him across the face. The sharp sound echoed through the kitchen.

He released her immediately.

April had often initiated fights with Raul. Many times he would strike her with no prior warning, for no discernible reason. It was like waiting for a bomb to go off, every single day. The anticipation was torture.

So she set the bomb off herself.

She would do things to make him angry, pick fights, talk back to him. Then, when he exploded, she felt an awful, inevitable relief.

Noah didn't explode. She stared at him in horror, her palm stinging from the impact. Its harsh imprint stood out on his cheek.

As soon as he lifted his hand, she flinched, cowering against the kitchen cabinets. But the blow she'd been expecting didn't come. She glanced up at him warily, realizing that he'd merely raised his fingertips to his face, touching the mark she'd made.

His gaze filled with sympathy, and she experienced a crippling wave of shame. She saw herself through his eyes—half crouched against the counter, panting in fear, as fractious as a wild animal.

She straightened, raking a hand through her hair.

When he reached out to her, she shied away again, her shoulders trembling. Undeterred, he stepped forward, wrapping his arms around her. Still lost in the flashbacks of abuse, she struggled to break free. Raul had done this. Hugging her close one minute, smacking her down the next.

Terrified and humiliated, she started pummeling his chest, fighting hard. Noah grabbed both of her wrists and held her arms behind her back.

She twisted to the side, bringing her spike heel down on top of his shoe.

He grunted in pain, but he didn't loosen his grip. "Stop," he said, pinning her against the counter. The blunt edge dug into her hip. Off-balance, her heels scraped the linoleum floor, useless. "I'm not going to hit you," he said, his teeth clenched. "But I won't let you hit me. Do you understand?"

Tears sprang into her eyes. She understood that he was incredibly strong and that resistance was futile. Already exhausted, she stopped fighting him and conserved her strength for the explosion.

It didn't happen.

Noah continued to steady her, his arms locked around her, his heart pounding in rhythm with hers. When she wilted against him, forcing him to bear her weight, he boosted her up on the countertop, keeping her wrists secured behind her back.

After a few moments his hold began to feel less restrictive. Like an embrace rather than a restraint.

With caution, he released her wrists. "Okay now?"

She nodded, trying to hold the tears at bay. But it was impossible, because all of her walls had come tumbling down. Giving in to her emotions, she pressed her face to his neck and cried, clinging to the front of his shirt. He made soothing sounds and rubbed her shoulders, gentling her. Although she was appalled by her actions, his touch felt good.

Incredibly good.

Her tears stopped flowing, little by little. In slow measures, she realized she was sitting on the countertop, her skirt hiked up to the point of indecency. He was standing between her splayed legs, his chest heaving against hers.

For a man who was no longer expending much energy, he was breathing hard. "Raul . . . abused you?" he asked.

"Yes."

"I'm sorry."

She didn't know how to respond to that or where to start. He'd asked for the truth, so she made an attempt to tell it. "When Raul became . . . violent, Eric often tried to protect me. He was only a kid at the time and no match for his brother physically, but he would put himself between us. Once, Raul held a gun to his head for interfering." Her eyes searched his. "I don't know how Eric makes his money. I wouldn't tell you if I did. He's like a brother to me, and I would *never* betray him."

Noah paused before he spoke, letting her words sink in. "What if I asked you to stop accepting money from him?"

She slid her hands over his shoulders, smoothing the wrinkles her fists had made. "Are you asking because you're jealous or because you don't want me involved with something illegal?"

"Both," he admitted. "I don't want another man . . . taking care of you."

"Even Raul? If he paid child support?"

"If you were mine, I'd give you everything you need."

Her heart warmed at the sentiment, even while her mind rejected it. "I'm not yours," she said, placing her fingertips on his jaw. "I can't be yours."

He went very still. Their lips were less than an inch apart, and he obviously longed to close the distance. But getting together wasn't really an option for either of them right now. Being with her violated his code of ethics. Being with him threatened her sense of independence.

"Why are you here?" she whispered.

"I wanted to get your side of the story."

"And to break up with me in person?"

He couldn't deny it. "I know I should have stayed away," he said instead, his eyes locked on hers. "But I can't stop thinking about you. I lie awake at night, aching for you. I fantasize about making you come, over and over again."

April smothered a moan, because she'd been suffering from the same problem. Last night she'd woken with his name on her lips, writhing against the sheets. She couldn't imagine finding another man she connected with on so many different levels. It might be five more years before she came close to sexual intimacy again.

"Before you leave, do me a favor," she murmured, dipping her head to taste the warm skin at his throat. His pulse throbbed beneath her lips, and his salt tingled on her tongue. She could feel the heat of his erection jutting against the juncture of her thighs.

If they couldn't have a relationship, maybe they could have *this*.

"What?"

Her mouth touched his ear. "Fuck me."

His body shook against hers, his resolve crumbling under the weight of his desire. He lifted his hand to her nape, fisting it in her hair. She couldn't have said why, but the action excited her beyond belief. Her panties were damp, her flesh swollen and achy.

When he tilted her head back, she moaned and clutched the edge of the counter, steadying herself for his kiss.

His technique wasn't graceful. He devoured her mouth, thrusting his tongue deep inside, possessing her completely. She wrapped her legs around his waist and grabbed handfuls of his shirt, loving every second of it.

One of them knocked over the sugar bowl. Its contents spilled across the counter, dusting the tile surface.

They didn't waste much time with foreplay. She tugged off his shirt, her fingertips dancing over the muscles in his chest. He reached under her skirt, yanking her panties and stockings down her thighs, just far enough to give him access. The countertop felt cool against her bare bottom. He jerked open the fly of his pants, and then the blunt tip of his erection was right there, pressing against her.

"No," she said, pushing him back.

His eyes flashed with anger. "No?"

"Not without a condom," she clarified.

He shook his head, as if to clear it. "Right," he muttered, reaching into his front pocket. "I, uh, agree."

While he took care of that, she kicked off her shoes

and finished removing her panties and stockings. Then she pulled her top over her head and unhooked her bra. It fell away from her body, her breasts tumbling free.

Her nipples stood out like pebbles, begging for his touch.

Moistening his lips, he rolled the condom down himself, looking from her mouth to her breasts to the dark triangle between her legs. His eyes were hungry, as if he wanted to taste everything at once.

Impatient, she flattened her palms on the countertop and parted her thighs.

He groaned, stepping up to the plate. Bracing one hand on the cabinet above her head, he guided himself into her with the other. Although she was very wet, she didn't accept him easily. She wrapped her legs around his waist, squirming for a better angle. He found it, burying himself to the hilt in one smooth thrust.

"Oh, my God," she moaned.

"I like it when you say that."

She dug her fingernails into his bare shoulders, panting against his throat. After a long stint of celibacy, she felt an almost painful sense of fullness. He was big, but not so big that she couldn't take him. Her body stretched to the limit, accommodating his size.

"Am I hurting you?"

"It's a good hurt."

He clenched his teeth, obviously wanting to pound her into oblivion. Instead, he skimmed his hands along her sides, cupping the soft weight of her breasts. He unwittingly transferred some spilled sugar from the countertop to her skin. The granulated particles clung to her stiff nipples, abrading her sweetly.

When he bent his head to lick the sugar-dusted tips, she gasped with pleasure, her hips jerking forward. He withdrew from her a few inches and drove himself deep again, plunging into her slick heat.

"Oh, God," she said, clinging to the edge.

She wanted more thrusting, just like that, but he set a slower pace. Framing her face with one hand, he rubbed his thumb over her parted lips. Tasting sugar, she sucked on the pad, watching his eyes go dark. It was almost too much to bear, having him in her mouth that way, his thumb mimicking the slide of his cock.

She was so close.

Dragging his thumb from her mouth, he placed it over her clitoris, stroking her in languid circles. She felt a rush of moisture and every inch of his thick length pulsing inside her. Sagging against him, she cried out, unraveling in delicious spools.

"You are so fucking hot," he growled, lifting her off the counter. He spun around, propping her back against the refrigerator. The position allowed him to thrust harder, and he did, slamming into her again and again.

Refrigerator magnets and papers were dislodged. A cereal box fell to the floor.

Amazingly, she kept peaking. Her inner muscles clenched around him once more, and this time he came with her. With a strangled groan, he buried himself deep, his body shuddering as he found his own release.

When it was over, she glanced around guiltily. They were in her kitchen. Sugar littered the countertop. She was naked, her skirt shoved up to her waist. He was holding her up against the fridge, his pants around his ankles.

One of Jenny's drawings had been trampled.

"Put your feet on the floor," he murmured, letting her down.

She stood on tiptoe, watching while he wrapped his hand around the base of the condom and withdrew from her. Her oversensitized flesh whimpered in protest. She felt like she'd been . . . rode hard.

While he went to dispose of the condom, April tugged her skirt down her thighs and searched for her top on the floor. Shaking the sugar from the fabric, she put it on, not bothering with panties or a bra.

He came out of the bathroom a moment later, shirtless. Beautiful.

Swallowing drily, she sat down at the table. As soon as the sex high wore off, she'd be embarrassed. For now she admired the view.

He put his shirt back on, ruining it. "I have to go."

She drew in a sharp breath. His words were like a splash of cold water, reminding her of their argument. "I'm sorry I hit you."

He shrugged, as if the slap hadn't bothered him.

She stared at the surface of the table. "It won't happen again."

"No. It won't."

Because he wasn't coming back.

April's stomach dropped. Too late, she realized her mistake. She'd thought all she wanted was sex. She was wrong.

She needed to be held.

More ashamed of this feeling than she was of her

brazen behavior or her violent reaction to their fight, she crossed her arms over her chest, hiding her shaking hands.

"I shouldn't have come over," he said finally, his voice hoarse with emotion. "I can't be near you without wanting to touch you."

Her heart clenched at his words. She bit down on her lower lip, fighting tears.

"God damn it, April! I won't apologize for giving you what you asked for."

"Just go," she cried out, gesturing toward the door.

Appearing as unhappy as she was, as if the brief encounter hadn't been enough for him, either, he nodded curtly and walked out on her.

18

🌿 Arranging a midweek visit with Raul was difficult but not impossible.

Donovan Prison, the maximum-security facility where his brother had spent the past three years, allowed visitors only on the weekends. If Eric had submitted a formal request for an emergency meeting, he probably would have been denied.

Luckily, he knew another route. Like most prisons, Donovan had an underground system of criminal activity, run by opportunistic guards. For a price, one of them had set up an after-hours visit in a room normally reserved for legal counsel.

His brother was happy to see him. After the guard removed Raul's cuffs and left them alone together, Raul wrapped Eric up in a bear hug. The embrace made him uncomfortable, but Eric didn't have the heart to pull away. He was Raul's only contact with the outside, the only person he felt safe with.

"You didn't come on Sunday," Raul said.

"I got tied up."

As soon as they sat down, Eric passed him some cash

under the table. It was their typical routine. Eric supplied his brother with the tithe for *Dos Emes* and paid the guard to look the other way. Raul, in turn, skimmed a portion of the cash for his drug habit, which had only grown worse in prison. The same guards who could be bribed to ignore handoffs and set up meetings also made a tidy profit from drug sales.

As always, Eric felt conflicted about giving Raul money. Without it, his brother's position in the prison gang was negligible. The tithe was Raul's lifeline, but it was also a rope with which he seemed intent on hanging himself. Eric suspected that Raul was keeping a larger percentage every time, digging his own grave.

"What's up?" Raul asked, his eyes darting around the room. He was probably thinking about his next hit rather than the reason for Eric's visit. On rare occasions, he asked how Jenny was doing. Most days he didn't seem to care about the outside world. He hadn't even remembered to send a card on her last birthday.

Every year that he was locked up, he became less . . . human.

Eric studied Raul from across the table, wondering if he was looking at a future version of himself. They had the same dark coloring, the same basic height. Despite his drug use, his brother was in good shape physically. The short sleeves of his chambray work shirt showed muscles that bulged from lifting weights. He sported a thick mustache and goatee, though his head was shaved clean.

Eric used to think the sun rose and set with Raul. His brother had been his unofficial guardian, his vigilante knight. The only life Eric had known before Raul took him in was one of constant turmoil. His father had abused his mother—and she'd loved him anyway. When his dad died in a prison brawl, she'd gone back to Mexico, shattered.

At ten years old, Eric had decided he didn't need parents. He stayed in Chula Vista with Raul. His brother never told him what to do. He treated Eric like an adult. A crew member. It wasn't until Raul descended into drug addiction and became violent with April that Eric began to question his brother's character.

Now, when he looked at Raul, he saw their father.

"Junior's sister was murdered," Eric said.

"I heard about that."

"He wants to find the killer."

"How?"

Eric moistened his lips. This was tricky. If Raul suspected him of working with the police, he would get very angry. "She was strangled, I guess. He thinks it might be . . . that guy. He asked me to talk to you about it."

Raul gave him a blank look. "What guy?"

He switched to Spanish. "The one in the mask. He paid you for the girl. That night in the abandoned house."

Raul's eyes flickered with surprise. "Junior told you about that?"

"No. I was there."

Raul leaned back in his chair, smoothing a hand over his bald head. "Fuck Junior," he said, dismissing the threat. "Word around here is that he went *loco*, shooting wild at some *chavala*'s house. He should be worrying about how he's going to avoid lockdown, not chasing shadows."

Eric tried a different tactic. "Tony Castillo's girl got killed, too. He was there that night. You don't think it's suspicious?"

Raul crossed his arms over his chest. "Suspicious," he repeated, squinting at the ceiling. "Like you coming here on a weekday?"

Eric started to feel nauseous. He knew exactly what Raul was capable of when angered. And the guard he'd paid to wait outside wouldn't give a damn if they scuffled in here. "Two neighborhood girls are dead. One of them was my friend's sister. The other worked with April. Why shouldn't we want to find the guy who did it?"

"And then what?"

"Take care of him."

Raul smiled, but the expression was cold. "From Junior, I might buy it. He always had more balls than you."

"Tell me his name."

He reached out, grabbing Eric by the front of the shirt and dragging him across the table. "He doesn't have a name," Raul said, speaking directly in his ear. "He doesn't even exist. That night never happened, *hermanito*. If you ever mention it again, *you* won't exist."

Eric wasn't a little kid hanging on his father's arm to slow his blows anymore. He wasn't a skinny teen begging Raul not to hit April. He was a grown man who knew how to defend himself.

Proving it, he drew back his fist, punching his brother in the jaw.

Raul's head snapped to the side. He seemed stunned,

but only for a second. With a low growl he retaliated, slamming his fist into Eric's mouth. Pain blossomed on impact, vibrating through Eric's skull, rattling his teeth.

He fell off the end of the table, dazed. Raul didn't pursue, but he didn't have to. His point was made. He was stronger, more powerful.

Ruthless—even with his own brother.

Eric rose to his feet, wiping his mouth with the back of his hand. "I can't believe I used to look up to you."

"Fuck you, *dedo*. You think I don't know why you're really here?"

"To bring you drug money?"

"You're talking to the cops."

"Not yet. I might have to, if you don't tell me who he is."

Raul didn't fall for it. "Get the fuck out of here," he said, lifting his chin. "I'll see you in the joint, *puto*. A pretty boy like you will attract a lot of attention, but I won't have your back. Nobody protects snitches."

He nodded slowly, smoothing his rumpled shirt. At that moment, any love he had for his brother died. There was nothing left inside him but resentment. On his way out, he said, "Find someone else to support your habit, you fucking junkie."

Raul threw his chair at the door.

Eric felt the walls closing in on him as he was escorted from the facility. He had no avenue of escape. No information to use as a bargaining chip. No friends left on either side. Junior, Tony C, and Raul used to be in his circle of trust. Talking to the police would fuck them all over. But how could he stay quiet?

He was going to end up in prison, being somebody's

bitch. Sucking cocks, if he was cooperative; getting butt-raped if he wasn't.

And he couldn't imagine being cooperative.

"Shit," he muttered, pacing the parking lot. Junior didn't know the masked man's name. Raul wouldn't tell him. There was one other person who'd been there that night—Tony Castillo. Maybe Tony had some information about the masked man or his young victim.

If the recent killings were related, Eric had to find out everything he could and pass it on to Officer Young. For Cristina's sake and his own. For the other girls in the neighborhood, none of whom deserved to be next.

But also for the one he hadn't helped, so long ago.

Visiting Tony in county jail wouldn't be a problem. The real trick would be walking back out again, a free man.

"This is crazy," he said, shaking his head. He had to discuss an unsolved murder with his former trafficking partner, a current inmate.

Without getting caught.

Noah's conscience was killing him.

He reported for duty on Wednesday afternoon, feeling like a criminal. Patrick's empty desk mocked him. Although Noah was often at odds with his partner when he was around, he found himself missing his companionship now that he'd gone.

He could use a friend right now.

Sighing, he logged on to his computer, doing a detailed search of cold-case murders from the previous decade. There were several that appeared to be gang-related, and one case stood out from the rest. Eight years ago, an unidentified young woman had been found by a construction crew, her body buried in an empty lot. Decomposition made the cause of death difficult to determine, but a plastic bag covered her face.

She also had a brown bandanna tied around her neck.

Eric Hernandez might have information about this particular case, but Noah doubted it. He probably knew a few minor details about a shooting or beating death.

Or he was yanking Noah's chain.

At this point, he wasn't sure he should pursue any investigation that concerned Eric. Meghan was involved. April was involved. *He* was involved. Last night, his behavior had been so inappropriate, it was insane.

He bolted away from his desk, heading straight to Santiago's office. When he knocked on the open door, the detective took off his glasses and massaged his eye sockets, motioning for Noah to come inside.

"Can I speak with you for a moment, sir?"

Santiago smothered a yawn. "Of course."

Noah sat in the chair across from his desk. "After our conversation on Monday, it occurred to me that I have something to disclose."

He tilted his head to one side, listening.

"The first night of the investigation, Patrick and I interviewed the staff at Club Suave. One of the waitresses, April Ortiz, gave me a tip. It led to Tony Castillo's arrest."

Santiago already knew this. "And?"

Feeling his neck grow warm, Noah tugged at his

uniformed collar. "I ran into her again, off duty. We've been . . . seeing each other."

"Romantically?"

"Yes."

Santiago smiled. "Congratulations."

Noah cleared his throat. "She has gang connections, sir. Some documented members are related to her. I thought it might be a problem."

Santiago leaned back in his chair, folding his hands across his chest. "I met my wife on patrol."

That threw Noah for a loop. "Really?"

Santiago rifled through his top drawer, finding a framed photo. "I pulled her over on a speeding charge. She took the ticket and asked for my phone number. I was very flattered." He handed the picture to Noah. "That sort of thing might happen to you all the time, Officer Young, but homely guys like me don't get hit on."

He accepted the photo, intrigued. A less weathered Santiago stood at the altar with his young bride. It was a serious moment. A committed moment. "She's very pretty."

"Yes. Unfortunately, I couldn't hang on to her."

Noah murmured his condolences. He hadn't known Santiago was divorced.

"She got tired of me working so many long hours and left. I promised to be more attentive, but I never followed through." He put away the photo, his face drawn. "This job is hard on families."

"I've heard that."

"This girl from the club is someone special, isn't she? Otherwise you wouldn't have come to me."

Noah hesitated. If she was special, why had he treated her so casually? If she wasn't, why hadn't he been able to stay away? "I came to you because it's a conflict of interest. I wanted to be up front."

"Let's keep it between us," Santiago suggested. "Sergeant Briggs might be less understanding, considering that recent fuckup with Officer Shanley."

"I'm sorry that happened, sir."

"You're applying to the homicide division, is that correct?"

"Yes, sir. As soon as I qualify."

"Shanley spoke to me about your interest. He asked me to pass you over, in fact."

Noah went still with shock. "Did he say why?"

Santiago leaned forward, his dark eyes searching. "He said you had too much heart. There's a certain amount of detachment a man needs for this job, Officer Young. Sometimes I feel more dead than alive."

"I'll deaden up, sir."

Santiago laughed. "Are you sure you want to? Do you want to see images of corpses every time you close your eyes? Bring the stench of death home to your family? There comes a point when you feel as though you're going to taint them with it. So you disengage."

Noah knew Santiago was telling the truth. Homicide wasn't a department for weak stomachs or half efforts. It required an intense commitment. Noah didn't like the suggestion that he wasn't tough enough, but he couldn't dismiss it outright.

Maybe he *was* too trusting. He would work on that.

Noah wanted a challenging job, and he was ambitious. He'd never wondered how the choice would impact his personal life. Before he met April, having a wife and children had seemed like a vague possibility, years ahead of him. Two weeks ago he hadn't needed to worry about how his long hours affected Meghan.

Did he want to be the kind of man who put his career ahead of his family?

"Next to Patrick, everyone seems kindhearted," Noah said. "But I appreciate your honesty, and I'll give your words some serious thought."

"Good, good. Don't think I'm trying to talk you out of applying. I can always use smart, well-educated officers on my team."

"Thank you, sir. One more thing . . ."

"Yes?"

He gave Santiago a copy of the autopsy report he'd been viewing. "I found this in the cold-case files. The victim is an unidentified female, approximate age fourteen to seventeen, possibly strangled by a brown bandanna. She was also buried with a plastic bag over her head."

Santiago glanced at the printout. "Lots of bodies get buried in plastic, Young. Fluid from the head is messy."

"Right," Noah said. "Even so, there's no blunt-force trauma. No evidence of knife or gunshot wounds."

"Eight years ago." He shrugged, obviously considering it a long shot. "I hadn't looked back that far. I've been slogging through local unsolved murders from the past five years. There are many." To demonstrate, he pulled up a slide show of the gruesome crime-scene photos he'd been browsing on his computer.

Noah swallowed hard, trying not to grimace.

"Considering the likely gang ties and the victim demographic, this is well worth following up on." Santiago handed back the printout. "Go ahead."

"You want me to look into it?"

"Why not? You've got great instincts, and you need the experience. To be honest, we're hurting for more hands. With a possible serial murderer on the loose, my team is working around the clock. Everyone is swamped."

Noah thanked the detective and left his office, excited by the opportunity to explore a new lead on his own. He probably should have mentioned his talk with Eric Hernandez, but he was glad he hadn't.

He didn't want to press his luck.

He was also surprised by Santiago's reaction to the disclosure about April. He'd expected stern disapproval at the very least. Santiago hadn't seemed concerned. As long as he was discreet, Noah could continue dating her.

If she'd let him.

His gut clenched in anticipation of seeing her again. He hadn't shown "too much heart" last night. Pinning her arms behind her back, screwing her against the refrigerator. He'd been so intent on having her that using protection had almost slipped his mind. He'd wanted to plow into her, with no barriers between them, and damn the consequences. The condom hadn't slowed him down much, either. He'd taken her fast and hard.

God.

He'd never been so rough with a woman before. The fact that he'd treated *April* that way tore him apart inside. She'd opened up to him about the abuse she'd suffered. And what had he done in return? Banged the hell out of her.

He was sorry he'd left so abruptly, but he couldn't regret the encounter. He'd enjoyed it too much. Besides, she'd practically begged him to continue.

Damn. That had been off-the-charts hot.

Stifling a groan, he shelved the memory. Tomorrow he would stop by her house, try to talk to her. Maybe he could find a way to smooth things over. For now he had an investigation to reactivate.

Cautiously optimistic, he went down to the archives to pull the cold-case file.

19

🌿 Meghan rode her bike to Cristina's viewing.

The funeral parlor was five miles away from Noah's house, in a quiet residential neighborhood. She stopped at a shady little park across the street to drink cool water from the fountain and lock up her bike in the rack.

The funeral Mass would take place on Saturday, complete with a Catholic service and cemetery burial. She planned to attend with Noah. Today's viewing was a less formal occasion. Anyone could drop by and visit the body, from early afternoon to late evening.

Meghan felt apprehensive about seeing Cristina. She wasn't sure why she'd come. Morbid curiosity, she supposed. And a bellyful of guilt.

When she stepped inside the parlor, it was just past 4:00 P.M. She smoothed her hair away from her flushed forehead. Riding a bike in appropriate attire was difficult, so she'd worn knee-length black leggings beneath her lightweight summer dress. The air-conditioned interior felt chilly against her sun-warmed skin.

She rubbed her bare arms, self-conscious.

There were three middle-aged women in the waiting room, faces crumpled, tissues fisted in their hands. She nodded politely as she passed by. Near the entrance, a table had been set up for flowers and cards.

Meghan signed the guestbook, automatically perusing for Eric's name.

It wasn't there.

Pushing her thoughts of Eric aside, she crossed the room, pausing before a set of closed doors. She tried to imagine what was on the other side. She'd never seen a dead person before. Would Cristina look peaceful?

She hesitated, glancing at the other women. Cristina's relatives were having a private conversation in Spanish, their voices choked with sorrow.

Meghan looked away quickly, feeling out of place. She didn't belong here. She'd known Cristina for only a week. These women were in pain, and Meghan was intruding on their grief.

But she couldn't leave now without paying her respects.

Heart pounding with trepidation, she went through the door and slipped into the viewing room. A short aisle separated two groups of empty chairs. An open casket was set up on a raised platform.

She walked forward on unsteady legs, her palms slick with sweat. She felt strange and light-headed, almost as if she'd taken another puff of Jack's weed. Her eyes had trouble adjusting to the softly lit interior of the building.

Taking a deep breath, she approached the casket.

Cristina lay inside the velvet-lined box, wearing a demure blue dress with a high lace collar. Her eyes were closed and sort of sunken-looking. The youthful buoyancy had been stripped from her face, and no amount of makeup could replace it. Her features were slack, almost unrecognizable.

She didn't look like she was sleeping.

When Meghan pictured Cristina's vibrant smile and mischievous eyes, her chest tightened with sadness.

This was horribly unfair.

Her gaze slid down to the lace at Cristina's throat, because it seemed so incongruous with her fashion sense. Meghan realized that the accessory covered a skin discoloration. And just like that she was taken back to that terrible night, assaulted by memories of Jack. She felt his knuckles digging into her collarbone, his hand fisted in her tank top. She felt him behind her, ripping her underwear and yanking down her pants.

How much worse it must have been for Cristina! Her attacker hadn't been thwarted. He hadn't only stripped her clothes. He'd pushed inside her, violating her body, tearing her open. He'd held her down and choked her, stealing her last breath.

Imagining Cristina's final moments, Meghan stifled a sob with the back of her hand. It might have happened to her if Eric hadn't come along. Overwhelmed with terror and guilt and relief, she turned away from the casket, sinking into a nearby chair.

At the bonfire, she'd been jealous of Cristina. She'd wanted to take her place.

Now she buried her head in her hands and cried. She didn't know if she believed in God anymore, but she begged for his forgiveness.

Maybe she'd been wrong to leave her parents' house

in Cedar Glen. She felt so lost and alone. The elements of the city that had seemed exciting to her a few days ago now seemed cruelly foreign. Her only friend had been murdered. On the way to the viewing, she'd passed a hundred strangers, no one her age, no one who spoke her language.

She sat there for a long time. Crying for Cristina, for herself.

A few minutes later, a young man came in to pay his respects. He knelt at the casket for several long moments, murmuring a prayer. When he was finished, he drew a chain from beneath his shirt, touching the cross to his lips.

It was Eric.

He must not have noticed her as he came in, but he saw her then. Letting the crucifix fall under the collar of his shirt, he stood. His dark gaze wandered over her, taking in her anguished eyes and tearstained cheeks.

"Come," he said, holding out his hand.

She walked with him into the sun-dappled gardens. There were several headstone samples beneath a shady oak. The sound of rush-hour traffic on the freeway overpass seemed to insulate the space rather than detract from its quietude.

"Do you believe in God?" she asked.

"Yes."

"Why?"

He thought about it for a moment. "Because I'm alive."

"Haven't you ever been uncertain?"

"No."

"When something bad happens to you, don't you wonder if God has forgotten you? Or if he even exists?"

Eric shrugged. "Not really. I don't blame God for any of my problems. Everything bad in my life, I've done to myself."

"So . . . you believe that people deserve their suffering?"

"No," he said softly, watching the passing cars go by. "Most of the time, no. Life isn't fair that way. But I don't think it's God's fault."

"It isn't his plan?"

"I don't know."

"I hate God."

He laughed, putting his arm around her shoulders. Although his touch thrilled her like nothing else ever had, she was disturbed by the contrast between his handsome vitality and Cristina's untimely death. It seemed wrong for Eric to smile so easily and for Meghan's breath to catch at the sight. "It's not funny," she murmured.

"Sorry," he said, sobering. "I never thought I'd see you again, Mía. But here you are. Being with you makes me happy."

Her heart sang to hear that. She leaned into him, basking in his warmth. "When I was a little girl, my mother told me that she loved God more than she loved me. She said all good Christians did. Do you think your mother felt that way?"

His eyes searched hers, seeing her pain. "No," he said, after a pause. "She's very religious, but no. I think she loved my father more than she loved me, though. And he was as far away from God as a man could be."

Meghan didn't know if that answer made her feel better or worse. She only knew that she felt connected with him. Getting closer still, she slipped her arms around his neck. "I'm sorry, Gusto."

They stayed that way for a short time, finding a measure of peace. Meghan hoped Cristina wouldn't have felt dishonored by their actions. After coming face-to-face with death, it seemed more important to cherish special moments, to embrace life.

"Your brother is going to arrest me," Eric said.

"For what?"

"Lots of things."

"Are you guilty?"

"Yes."

She sighed, pressing her face to his collar. He was dressed nicely today, in dark jeans and a button-down shirt. "I don't believe you."

"Your judgment is off. Way off."

"How did you get here?"

"I drove."

"You have a car?"

He hesitated, skimming his hand down her back. "Yes."

"Take me someplace."

"Where?"

"Anywhere."

He walked her out to the parking lot, where a shiny brown car rested in the shade. It was an older model, sleek and fast-looking.

"Did you steal this?"

With a wry smile, he opened the passenger door for her. "No."

She sat down on the black vinyl bench seat, securing a lap belt across her waist. It felt . . . dangerous.

They drove down the freeway, windows open. Jay-Z and Beyonce's "Bonnie and Clyde" played on the radio. The late-afternoon breeze rippled through her hair, plastering the front of her dress to her body. She thrilled at the sensation of being totally free, living for the moment, leaving her troubles behind.

He took her to Balboa Park, in downtown San Diego. She'd been there several times with Noah. It was a huge space, encompassing acres of botanical gardens, various playhouses and music stages, and more than a dozen museums.

Meghan didn't ask what they were doing. She didn't care.

At one of the smaller museums, there was a photography exhibit. Eric paid a small price at the entrance and escorted her inside. The ambiance was casual. A handful of chic twentysomethings stood around, talking about art.

Eric ignored them.

The exhibit featured local graffiti. She'd seen the scrawled tags on the underpasses, along block walls, and on fencing slats. Before now she hadn't considered it art. Upon closer inspection, some of the workmanship impressed her. There were colorful geometric shapes, intricate block lettering, whimsical details.

The accompanying images were disturbing, urban, violent, religious.

When they stood before a beautiful interpretation of a thorn-studded heart, Eric glanced sideways at her, gauging her reaction.

"Did you take these photos?" she whispered.

"No."

She looked closer, trying to understand his connection to the work. At the bottom of the heart, she noticed a cryptic lowercase *e*. "You did this," she realized, searching for his signature on the other pieces. "You did almost all of these."

He gave the group of photography students a warning look, conveying a silent message not to approach. "Shh. I don't want anyone to know."

"Why not? These are amazing, Eric. Obviously the photographer thought so, too."

He shrugged, uncomfortable. "It's illegal."

She gave each of the images he'd created another examination. The subject matter was decidedly adult. Prostitutes on a street corner, waiting for customers. A man tying off the vein in his arm to shoot up.

The work revealed a lot more about Eric than his artistic talent.

"You could get paid to do this," she said. "Graphic design, murals. Have you ever thought about going to art school?"

Instead of answering, he took her by the hand, ushering her outside. "Did you hear those kids? They were talking about styles, and symbolism, and . . . time periods. I can't do that. I'm just a tagger from the ghetto. They're from . . . Hillcrest or some shit."

She smiled, finding it ironic that a boy from Castle Park could be intimidated by residents of a quirky, gay-friendly community. "Why did you bring me here?"

"I guess I wanted you to see a different side of me. To

pretend, for a little while, that I was an artist instead of a criminal."

"I like all the sides of you, Eric."

"You don't even know me."

The assertion stung. She glanced toward the exhibit entrance, deliberating. "Is that stuff autobiographical?"

He avoided her gaze. "I don't know what you mean."

"Yes, you do."

"It's based on things I've seen and done. Real life."

"Do you sketch first?"

"Sometimes."

"What's your favorite surface?"

The corner of his mouth tipped up. "Smooth-finished concrete's pretty sweet."

"Are you making a statement about society?"

"Shit," he said in a dismissive tone.

"You can keep up with art students, Eric. You can do anything you want to."

His eyes cruised over her body in a slow caress. "I wish."

Her pulse kicked up a notch. "I'm flattered that you shared your work with me," she said, fingering the buttons on the front of his shirt. "And I wouldn't mind continuing this discussion . . . in private."

His brows rose at her insinuation. The other night he'd been reluctant to touch her, maybe because they were in Noah's house. Today he seemed different. More willing to go after what he wanted.

Nodding his agreement, he led her back to his car. At dusk, the parking lot was almost empty. He drove to a quiet corner, facing a slope of bottlebrush trees, and killed the engine. "Is this private enough for you?"

There was no one around right now, but they could get caught by a random passerby at any moment.

"It's perfect," she said.

He glanced out the back window, making sure they were alone. Meghan started to unbutton the front of her dress. He watched intently as her bra came into view, his eyes lingering on the lacy cups.

"What's this?" he asked, sliding his hand beneath a synthetic string that was hanging from her neck.

She'd forgotten she was wearing the whistle he gave her, tucked into her bra. When he tugged, it popped free, the metal mouthpiece warmed from her flesh. He lifted it to his lips, testing the heat.

Her tummy fluttered at the sight.

"Why do you have this on?" he asked, encircling the object in his fist.

She cupped her hand around his knuckles. "Because it's yours."

He pulled on the string again, until his mouth was just inches from hers. "Why are you here with me?"

She moistened her lips. "Because I want you to touch me."

His gaze dropped to her half-exposed breasts. "I'm going to hell anyway," he muttered, lowering his head to kiss her. But he winced slightly as his lips met hers, as if the pressure pained him.

"Are you hurt?" she asked.

"Nothing serious."

Upon closer inspection, the corner of his mouth looked red and swollen. Realizing that he'd been fighting—again—a wave of protectiveness washed over her. She proceeded to kiss him in a way that wouldn't bother his injury, flicking her tongue hotly against his. With a low groan, he followed suit, kissing her with a wet, open mouth.

The shallow strokes were very arousing. Perhaps because he couldn't crush his mouth over hers like she wanted him to, the rest of her body ached for a more complete satisfaction. She panted against his lips, working on his shirt buttons.

He moved away from the steering wheel to give her easier access. She pushed his shirt off his shoulders and straddled his lap, smoothing her palms over his taut, well-muscled chest. "You have a beautiful body."

His hands gripped her hips, pressing her down on his erection. "Fuck."

Keeping her dress on would give them a modicum of privacy, but the voluminous fabric annoyed her, so she yanked it over her head. He filled his palms with her breasts, squeezing her tingling flesh. Lost in sensation, she wrapped her arms around his neck and arched her back, squirming on his lap.

He tugged down the cups of her bra, his breath fanning her nipples. His hot mouth closed over one pink tip, then the other. She moaned, raking her nails across his bare shoulders, caressing the back of his skull.

Without warning, the interior of the car brightened. While they'd been getting friendly, darkness had fallen.

Meghan froze, trapped in the headlights of an approaching vehicle.

Eric pushed her down on the seat, holding her beneath him until the threat was gone. His heart was pounding against hers—he'd really been startled by the other car. She pressed her face to his chest and giggled hysterically.

When she quieted, he shifted to the side, finding them a more comfortable position. She nestled into the crook of his arm. Maybe doing it in a public parking lot wasn't the best idea they'd ever had.

He kissed the top of her head, sighing.

She trailed a circle around his flat nipple, admiring a finely etched tattoo of two praying hands on his upper chest. Moving on, she tried to read the cursive script around his biceps. "What does this say?"

"*Perdóneme, Padre, porque he pecado.*"

"What does it mean?"

"Forgive me, Father, for I have sinned."

"You aren't wearing your wristband," she noted.

"No."

"Are you out of the gang?"

"I don't know."

"Don't you have to get jumped out?"

"I was never jumped in."

"How'd you get in?"

He shrugged. "I was born in, I guess. My dad, my brother . . . all of my male family members were already in."

"How do you get out when you're born in?"

"You move away. Or die."

Meghan lifted her head, seeing that he was serious. "Are you going to move away?"

"Maybe I won't have to. There's something I need to figure out. A deal I might be able to make."

Troubled by his words, she rested her cheek over his

heart. "I don't want you to die," she murmured, fingering his crucifix.

He slid his hand down her arm, stroking her skin. "Let's talk about something else. When I'm with you, nothing else matters."

She let her fingertips wander down his rib cage, along his clenched stomach muscles. "We don't have to talk at all."

He trapped her hand before it went farther. "Meghan—"

"My ex-boyfriend cried the first time we had sex. Is that normal?"

"Uh . . . no."

"He said that we needed to get married to absolve the sin."

"No offense, but he sounds like a wimp."

She laughed a little, relieved. "I thought I did something wrong."

"Like what?"

"I don't know. I didn't enjoy it much."

He didn't seem surprised by that, but he looked interested. And he *felt* interested, his abdomen taut beneath her palm.

"Maybe I need more practice," she whispered, kissing his chest.

He sat up abruptly, moving her hand away from his belt. "This isn't a very secluded place—"

"I don't care."

Moistening his lips, he studied the cramped space inside the cab. "Okay," he said, sliding over to the passenger side once again. Then he pulled her into his lap, facing away from him.

Meghan went still, uncomfortable with the posit
It reminded her of Jack, of being grabbed from beh
But this was Eric, and his touch made her feel safe.
instant his lips met her exposed nape, she me
against him.

His open mouth found sensitive spots she ha
known existed. He kissed each shoulder, slipping
bra straps down. His lips touched the ridges of
spine and the dips of her shoulder blades. By the t
his mouth returned to her neck, her nipples were ti
jutting against the lace cups of her bra, and her
pulsed with awareness.

She moaned in frustration, wriggling on his lap.
erection pressed hard against her bottom, teasing h

He slid his hand between her legs, rubbing
through the thin fabric of her leggings. Pleasure b
somed from the spot, making her gasp. The contact
incredibly arousing, but she wanted more.

Instead of giving it to her, he lifted his hands to
breasts, tugging at the cups of her bra. He scraped
teeth over her nape, pinching her nipples gently.

"Oh!" she breathed, digging her nails into the v
seat.

Finally he went back down, slipping his finger
under the waistband of her leggings, into the from
her panties. He groaned when he encountered her
swollen flesh. She grabbed his wrist and held him th
panting with excitement. He alternated between
ping his fingers inside her and stroking her with
slick fingertips until she bit back a scream, shatterin
his arms.

When it was over, she rested her head against

shoulder, her pulse throbbing. She could hear the buzz of insects outside, the sound of a summer night. "Is that it?"

He laughed roughly, pushing her off his lap. "Are you disappointed?"

"No," she said, very aware that the pleasure had been one-sided. "I mean, yes. You didn't finish."

"There isn't enough space in the cab for that."

"Hmm," she said, sliding down to the floorboards, kneeling between his splayed knees. "Plenty of room here."

A muscle in his jaw jumped as he took another glance out the back window, checking the deserted parking lot. "We're going to get caught," he murmured, but it was a token protest. He wanted this. When she took off her bra, his eyes glazed over.

Smiling, she bent forward, pressing her lips to his abdomen. "No one can see me."

He stared at her mouth, swallowing hard.

Delighting in her feminine power, Meghan unbuckled his belt and lowered his zipper. "Tell me what you like."

He said something in Spanish, more a curse than an instruction.

She tugged down the front of his boxer shorts and circled her hand around him, squeezing and stroking. He watched her tentative motions, mesmerized. When she bent her head to him, tasting the hot skin, he shuddered. Emboldened by his response, she swirled her tongue around the blunt tip.

"Fuck," he choked, threading his fingers through her short hair. "Open your mouth."

She complied on instinct, taking him deeper than she'd imagined was possible. Letting him guide her, she moved her wet mouth up and down his length, sucking firmly. It was a fairly intuitive act, and he appeared to have no complaints about her technique.

She reveled in his whispered curses, his masculine taste.

"Stop," he said suddenly. "Stop!"

She lifted her head, questioning.

He grabbed his bandanna and wrapped the cloth around himself, spilling into it with a strangled groan.

"Why did you do that?" she asked.

He closed his eyes, breathing hard. "Did you want me to come in your mouth?"

"Yes."

Leaning his head back against the seat, he laughed. "I was trying to be polite."

Pleased with herself, she refastened the front clasp of her bra and found her discarded dress on the floor.

He straightened also, shoving the bandanna into the empty ashtray. She stared at his exposed body, curious. His lean, muscular torso narrowed to a trim waist. A line of dark hair ran from his navel to his groin. His penis, which had softened some, twitched at her perusal. Scowling, he put it away.

"What now?" she asked, afraid that their time together had drawn to a close.

He seemed as uncertain about the next step as she was. Instead of making promises, he gathered her against his chest and held her, savoring these stolen moments. Protecting her from the outside world, where the odds continued to stack against them.

20

Noah hadn't called.

April tried to push thoughts of him from her mind, but her eyes kept straying to the kitchen countertop, the sugar bowl, the refrigerator. She felt sad and sluggish. Jenny was sitting beside her on the couch, watching a SpongeBob marathon.

Sighing, April took her coffee to the kitchen window and stared out into the backyard. The grass was overgrown, the flower planter full of weeds. She needed to do some gardening. In a few hours the morning sun would burn through the marine layer, but right now the weather was cool enough for the task.

"Let's go outside," she said, clicking off the TV.

Jenny made a sound of protest, but her attention was easily diverted. "To play?"

"To work."

Jenny liked helping April in the garden. Excited, she leapt up from the couch and ran to her room to get dressed. She put on an orange T-shirt and pink shorts, old clothes that didn't matter. "Don't forget your shoes and socks," April said, ruffling her hair. Jenny would go barefoot all day if April let her.

April donned her own "play clothes," a pair of torn jeans and an old tank top. Tugging her hair into a ponytail, she went to the garage for her gardening tools.

Working outside felt therapeutic. She cut the grass with her old-fashioned push mower. The only tree in their backyard, a California pepper, also needed trimming. It offered a nice amount of shade and a sturdy limb for Jenny's swing, but the tiny yellow flowers attracted bees, and the shedding leaves created a lot of debris.

While April clipped the drooping branches, Jenny raked up the leaves. Together, they shoveled the green waste into a garbage bin. By the time April put on her gardening gloves to tackle the flower planter, the sun was high and hot overhead.

"Can I fill up the pool?" Jenny asked.

Using the back of her wrist, April pushed a lock of hair off her sweaty forehead. "Sure. Go put your suit on."

The kiddie pool was about four feet wide, just big enough for Jenny to stretch out in. At the end of the season, it was showing some wear and tear. Next summer April would have to buy the next size up.

April continued to pull weeds while Jenny rinsed the grit from the bottom of the pool and filled it with clean water. "How is everything at Consuela's house?" she asked. "Do you still like it there?"

"It's okay."

"Are the girls nice?"

"Yes. Well, Fabi pinched me yesterday."

April looked over her shoulder. "That's enough water," she said, turning off the spigot. "What did you do?"

"Nothing. It didn't hurt."

"You'd tell me if someone hurt you, wouldn't you?"

Jenny brought her beach toys to the pool. "Uh-huh."

April had asked the question before, when Jenny attended the on-campus day care. She'd also asked if Josefa ever spanked her or lost her temper. Jenny said no. April didn't want to dwell on the dark subject, but she felt compelled to bring it up on occasion.

Josefa had left April with a couple of inappropriate caregivers while she was growing up, including one of her loser boyfriends. April remembered agonizing over the decision to tell her mother what he'd done. Luckily, Josefa had taken April's word over his and thrown the sorry bastard out.

But the shame she'd felt hadn't left with him. It had eaten her up inside, convinced her that she'd invited his attention. The shame had made her vulnerable to more abuse. And, when Raul struck her for the first time, it had kept her quiet.

"You can tell me anything," April said.

"I miss Abuelita."

"So do I, *m'ija*."

"When will she come back?"

"I don't know. Maybe next summer."

Jenny started to chat about plans for her sixth birthday, which was ten months away. She wanted horse rides, and an inflatable jumper, and a giant chocolate cake. April turned back to the planter, smiling. "We can have the cake, for sure."

A few minutes later the doorbell rang.

"Can I get it?" Jenny asked.

April rose, dusting off the knees of her jeans. "No. I don't want you dripping water all over the floor."

"Okay." Manipulating the arm of her Little Mermaid doll, she waved goodbye.

Feeling a twinge of apprehension, April walked through the house, checking the peephole before she answered the door.

It was Noah.

She'd been thinking about him constantly, tortured by regrets. He'd treated her badly. She'd treated him worse. Then they'd—oh, God. He wasn't perfect, but he *was* good. And he'd break her heart if she let him.

His eyes traveled over her face, her gardening attire. "Hi."

She gave him a similar perusal. He was wearing jeans and a T-shirt, carrying a brown paper bag at his side. "Hi."

"I was a jerk to leave you like that the other night."

In her fantasies of this moment, he apologized and she slammed the door in his face. In reality, she left it open. "Jenny's in the pool," she said, glancing toward the backyard. "I have to watch her."

"Can I come in?"

"I guess."

He followed her out the back door, where Jenny greeted him with a delighted squeal. "Noah! I've been practicing the stuff you taught me. Look, I can float." She demonstrated as well as she could in the shallow water. "And blow bubbles!"

"Wow," he said, smiling at her. His eyes were brilliant, his hair dark gold in the sunlight. "You're like a dolphin in there. I hardly recognized you."

She made a squeaky noise and plunged underwater, inspired.

Noah returned his attention to April, lifting the bag he was carrying. "I brought you something."

"Is it lunch?"

He laughed, massaging the bridge of his nose. "No. Sorry."

Tugging off her gardening gloves, she sat down in a plastic lawn chair. He took the other, which looked too insubstantial for his size. Inside the bag there was a purple backpack. April pulled it out.

"That's for Jenny. She's starting kindergarten soon, right?"

"Right." April pictured her daughter wearing the backpack, disappearing into a crowd of students. She blinked the image away, disturbed.

"Can I try it on?" Jenny asked, scrambling out of the pool.

"If you dry off first."

Jenny let April give her a quick rubdown with a bath towel, and Noah helped her put the backpack on, adjusting the shoulder straps for her. "I want to look in the mirror," she said, her eyes bright.

April forced a smile. "Why don't you tell Noah thank you first?"

"Thanks, Noah!"

"You're welcome."

They both watched her run inside the house.

"You don't like it," he murmured.

Her throat closed up. "No, it's adorable. I'm just a little anxious about her going to school."

"Ah," he said, his expression softening. "She'll be fine."

April brought the second package out of the bag. This one felt heavier. Wrapped in tissue paper was a sleek leather briefcase. It was sturdy and professional-looking, but it also managed to appear stylish and feminine.

"Do you already have one?"

"No," she said, stifling the urge to hug it.

"You'll need one for work or classes."

She checked the inside liner. "This looks expensive."

"Not really. My sister helped me find it. She has good taste."

A white card accompanied the briefcase. His elegant scrawl read, *I'm sorry. If you don't accept my apology, please accept this. Love, Noah.*

Love.

She ventured a glance at him. He was gauging her reaction. Everything depended on this moment—saying yes meant accepting his apology, the gift, maybe even his heart.

April wasn't ready to do that.

He'd walked out on her the other night. He'd said his unit wouldn't approve of him dating a woman with gang connections. They had some serious issues to discuss before she'd decide to take a chance on him again.

"What about your job?" she asked, replacing the briefcase.

"I spoke to one of my bosses. My prospective boss, actually. Detective Santiago. He was fine with it."

"And your partner?"

His eyes darkened. "Forget him. I don't care what he thinks."

Frowning, she looked away. She didn't want to create conflict between him and Shanley. His workday was already fraught with danger.

She was also troubled by how quickly he'd changed his mind about their relationship. He expected to waltz back into her life, sweep her off her feet, and make everything better with a romantic gesture.

It wasn't that easy.

He took her hand in his. "I don't care what anyone thinks, April. I want to be with you. We should probably keep this quiet, at least until the case wraps. But I can't stay away, not even for a little while."

She moistened her lips, hesitant.

Jenny came barreling out of the house, oblivious to their heartache. "Push me, Noah," she said, running toward her swing.

He rose to his feet, giving April a plaintive look.

She watched him push her daughter higher and higher. Jenny's face showed the unrestrained joy only children could feel.

Tears blurred April's vision.

Noah wasn't perfect, but he was still too good to be true. He was too sincere, too giving, too handsome, too honest. He also had a too-easy way with women. She supposed he'd settle down someday, but she doubted it would be with her.

She'd rather he moved on now, before she got attached.

Before *Jenny* got attached.

The phone rang, interrupting her thoughts. Noah continued to push Jenny on the swing, so April went to answer it.

"Hello?"

"Miss Ortiz?"

"Yes."

"This is John Sullivan, the warden at Donovan State Correctional Facility. I have some bad news."

Her stomach twisted with unease. "About what?"

"One of our inmates, Raul Hernandez, passed away last night."

April felt the phone slide out of her slack hand. It bounced on the linoleum. She knelt to pick it up.

"Ma'am?"

"Wh-what did he die of?"

The warden cleared his throat. "There are no obvious injuries. We suspect drug usage. Sometimes inmates are able to smuggle in controlled substances."

"Oh, my God," she whispered.

"An autopsy is being performed. We'll let you know the results. Jennifer Ortiz is listed as the recipient of his effects."

"That's my daughter."

"Yes, ma'am. I've also contacted Eric Hernandez, his next of kin. He'll be taking care of the funeral arrangements."

She nodded mutely.

"I'm sorry for your loss."

The platitude seemed incongruous with the situation. Raul's death—a loss? Feeling numb, she murmured "thank you" and hung up.

Noah stood in the doorway. "Are you all right?"

"Yes," she said, glancing past him. Jenny was still on her swing. Although she needed help to get going, the little girl could pump her legs and keep swinging for a long while. "That was the warden from Donovan Prison. Raul died."

His gaze sharpened. "Of what?"

"Drugs, they think."

He relaxed some, dropping the cop attitude. "I'm sorry."

"I'm not."

He wrapped his arms around her, comforting instead of judging. After a brief hesitation, she lifted her hands to his sides, returning the embrace. "The last time I saw him, he'd been up for days on crystal meth. He came to the house at three A.M., banging on the door, demanding to see Jenny. I didn't let him in."

He stroked her back, listening.

April felt tears leak out of her eyes, because the memory was excruciating. "He wanted to take her away. He started circling the house, tapping on the windows. Saying he was going to shoot the door down. I called the police."

"Good."

"It took them forever to get here. My mom wasn't home. We hid in Jenny's closet until they came. I was terrified."

"Who was the arresting officer?"

"Shanley. But no arrest was made. Raul was gone by the time he arrived. He told me to get a restraining order and left."

Noah cursed his partner fluently.

"Raul was arrested for armed robbery a few weeks

later. I hoped he would turn his life around in prison. Get sober, for Jenny's sake. Obviously, he didn't." She pressed her face to his shirt. "Sometimes he sent her letters. Birthday cards. I don't think she remembers much about that night, because she loved him. I couldn't bear to tell her that her father was a . . . horrible person. She's half him, so what does that make her?"

"A great kid. Beautiful and kind, just like you."

"I'm glad he's dead," she said, lifting her head. "I hated Raul, and I'm glad he's dead."

"Who's dead?"

April gasped, turning to see Jenny in the doorway.

"Are you talking about my daddy?" she asked, her eyes filling with tears.

Horrified by what her daughter had overheard, April rushed toward her. "Honey—"

"I knew you hated him!" she accused, backing up a few steps. "You sent him away. He wanted to see me, to give me presents and throw me a big birthday party, and you locked me in the closet."

April's mouth dropped open. She knelt in front of her daughter, holding her upper arms. "That is *not* what happened."

Jenny twisted out of her grasp. "You sent him away! Now he's dead, and I'll never see him again. I hate you!"

April hugged her, sobbing out loud.

Jenny screamed and kicked. "You sent Abuelita away, too. Why are you so mean? You send everyone away to die."

Noah stepped between them, trying to defuse the situation. Jenny started pummeling him with her fists.

"I hate you, too! You're not my daddy! I want my daddy!"

There was a muted knock at the front door, and Eric let himself in. The instant Jenny saw him, she held out her arms. "I want Eric!"

He came forward, extracting her from Noah easily. She clung to his neck and wrapped her legs around him, hugging him with her entire body. "I'm here," he said, his voice rough. "I'm here now. Everything will be fine."

Jenny pressed her face to his neck and bawled.

Eric looked from Noah to April. Behind the pain in his expression, there was curiosity and a little surprise. "I'll take her to her room."

April nodded her permission. With one last glance at Noah, Eric carried Jenny to her bedroom, shutting the door.

Noah looked . . . flattened. The other night, April had chosen Eric over him, in effect. Now Jenny had done the same.

Although April knew he felt awful, she was too traumatized to reach out to him. In front of Jenny, she'd said she hated Raul. She'd said she was glad he was dead. Jenny would never forgive her.

She was the worst mother in the world.

Sinking to the floor, she covered her face with her hands and cried. When Noah touched her shoulder, she jerked away, burying her head in her arms. She didn't deserve his sympathy. She didn't deserve *him*.

"Please," she said, aching with emptiness. "Leave me alone."

And, after a long, painful moment, he did.

21

Eric held Jenny until she fell asleep.

When her breathing slowed, he sat up, smooing the damp hair away from her brow. She had a le from Raul crumpled in her half-closed fist. Before cried herself to sleep, she'd asked Eric to read all cards her father had sent. There were pitifully few.

Jenny had saved his correspondence in her drawer. There were two birthday cards, a Christr card, and some rambling letters. Raul's messages w vague but positive. *Best wishes, take care, thinking you.* There were no apologies, no regrets.

Even to Eric, Raul had never admitted to any wro doing. Raul was misunderstood, a product of streets, a victim of the system.

Of course Jenny felt confused. She didn't really kn her father or understand what he'd done to April. It only natural that she blamed her mother for "send him away." Later in life, Jenny would be grateful for mother's protection. Now there was no use telling the truth about Raul.

Her father was an abuser, a rapist, a drug addict, a criminal.

"Did my daddy love me?" she'd asked, her voice breaking.

"Very much," Eric had answered, getting a little choked up himself. "And your mom loves you. And I love you."

She'd hugged him closer. "I love you, too."

Wiping the tears from his eyes, Eric gathered up the letters and put them back in the drawer. There was one he hadn't noticed before, set apart from the others. It said, *Have fun at Wave City! Love, Meghan.*

He closed the drawer quietly, careful not to wake her as he let himself out.

April was reclining on the couch, a diet soda in one hand, a folded dish towel over her eyes. At her feet there was a large brown gift bag. Officer Young was gone. Eric hoped he wouldn't come back in uniform.

She took the towel away from her face. "How is she?"

"Fine," he said, shoving his hands into his pockets. "Asleep."

"She overheard me say I'm glad he's dead."

Eric wasn't surprised by the sentiment, although he didn't share it. He wished he could. He'd have welcomed some relief. "She'll forgive you."

"Someday I'll have to tell her what he did."

"Wait. It's hard for a kid to grow up knowing their dad is a monster."

April knew he was speaking from experience. She stared up at him in sympathy. "I'm sorry you had to go through that."

Eric didn't want to talk about it. He sat down on the

couch next to her, doing a quick survey of her appearance. The knees of her jeans were dirty, her eyes were swollen from crying, and she had leaves in her hair. She looked totally wiped out. Eric wondered if Meghan's brother was responsible for some of her distress.

A couple of weeks ago she said she'd given a tip to a cop—Young, he surmised.

"So, what's up with you and Mr. Patrol Officer? Have you two been rolling around in the backyard together?"

"Of course not," she said, running a hand through her hair. But her eyes drifted toward the kitchen as she tidied her ponytail.

Eric followed her gaze. "On the dinner table?"

She flushed with guilt, though he'd been joking.

"Well, damn," he said, getting the picture. As far as he knew, April hadn't let a man near her since Raul. Meghan's brother must have the magic touch.

She nibbled on her lower lip. "Do you mind?"

"Why would I mind?"

"Because of Raul."

"I never thought you'd get back with him. I was afraid you'd be scared of men forever because of what he did, so I'm glad you're seeing someone. You should be happy." He frowned at her tearstained countenance. "Are you?"

Sighing, she reached into the gift bag at her feet. "He gave me this."

Eric inspected the briefcase, impressed. It was a thoughtful, expensive purchase, suggesting they already knew each other well. He read the card. "What's he sorry about? Did he treat you wrong?"

She hesitated. "We had a fight. We were . . . both wrong."

He considered the way Young had looked when Eric walked in, as if his entire world had been disrupted. "Is he in love with you?"

Her face crumpled in dismay.

"Why are you so sad?"

"I don't know what to do!"

"Well, if you're not that into him—"

"I'm into him," she said, miserable.

"Then what's the problem? Not the gift, I assume."

"What's the problem? He's a cop, Eric. We're from two different worlds. He doesn't understand . . . hard times."

"You think he'll judge you?"

She shrugged, looking away. "I've made some really bad choices. He's probably never even had a misstep."

Eric thought April was being too critical of herself, but he could sympathize with her situation. He knew damned well that he wasn't good enough for Meghan. Compared to April's, his bad choices were epic.

"How could we possibly make it work?" she asked.

"You don't have to marry him, April. It's okay to have fun."

She was silent for a moment. "He asked me if you sold drugs."

Eric's stomach sank. "What did you say?"

"That I didn't know."

"Don't lie for me. Please. I don't want you to."

"Are you in some kind of trouble?"

He stood, pacing the living room.

"Get out of the gang," she pleaded, crushing a wad of

tissues in her fist. "Now, before it's too late. I can't bea
the thought of you ending up in jail. Or worse."

"I'm working on it, okay? Did he say anything abou
me and Meghan?"

"Meghan?"

"His sister."

Her mouth went slack. "No. Eric—you didn't."

He refused to regret his actions. Although he'∂
promised not to touch Meghan, he wasn't sorry he had
He'd do it again if he got the chance. Hell was worth it

"You *did*. Are you crazy?"

"He's going to kill me," Eric said. "Arrest me and then
kill me."

"What can I do?"

"Ask him to give me more time. I'm trying to ge
some information for him. I have to go do that righ
now, actually."

She rose to see him out. "Be careful."

On the front step, he paused. "Did the warden tel
you what caused Raul's death?"

"Drugs, they think."

Eric nodded. He'd been told the same thing. "I gav
him money. Two nights ago."

April reached up, touching his jaw. Forcing him t∘
meet her eyes. "Don't you dare blame yourself. It's no
your fault."

He cleared his throat, trying to believe her. When sh
pressed her lips to his cheek, he noticed a white Mont∘
Carlo cruise by, slowing at the curb. There was a gu
with a shaved head in the passenger seat. Eric recog
nized him from the taco shop and knew immediatel
that this was Oscar Reyes.

"Go inside," he murmured.

She glanced past him. "Eric—"

"Go!"

Perhaps because of Jenny, she didn't argue further or ask him to come back in with her. Eric strode toward his Chevelle, which was parked down the street, and gestured for Oscar's crew to follow. His heart hammered against his chest as he closed the distance.

When they were no longer in front of April's house, and his car was nearby, Eric approached the Monte Carlo's passenger side. There were three men in the vehicle, all Eastside members. The one in the backseat had a 9mm, holding it low.

Eric kept his focus on Oscar. *"Qué honda?"*

Surprise flickered in Oscar's eyes. Maybe he hadn't expected Eric to be so straight up. "You owe me a car, *ese.*"

Eric didn't ask how he knew. The street had big ears. He also didn't bother to explain that Junior had been trying to avenge his sister or that Eric had tried to stop him. Nothing mattered to men like this except action.

Talk was cheap.

"Your girlfriend has a nice ass," the driver said, glancing toward April's house. "I think I'll come back and tap it later."

Eric's jaw tightened. *"Déjala en paz.* She's not my girlfriend."

"Oh, sorry. Your *puta,* I mean."

He forced his attention back to Oscar. "Let's bury this."

"How about we bury *you*?" he replied, his lips curling into a sneer.

Eric had his back pressed against the wall. They were threatening April, threatening him. If he didn't settle his debt, they might come after her.

"Brown Field, tomorrow night," Oscar offered, a glint in his eyes. "Just you and me, mano a mano."

Eric didn't want to fight, but he had no other choice. "If I win, I walk away. It's over."

"And if I win?"

He jerked his chin toward the Chevelle. His pride and joy. His only asset. "She's yours."

Oscar laughed, revealing a gold cap on one of his incisors. "They're going to scrape little pieces of you off the ground when I'm done."

Eric knew the matchup was uneven. Oscar outweighed him by at least forty pounds, and he was solidly built. "Then you have nothing to lose."

"*Bueno,*" Oscar said, accepting the terms. He slapped his hand against the passenger door, indicating that he was ready to go, and the driver stepped on the gas.

Eric watched the car speed away. He supposed he could have just handed over the keys and been done with it. But in order to survive in the barrio, a man had to be able to hold his head high. Sometimes he had to take a beating.

He'd made a fair deal.

Cursing under his breath, he climbed into his Chevelle and started the engine. He merged onto the freeway and headed east, his mind racing. He had a shitload of things to do before he met Oscar tomorrow night.

At San Diego County Jail, he waited more than an hour to see Tony Castillo, sweating bullets the entire time. If his name was flagged, he'd become a guest of the facility rather than a visitor. Eric must not have been listed as a person of interest, though, because he was led back to the visiting room without incident. He'd been there before. Unlike the communal area at Donovan, this space had Plexiglas dividers and telephone head-sets.

Tony wasn't happy to see him. He'd kept his mouth shut about Eric for a reason. If he had no trafficking partner, there was no one to pit against him, and he had a much better chance of beating the charge.

"What the fuck are you doing here?"

Eric didn't take the attitude personally. "I need to talk to you."

"We have nothing to talk about."

"Raul's dead."

Tony flinched. For the first time in Eric's recent memory, Tony looked sober. And sad. Maybe he was still grieving for Lola. "I'm sorry," he muttered, sounding sincere. He and Raul had been best friends.

Eric had known Tony most of his life. Like Raul, Tony was a drug addict and a thug. Not exactly a great role model. But there was a small glimmer of humanity in him, Eric suspected. "We're all fucked," he said flatly. "Me, you, Junior. But I thought of a way out."

"What?"

"We talk about the girl. From that night."

Tony leaned back in his chair. "No. Hell, no." His eyes darted around, checking the cameras that were probably recording their conversation. "I don't know what the fuck you're talking about. What night?"

"We didn't do anything wrong."

"You mean *you* didn't do anything wrong."

"Don't you want to make a deal? His name, in exchange for your freedom. At the very least, you'll be looking at a reduced charge."

Tony's mouth thinned. He shook his head, refusing to consider it. "I don't know what you're talking about."

"He choked her, man. Maybe he's the same one who did Lola."

"No," Tony whispered, his eyes swimming with tears.

"We can go to the cops, explain what happened. I know they'll take it seriously, do an investigation and all that. They might even catch the killer, because of us. We could do the right thing. For once."

Tony wiped his eyes with the hem of his shirt, letting out a harsh laugh. "No cop in the world would touch this."

"Why?"

"Because Raul took his name to the grave. I heard him speak of that guy only one time. You know what he called him?"

"What?"

"*El patrullero.*"

Patrol officer.

Noah had a couple of hours to kill before his shift started, and he was too restless to spend them at home.

Meghan had been a little less distant lately. He suspected she was still seeing Eric, but he didn't want to know for sure. He was damned tired of getting tossed aside for that wall-painting, drug-dealing little bastard.

His sister preferred Eric's company to his. April

would protect Eric at all costs. Jenny had screamed for Eric to hold her.

Everyone loved *Eric*.

Noah had left April's house with his spirits low. He'd never had a woman cut him off at the knees so completely. This was why he dated women with no baggage: amicable breakups. There were no emotional scenes, no groveling.

There was no spur-of-the-moment sex against the refrigerator, either.

"Damn it," he groaned, raking a hand through his hair. On impulse, he took the next freeway exit, heading to Patrick's house. He had a few questions to ask and some aggressions to work out. Maybe he just needed to talk to someone, too.

Despite their last argument, Noah still considered Patrick a friend.

Patrick's house looked the same as always. His front yard was clipped, green, precise. The *Aurora Lee,* his fishing boat, gleamed in the noonday sun. Noah parked at the curb and strode up the sidewalk, feeling surly.

Patrick answered the door in the same mood. He was wearing flannel pajama pants and a gaping robe. His eyes were bloodshot, and he smelled like booze.

"Can I come in?" Noah asked.

"Suit yourself."

The interior of the house wasn't quite as tidy as the outside. It was dark and depressing. The curtains in the living room were tightly drawn. There was a faint, musty odor Noah associated with old men. A mixture of unwashed skin and mothballs.

He didn't feel like sitting down.

"Want a beer?"

"No. I have to work."

Patrick snorted. He grabbed himself a can, popped it open, and sat down on his recliner. Taking a sip, he stared at the blank television screen.

"I had a talk with Santiago yesterday."

He kept drinking and staring.

"He said you asked him to turn down my application."

Patrick leaned back in his chair. "So?"

"Do you have a reason for going out of your way to fuck me over," Noah asked quietly, "other than not wanting the hassle of training a new partner before you retire?"

He pointed a thick finger at Noah. "My recommendation was based on your performance, short pants. You're not tough enough for homicide."

"Because I'm not a racist asshole like you?"

Patrick scowled. "You think all these Mexi kids are misguided—"

"They are."

"Even the one who pulled a gun on you?"

"An isolated incident," Noah said. "Why would I judge an entire group of people based on the actions of one?"

"You're going to get yourself killed," he yelled, his voice breaking. "I asked Santiago to pass you over for your own good. Because I care about you, you shithead." He took another swig of beer, chagrined by his emotional outburst. "I think you need a few more years on patrol. You're too trusting."

Noah sank down on a brown wool couch, feeling

some of his anger seep away. If Patrick had done what he thought was right, Noah couldn't fault him for it. On the other hand, Patrick's judgment was biased. He assumed every kid on the street was a threat and every woman a whore. He'd lost his ability to relate to honest, law-abiding citizens.

How could a cop protect and serve a community he hated?

Noah wished Patrick was more like Santiago. Tough but fair. Kind, even. Although they'd spoken only a handful of times, Noah respected his prospective boss much more than his current partner.

"I told Santiago about April. He didn't seem to think it was a problem."

"Maybe he's setting you up."

"Why would he do that?"

Patrick made a sour face. "To have a convenient fall guy when the investigation goes nowhere. Don't you think it's odd that he assigned two gang-unit cops so much responsibility in a high-profile case?"

"The department is shorthanded. And . . . he thinks I have good instincts."

Patrick smirked drunkenly. "Good instincts? You wouldn't know a perp if he was sitting right in front of you."

Noah's patience expired. "What's your real beef with Santiago? Did he call you out on your prejudices, when the two of you were partners? Admit it—you can't stand to see a brown-skinned man move up in the ranks."

Patrick shook his head, drinking more beer. "I didn't want that job, anyway."

"That's it," Noah said, astounded. "You both applied to homicide at the same time, and he was promoted instead of you."

"Only because I'm white."

"You're pathetic."

With a strangled sound of rage, Patrick lumbered to his feet. Alcohol made him slow, but it didn't rob his strength. He grabbed Noah by the front of his shirt, drawing back his meaty arm to take a swing.

Dodging the clumsy blow, Noah shoved him off.

Patrick stumbled back into his chair. His beer can tipped over, its contents fizzing on the blue carpet.

"If you ever try that again, I'll request reassignment."

"Don't bother," Patrick muttered, out of breath. "I resigned."

Noah stared back at him in disgust. He couldn't respect a man who refused to own up to his mistakes. According to Patrick, his ethnicity, not his attitude, had kept him from succeeding. His "cheating, no-good" wife had left him.

Now he had nothing. No career, no family. Just a dark, empty house and a fishing boat named after a woman he let get away.

"I'm sorry it ended like this," Noah said, and let himself out.

Noah's patrol shift dragged that evening. He tried not to replay the emotional scenes between April and him, or his caustic argument with Patrick.

An impromptu DUI arrest ate up only half the night. Santiago's team had been consulting with the FBI and following some new leads, but they weren't keeping Noah in the loop. The cold-case file he'd been studying offered little information. Although the body was in an advanced state of decomposition when it was found eight years ago, swabs had been taken and sent to the crime lab for DNA analysis.

The file showed no record of the results.

Noah left a voice-mail message at the lab, wondering if there had been a mix-up with the paperwork.

Both of the recent victims had tested negative for DNA. Using a condom might be part of the killer's m.o. If Noah could find another connection, linking the cold case to the current murders, he'd have a great lead.

When his shift was over, he showered and changed into his street clothes, thinking about April. When he'd left her, she was hurting. That didn't sit well with him. He decided to stop by her house again on his way home.

He wanted another chance to win her over.

Thankfully, she was home and awake. She answered the door in pinstriped pajama bottoms and a ribbed tank top. Although she wasn't wearing a bra, and an inch of smooth belly was visible above the waistband of her pajamas, he was riveted by her face. Clear of makeup, she was breathtaking.

Not that he didn't like her smoky eyes and painted lips. But this stripped-bare April appealed to him on a deeper level.

She stepped aside, letting him in.

"You didn't work tonight?"

"No. I wanted to be here for Jenny."

"How is she?"

"Distraught," she said, sitting down on the couch. "It took her a long time to fall asleep." Tucking her legs under her bottom, she picked up a steaming mug from the end table, wrapping her hands around its warmth.

He sat down next to her, resting his arm on the back of the couch. "How are you?"

She took a sip of tea, her brows lifting. "Me? I'm okay."

Noah smiled at her surprised expression. He supposed that she was so used to taking care of others and considering their needs that she rarely thought of her own.

"My father died when I was two," she said after a pause. "I never knew him. *Mamá* didn't talk about him at all, so I created this character in my head. Someone who walked me to school and read me bedtime stories. It was silly."

"No," he said.

"I should have expected Jenny to do the same. To imagine a kinder, gentler Raul. It's going to crush her to find out the truth, but I have to tell her someday. I want her to know what happened, to protect her from making the same mistakes."

Noah wondered if he'd ever faced such a difficult decision. Keeping Meghan's secret came close.

"What's your dad like?" she asked.

He didn't want to give a pat answer, so he replied honestly. "Difficult," he said. "Distant."

"Did he read bedtime stories?"

"No. Most of his time was spent on church business and sermons. But he did throw the baseball at me every once in a while."

"That sounds nice."

He shrugged. "I remember one day he was hitting grounders for me in the backyard. I was wearing my favorite shirt, and I didn't want to get it dirty because I was going to the movies with Jamie Simpson afterward."

"Jamie Simpson," she scoffed, taking another sip of tea. "How old were you?"

"Thirteen, I think. Anyway, he kept hitting them out of my range, telling me to quit whining and run hard. I dove for the next ball." He showed her the thin scar on his elbow. "Ten stitches. Hit a rock."

"Did he feel bad?"

"Hell, no. He laughed and said, 'Atta boy.'"

"Was your mom upset?"

"Sure. I ruined a new shirt."

"Hmm. Are you trying to say that your childhood wasn't perfect?"

"It was pretty good," he allowed. "Better than a lot of kids get."

April had obviously been one of the unlucky ones, but she didn't admit that, and he didn't press her for details.

He hadn't come here to make her cry again.

They fell into an awkward silence. Noah didn't know what else to say. He'd apologized and brought gifts. He wanted to be with her, desperately, but she seemed more reluctant than ever to take a chance on the relationship.

While he studied her, wishing she'd give him another shot, she stared back at him, moistening her lips.

She had the sexiest mouth he'd ever seen.

"I forgot something earlier," he decided.

She set her tea aside. "The briefcase? I'll get it."

"No," he said, reaching out to cup her face. He slid his hand along the side of her neck, his thumb brushing her cheek. Maybe it was cheating to kiss her when she was vulnerable. But he would do anything to make her his again. "This."

He lowered his head, covering her mouth with his.

She tasted hot and sweet, like honey. Her lips trembled, parting for his tongue, and he swept inside, coaxing her. Coercing her. She lifted her hands to his hair, threading her fingers through it, and he moved closer, deepening the kiss.

Then she placed her hands on his chest, halting his progress. "Is that all you forgot?"

His gaze dropped to her lips. They were swollen from kissing. He remembered what she'd whispered in his ear the other night and felt heat pool in his groin. "I was hoping you'd ask me for another favor before I left."

Her eyes darkened. "You liked that?"

"Yes," he said in a hoarse voice, dragging her hand to his lap. He shaped her palm over his erection, showing her how much he liked it.

She trailed her fingertips along his fly, squeezing him firmly.

With a groan, he kissed her again, tasting every inch of her delicious mouth. When they came up for air, she said, "My request is a little different this time."

As long as it required use of her bedroom, he was game. "I can't wait to hear it."

She touched her lips to his ear. "Make love to me."

Noah went stock-still and stone-hard. He didn't

know how any command could be sexier than "fuck me." Somehow, this one was. She was giving him permission to take his time, to make it meaningful.

He couldn't wait to do her bidding.

Picking her up off the couch, he carried her into the bedroom, tossing her on the mattress. A lamp on the nightstand lent the space a warm glow. "Lock the door," she said, tugging off her tank top.

He did, pulling his shirt over his head.

In the next instant, her lush body was stretched out beneath his. She wrapped her legs around his waist and arched her back, rubbing her stiff nipples against his bare chest. Shaking with anticipation, he took her mouth again. He molded his hands over her bottom, holding her in place for his thrusts.

It occurred to him that he was close to losing his control. He'd never wanted a woman with such intensity, and it drove him right to the edge. The urge to tear her pants off and bury himself in her was hard to resist.

He shifted his weight to the side, trying to set a slower pace. Moving his mouth from hers, he kissed his way down her body. His lips touched the hollow of her throat, her collarbone, the inner curves of her breasts, her pouting nipples. At her sleek belly he paused, nuzzling her navel. Untying the drawstring at her waist, he tugged her pajamas down her hips.

Her panties were very white and very brief. The scrap of lace cupped her femininity, framing the juncture of her thighs.

Noah's breath caught in his throat.

He kissed the front of her panties, feeling her heat

against his lips. He looked up at her, gauging her rea‐
tion. "Any . . . other requests?"

"That," she said.

He stripped her panties off. Her naked body was
lovely, he just wanted to stare at it. Although his co
was straining against his fly, throbbing for attention,
couldn't resist drawing out this moment.

Putting his hands on her hips, he brought her to
edge of the bed.

She sat up. "Wh-what are you doing?"

He slid to his knees on the hardwood floor a
nudged her thighs apart with his hands. She was gl
tening, wet for him, her sex pouty and swollen. Gla
ing over his shoulder, he noted that the vanity mir
caught her reflection.

Her lips parted as their eyes met.

The position fulfilled him in a way he couldn't
plain. She was sitting up, legs spread, her sweet lit
pussy exposed for them both to see. He pictured
watching him kiss her there and groaned out loud.

He'd never been so aroused in his life.

Bending his head, he placed his open mouth agai
her quivering inner thigh. When she moaned, beggi
for more, he tasted her slit, slipping his tongue insi
She fisted her hands in the comforter, gasping.

He stopped teasing and settled his mouth on her
toris, sucking gently. When she began to tremble,
backed off, because he wanted to make it last. Looki
in the mirror again, he saw that her head was thro
back, her nipples jutting forth. He slid two fingers
side her, working them in and out. She was so hot.

"Please."

He glanced up at her face. "Please what?"

"Lick me."

Holding her gaze, he lowered his head again, flicking his tongue over her clit. She cried out, threading her fingers through his hair and pressing herself harder against his mouth. He gave her what she wanted, in bold strokes. Her moisture slicked his fingers. He felt her shivering tension, her exquisite tightness.

With a hoarse scream, she went over the edge, locking his head between her thighs and clutching his hair, convulsing with pleasure. When the earthquake was over, she fell back on the bed, panting.

He wiped his mouth and lay down beside her, supremely self-satisfied. His cock felt differently, but he ignored it.

She murmured something unintelligible, snuggling closer to him.

Although his body ached for release, it seemed more important to let her rest. For the first time in his life, he wasn't concerned with his own needs at all. He wanted to give her everything, earn her trust, win her heart.

Content to wait, he listened to her soft breathing as she fell asleep.

22

April awoke with a start, instantly alert.

The room was blush with predawn light. She slept only a few hours, and it wasn't yet time to get u Sometime last night Noah must have turned off t lamp and covered her with a soft blanket.

But he hadn't left.

The bed was warm from his body.

Clutching the blanket to her chest, she glanced ov her shoulder. He was lying on his back, eyes closed. O arm was tucked behind his head, revealing a dark tuft hair underneath. The other rested on his flat abdome

He was still wearing jeans. His fly was undone, as he'd needed to make things comfortable down the before he fell asleep. A flush rose to her cheeks as she r membered the state she'd left him in. Cupping a ha over her mouth, she stared at the vanity mirror.

Oh my God.

Heart pounding, she eased off the mattress. Aba doning his warmth, and the cozy blanket, she tipto across the room, naked. Grabbing a short robe off t hook by the door, she slipped outside and walked down the hall.

Jenny's door was shut. April normally left it open, but she'd closed it before she let Noah in last night. She turned the knob quietly, peeking inside.

Her daughter was sound asleep, snug as a bug, hugging Lalo.

April closed the door again, smiling. She ducked into the bathroom for a quick toilette. After using the facilities and checking her reflection in the mirror, she went to the kitchen for a glass of water.

They had at least an hour before Jenny woke up.

Sneaking back into her bedroom, she locked the door behind her. Noah was still asleep. She set her glass of water on the nightstand and stretched out on the bed next to him, drinking in his beauty. With his face relaxed, and his hair sticking up, he was irresistibly handsome. A shadow of beard stubble covered his angular jaw. Although she'd seen him shirtless several times now, she found her gaze lingering on his bare chest.

He was taut and toned, more lean than muscle-bound. With his right arm bent behind his head, his biceps bulged. There was something fascinating about his armpit hair. It was several shades darker than his golden head.

Her eyes drifted lower, to the hand that lay across his abdomen. There was more hair there, swirling around his belly button. Moistening her lips, she stared at his open fly. A pair of blue boxer shorts obstructed her view.

She wanted to tug down the waistband and see the rest.

Closing her eyes, she pondered her next step. Last night she'd broken her rule about having a man in her bedroom while Jenny was home. She definitely had to get him out of here before Jenny woke up.

Beyond that, what was she doing? She hadn't really accepted his gift, or his apology. But she'd accepted his tongue between her legs. Her cheeks heated as she pictured her sultry expression in the mirror. She'd watched him go down on her!

And she was more aroused by the memory than ashamed. She was very aware of her naked body beneath the silky fabric of her robe. Her nipples pebbled, and a sweet ache began to throb at the juncture of her thighs.

Maybe she moaned out loud, because he stirred, sitting up.

She looked into his startled blue eyes, her throat going dry. Stalling for time, she drank a sip of water.

He gestured for it, and she handed him the glass, watching him take a few long swallows. As soon as she replaced the glass on the nightstand, he reached for her. Their mouths were cool from the water, but for only a second.

He buried his hand in her hair, kissing her deeply. She wrapped her arms around his neck and pressed her breasts to his chest, squirming against him.

"Should I leave?" he asked, between kisses.

She glanced at the locked door. "We have to be quiet."

Nodding eagerly, he kissed her again, his hands sliding over her bottom. When he found it bare beneath her robe, he made a growl of approval, squeezing her supple flesh.

"Wait," she whispered, putting her hands on his shoulders and giving him a light shove. "I think I owe you a favor."

After a brief hesitation, he lay back, resting his weight on his elbows.

April felt a thrill she'd never known before. He was letting her call the shots. It was unbearably exciting.

She sat up, pushing the robe off her shoulders. His gaze darkened as he stared at her exposed breasts, her stiff nipples. Continuing the show, she untied the sash at her waist, tossing the robe aside.

His eyes devoured her, lingering at the apex of her thighs. She noted the outline of his erection beneath his blue boxer shorts, the tension in his stomach muscles, and his flexing hands at his sides.

She cupped her breasts, pushing them together.

His throat worked while he watched her touch herself. He looked as if he wanted to pounce on her, but he didn't. She admired his control.

Teasing him further, she smoothed her hand down her belly. Opening her thighs for him, she dipped one finger inside.

He let his head fall back against the pillow, groaning.

She brought the finger to her lips. "Shh."

That must have been his breaking point, because he kicked off his jeans and boxer shorts, impatient.

Her mouth went slack as she stared at his jutting erection. It was very thick.

Holding her gaze, he wrapped her hand around him in a tight grip. She pumped him in her fist, marveling at the sight. When a bead of moisture appeared at the tip, she leaned forward, licking the salty drop. He inhaled sharply, cupping his hand behind her head. Although he didn't push her, she knew what he wanted. Her dark hair spilled across his thighs as she closed her mouth around him. Hollowing her cheeks, she drew him deep, watching his face while she sucked and stroked him.

Receiving oral sex was unfamiliar territory for her. This, she knew. And with Noah, she actually enjoyed it.

She wanted to blow him away.

He didn't let her.

Just when she was really getting into it, making throaty sounds of pleasure, he threaded his hand through her hair and pulled her head up.

Raul had never done that, either.

"I love your mouth," he murmured, kissing it.

"Mmm. I like yours, too."

He gave her bottom a light spank. "There's a condom in my pocket."

She crawled to the side of the bed and reached for his jeans, finding the square package. It took her at least a minute to put the condom on him, and she dragged the process out. When she was finished, she cradled his testicles in her palm, testing their weight.

Making a strangled sound, he grabbed her by the upper arms and moved over her, parting her legs with his thigh. In the next breath, he was inside her.

April gasped, clinging to his shoulders. This time, her body accepted him easily. They were a perfect fit.

"You're so wet," he panted. "I'm not going to last."

She writhed underneath him, restless. "Just do it."

He did.

Withdrawing almost all the way, he surged forward, driving deep, filling her to the hilt. The bedsprings creaked under their combined weight and she cried out in pleasure, digging her nails into his skin.

"Quiet," he reminded her, glancing at the door.

"More," she moaned, wrapping her legs around his waist.

With a low groan, he changed positions, bringing her on top. Too enthralled to protest, she lifted herself up and slid back down his entire length, seating herself fully. The bedsprings made less noise, but the sensation was just as intense.

She impaled herself on him again and again, shivering with pleasure. He studied her motions through half-lidded eyes, tracing the curve of her bottom, squeezing her waist. When he pinched her stiff nipples, applying gentle pressure, her hips bucked forward.

"Oh, God," she said.

Glancing down at the juncture of their bodies, he licked his thumb. Her slick, sensitive flesh was stretched around his thick base, her moisture making him wet. "Say something in Spanish."

She blurted out the first phrase that came to mind, desperate for him to continue. The instant he placed his thumb over her clit, she started to come. Her inner muscles clenched around him and she sagged forward, biting back a scream of pleasure. He shoved his hand in her hair and brought her mouth down to his, smothering both their cries while his cock jerked and pulsed inside her.

Totally spent, she collapsed against his chest.

For several languid moments, he stroked her tangled

hair, trailing his fingertips over her naked back. "So . . . you want me to fuck you a thousand times?"

She lifted her head. "What?"

"That's what you said."

Giggling helplessly, she said, "I didn't know you understood Spanish."

"Well, I do. And I'm holding you to it."

She slid off him, still laughing, and rolled over to grab the wastebasket beside the bed. "Here," she said, passing it to him so he could dispose of the condom. When that was done, he pulled her into his arms, spoon-style, and covered them both with the blanket.

"Tell me more about Cedar Glen," she said, snuggling into him.

"It's a typical small town in the mountains. Picturesque . . . boring."

"Sounds nice."

"I'll take you there," he promised.

"Really?"

"Sure. I always go back for Thanksgiving and Christmas. Sometimes a week in the summer, too."

"You'd introduce me to your parents?"

"Of course. But we could just see the sights, if you'd rather. The lake has a designated swimming area, and the ski slopes open when it snows."

"I've never been skiing," she mused.

"I have to warn you, my parents are very old-fashioned. They won't let us stay in the same room."

"How do you know?"

He didn't answer right away.

"How many other girls have you brought home?"

"A few," he admitted.

"What happened to them?"

"Nothing, really. They just . . . weren't you."

She tensed at the simple statement, glancing over her shoulder at him. As always, he was relaxed, sincere, completely unguarded. April wondered what it was like to be so fearless with affection. To leap without looking.

"You've had a lot of girlfriends," she surmised, settling against him.

"Not that many."

"Anyone serious?"

He deliberated for a minute. "I wanted to be serious with a couple of them. Maybe I didn't try hard enough."

"Why not?"

"I've always been more focused on my career," he said. "If a relationship didn't work out, I'd feel disappointed, but I never . . . obsessed about it." His arm tightened around her waist, as if he couldn't bear the thought of letting her go.

She stroked the back of his hand, tracing his fingers absently. "You're obsessed with me, is that it?"

"Mmm-hmm," he said, kissing her bare shoulder.

"You wouldn't be, if you knew me better," she whispered.

He went still. "Try me."

She fell silent, not wanting to ruin the moment. But she suspected that she had to come clean, in order to move forward.

"Hey," he said, turning her toward him. "There's nothing you could say that would change the way I feel about you."

She shied away from him, wishing that were true.

"I'm a police officer, April. You can't shock me."

Rising from the bed, she wrapped the robe around her naked body. "I did drugs when I was pregnant."

Noah didn't recoil in disgust or cast aspersions on her. He sat up straight, waiting for her to continue.

"I—I knew Raul was into drugs when we met," she said, backtracking a little. "He was also a few years older than me, but I didn't care. In some ways, he reminded me of my father—what I thought my father was like, anyway."

"A gang member?"

She closed her eyes, ashamed of the family legacy. "Yes. He also had a lot of money, or it seemed that way. He bought me frivolous things. My mother hated him. I thought it was all very . . . edgy and glamorous."

"Go on," Noah said.

"About a month after we started dating, I moved in with him. He sold drugs, so there were always people coming and going. It was a nonstop party. I started using pretty heavily, and we argued about it. One day, when I yelled at him in front of his friends, he just . . . snapped." She lifted a hand to her cheek, remembering the blow. "He said he was sorry later, and I forgave him. But he did it again, and again, and again. After a while I started to think I deserved it. That I *asked* for it. I often instigated the attacks."

Noah's mouth thinned with anger. "He should never have put his hands on you. No matter what."

She paused, studying him. "The other night, when I slapped you . . . I guess I was looking for your breaking point."

"I'd die before I hurt you. I told you that."

She nodded, believing him this time. "It's hard for

me to trust you, because of what I've been through. Not just with Raul, either. My father was never there for my mother. And some of the men she dated . . ."

His eyes narrowed. "Did they touch you?"

"One of them tried to. I told my mom about it, and she kicked him out."

"Motherfucker," Noah swore, his face dark with fury. "What's his name? I'll run it as soon as I get to the station."

April gave him the information and moved on, needing to finish the story. "When I found out I was pregnant with Jenny, I was horrified. I'd been high on crystal meth for days. I thought I'd already . . . screwed her up." She pressed her fist to her lips, trying not to cry. "The only person I told was Eric. He went with me to the clinic. The moment I saw Jenny on the ultrasound screen, I felt this . . . connection. I knew I wanted her. I wanted to change."

Noah swung his legs over the side of the bed and pulled her close, comforting her.

"I went home and packed my things," she continued, feeling numb. "Raul caught me leaving and went crazy. Eric grabbed him by the arm, telling him to lay off because I was pregnant. He ignored Eric and slammed me against the wall, said I wasn't going anywhere. When Eric tried to step in again, Raul pulled a gun on him. I ran away while they were arguing." She met Noah's steady gaze. "Eric saved my life."

He lifted his hand to her cheek, stroking his thumb over her jaw. "I'm glad he was there for you. I wish I could have been."

She took a deep breath, tears leaking out the corners

of her eyes. "I've never talked about that. Not even with my mother."

"Did you really believe I'd think less of you for it?"

She shrugged, looking away.

He held her chin, urging her to face him. "I don't. I admire you for being able to turn your life around. I know how hard it is. Most teen mothers don't even graduate high school, let alone go on to college. You're a strong person. And a great mom."

Her heart swelled at the words. After yesterday's tragic events, she needed to hear that. With a muted cry, she wrapped her arms around his neck and pressed her nose to his throat, sharing her emotions with him, letting him in.

He hugged her for a few moments, smoothing her hair while she cried. Then he cupped her face very gently and kissed the tears away. She kissed him back, moaning a little, and soon he was stretched out on top of her, slipping his hands inside her robe.

"Wait," she said, tearing her mouth from his. "We can't. Jenny will be up soon, and I don't want her to see you."

He groaned, resting his forehead on her collarbone. "Are you working tonight?"

"Yes."

"I'll try to stop by the club, make sure you get home safe."

April didn't have to ask why. It was Friday: time for another murder.

She knotted the belt around her waist, watching him get dressed. When he sat at the edge of the bed to put on his shoes, she stared at his handsome profile, stifling the urge to lace her arms around his neck and nibble his ear.

"So . . . are we going to do this?" he asked, glancing at her.

"Do what?"

"Be together."

The straightforward question shouldn't have surprised her. He was always catching her off guard, slipping past her defenses. "What about Eric?" she asked, wanting to know where they stood on that issue.

His mouth hardened. "I'm still not comfortable with you accepting his money."

"I was going to stop doing that anyway," she said, furrowing her fingers through her hair. "I asked him to get out of the gang."

"What did he say?"

"That he's trying to get you information. I'm scared for him."

Scowling, he rose to his feet. "I can't promise anything, April. I let him off the hook once, and that was against my better judgment. He's involved in illegal activities." There was a tic in his jaw. "I can't bend the rules just because you love him."

She heard the jealousy in his voice, saw it in his fierce expression. Noah envied her emotional connection with Eric. Which was pretty ironic, considering that she was head over heels in love with *him*.

April almost gasped aloud at the realization. This morning she'd bared herself to Noah, body and soul. She'd told him about her darkest hour, her deepest shame. There was nothing left to hide behind. No more walls between them.

Although she wanted to reveal her feelings, she hesitated. It seemed like such a huge, frightening step.

And Jenny could wake up any second.

"We'll talk about this later," she said, her mind reeling.

At the door, he leaned in to kiss her, his mouth lingering on her lips. When he raised his head, she saw the raw emotion in his eyes. She waited for him to utter the words she longed to hear, the words she longed to say.

Perhaps because he thought she didn't share the sentiment, he said only, "Goodbye."

Not sure if she should feel relieved or disappointed, she locked the door behind him. Her chest ached with longing and her throat felt tight, as if she might burst into tears. Falling in love was terrifying.

Drying her sweaty palms on her robe, April went to the kitchen to make a pot of coffee. While she waited for it to brew, staring blankly at the upper cabinets, she remembered a box of photos she'd stashed in there one day.

Moving aside the flower and sugar tins, she found the box. She took it to the couch with her, bringing along a cup of coffee.

She'd barely opened it when she heard Jenny stir. "Mommy?"

April went to her room immediately. Jenny was wrapped up in the blankets, her hair adorably mussed. "Yes, *pepa*?"

"I need help getting up."

Smiling, April held out her hand. When Jenny grabbed it and pulled her down on the bed, April tickled her until she screamed for mercy. Then she hugged her daughter tight, tears forming at the corners of her eyes.

"Why are you crying, Mama?"

She kissed the top of her sweet head. "Because I love you so much. It makes me mushy." Wiping the tears away, she sat forward, gesturing for Jenny to climb on her back. "Piggyback," she said, giving her a ride to the couch.

"What's this?" she asked, seeing the box.

"Some old pictures."

"Can I look?"

"Yes."

April had brought the box with her when she left Raul, but she'd never gone through it. Not all of the photos were appropriate for Jenny's eyes. The first showed April and a couple of girlfriends, their hair sprayed into stiff peaks, hands forming gang signs.

She put the picture back in the stack before Jenny recognized her.

April hadn't been a true member of CVL. Raul had been adamant about her not joining. Girls were either jumped in or "sexed" in—literally gangbanged. He had refused to allow it. April guessed she should be grateful for that small favor.

She handed Jenny another photo, pushing those memories aside.

"Who's this?"

"Your grandfather," she said, studying it with her. "My dad." Mariano Ortiz was kneeling next to a blue El Camino, his arms crossed over his chest in a proud pose. He was only twenty when he died. Next, April gave Jenny a black-and-white photo of Josefa, gorgeous and lush at eighteen.

"Is that you, Mama?"

"No, it's Abuelita. Does it look like me?"

"Uh-huh."

There were many photos of Raul, and they caught Jenny's full attention. She pored over each one, as if the secret to his short existence could be solved by her intense concentration. Many showed Raul in his typical state—surrounded by a rowdy crew of young men, a forty-ounce bottle of beer in his hand.

April watched Jenny look at them, trying to gauge her reactions.

"Was my daddy sick, like Abuelita?"

"Yes," April said, her heart twisting. "But he never got better."

"Will Abuelita get better?"

"I hope so, *pepa*," she said, smoothing her hair. "I sure hope so."

23

Eric spent most of the day handling Raul's burial arrangements.

The cemetery plot cost a fortune. After spending most of his money on the least expensive spot available, he couldn't afford a proper coffin or a fancy grave marker. For a fraction of the cost that the funeral home had quoted, he could get a simple pine box and a standard marble headstone in Tijuana.

He crossed the border to pay for the items and pick up his mother. They waited for two hours at San Ysidro, the sun beating down relentlessly, street vendors peddling *paletas* while his mother wept into an embroidered hankie.

When they were finally across the checkpoint, he stepped on the gas, picking up speed. With the coastal breeze drying the sweat from his T-shirt, Eric broke the other bad news to her. "Grandma has to go back with you," he said in Spanish. "I can't take care of her anymore."

She dabbed at her eyes with a tissue. "Why, *m'ijo*?"

"The plot costs two thousand dollars. I won't be able to pay rent."

His mother was a pragmatic woman and too proud to borrow from relatives, most of whom were worse off than Eric. "We'll bury him in Mexico, with your father."

"No. I want Jenny to be able to visit him here."

There was a heavy pause. "Whatever you think is best."

Eric had heard that before. He'd been the financial head of the family since he was seventeen, so he was often called upon to make the tough decisions. At times like this, the responsibility was wearing.

He had so many other things to think about.

At home, a small group of friends and relatives greeted them. In many ways it was a typical Mexican get-together. There were cousins he'd never seen before and more food than anyone could eat. With some livelier music, they could call it a party. Thankfully, his mother fielded most of the condolences. Eric couldn't bear to keep up the pretense that Raul was a decent human being, worth mourning.

And yet, despite his brother's lack of redeeming qualities, Eric was devastated by loss. Yes, his brother had been a monster. But Eric had loved him, just the same.

Tonight, the crowd would become larger. Everyone would share stories of Raul, and most of the men would get drunk. The burial wasn't scheduled until Sunday afternoon, so they had a long weekend of liquor-soaked reminiscing ahead.

Eric had avoided this kind of scene at Junior's house, and he was even more uncomfortable dealing with it at his own. He slipped out the back door as quietly as possible, plotting his escape.

But his uncle Ramón was standing there, smoking a cigarette. "You want one?"

"No."

Ramón took a wad of cash out of his pocket. "Your mother told me you could use some help with the funeral costs."

It was at least a week's worth of pay, and his uncle needed it far more than Eric did. The display of generosity brought tears to Eric's eyes. "Give it to my mom," he said, clearing his throat. "Can you take her to pick up the coffin and headstone?"

"*Claro,*" Ramón said, taking another drag of his cigarette.

Eric pulled the receipts out of his pocket, giving them to his uncle. "I have some more stuff to do."

"Why don't you go back inside first, have a drink?"

He felt as if he was hanging on by a thread, barely able to hold himself together. One more kind word or gentle touch and he'd fall apart. "No. I can't stay. Tell everyone I said goodbye, okay?"

With a reluctant frown, Ramón nodded.

Eric hugged his uncle and left before anyone else could detain him. He climbed behind the wheel of his car and started the engine, breathing a sigh of relief. His guilt over walking out on his brother's gathering lasted for only a minute. As soon as he was out on the open road, windows rolled down, radio turned up, he felt better.

"I'm going to miss you, *chica,*" he said, slapping the

dash. If only he could keep on driving and leave all of his troubles behind.

He hadn't lied to his uncle. There was one last thing he had to do before his appointment with Oscar Reyes. Although it involved seeing Meghan again, he wasn't looking forward to it. In fact, he was filled with dread.

Palms sweating, he called her on his cell phone. "Is your brother home?"

"No."

"I'm coming over."

Meghan didn't play coy. "Okay."

He parked by the curb, glancing around warily as he approached the front door. She answered before he knocked, launching herself into his arms. "It's good to see you," she said, pressing her lips to his.

Eric hadn't come for this, but he couldn't resist kissing her back, with a little more relish than was wise. Before his thoughts—and his hands—could wander too far, he released her. "Let's go somewhere."

"Where?"

"Anywhere."

She looked a little disappointed. "Hang on a minute." After scribbling a note for her brother, she grabbed a purse the size of a paperback. He studied her vintage T-shirt and plaid shorts, admiring her style. With her quirky haircut and modish clothes, she'd fit in with those smart kids at the photography exhibit.

She didn't belong with a loser like him.

They had only a short time together, and he couldn't bear to ruin it all. So he drove her to the beach and they strolled along the shore, hand in hand. She kicked off her shoes, testing the water. They watched a pelican catch a fish and spotted several arcing dolphins. When Eric pointed out a hermit crab, Meghan squealed and ran back toward him, afraid for her toes.

It was a golden hour. An utter fantasy, framed by sunset.

"I have to talk to you about something," he said finally.

She slipped her arm around his waist. "What?"

They were almost at the pier. Unsettled by its presence, Eric turned around, heading in the opposite direction. "The other night, I promised your brother I'd give him some information in exchange for not arresting me."

Her gaze clouded. She didn't want this. Like him, she preferred the fantasy. "Information about what?"

"A murder."

"A murder," she repeated thinly, dropping her arm.

"I'm going to tell you everything I know, and I want you to relay it to him. Tonight, if you can. It's important."

"Why can't you tell him?"

"Because I'm afraid he'll arrest me anyway. At the very least, he'll take me down to the station to make a statement."

"So? You can do that anonymously."

"No. I can't."

She stared out at the ocean, her chin lifting. "Fine. Tell me about this murder you committed."

He didn't bother to correct her wording. "When I was ten, my dad died, and my mom went back to Mexico. My brother was eighteen at the time, so I stayed here in Chula Vista and lived with him. There were no rules at his house. He didn't make me go to school regularly. We stole things, and stayed out all night, and did drugs."

"When you were ten?"

"Yes. I did whatever he did. Even then, I was a good tagger. They thought it was funny to get me stoned and give me a can of spray paint."

Her eyes widened with concern. He wished it wasn't true.

"One night Raul planned something . . . really bad."

"What?"

Eric looked away, swallowing hard. "A girl from the neighborhood wanted to be in our clique. She didn't have many friends, and her mom didn't pay much attention to her. She was one of those girls who would . . . do anything."

"Like what?"

"Any drug, any guy." He paused for a minute, collecting himself. "Raul told her she could be a member. We picked her up and took her to this abandoned house. The place was trashed. Everyone was drinking. He tied her up."

"Why?"

He forced himself to meet her eyes. "Because that's how girls get initiated."

"No," she said, shaking her head. "With rape? You haven't done that. Tell me you haven't done that."

"Raul went first. Then Tony. Then Junior."

Her lips trembled. "Not you. Please not you."

"No. But I might as well have, because I didn't do anything to help her. I watched it like a movie."

"She agreed to it? She knew what they'd do?"

"I think so, but she didn't *like* it. She screamed, especially with Junior. It was his first time, and he was . . . overeager." Disturbed by the memory, he moved on. "I thought they were going to untie her, but Raul left her like that. Another man came to the door, wearing a mask. He gave Raul money to take a turn."

Meghan covered her mouth with one hand, horrified.

"Even though Junior had just done the same thing, he was furious with Raul. I think he felt some remorse, because he didn't want the girl to get sold like that. They started fighting, really fighting, knocking holes in the walls. Me and Tony broke them up." His stomach clenched with nausea. "About this time we realized that the girl wasn't screaming anymore. Raul kicked the door down, but the man was gone. And the girl was dead."

"Oh, my God," she whispered.

"She had a plastic bag over her head and a bandanna around her throat. He'd choked and suffocated her. Raul pounded on her chest a few times, but she wasn't breathing and her heart wasn't beating. We didn't know what to do. Calling the police was out of the question. Finally my brother wrapped her up in an old piece of carpet, and we carried her into a copse of trees behind the house. I helped dig the hole. We buried her, right there."

Meghan sat down on the beach, stunned. "Where was the house?"

"On Sycamore. A construction crew found the body a few years later."

"What was the girl's name?"

"Maggie. Magdalena, I think."

"The case is still open?"

"Unless the mystery man confessed. More likely he kept on killing. Maybe he's the one who got Cristina."

"But you don't know his name or what he looks like."

Eric made a gesture of frustration. "No. I don't. I've been trying to get more information all week, with fucked-up results. Junior put a gun to my head. Raul busted my lip. And Tony C had only one clue."

"What?"

"He said the killer was a cop. A patrol officer."

"Like Noah?"

"I don't know. It might be bullshit. Between you and me, his brain is fried."

She reacted the way he'd anticipated—with horror and disgust. A mere week ago, Meghan had been assaulted right here, under the pier. Maybe that was why Eric had brought her to this particular location. To show her that his entire life was like her worst memory. A collection of ugly scenes, a series of physical attacks.

After a few tense moments she looked up at him, holding out her hand. Surprised, he took it, and she tugged, encouraging him to sit down next to her. "Do you think your brother knows his name?"

Eric hesitated, feeling his throat close up. "I went to see him the other night. Before he punched me in the mouth, I gave him some drug money." Struggling with the words, he said, "He overdosed the next day. He's dead."

She put her arms around him. "Oh, Eric. That's awful."

He shrugged her off. "I just told you that I stood by and let a rape and murder happen. Did you hear what I said?"

"You were only a boy," she said.

"And you think I haven't done anything wrong as an adult? I'm a hard-core criminal. I've robbed and beaten innocent people. Sold drugs to kids. Smuggled guns over the border. I'm a bad person, Meghan."

She studied him, questioning his sincerity. "Are you sorry?"

He wanted to say no, but he couldn't.

"Everyone makes mistakes."

"Not these kinds of mistakes."

She rubbed his shoulders, refusing to believe the worst of him. "You're not a bad person. A bad person wouldn't *feel* bad. A bad person wouldn't have saved me from Jack, or tried to make amends, or risked his life to find a killer." When he glanced away, she cupped her hands around his face. "Your brother was bad. Not you."

The tears that had been threatening all day pressed close, looming behind his eyes.

"A bad person wouldn't mourn a brother who trained him to be a criminal or be able to forgive a mother who abandoned him when he was ten years old."

When she slipped her hand around the nape of his neck, urging him forward, he couldn't fight his feelings any longer. He cried on her shoulder, literally, with strangers passing by and waves crashing in the background.

Then she wiped his tears away, and he covered her

mouth with his, shutting out the world around them with a tender kiss.

"Take me home," she said in his ear, after they broke apart.

Eric knew what she was asking for and that he shouldn't give it to her. Only a selfish man would use her body and leave her. His odds for walking away from tonight's fight unharmed and evading arrest were abysmal.

But she touched her lips to his throat, tasting his skin, and he wavered, remembering the hot slide of her mouth as she went down on him. He wanted that again. He wanted all of her, trembling beneath him.

He wanted one last escape.

So he nodded his agreement and rose to his feet, unable to deny himself the pleasure.

Meghan took him upstairs, her heart pounding with anticipation. Eric walked in first, and she shut the door behind them.

He sat down on the bed, silent.

Feeling nervous, she went to her desk to turn on some music. She'd found an old record player at the secondhand store, along with a handful of classics. Choosing "In My Room" by the Beach Boys, she put the needle in place and stepped away.

"Is this okay?" she asked, undressing.

He watched her clothes fall to the floor, his Adam's apple bobbing. "Yeah."

After she stripped down to her bra and panties, he

rose and pulled his shirt over his head. At just past sunset, there was still enough light for her to see his finely etched muscles and scripted tattoos.

He stood as still as a shadow, letting her come to him.

She crossed the room, smoothing her hands across his chest, touching the thin silver chain that held his crucifix. As she trailed her fingertips over his torso and down his taut abdomen, she felt his eyes on her body. Her nipples peaked against the soft cups of her bra, and a beat pulsed between her legs.

Groaning, he filled his hands with her mostly bare bottom and lifted her against him, kissing her hungrily. They fell back on the bed together, arms and legs entwined. A few days ago she'd been uncomfortable in this position. Now, when he settled on top of her and his erection nudged the cleft of her sex, she felt only pleasure.

Plumbing the depths of her mouth, he shoved his hand down the back of her panties, squeezing her bottom. She dug her fingernails into his shoulders and arched like a cat, rubbing her breasts against his chest.

Long before she was ready to stop kissing, he tore his mouth from hers, breathing hard. Shifting his weight to the side, he tugged her panties all the way off.

The sensation of being nude from the waist down was strangely arousing. His gaze lingered on her pale belly, her naked hips, the apex of her thighs. Her breasts strained against the confinement of her bra, her nipples tingling for his touch.

She reached behind her, unhooking the clasp. When her breasts tumbled free, he moistened his lips.

"Touch me," she said, parting her thighs.

He put his hand between her legs, eager to please. Sliding one finger inside, then another, he tested her heat. At the same time, he lowered his mouth to her breasts, swirling his tongue over the puckered tips.

She spread her legs wider, begging him for more.

Lifting his head, he looked from her wet nipples to the juncture of her thighs. "I want to fuck you so bad."

"Yes," she panted.

But he continued to touch her, stroking her slippery flesh until she cried out, shuddering with pleasure. When she opened her eyes again, he was watching her face intently, as if he was trying to memorize her expression. While she stared back at him, senses reeling, he took a condom out of his pocket and unbuttoned his fly. Positioning himself over her, he wrapped his hand around the base of his erection and guided it inside.

It hurt. Not as much as her first time but enough to give her pause.

Eric went very still. "Are you okay?"

She felt pinned to the mattress, her heart fluttering madly in her chest. Realizing that she'd tensed up as soon as he entered her, she tried to relax. Unclenching her fists, she lifted her knees higher. "I think so."

Cursing in Spanish, he drew back a little and slid in again.

The pain receded into a sweet, hot ache. She hooked her legs around his waist and twined her arms around his neck, clinging to him. With each thrust, her body accommodated his more comfortably. "Yes, Eric. Like that."

With a low groan, he drove deeper, watching her breasts bounce as he plunged into her. She was fascinated by his flexing muscles and lust-dark eyes, his guttural curse words and clenched teeth. His excitement thrilled her. She wondered how it would feel if he took her hard and rough, holding nothing back.

He found his release quickly, and somewhat apologetically, as if he regretted not being able to make it last longer. Gripping her hips in his hands, he buried his face in the crook of her neck and came.

For a few moments, he lay on top of her, sweating. "Hang on a second," he said, removing himself from her carefully. Hitching his pants up his hips, he walked to the bathroom to dispose of the condom.

Meghan smiled, hugging a pillow to her chest. When he came back into her room, he yanked the pillow away from her and wrestled her down on the bed, kissing every inch of her body while she bucked and squealed.

Breathless, they stretched out side by side. She couldn't think of a time she'd felt more alive. "I love you," she said, touching his handsome face.

He grabbed her wrist, lightning-fast. "You can't."

She pulled her hand back, her smile fading. "I can, and I do."

After an, awkward pause, he looked away, shaking his head. "I have to go. Don't forget to tell your brother what I told you."

She was stung by his careless attitude, almost speechless. "Are you too much of a coward to tell him yourself?"

Jaw clenched in anger, he rose from the bed, finding his T-shirt on the floor.

"So this didn't mean anything to you?" she whispered, covering herself with the blanket. "I don't mean anything to you?"

His T-shirt was inside out, so he righted it. "You were okay."

She wanted to slap him. "You look like a scared little boy right now, Eric. Afraid to admit your true feelings, afraid to get out of the gang. What are you going to do tonight? What's so important that you have to run away?"

"I'm not running away—and I'm not a coward." He pulled his shirt over his head, nodding a curt goodbye. "Maybe I'll see you around sometime."

"Where's your necklace?"

He waited a beat too long. "What necklace?"

"Your cross. You never take it off." She looked around for it, but he was already turning his back to her, walking out the door. Dragging the blanket along with her, she raced after him, checking the bathroom in the hall.

The silver crucifix was there, sitting on the surface of the counter. She picked it up, almost tripping over her own feet as she rushed down the stairs. "You left it here on purpose! Why did you do that?"

He paused, his hand on the doorknob. "Because I might not come back again," he said, glancing over his shoulder at her. "And I wanted to give you something to remember me by. Now I really do have to go."

She ran to him, tears filling her eyes. "Where?"

Avoiding her gaze, he refused to answer.

"Don't do it," she said, holding the blanket up with one hand, his chain in the other. "Please, Eric. Whatever it is, don't do it."

He hesitated another moment, searching for the right words. "I lied to you upstairs. I thought it would be easier to leave you that way, but it isn't. So the truth is this—you've been the best time of my life. And I wish I could be the person you think you love." He kissed her stunned cheek and walked out the door.

Noah had a voice mail waiting for him when he arrived at the station. The lab director informed him that the samples from the cold-case file he'd been working on had been archived, untested, at the department's request.

He listened to the message twice, nonplussed. Only a lead investigator could halt testing, usually because a case had closed. Budget issues were always a concern, and DNA analysis was expensive. Maybe someone had decided the cost outweighed the benefit. It was even more likely that a simple miscommunication had occurred. With thousands of samples to process, some orders fell through the cracks.

Noah would have to track down the source of the problem and submit a new request. Making a note to ask Santiago about it, he left his desk.

The cold case would have to wait until Monday morning.

Tonight he was involved in a routine sweep operation. Every few months the gang unit came together in a concentrated effort, combing the streets for documented members. They collected intelligence, visited known hangouts, and made multiple arrests.

Without Patrick, there were five GU officers on the team rather than six, so they had their work cut out for them. Noah was growing accustomed to riding solo and even enjoyed the independence. Although he missed having a partner at his side, he felt more confident in his abilities as a police officer now.

At times, Patrick had been a burden.

The night was really beginning to heat up when Noah got interrupted by dispatch. "Officer Young, I have an urgent request from Meghan that you call home."

Thankfully, he was on the freeway, not engaged with a suspect. Acknowledging the dispatch operator, he picked up his cell phone and stabbed the home button.

It rang only once.

"Noah?"

His gut clenched at the sound of her voice. She'd been crying. "What's wrong?"

"I need to talk to you."

"About what?"

"Eric."

"Is he there?"

"No, but he told me something . . . really bad. I think you should come home."

Cursing, he glanced into his rearview mirror. He'd passed his exit. "Okay. I'll try."

"Is anyone with you right now?"

"No."

"Not even Patrick?"

"I'm alone in my squad car. Why?"

"Come home. Please. It might have something to do with the recent murders."

"I'll be there in five minutes," he promised, hitting his lights. After notifying his fellow officers of a family emergency, he exited the freeway and headed west toward his neighborhood in Imperial Beach.

Inside the house, Meghan was sitting at the base of the stairs, a blanket wrapped around her slender body. Her eyes were puffy and her shoulders bare.

She had a crucifix cupped in the palm of her hand.

Noah didn't need any special cop intuition to understand what had happened. Eric had touched his baby sister, after giving his word not to. "Mother*fucker*," he said, wanting to punch a hole through the wall. "Did he hurt you?"

"No. I'm just . . . upset."

He swore again, furious. When he caught up with Eric, he was going to wring his neck. "What information did he give you?"

Tears leaking out her eyes, she began a very disturbing story. With each chilling detail, Noah felt more loathing toward Raul and a renewed empathy for April. Even his anger toward Eric dissipated some. "Did he describe the killer?"

She shook her head. "He was trying to get more information from his friends. He said that Junior put a gun to his head for asking, and that his brother punched him. But a guy named Tony told him the killer might be a patrol officer."

A cold bead of sweat trickled down his spine. "Tony Castillo?"

"I guess. Eric wasn't sure about the patrol-officer part. He said Raul was the only one who really knew anything."

"And he's dead."

"Right."

Noah raked a hand through his hair, his mind racing. There were dozens of patrol officers on the CVPD. San Diego had hundreds. Like Eric, Noah was also skeptical of the source. Tony Castillo had pulled a gun on him two weeks ago.

"He told me the girl's name," she continued. "Maggie or Magdalena. Her body was found by a construction crew a few years later but never identified."

Noah knew with absolute certainty that this girl was the subject of the cold case he'd been studying. Eric seemed to think the murders were related, and maybe he was right. This victim had a plastic bag over her head and a CVL bandanna around her neck.

"Fuck," he said, considering the implications if the killer really *was* a cop. Maybe the DNA analysis hadn't been canceled by accident. "Fuck!"

"You're scaring me," Meghan sobbed. "I want you to find Eric. I think he's going to do something dangerous, like get jumped out of the gang."

Noah had been hitting the streets all night, and he hadn't heard any news about a jump-out. He had, however, collected some intel about a rumble between Eastside and CVL. Supposedly two top guys from each crew were going to brawl it out. No one had named the participants or mentioned where this fight would take place.

"I'll look for him," he said, kneeling before her. "Are you going to be okay?"

She nodded, her face scrunched up. "I love him."

"Oh, Christ," he muttered, giving her an awkward hug. This was a disaster. He couldn't recall Meghan ever saying she was in love before. The fact that she'd fallen for a gang member who was headed for death or jail boggled his mind.

What was so fucking special about Eric Hernandez?

Noah didn't have time to deal with Meghan's misplaced affections. He made her promise to stay put and returned to his squad car. After contacting his unit, requesting that they be on the lookout for Eric, he ran a search for the name *Magdalena* in the system.

He got lucky.

There was no recent information, but he found a decade-old arrest report starring Magdalena "Maggie" Chavez. He couldn't access a full record of the juvenile offense or the accompanying mug shot, but he was able to track down a last known address and next of kin. Her mother, Elvia Chavez, was still listed at the same address.

Noah decided to pay her a visit.

The small house near Castle Park High School was in a sad state of disrepair. The paint was peeling and the yard was dead. It looked abandoned. Noah parked by the curb and approached the front door with caution, his hand on his holster.

He glanced through the torn mesh screen, detecting movement. "Mrs. Chavez?"

A middle-aged woman appeared on the other side. "*Sí.*"

"I'd like to speak with you about Magdalena."

She opened the screen door, letting him in. When his eyes adjusted to the dim lighting, he realized that she was in her forties, younger than he'd estimated. Her disheveled hair and coarse complexion added years. She had the bleary-eyed, red-nosed look of a wino.

"Have you found my daughter?"

Noah couldn't answer that. "How long has she been missing?"

"Ten years."

"Did you file a report?"

"Twice. They said they lost the first one."

The second must have suffered the same fate, as it wasn't in the system. "Can you tell me about her?"

The woman frowned, crossing her arms over her chest. "She was a good girl, but she ran around with bad boys. Gangbangers."

He took out his notebook. "Do you remember the names of any of her friends?"

She shook her head sadly.

"When was the last time you saw her?"

Mrs. Chavez walked away from Noah, into a dark living room, and sat down. The space was crammed with broken furniture and random junk. It smelled like dusty carpet and cat urine. Staring off into a corner, she lifted a small glass from the coffee table and drank from it. "Summer of 2000. She was sixteen."

"Did an officer come to your house when you reported her missing?"

"Two officers came. One of them was quiet, nice. He didn't talk much. The other told me that kids in gangs were taking over the streets, and there was nothing they could do about it. He said she'd turn up eventually. Shanley, I think he called himself. For all I know, he threw that first report away."

Noah thanked her for her time, his heart racing from shock. He didn't mention the cold-case murder, but he left his card, saying he would be in touch.

Outside her house, he took a few deep breaths, wondering what to do next. He felt as if he was stuck in a nightmare. Patrick's last words came drifting back to him. *You wouldn't know a perp if he was sitting right in front of you.*

He'd suspected his partner of being a racist, a woman-hater, and a piss-poor police officer, but a murderer?

It was unfathomable.

He put in a call to Santiago, leaving an urgent request to speak with him. He also left a message with April, although he doubted she knew where Eric was.

Trying to remain calm, he considered his options. This was an incredibly sensitive situation. He couldn't waltz over to Patrick's house and pop off accusations. Nor could he announce that he was looking for a serial killer/cop over the wire.

He had to find Eric. *Now.*

Picking up his radio, he contacted his unit. "Any word on the Eastside rumble?"

"Yes, actually. Rumor has it that a fight's going down at Brown Field."

"Between who?"

"Oscar Reyes and an unknown CVL member. We think it might be the mysterious third passenger from last weekend's drive-by. As soon as we're finished with the sweep, we'll be en route to that location."

"I'll meet you there," Noah said, signing off. Brown Field was a section of land behind the municipal airport. With its dusty hills and intricate back roads, it was an ideal place for a clandestine meeting. Lots of cover, plenty of space.

He could attempt to track Eric's cell phone, but that brought up some touchy legal issues. Unless Noah could prove that Eric's life was in danger, accessing his personal information required a court order.

April called him back a moment later. "What's up?"

"Do you know where Eric is?"

"No."

"Is he planning to fight someone tonight?"

"I wouldn't be surprised," she said, sighing. "Yesterday three men drove by the house while we were saying goodbye. He told me to go back inside."

"What did he do?"

"He went right up to the car! They talked for a minute, at the most."

"Can you describe the car or the men inside?"

"White Monte Carlo, at least ten years old. Mexican guys with shaved heads."

He made a note of the description. "Is there a special place Eric would meet them? Designated turf for a fight?"

She thought for a second, cursing Eric's recklessness in two languages. "The only place I can think of is near the southern border of Brown Field. CVL and Eastside used to have *broncas* there, back in the day."

Noah thanked her for the info. He'd heard about the

old-school fistfights, and now he had a more speci██
area to search. "Go straight home after work," he sa██
pulling away from the Chavez residence. "I'll call y██
back as soon as I can."

"Be careful," she said softly.

"I will." Although he wanted to say more, it was██
the right time, so he ended the call and headed sou██
toward Brown Field.

Eric traveled east on Otay Mesa Road, slowing as ██
passed Brown Field.

There was a large, hilly area behind the airport whe██
Raul used to give him boxing lessons. The space v██
open but secluded, offering endless escape routes ██
dirt-bike paths and gravel roads. In the past few year██
had been claimed by the Otay crew, an upstart ga██
that both CVL and Eastside looked down on.

They weren't here tonight.

Not that Eric cared one way or another. If he s██
them, he'd just move to a deserted part of the field.

He didn't expect Oscar to be waiting for him, and ██
wasn't. He parked near a flat area that couldn't be se██
from the main road and left his lights on. He'd been t██
nervous to eat dinner, so he grabbed some beef je██
out of the glove compartment, chewing and swallowi██
mechanically, chasing it down with a Coke.

Thinking about the fight made him anxious, so ██
replayed the high points of his afternoon with Megha██
For some reason, his mind kept returning to their st██
on the beach rather than the very satisfying mome██
he spent on top of her.

"*Baboso,*" he called himself, closing his eyes and continuing to picture her face, her smile, the way she said, *I love you.*

An hour later, when someone tapped on his window, he jerked awake with a start. "*Listo, cabrón?*"

Eric straightened in his seat. A group of cars were parked in a half circle, front ends pointed toward the flat, open area. With a full moon in the sky, there was no need for headlights to illuminate the space.

He drained the last of his soda and got out.

Oscar was leaning against the hood of a white Monte Carlo, his arm draped around a homegirl. Eric wondered if she'd been inside the house when Junior did the drive-by. She was pretty and slim, too young for her heavy makeup and hard eyes.

"*Estás solo?*" Oscar asked.

Eric held out his arms. Obviously he was alone.

"You're not with CVL anymore?"

He shrugged. "What difference does it make?"

"Your boy shot up my car, *ese.* He fucked with my family. Just so we're clear, this takes care of your debt only—not his."

"He thought you hurt his sister."

The girl beside Oscar frowned at him.

He spat on the dirt. "I didn't do shit. Fuck him. And fuck you."

Eric fell silent. Telling Oscar how it went down might help Junior later, but it wasn't going to change anything tonight.

"Where's the pink slip?"

"In the glove compartment, signed. The keys are in my pocket."

"Do you really want to do this, *chacho*? Why don't you hand them over and walk away while you still can?"

Eric glanced around the small crowd, considering. They would probably beat him up no matter what. And, although he had distanced himself from the Locos, he still represented their clique. He could end this conflict like a man, and leave the barrio with honor, or run away and watch his back forever.

"You'll have to take them from me," he decided.

Oscar smiled coldly. *"A que quieras, güey."* He stepped into the ring, pulling his T-shirt over his head. He'd done time in prison recently, and it showed. He was ripped. His shaved head gleamed in the moonlight, and his muscles bulged.

Eric's stomach clenched with apprehension. Swallowing drily, he removed his own shirt, tossing it on the hood of his car. His lean body inspired laughter rather than awe. Only Oscar's girl looked at him with a glint of appreciation, which was fine. He didn't want to be admired by these men; he wanted to be underestimated.

"My homie will check you," Oscar said.

Eric bent forward, bracing his hands on the hood while some cockhead patted him down. He stared at Oscar without really seeing him, enduring the indignity. Oscar's girl watched the proceedings, moistening her lips.

When the kid was finished checking Eric for weapons, Oscar turned to his girlfriend. "Show him I'm clean."

Giving Eric a sultry smirk, she knelt behind Oscar, encircling his ankles, lifting the cuffs of his jeans. She slid her hands up the insides of his thighs, moving slowly. Then she stood, reaching around to cup his fly. "It's all you, baby."

Eric wasn't impressed by the display. She reminded him of the girls Junior screwed in front of everyone.

"Ready?" Oscar asked.

Eric came forward, his heart in his throat, blood pumping with adrenaline. Although Oscar outweighed him, Eric was several inches taller, and he had a longer reach. He was also quicker and lighter on his feet. Bulky men weren't necessarily good fighters, he assured himself. They often lacked finesse and endurance.

Power for power, they were a poor match. The first time Oscar landed a solid hit, Eric would probably go down for the count. But if he dodged the blows, he had a chance of wearing down the bigger man.

As they circled each other, fists raised, Eric began to reassess his opponent. Oscar Reyes was not a graceless brute. He didn't exactly float like a butterfly, but he wasn't clumsy. Dancing around him no longer seemed wise.

So Eric struck first, trying to stun him with a quick left. Oscar evaded the punch easily. Taking advantage of Eric's proximity, he retaliated with a big hit to Eric's stomach, followed by a painful knock on the chin.

Eric stumbled backward, in danger of losing his footing. He held a hand over his burning midsection, gasping for breath.

Oscar laughed, still circling.

Knowing he didn't have much time to regroup before Oscar struck again, Eric nevertheless hesitated, exaggerating his weakness. His opponent fell for the trick.

Instead of proceeding with caution, Oscar moved in for the kill.

Eric ducked the next blow and came up swinging. He connected with Oscar's jaw twice, a hard one-two punch.

Oscar's head snapped back, and he staggered sideways.

Eric felt as if he'd broken a few knuckles, so he figured Oscar was seeing stars. He advanced again, doubting he would find a better opening. As soon as he slammed his fist into Oscar's ribs and heard a satisfying crack, Oscar threw an arm around Eric's neck, taking the fight to the ground.

Good. Eric was a better grappler than a boxer.

Unfortunately, Oscar had better positioning, and he used it wisely, holding Eric down and pummeling his left side.

Fuck, it hurt.

Eric couldn't breathe. His knuckles were throbbing, and his chin was on fire. Sharp rocks stabbed his back, cutting into his skin. Grunting with exertion, he wrapped his legs around Oscar's midsection, using his thighs to crush his rib cage.

"*Puta madre!*" Oscar said, drawing back his arm to punch Eric in the face.

It was a devastating blow.

Eric loosened his grip, panting. God *damn*. He was so jacked up, he couldn't see straight. Blood was dripping down his cheek, and his brain felt like jelly. But he still had his legs around Oscar's ribs, and he continued to exert pressure.

"Kill this motherfucker," one of the other guys said,

handing Oscar a blade. It flashed in the moonlight, slim and deadly.

Oscar didn't hesitate. In fact, he may have planned this finish. The knife arced downward toward Eric's chest, and he was almost too winded to defend himself. Then panic seized him, compelling him to act. He grabbed Oscar's wrist and twisted sideways. The blade nicked Eric's ribs, scraping along the bone, creating an agony he'd never known before. He screamed in pain, clenched his fingers around Oscar's wrist.

Oscar rotated the knife just slightly, baring his gold tooth in a menacing grimace. The sensation was immense, sickening. Black spots wavered before Eric's eyes. He knew he was on the edge of consciousness.

"*Dios*," he whispered.

"*Dios te lleve!*" Oscar shouted back. *God take you!*

Summoning every ounce of his remaining strength, Eric pushed the knife away from his body, feeling a warm trickle in its wake. Tilting the tip of the blade toward his attacker, Eric rolled on top of him. The sudden change of leverage and momentum sent the knife forward, thrusting between Oscar's ribs.

All the way to the hilt.

"You first," Eric said, holding it there.

Blood gushed over his hand, warm and wet. More sputtered out of Oscar's mouth. His eyes widened with shock, then glazed over.

His body convulsed beneath Eric's as God took him.

Eric let go of the knife handle and fell to the side, his lungs burning. "*Perdóneme*," he prayed, waiting for darkness to descend upon him.

25

Noah didn't see any sign of a disturbance at Brown Field.

He drove along the dirt road behind the municipal airport, searching for lights or movement. The place was quiet and deserted. Just when he was about to check a different location, a black SUV came rolling down the hill, kicking up dust.

He followed its tracks to a clearing.

The instant Noah's headlights hit the area, people scattered, getting into their cars and fleeing the scene. Only Eric's Chevelle remained. And two bodies, motionless and bloody, lying on the rock-strewn dirt.

One had a knife sticking out of his chest.

Noah called dispatch, reciting license plate numbers and vehicle descriptions, but he didn't pursue the suspects. After requesting backup and an ambulance, he exited his squad car, approaching the prone figures with caution.

The man with the knife wound was Oscar Reyes. The ground beneath him was soaked with blood, and his dead eyes stared up at the night sky.

The other body belonged to Eric. He was lying in the fetal position, his hands curled around his head. There was a jagged laceration on his side and smaller cuts all over his back. His hair was caked with dirt, his naked torso covered in boot prints.

He'd been beaten to death.

Noah's gut clenched at the sight.

"You stupid, stupid kid," he said in a low voice, fighting tears. Meghan and April were going to be devastated. When Noah knelt beside him, touching the radio at his shoulder to relay the details of the scene to dispatch, Eric coughed.

Noah almost jumped backward in surprise.

He was alive!

Eric moved his arm away from his head, moaning. Blood dripped from his mouth, and his eyes were swollen shut.

"It's Officer Young," he said, knowing Eric couldn't see him. "It's Noah."

"Am I dead?"

"No."

"Kill me."

Noah patted his shoulder, not sure if he should laugh or cry. "Hang on, man. The ambulance will be here any minute."

"Is Oscar dead?"

He glanced at the other body. "I don't know," he lied. "What happened?"

"I stabbed him."

"Shit," Noah muttered, rubbing a hand over his face. For that simple statement, Eric could go to prison for the rest of his life. If he lived, that is.

"I want to die."

"Well, too bad," Noah said. "You're not going to

Eric shuddered, vomiting a watery mixture of b and bile.

Noah didn't have a second to waste, so he cou indulge Eric with kind words. "Shut the fuck up a Oscar until you get a lawyer, and listen to me very fully. I need you to tell me about the guy who k Maggie Chavez."

He moaned in protest.

"Meghan said you didn't see his face. Describe e thing else. Did you hear his voice? Was he dark-h or light? Tall, thin? Black, white, Hispanic?"

"Medium height. Average build. Dark . . . hair."

Noah's mind raced with confusion. "Are you su

"Yeah."

"What else?"

"I think he was . . . one of us."

Noah leaned close, fearing that Eric would lose sciousness again. "A gang member?"

"A . . . Mexican," he said, and passed out.

He stepped away as the ambulance arrived, le the EMTs stabilize Eric's condition. For all Noah k the kid had internal injuries. He'd been kicked stabbed and beaten by a crowd of angry young me

If Noah had arrived a moment later, Eric might died. He still might.

"I thought you had a family emergency to take of," one of his fellow gang-unit officers comme surprised to see him there.

"I got sidetracked," he muttered.

Noah climbed behind the wheel of his squad car

sanitized his hands, thinking about Eric's last words. No one could confuse Patrick for Mexican. His former partner was tall, heavyset, light-skinned, and light-haired.

"God damn it," Noah muttered. He was back to square one.

Despite the city's largely Spanish-speaking population, Hispanic officers were a minority in the Chula Vista Police Department. Noah had no idea how many Mexican patrol cops had been on staff ten years ago, but he figured it was a low number.

He could generate a short list of names in minutes. And then what?

Again he questioned the source of the tip. Raul Hernandez had allegedly told Tony Castillo that the killer was a patrol officer. But both men were hard-core drug addicts and lifelong criminals.

What were the odds that one of them was lying?

Even if the information was accurate, the lead would be difficult to follow. Noah couldn't tell his fellow officers about it. He'd have to go down to the station and snoop around, searching through the employee files and missing-persons reports.

He should contact internal affairs.

"Fuck," he said, resting his forehead against the steering wheel.

In the meantime, it was Friday night. There'd been two murders in two weeks, both committed in the wee hours of Saturday morning. There was no doubt in Noah's mind that the cold case was connected, probably by a common perpetrator. He'd strangled three young women, all of whom were affiliated with CVL.

Where would he strike next?

April had a disastrous night at work. She mixed up drink orders, calculated tabs incorrectly, and spilled beer.

Even before Noah called, she'd been scattered. After, she was completely worthless. Too distracted to take care of her customers properly, she scurried from table to table, trying to sort through the chaos she'd created.

When she delivered a round of tequila shots to a group of ladies who'd ordered white zinfandel, she wanted to cry in frustration. "I'm so sorry," she said, putting the shot glasses back on her tray. "I'll get your wine right now."

On the way back to the bar, she glanced over her shoulder, seeing a trio of annoyed female faces.

And ran right into Eddie.

The tray tilted, spilling gold tequila all over his cream-colored shirt. The shot glasses shattered on the floor.

April burst into tears.

Any other night, Eddie would have dragged her back to the kitchen and yelled at her. He'd have fired a new girl on the spot. Someone like Lola might have been directed to his office for a very special apology.

"*Hijo de puta*," he swore, grabbing a towel from behind the bar. To her surprise, he yanked the tray out of her hands and knelt to pick up the pieces of glass for her. "Take a break," he ordered, signaling at Carmen to go with her.

Shoulders trembling, April walked away with the other waitress. Carmen sat her down at the table in the kitchen and took the seat directly across from her, their knees almost touching. "What's wrong? Is this about Raul?"

"No," she said, dabbing at her weepy eyes with an apron. In between sniffles, she told Carmen about Josefa's disappearance and Eric's trouble with the law. She felt as if her entire life had been turned inside out and upside down. "It's all Noah's fault." Before he came along, she'd never lost her composure at work.

"What did that bastard do to you?"

April smiled through her tears, knowing she sounded melodramatic. "Yesterday he bought me this really nice briefcase, and the card said *Love, Noah.*"

"*Que barbaro.* The nerve of some guys."

"It's too soon, Carmen. It feels like too much."

"Why? Is he pushing you?"

She shook her head. "He's persistent, and he goes out of his way to spend time with me, but I wouldn't call him pushy."

"Does he have a life outside of work?"

"Yes, actually. He has a lot of other stuff going on. If anything, he's stretched too thin."

Carmen held her thumb and forefinger a few inches apart. "Too small?"

"No! God, no."

"Selfish? Clumsy?"

April blushed, thinking of the times he'd seen to her pleasure instead of his own. "No, and no."

"Too gentle. Boring. Uninspired."

"Definitely not."

"Let me see if I understand the problem," she said, clasping her hands together. "He's handsome, sexy, and

caring. He's got a good job and he's great in bed. F
you don't want to be with him."

April's eyes filled with tears again. "I don't want
get hurt."

Carmen leaned forward. "Would you rather tak
chance or continue as you were—cold, closed off, a
alone?"

"I like being cautious. It makes me feel safe."

"Come on, April. You're a beautiful woman with
body to die for. Don't hide your bush under a barrel,
whatever that saying is. It's not natural."

She knew Carmen was speaking from the hea
Women of their culture prided themselves on bei
passionate. Even the most demure Latinas valued se
suality. "You don't think we're moving too fast?"

Carmen arched a brow. "Not if he knows what
wants."

April nodded, twisting the apron in her lap. No
made decisions quickly, but he had strong convictio
He was honest, and loyal, and trustworthy. She cou
count on him. "You're right. I have to tell him how
feel."

Carmen gave her a quick hug. "Good girl. I hate
see you throw away a keeper."

April thanked her and rose to her feet, taking
compact mirror out of her purse to check her refl
tion. After she fixed her mascara, they walked back
onto the floor together. A woman in a flashy silver
caught April's attention. The sight filled April with
mixture of dread and relief. "Oh, no."

"What?"

"It's my mother," she groaned, holding a hand o

her forehead. What a nightmare this evening had been! She was glad Josefa was okay but certain that she'd embarrass April with her outrageous behavior.

Carmen searched the crowd, narrowing her eyes. "I'll take care of her."

April had other customers waiting, and it was almost last call, so she hustled to fill the final drink orders. She delivered her usual excellent customer service, working double time to correct her earlier blunders.

At the end of the night, she made out okay, as far as tips went.

Josefa had also done well for herself. A group of young men were flocked around her. One kept touching her lower back while she sipped her drink and laughed. When the closing lights came on at 2:00 A.M., the men left, but Josefa stayed put.

Carmen gestured at April, rubbing her fingers together. *No money.*

What a surprise.

Straightening her shoulders, April approached her mother. Even under the unflattering fluorescent lights, she looked good. Drugs and alcohol hadn't ravaged her beauty or ruined her figure. Yet.

"How are you?" April asked, setting her tray down on the bar.

Josefa gave her a brittle smile. "Broke."

April looked across the room at Eddie, who shook his head. This was so humiliating. When a customer couldn't pay, he called the police. But if April covered the tab, her mother would come back every night.

"Raul died," she said, changing the subject.

Josefa's brows rose. She drained the last of her drink. "Good riddance."

April nodded in agreement. "Jenny misses you."

Those words seemed to penetrate her mother's devil-may-care façade. Her eyes softened. "I'd love to see her," she whispered.

April's throat closed up. She said nothing.

The young man Josefa had been flirting with ducked his head inside the front door, as if he'd been waiting for her. "Coming, sweet thing?"

After a long pause, in which April refused to meet her mother's pleading gaze, Josefa slid off the bar stool, sauntering toward her mark. She whispered something in his ear, probably a request that he pick up her tab. He gave a few bills to Carmen and put his arm around Josefa. They walked away together, into the night.

Eddie appeared beside her. "You okay?"

April glanced at him, considering. It hadn't escaped her attention that he'd been sober the past couple of weeks. Maybe Lola's death had turned him around. "I'm fine," she said. Actually, she felt better. She'd have preferred to watch her mother check into rehab rather than sell her body to a stranger, so this ending was bittersweet.

It was hard to do the right thing.

She hugged her arms around herself, wanting Noah. She longed for his warmth, his strength. As soon as she was finished wiping down her tables, she grabbed her purse and said good night, checking the messages on her cell phone as she walked outside.

No missed calls.

Maybe he was waiting at home for her. Eager to see

him, she unlocked her car and tossed her purse inside. She drove out of the parking lot, filled with nervous energy.

Noah's truck wasn't in front of her house, to her disappointment. Instead, a sleek black Audi idled there. April pulled into the garage, casting an anxious glance in her rearview mirror. A man got out of the car, flashing a badge.

"Shit," she said, raising her hands over her head.

"Miss Ortiz? Can you step out of the car?"

April followed his instructions, keeping her arms up.

He seemed to find her actions amusing. "You're not in trouble. Officer Young asked me to stop by. There's been an accident."

Her heart twisted. "Is Noah hurt?"

"No, ma'am. It's Eric Hernandez."

"Oh, my God," she breathed, dropping her arms. "Where is he?"

"An ambulance is taking him to Sharp, and I'm on my way there to question him. Would you like to come with me?"

She reached for her purse. "Of course. Thank you."

He opened the passenger door, his demeanor calm and self-assured. It occurred to her that she'd seen him before. She never forgot a face.

"I'm Detective Santiago," he said, smiling politely.

She sat down. "You used to be on the gang unit with Officer Shanley."

Closing her door, he walked around to the driver's side and got behind the wheel. "You have a good memory. That was years ago."

"Is Eric going to be okay?"

He checked his rearview mirror and pulled forwar driving down the street. "I don't have any details on I condition."

April took a deep breath, trying to relax. She hat being in a car with a stranger, even a mild-manner police officer.

A moment later, when her cell phone rang, she sta tled.

"Do you mind turning that off? It interferes with r scanner."

Although she knew it was Noah calling, she did dare refuse. Detective Santiago was his boss, or wou be someday. She switched off her phone and slipped back inside her purse, every nerve in her body on ed

After they'd gone a few miles, she realized that th weren't anywhere near Sharp Medical Center. S frowned at the dark, curvy road, wondering if th was a shortcut. An intense wave of foreboding pass over her.

She'd made a mistake.

As if sensing her discomfort, Santiago rolled do his window. Yanking her purse from her clutch hands, he tossed it out on the street.

April gaped at him in horror, realizing she was sta ing into the face of a killer.

26

When Noah tried to call April, she didn't answer. He dialed again, starting to panic when her voice mail picked up.

"Fuck!"

After leaving a message for her to call him back immediately and to not go anywhere *with anyone*, especially a police officer, he tossed the phone aside. Then he started the engine and drove away from Brown Field.

Abandoning a crime scene without speaking to investigators or checking the condition of the victim was the craziest, most inappropriate thing he'd ever done on duty.

But he didn't think twice.

In the next few minutes, his suspicions snowballed into full-blown certainty. There was only one man in the department who fit the description Eric had given. He had more than enough authority to halt DNA analysis. He'd been a patrol officer when Maggie Chavez disappeared and a homicide detective by the time her body was found.

Patrick's former partner and current nemesis: Victor Santiago.

Every cop instinct Noah possessed was on red alert, telling him that April was in danger. The previous victims were pretty, dark-haired young women connected to CVL. April's relationship with Raul—and Eric—made her a likely target.

He turned on his emergency lights and drove as fast as he dared to April's house, hoping he wasn't too late. He should have told her this morning that he loved her. Or said it on the phone earlier tonight. Why hadn't he done that?

When he pulled up to the curb and saw her car parked in the garage, he was so relieved he thanked God out loud. Leaving his engine running, he jogged up the front walk and knocked on her door insistently.

She didn't answer. The windows were dark.

He walked around the side of the house, calling her name. It was unusual for the garage to be open. Her car door was slightly ajar. He glanced inside, noting that her purse was gone. Stomach sinking, Noah checked the door that led into the kitchen. It was locked.

She'd never gone in.

Chilled to the bone, he ran back to his squad car, glancing across the street at her neighbor's house. It was also dark.

She wasn't here.

Noah contacted her cell phone service provider immediately, giving his badge number and demanding the signal information. While he stood there, cursing God and Santiago and the motherfucking phone company for taking so long, an operator triangulated her location.

"The latest signal is from the 2000 block of Hollister," she said finally.

"Keep tracking it. I'll call back."

Hollister Street went past Southwest High School into the Tijuana River Valley, skirting the border. It was the edge of the United States, the end of the world. He drove 120 mph on the 905 westbound, passing cars like they were standing still.

Before the turnoff, he called Patrick.

"Hello?" his partner answered, sounding drunk.

"Why do you hate Santiago?"

Patrick was silent.

"I'm serious, asshole! What's your gut feeling about him?"

"I never liked him."

"No shit," Noah said, impatient. "Why?"

Patrick paused, as if reluctant to answer. "I think he's a perp," he said in a gruff voice, laying it out there.

Noah took a deep breath, trying to stay calm. "What do you mean?"

"He loves dead bodies, practically drools on rape vics. Everyone says he's so dedicated. I always thought he was a creep."

"Motherfucker!" Noah hit the brakes hard, taking a left on Hollister. "Now you tell me! Why didn't you say anything before?"

"Would you have believed me?"

"Fuck you," he said, ending the call. He slammed his palm against the steering wheel. "Fuck!"

Noah didn't see a soul on the 2000 block of Hollister,

but there was a homeless guy near the corner of Suns
and 2200. He was sitting at the side of the road, next
his overloaded bike, rifling through a small black purs

Noah squealed to a stop, getting out of his squad ca

The man's eyes were as wide as saucers. "I just four
this. I swear."

Noah took the purse away from him, glancing insid
April's cell phone and wallet were still there. "Where?"

"Right here. On the grass."

He looked down the street, seeing a sign denotir
the Tijuana River Valley regional park. It was a remo
area, encompassing several miles of marshland, use
mostly for bird-watching. "You know who dropped it

"No, sir."

"Did you see a car pass by?"

"Yeah. A nice black one. Mercedes maybe. Went tha
way." He pointed toward the park entrance.

"Thanks," Noah said, getting back inside his squa
car and making an all-units request for assistance.

He didn't answer the rash of queries that flooded th
radio, and he didn't wait for backup. Killing his head
lights and drawing his weapon, he drove down the par
road in stealth mode, searching for Santiago's car.

Santiago took her to the Tijuana Estuary.

It was a quiet nature preserve, seldom visited durin
the day. At this time of night, the place was totally dead
He pulled over in a secluded spot, parking under a dar
veil of willow branches. April stared into the blacknes
outside her window.

No one would even hear her scream.

Santiago removed a gun from the holster at his waist. "Get out."

Her stomach dropped. "You're going to let me go?"

"No. I'm going to kill you outside."

April pictured Jenny's face, and tears sprang to her eyes. She couldn't bear the thought of leaving her. "Why?"

"Easier cleanup."

"Why *me*," she clarified, frozen to the spot. If he wanted to kill her out there, she was staying right here.

"Don't you know?"

As she shook her head slowly, it dawned on her that she'd seen him with someone besides Officer Shanley. "You knew Raul. I remember you visited him once. You gave him . . . drug money."

"Hush money, actually."

"For what?"

"A deal we struck. He didn't tell you?"

"No."

Santiago seemed as calm and reserved as he had been when he'd picked her up, a nice gentleman in black-framed glasses. The contrast between his sedate expression and the deadly barrel of the gun terrified her.

He wouldn't kill her politely.

"I guess he kept the secret, after all," he mused.

"Wh-what secret?" she asked, trembling with fear.

His gaze slid down her body in a cold caress. "A long time ago, he sold me a girl from the barrio. It was a very disappointing experience. She was tainted, you see. They gang-raped her before I got there. Ruined everything."

"I'm sorry," she murmured, nauseous.

"I strangled her anyway, just for practice. It was a difficult task, and horribly unsatisfying. I didn't use her sexually. The bandanna wouldn't work. Finally I grabbed a plastic bag to finish her off. That was the only bit of serendipity."

She stared at him in horror.

"I was so disillusioned by the incident that I almost gave up my craft. For years I fantasized about killing again, doing it right this time. Working on homicide fulfilled my obsession in some ways, and I enjoyed being meticulous."

April nodded, as if she sympathized with him. In truth, she was too terrified to make sense of his words. He was so close she could see the pores in his skin, smell his antiseptic breath. Her flesh crawled at the thought of him touching her. She tried to appear serene, but her face felt numb.

At any moment he could reach out and grab her wrist. Or pull the trigger.

"After a while, the fantasies weren't enough. A few weeks ago Raul tried to extort me for more money, and that was the last straw. His crew had violated my first love, my first kill. So I decided to do the same to their loved ones."

"Raul's dead," she said, moistening her lips. "Isn't that enough?"

"No. Killing men gives me no pleasure. But you"—he pressed the gun to her head, stroking her hair with the barrel—"are very much my type."

"You killed Raul?" she whispered, cringing in fright.

"I arranged for his demise, yes."

"Please. Let me go."

He smiled indulgently. "I'll give you a head start."

April reached for the door handle. Staying inside no longer seemed like a winning strategy.

"I cherish death," he said, placing a palm over the middle of his chest. "I'm giving honor to women who had none in life."

"I'm tainted," she babbled, her sweaty fingers slipping on the handle. "You wouldn't believe how tainted I am."

"Compared to the others, you're immaculate," he said, gesturing with the revolver. "Now, run."

"Noah will come for me."

Santiago laughed. "That would be convenient for my purposes but not likely. He'll be tied up at Eric's crime scene for hours, and he has no idea where you are. We have plenty of time together."

Making a strangled sound of despair, she finally managed to lift the handle and shove the door open. She exited the vehicle, stumbling on her way out.

"I'll give you five seconds," he offered.

Her heels found unsteady purchase in the wet soil, and the smell of thick mud drifted up, dark and stagnant. Although there was no one around to hear her, April screamed. The sound was absorbed by the heavy vegetation and sultry night air.

Run!

She'd gone only a few steps when she was faced with a heart-stopping dilemma: head down the road, where she would be completely exposed, or take cover in the salt marsh, where she would most certainly get stuck.

She chose the marsh.

The path of most resistance was her only chance of escape.

Keeping most of her weight on the balls of her feet, so her heels wouldn't sink, she ran as fast as she could through the knee-high grass, gasping for breath. The blades whipped across her ankles and calves, tearing her stockings and stinging her skin.

The only trees in sight were near the road. They were too sparse to hide among, but the marsh had plenty of dips and valleys. As soon as she put some distance between them, she could drop to her belly and crawl through the grass.

At least, that was her plan.

"Time's up," he called, sending chills down her spine.

Without looking back, she knew he was closing in on her. She was sobbing out loud, crashing through the grass, incapable of fleeing quietly. Santiago, in contrast, pursued her with silent ferocity, gaining on her in strides.

Like a killing machine.

In her panic to get away, she ran harder, her chest burning from exertion. Her right heel sank into the mud, and her ankle twisted, refusing to support her.

With a sharp cry, she fell to her knees.

Knowing she had to get up and run or die now, she reached down to her throbbing ankle, trying to take off her shoes.

She'd removed only one when he tackled her at full force, knocking her flat. His body was harder than it looked, streamlined and strong. He grabbed her by the hair and shoved her face in the mud, using his weight to trap her underneath him.

April couldn't scream. She couldn't even breathe. If Santiago continued to hold her in this position, she'd lose consciousness.

But he wanted to toy with her, so he let her up.

"Bastard," she panted, spitting out mud. Dragging herself forward, she slithered like a snake in the grass, her teeth clenched with determination.

Although she knew she had little chance of survival, April refused to quit. Every abuse she'd suffered at Raul's hands came rushing back to her, driving her on.

Never again, she promised herself. Fueled by rage and adrenaline and twisted memories, she tightened her grip on her high-heeled shoe, anticipating Santiago's next move. When he grabbed her sprained ankle, squeezing so hard she screamed in pain, she turned and swung, trying to jam the spike heel into his face.

She missed. Sort of.

The heel sank into his left ear, by some sadistic miracle. He released her ankle, shrieking like a banshee.

While he jerked the shoe from his punctured eardrum, she scrambled away. The instant she came to her feet, her ankle buckled again. She cried out in agony, but she didn't stop. Having no other option, she crawled through the wet grass on her hands and knees, trembling uncontrollably.

There was a river tributary close by, a serpentine oxbow painted silver by the moonlight. Having no choice but to wade through it, she toppled over the edge, falling into the shallow stream face-first.

Cool water rushed around her, gushing into her eyes and nose. Her hands found the silt-covered bottom and she pushed herself up, sputtering. The current was too weak to take her anywhere, the water too shallow for swimming. Shoving the wet hair from her eyes, she found her feet and continued on, crawling up the opposite bank.

Santiago leapt over the narrow stream entirely. He landed on top of her with a brutal slam, knocking the wind from her lungs.

They fell back into the water together, arms and legs entwined. She tried to choke in a mouthful of air, her chest seizing.

Again he had a chance to end it. Obviously he had something else in mind, because he didn't attempt to drown her. Instead, he grabbed her by the front of her shirt, lifted her up, and backhanded her across the face.

She sagged against him, stunned by the blow.

Pushing her onto the riverbank, he climbed out, his trousers soaked. "Bitch," he panted, his black eyes glittering in the moonlight. Blood dripped from his ear, splashing her cheek. "I should just shoot you."

He started to tear off her clothes.

April felt separated from her body. Rape hadn't always been a part of Raul's repertoire, but he'd done it a few times, near the end, when his drug addiction and violent tendencies had skyrocketed. Once had been enough to devastate her.

As if she were looking down on the scene, rather than experiencing it firsthand, she watched Santiago take some crumpled plastic from his pocket. Before she had a chance to react, he put the bag over her head and twisted it around her neck, cutting off her air supply.

The action jolted her back to reality.

Although her mind screamed in protest and her lungs strained for oxygen, she forced herself to lie still. He held the bag at her neck with one hand and unfastened his pants with the other. She couldn't reach his gun or her other shoe, so she felt around on the ground, searching for a rock to brain him with.

Nothing.

She let her head loll to the side, pretending to pass out. The instant he loosened his grip on the bag, bracing his weight on one arm to guide himself into her, she struck with the only weapon she had: her fists.

Tearing the plastic away from her face, she boxed his bloodied ear repeatedly, hitting him with all of her might.

Perhaps his equilibrium was off, because the blows affected him more than she'd anticipated. Seeming disoriented, he slumped sideways. She scrambled out from underneath him, feeling a surge of energy.

When he tried to catch her ankle, she kicked him in the teeth with her remaining heel. Roaring in pain, he fell back into the tributary.

Yanking her shoe off but keeping it clenched in her fist, she rose to her feet, struggling for breath. She half-ran, half-limped through the thick marsh, heading back toward the road, her heart thundering in her chest.

Jenny. She had to live, for Jenny.

Santiago came out of the water, cursing her. No longer interested in savoring his kill, he started to shoot.

———

Noah spotted Santiago's car parked at the side of the road. Gun drawn, he got out to search the immediate area.

The grass was bent in a telltale formation, creating a disturbance that led away from the vehicle into the salt marsh.

Blood pumping with fear and fury, Noah followed the trampled grass, moving swiftly. Less than a hundred feet in, he heard the shots.

About a quarter mile away, a muzzle flashed.

"No," he yelled, taking off at a dead run. He cut through the grass like a knife, pursuing the source of the flash.

When he caught up to Santiago, he was going to empty his clip in him. A thousand deaths wouldn't be enough.

More shots rang out, and he heard a woman scream.

He looked around for her, his chest bursting with hope. "April!"

She was between him and the shooter, flat on her belly in the thick grass. Smart girl. Her eyes were wide with fright, she was covered in mud, and her hair was wet, but she was alive. Thank God, she was alive.

Santiago staggered toward her, holding his revolver steady. His face looked maniacal, his eyes wild.

Noah kept running forward, meeting him head-on. "Drop your weapon!" he said, entering Santiago's range. Noah was wearing a bulletproof vest, a required component of his uniform, while the other man was in plain clothes. "Stop or I'll shoot!"

Santiago paused, considering.

"Put the gun down," Noah shouted, holding his ground.

His former idol nodded his acquiescence. With slow deliberation, he bent forward, making a show of setting the gun aside.

A month ago, Noah might have relaxed his stance and taken the move at face value. Most of the time, a suspect complied with police. He had made it a point, over the course of his career, to treat even the most dangerous criminals with courtesy. Excessive force wasn't necessary.

This situation was different. Santiago's crimes had been shockingly violent, and he'd fooled an entire department of officers. Noah believed him capable of anything. The close call with Tony Castillo had also taught him to never let down his guard.

So he didn't.

When the gun was just inches from the grass, Santiago pointed the muzzle in Noah's direction and pulled the trigger.

Noah didn't hesitate to return fire. He squeezed off five shots, several of which struck his intended target.

Santiago fell back in the grass, motionless.

His bullet had hit Noah's left upper arm, tearing through his uniform biceps. Ignoring the sting of pain, he gestured for April to stay put and strode forward, taking his flashlight from his utility belt. Holding it in tandem with his Glock, he approached the fallen man with extreme caution.

Santiago wasn't breathing. There were four bullet holes in his upper chest, and they weren't even bleeding. He'd been dead before he hit the ground.

Noah checked his pulse, just to make sure, and touched the radio at his shoulder, notifying dispatch of an officer down.

When he turned to look for April, she was limping toward him, tears streaming down her face. Her hair was straggly, her clothes were torn, and her stockings hung in tatters from her mud-streaked legs.

He'd never been so happy to see anyone in his entire life.

Running forward, he swept her into his embrace, feeling blood seep from the wound on his arm and hot pressure behind his eyes.

God. He loved her so much.

She sobbed in his arms, overwrought. "I thought I was going to die. I thought I'd never see you or Jenny again!"

"Shh," he said, kissing the top of her head, fighting his own tears. "You're safe now."

She continued to cry, holding him tight.

"Are you okay?" he said, pulling back to study her face. Her cheek was ruddy and she had marks across her throat. "Did he rape you?"

"No. I—I got away."

He hugged her again, overwhelmed with love and pride and relief. She felt so damned small in his arms, yet she'd fought like a wildcat and given a serial killer a run for his money. "You're amazing, do you know that?"

She touched his wet arm, frowning. "This is a gunshot wound."

"Yes," he agreed. Now that he thought about it, he felt a little dizzy. "I probably need to get it looked at."

Her teary eyes widened. *"Ave Maria Purísima,"* she said, recovering from her emotions. "Lie down."

While he stretched out on his back, she ripped the already torn fishnet from around her thigh and took it off, wrapping the stocking around his upper arm. "I love it when you speak Spanish," he murmured, finding her impossibly sexy and resourceful.

"You called for backup, right?"

"Mmm-hmm."

"Noah!"

"What?" he asked, opening his eyes.

She was hovering over him, nibbling her lush lower lip. "I love you."

He smiled wryly. "I should get shot more often."

"Don't say that! I'm so sorry I pushed you away, and tried to start fights, and slapped you in the kitchen. I've been such a fool. Please don't die!"

"I'm not going to die," he said, gaping at her. "This is nothing."

"Are you sure?"

"Yes. Come here."

She leaned in closer, her attention rapt.

He lifted his right hand, cupping the back of her head. "I love you, too," he said, bringing her lips to his. Sobbing, she wrapped her arms around him and returned his kiss, while a dozen squad cars descended on the scene, sirens blaring.

27

After he received treatment, Eric was taken to a dark hospital room, where he drifted in and out of consciousness for hours.

In the morning, he awoke to a throbbing body and a clear head. Before he opened his eyes, he cataloged his injuries. His ribs were bandaged tightly across his upper chest, and the laceration on his left side ached. When he tried to reach across to feel the stitches, he realized that his right hand was wrapped in gauze.

He moaned, because trying to move hurt. From the corner of the room, he heard a nondescript sound, like a book closing.

"Eric?"

It was Meghan.

His face felt magnified, grotesque. He wanted to explore the injuries above his shoulders, too, but he was afraid of what he'd find. Very gingerly, he opened his eyes. Well, one eye. The other was taped.

He needed a few seconds to orient himself. Everything was fuzzy. Both of his eye sockets ached and had certainly been blackened. Some kind of ointment clung to his lashes, obscuring his vision.

Meghan came up next to him. He blinked a few times, and her features came into focus. "Eric?"

He tried to speak, but his throat was too dry.

She grabbed a cup from his bedside and brought the straw to his lips. He drank a little, feeling incredibly weak and awkward. She set the cup aside and took his left hand, watching him with a troubled expression.

"How do I look?" he rasped.

"Awful."

He closed his eye, resting. "Touch my side," he said after a moment. "Describe it to me."

Frowning, she tugged the blanket down to his waist, inspecting him. Her fingertips were cool against his skin. "There's a large white bandage covering the wound."

"Fuck."

"The doctor said your eye will be fine. As soon as the swelling goes down, they'll remove the gauze."

Eric was more concerned about the rest of his body. He felt as if he'd been thrown from a moving vehicle. "I have to take a piss."

"Oh! I'll find the nurse."

"No, wait. I think I can get up."

With her help, he lumbered to his feet. His legs held his weight, so the short trip to the bathroom was uneventful. Not bothering to close the door, he braced his injured hand on the sink and relieved himself awkwardly with his left. Pissing didn't hurt, and his male parts seemed to be in working order. Good to know.

Meghan assisted him back to bed, her cheeks flushed pink. "Better now?"

"Yeah," he said, wincing at the pain in his side as he reclined against the pillows again. "Am I under arrest?"

She nodded, her bangs falling over her eyes. "Unfortunately, yes. There's an officer stationed outside your door."

"What's the charge?"

"I don't know. Noah's here, being treated for a gunshot wound—"

"What? When did that happen?"

Meghan told him that April had been taken out to the salt marsh by the killer, Detective Victor Santiago. Noah went to rescue her and was shot in the process. Apparently the information Eric gave him helped to solve the case, and save April's life.

"Is he okay?"

"Oh, yes. He says it's just a scratch."

"What about April?"

"Her ankle is sprained, but she's fine otherwise. She was here earlier, with Jenny. You were asleep. Anyway, Noah told me you needed a lawyer. With the beating you suffered, and the first stab wound, of course, it's an obvious case of self-defense."

"No," he said immediately. "It isn't."

"What do you mean?"

"I agreed to the fight, Meghan. I threw the first punch. And I killed him."

"Who pulled the knife, Eric?"

He didn't answer.

"There are witnesses."

"A group of rival gang members who would never testify on my behalf."

She moistened her lips. "Noah gave a sworn statement. He thinks that your assistance in capturing the serial killer will make a difference with the DA. At the very least, the charges will be reduced, and you can have your say in court—"

"No," he interrupted, startling her with his vehemence. "I won't."

"Eric, if you plead guilty to murder, you'll get twenty-five years. Minimum."

He sighed, letting his head fall back against the pillow.

"On Monday, you can talk to a lawyer. Get this sorted out."

Eric didn't argue with her. There was nothing else to say. He would go to jail—and then on to prison. Eastside would be gunning for him. *Dos Emes* would approach him.

He had a future with the prison gang or none at all.

"April called your mother," she said finally.

"Shit," he groaned, closing his eye. He couldn't imagine what his mother was going through. One son not even buried yet, the other in the hospital, under arrest. "I have to go to Raul's funeral."

"When is it?"

"Tomorrow."

"I'll ask Noah what arrangements can be made," she promised, staring at him solemnly. "Do you want me to stay with you for a little while?"

"Yes," he said, his voice hoarse. "Please."

She sat in the chair at his bedside, holding his left

hand. After a few minutes, she rested her head on his thigh, hot tears spilling down her cheeks. He stroked her hair, comforting her as well as he could, but he didn't tell her not to cry.

If his eyes weren't so fucked up, he'd join her.

28
Epilogue

Noah took April and Jenny home for Thanksgiving.

She was nervous about meeting his family, so he promised a short visit. They would arrive this afternoon, have dinner, and spend the night—in separate bedrooms. The next morning, they would leave.

Meghan agreed to the plan readily, also preferring a quick stay.

Over the past few months, April and Meghan had grown close. They talked about Eric, and Meghan had even mentioned the sexual assault he'd saved her from. She admitted that she was reluctant to tell her mother about the incident.

April had hugged her, trying to give support instead of advice.

Meghan had also become fond of Jenny. She'd offered to babysit her for free. Noah said he would consider it work for rent, and April acquiesced easily. The arrangement was convenient and comfortable for all.

Now she and Jenny both slept over several nights a week.

Noah recovered from his gunshot wound quickly, and April's ankle was better in a few days. They spent a dreamy week together, lazing about on the beach. Then Jenny started kindergarten, and April went back to work. Her classes at San Diego State, which had also commenced, were both interesting and challenging.

Life was good. For the most part.

Josefa must not have hit rock bottom, because she was still up to her old tricks. April saw her at the club on rare occasions. She was hoping her mother would take the necessary steps to get sober, but she wasn't holding her breath.

And Eric . . . She wept for Eric.

Meghan had begged him not to plead guilty. April had asked him to reconsider. Even Noah had gone to visit him, speaking about the realities for a nice-looking boy in prison. Eric had refused to be swayed.

In a last-ditch effort to get through to him, April used her trump card: Jenny. She wanted Eric in her daughter's life, and she wouldn't let Jenny visit him behind bars. He finally agreed to plea-bargain for a lesser charge, voluntary manslaughter. The penalty for that crime carried a mandatory three years in prison, but he could do as many as eleven.

They had their fingers crossed for a light sentence.

Any amount of time in prison would be difficult for Eric, of course. April worried that he would need gang protection to survive, and wondered if he no longer valued his life. He'd been so emotionally detached since his arrest, ignoring his family members, ending his relationship with Meghan.

The breakup was in Meghan's best interests, of course, but April's heart ached for them both. Meghan was desperately in love with Eric, and he obviously felt the same way. She'd been listless and depressed. Although Noah was concerned about his sister's well-being, he'd never approved of the relationship and was relieved they were no longer together. He thought Meghan would get over Eric in a few more weeks.

April wasn't so sure.

Before they arrived in Cedar Glen, Noah stopped at an apple orchard so they could stretch their legs. Jenny was delighted by the prospect of picking her own apples. When April nodded her permission, Meghan grabbed a bushel and they raced into the orchard together, looking for the best trees.

April smiled at the sight of the two girls, one light-haired, the other dark, running hand in hand.

"I think she's been good for Meghan," Noah said.

"Meghan has definitely been good for Jenny." Noah's sister hadn't exactly replaced Josefa, and no one could fill the hole that Eric left, but Jenny adored Meghan. She spoke of the older girl incessantly and hung on her every word.

Noah had been good for Jenny, too. His easy affection for her daughter made April love him all the more.

She crossed her arms over her chest and looked around, enjoying the brisk air and bright sunshine. The apple orchard was like something out of a picture, with rolling hills, fruit-laden trees, and snowcapped mountains in the distance.

"How close is Cedar Glen?" she asked.

"Another half hour. What do you think?"

"It's beautiful."

"Would you like to live here?"

She glanced at him, surprised. He wasn't just making idle conversation. "Would you?"

He shrugged, shoving his hands in his pockets. "I'd rather live in Chula Vista. Or any good-size city with a homicide department. But I can always commute, and this is a great place to raise a family."

She couldn't guess what he was thinking. He looked so charming in this storybook setting, with his nice wool sweater and sincere blue eyes. "I'm already raising a family," she reminded him, tilting her head to one side.

The corner of his mouth tipped up. "And doing a fine job."

She waited for him to continue, bemused.

He cleared his throat. "Assuming you want to stay in Chula Vista for the time being, Meghan and I . . . well, we talked the other day, and you know she adores Jenny. We'd like you to move in with us. Jenny could take the upstairs bedroom."

April moistened her lips, her mind racing. "Where would Meghan go?"

"The den. It's a bigger space, actually, and more private."

April didn't know what to say. Moving was a huge decision for her. It would involve a school transfer for Jenny.

"I hate to see you struggling to make ends meet, April. I know you're exhausted, and you can barely keep up with your homework. If you moved in with me, you could quit your job and concentrate on school."

Her stomach twisted with unease. "Are you embarrassed of what I do?"

"No! You're a damned good waitress, and you work your ass off. I'm proud of you."

She relaxed a little. "I wouldn't mind working fewer nights."

"I'm going to do another year on the gang unit, anyway, so I'll be working nights myself."

"When did you decide that?"

"Just recently. Santiago's team is still recovering from his loss, and they would have trouble accepting me right now. Also, though I hate admitting that Patrick is right, I could probably use some more patrol experience."

"This is very sudden," she murmured.

He cupped his hand around her face, looking into her eyes. "April, you're the one. I want to spend the rest of my life with you. But I'm willing to start slow."

"Moving in together after three months isn't starting slow!"

"It's slower than an engagement ring."

She froze, realizing that this moment was even bigger than she thought.

Noah muttered something like *screw it* and got down on one knee. Taking a black velvet box out of his pocket, he opened it. She saw a sparkling white diamond on a slim platinum ring.

"Oh, my God," she said, her mouth trembling.

"Will you make me the happiest man in the world and say you'll be my wife?"

"Oh, my God," she repeated, looking around. Meghan was still picking apples with Jenny, watching them out of the corner of her eye.

"We don't have to get married right away," he promised. "But I would love to introduce you to my family as my fiancée."

"You just want to sleep in my room tonight!"

He laughed out loud, almost falling sideways in the autumn leaves. "I can't say the possibility didn't cross my mind," he said, eyes twinkling. "It's going to take years to hit the thousand mark you asked for, and I need all the opportunities I can get."

April removed the ring from the box with shaking hands and slipped it on her finger. Her throat closed up as she looked from the glittering stone to his handsome face. She nodded. It was the least cautious, most wonderful thing she'd ever done.

He leapt to his feet, wrapping his arms around her. "Yes? You said yes?"

She smiled through her tears. "You didn't think I would?"

"I thought you'd come around eventually, not the first time I asked!"

"Well, now you're stuck."

He swallowed, visibly choked up. "I love you."

She touched his face. "I love you, too, Noah."

He dipped his head to kiss her, and she melted against him, twining her arms around his neck, reveling in the warmth of his embrace. By the time the kiss ended, Meghan and Jenny were standing there with a bushel of red apples, their cheeks flushed.

"She said yes," Noah explained.

Jenny didn't have any idea what April had agreed to, but Meghan did, and her joy was infectious. She picked up Jenny and twirled her around the orchard, their laughing faces turned toward the sun.

Please read on for an exciting sneak peek of

Jill Sorenson's next sizzling novel,

coming soon from Bantam Books.

1

Karina Strauss approached the San Ysidro border crossing at a snail's pace, her cargo van idling among a thousand other vehicles.

There were twenty-four lanes on the Tijuana side, a massive snarl of traffic that found order in the last hundred yards. Before the inspection booths were visible, the dividing lines were ignored. Cars lurched forward in semi-regular intervals. While the most aggressive drivers cut in ahead of others, zigzagging through the chaos, street vendors walked up and down the narrow aisles, selling everything from *chicle* and cold drinks to silver jewelry and colorful hammocks. As always, the peddlers included elderly women, disabled men, and children whose shoulders barely cleared the hoods of cars.

Kari let out a slow breath, removing her sweaty hands from the steering wheel. She'd turned off the air-conditioning and rolled down the windows in hopes that her van wouldn't overheat. At just past noon, the summer sun was blazing. Her left shoulder, exposed by her sleeveless cotton top, felt burned.

As the crush of vehicles evened into single rows,

Kari became aware of impatient drivers angling toward the right. Her lane seemed more backed up than the others—not a good sign. Some of the inspectors were very thorough, checking the contents of each and every car. Normally, she appreciated their diligence.

Today she was desperate for lax security.

She put on her signal and tried to merge into the next lane, with no luck. A woman in a midsize sedan stole the spot, her radio blaring Juan Gabriel.

The space in front of Kari cleared and she was forced to move ahead in the same lane. Now there were only a few cars between her and the inspection booth. She met her startled reflection in the rearview mirror, swallowing dryly. Her heart slammed in her chest, beating too hard, too fast.

Stay calm, she told herself. Act cool.

The officer stationed at the booth ahead didn't appear lax in any way. His dark blue uniform fit well. He had short black hair and a stern face. She couldn't see his eyes behind the lenses of his authoritative sunglasses, but she'd bet they were brown.

Kari watched the man walk around a dusty Oldsmobile, gesturing for the owner to open the trunk. His short-sleeved shirt stretched across his back as he leaned forward to glance into the trunk's recesses. He looked strong, broad-shouldered, bronze-skinned. There was nothing unusual about him other than an eye-pleasing physique, but she sensed that he was sharp and precise.

Sweat trickled between her breasts.

Too nervous to sit still, she unfastened the top buttons on her blouse, searching the interior of the cab for a tissue to blot her nervous perspiration.

The line crawled forward again. Damn!

She used the hem of her skirt to wipe her chest and left the buttons undone. Maybe she could entice the inspector to look down her shirt rather than inside her vehicle. Tapping the gas pedal, she eased the van closer.

She'd been waiting in traffic for over an hour and the final moments were the most intense. Blood pounded in her ears, her temple, her throat. She took a small sip of water and fiddled with the radio, trying to disguise her fear. Her pulse was racing, her hands trembling. She didn't dare glance back into the cargo space.

At last, it was her turn. She pulled up to the inspection booth, which was underneath a shaded structure, and prayed for a wave-through.

"Citizenship?"

"U.S.," she murmured, handing him her passport. Most of the stamps marked her visits to Mexico. Others were from the Czech Republic, where she'd been born. She watched him handle her paperwork, fixating on the almost indiscernible grain of stubble along his jaw, the smoothness of his taut brown throat.

Officer A. Cortez, the name tag on his shirtfront read. He was Hispanic, but that didn't relax her. There was no room for mixed sympathies in his profession.

"Anything to declare?" he asked.

She fumbled for her inventory list. His voice was low and even, no trace of an accent. He was also disturbingly handsome. As she passed him the handwritten account of the items in her van—well, *most* of the items—she remembered her gaping blouse. The flat expression on his face suggested that he'd noticed, but wasn't impressed.

"It's all just stuff for my store," she explained, flush-ing. "Zócalo, on E Street?"

His gaze dropped to the insignia on the side of her van. *Authentic Arts and Crafts from Latin America*. The accompanying image was whimsical, a dancing skele-ton in a sombrero. In Mexico, even death was a fiesta.

"Please turn off the engine and step outside of the vehicle."

She nodded, curbing the urge to ask if she'd done something wrong. Better to stay mum. With numb fingers, she removed the keys from the ignition and opened the driver's side door. The instant she climbed out, her rubber flip-flops soaked up the heat of the as-phalt and a warm breeze rippled through her calf-length skirt.

She followed Officer Cortez to the rear of the vehicle, her heart in her throat.

"Open the doors, please."

Oh, God. What could she do? Refusing to cooperate was not an option.

As she approached the double doors on shaky legs, her keys slid from her slippery grip, clattering to the pavement. She bent to pick them up, aware that her thin cotton skirt was clinging to her backside.

Straightening, she unlocked the doors. Her eyes had trouble adjusting to the dim interior, but she could make out a few shadowy boxes and piles of textiles, her usual haul. She stepped aside, not allowing her gaze to linger.

Cortez glanced into the cargo space and then squinted down the line of cars, assessing the rows of vehicles. When he looked back at her, she shifted her weight from one foot to the other, self-conscious. He touched the radio at his shoulder and spoke into it, engaging in a clipped conversation she couldn't overhear.

Kari had to do something to distract him from the contents of her van. As he dropped his hand from the radio, she saw that he wasn't wearing a wedding ring. He had a lean, muscular build, and he was medium-tall, maybe six feet. Under different circumstances, she wouldn't have to feign interest.

"This must be an exciting job," she ventured, trying to sound fascinated.

He perused the cargo. "It has its moments."

"Have you handled any big loads?"

That got his attention. He gave her a bald look, obviously wondering if she meant to be suggestive.

She smiled, fanning her cleavage with one hand. "Hot, isn't it?"

Behind the dark lenses of his sunglasses, his eyes followed her movements. Although she'd dressed for comfort, not seduction, the outfit flattered her figure. Most men liked breasts, and hers were half-showing. Cortez was also fairly young, which worked in her favor. He might be an exemplary officer, but he wasn't immune to the stuff.

To her disappointment, he tore his gaze from her chest and continued the routine inspection, a muscle in his jaw flexing.

Her mind whirred with ridiculous options, like pretending to faint on the hot blacktop. Then a loud noise stole Cortez's attention. Several lanes over, a trio of vicious-looking German Shepherds were barking up a storm, straining at their leashes.

Alerting officers of illegal cargo.

Officer Cortez stepped away from her vehicle. "Have a nice day, ma'am," he said, handing back her paperwork. After calling for another uniformed man to cover his station, he walked toward the commotion in long strides.

Kari shut the back doors of the van, dizzy with relief. She walked around the driver's side and got in, ears peeled for shouts to halt. Thankfully, they didn't come. She turned on the engine and pulled forward, crossing the border into San Diego. Clear, organized roadways and a clean ocean breeze greeted her.

Freedom.

She stepped on the gas and inhaled deeply, letting the wind whip through her shoulder-length hair. Even after she'd gone a few miles, her heart wouldn't stop racing. She didn't dare glance back into the cargo space for fear she was being followed.

"Oh my God," she said finally, holding her palm to her forehead. "That was close."

Normally she went straight to her store, which was near Old Town, to unload the van. Today she drove to her quiet little house in Bonita. The tiny San Diego suburb was only a ten-minute trip from the San Ysidro port of entry. As soon as she came to a stop in her driveway, she scrambled into the cargo space, wading through cardboard boxes.

She tore open the largest box. "Maria?"

Her stowaway was hidden in a very cramped space, her slender limbs contorted in an uncomfortable position. As Kari lifted the top flaps of cardboard, Maria moaned, insensible. Her eyes were closed, her head lolled to one side.

"Oh shit," Kari cried, grabbing her bottled water. The box must have been hot, stuffy, and intensely claustrophobic. She poured water on the young woman's dark hair, trying to rouse her. Maria choked and sputtered, shaking her wet head. Kari put her arms around Maria and heaved, pulling the woman from the box. Although Maria was slender, she weighed at least a hundred pounds, and Kari could barely lift her.

For a moment, they lay together on the woven blankets, panting from exertion.

"*Aire,*" Maria rasped. "I need air."

Kari leapt to her feet and shoved open the back doors, glancing around the deserted neighborhood. There was a car she'd never seen before parked across the street, but it was empty. "This way," she said, helping Maria out of the van. They stumbled across the driveway and collapsed on the front lawn.

Maria rolled onto her stomach and retched, her slim back bowed, her arms trembling.

Kari retrieved her bottled water from the van and waited for the woman's nausea to pass, cringing with sympathy.

After a moment, Maria straightened, wiping her mouth with her hand. She accepted the water and took a small sip, studying their surroundings with wet eyes. Her gaze moved from the vibrant green blades of grass beneath her to Kari's front door. "This is your house?" she asked, pronouncing "this" as "thees" and "your" as "jour."

Kari smiled, finding her accent charming. "Yes. Do you like it?"

"It's beautiful," she said, tears spilling down her cheeks.

Kari glanced around the front yard, surprised. The neighborhood was middle class, at best, and her house a modest two-bedroom. It was Maria who was beautiful, with her lovely dark hair and serene smile. She had a slightly crooked tooth in front, a tiny imperfection that added to her appeal.

They'd met in La Bufadora, a poverty-stricken tourist spot near Ensenada. Powerful waves met steep cliffs there, creating a gust of ocean spray known as "the Blowhole." Kari bought crafts from the local women, but she also dropped off donations. She'd been a volunteer for a charity organization called Hands Across the Border for years, delivering clothes and school supplies to the needy.

Maria worked mornings at a nearby hotel and afternoons at a pottery kiln. The black volcanic sand of La Bufadora formed a very unique type of clay, and Kari was happy to pay a good price for one-of-a-kind creations. Whenever Kari came to the kiln, Maria went out of her way to accommodate her. She was charming and loquacious, a natural saleswoman. Over time, the two women had become friends.

Kari knew that Maria was supporting her widowed mother and younger siblings. Last week, over lunch, Maria had confessed that her family was in dire straits. Her sister needed medical treatment and her brother, who was only fourteen, was threatening to cross the border to find work. Maria had begged Kari for a ride to the U.S. In San Diego, she could make a week's wages in a single day. The extra money would go a long way.

Kari looked Maria in the eye, preparing to say no. She couldn't save the world. It wasn't possible to assist every person in need, and trafficking was against the law. But there was something special about Maria, an inner strength. She was desperate, and she was determined. Kari had heard the horror stories about single women who attempted to immigrate illegally, and she feared for Maria's safety.

Besides, Kari found it impossible to turn her back on a friend in need. Hoping she wasn't making the biggest mistake of her life, she said yes. They planned for Kari to transport Maria the following week. Today, as Kari was loading up her van, Maria had grabbed a beat-up duffel bag and climbed aboard.

"You've never been to the U.S. before?" Kari asked.

"Just once," she said, her smile fading. "I walked through the desert with a group. It was a long journey."

"What happened?"

She swallowed a few times, as if sickened anew by the memory. "I got separated from the others at night. I was lost for many days, I think. *La migra* picked me up and sent me back to Mexico."

The story wasn't at all uncommon. Dozens of illegal immigrants died every year making the same arduous trek.

Kari had never imagined that she was capable of smuggling a human being. Although she wouldn't choose to repeat the experience, she couldn't regret her decision. Maria reminded her of Sasha. She sensed a hint of sadness behind that disarming smile. Kari couldn't help her troubled sister; maybe she could help Maria.

"*Muchísimas gracias*," Maria said, giving Kari an enthusiastic hug. "I have waited years to return to the U.S.

I am so happy to be here, to find work and send money to my family. You are angel from heaven. God bless you."

Kari accepted the embrace awkwardly, remembering the last time she'd hugged Sasha. Her sister had tensed, holding herself at a distance. For years, Sasha had been closed off from Kari emotionally, a stranger with a familiar face.

When they broke apart, Maria noticed Kari's dishabille. "Your blouse needs repair. I will sew for you."

"Oh, no," Kari said, blushing as she buttoned up. "It's fine. I was just trying to distract the vehicle inspector."

Her elegant brows rose. "It worked, yes?"

"Maybe," she allowed, thinking about Officer Cortez's searing gaze. Hundreds of officers guarded the San Ysidro port of entry; she doubted she'd see him again. "What are your plans, now that you're here?"

The young woman shrugged. "Find job."

"Do you need to use the phone?"

"I have no one to call. I don't know anyone here."

Kari stared at her, incredulous. "Where will you stay?"

Maria smiled. "Good question."

"How old are you?"

"Twenty-four."

Sasha's age. Maria looked about eighteen, far too young to be wandering the streets, and much too pretty to go unnoticed. Kari didn't want her sleeping on a sidewalk. "Why don't you stay here? I have an extra bedroom."

It was meant for her sister, of course. Kari had finally come to terms with the fact that Sasha wasn't going to leave her drug lord boyfriend.

Maria's jaw dropped. "A bedroom? For me only?"

Kari nodded. "It's nothing fancy, a small bed and some basic furnishings. Would you like to come in and see?"

"How much I pay?"

She wondered what amount sounded reasonable. The house had been a bank foreclosure, and a steal, so her living costs were low, and Zócalo was turning a comfortable profit. "Half of the utilities," she said. "But don't worry about it until you get a job."

Maria was already on her feet, eyes bright with excitement. "I do housework. Laundry your clothes. Whatever you need."

Kari laughed, closing up her van and walking toward the front door. During the summer months, she worked about sixty hours a week at the store, so she wouldn't mind a little help around the house. "Can you cook?"

"Oh, *sí*," Maria said. "Anything you like."

They were discussing plans for lunch as Kari unlocked the door. The instant she crossed the threshold, a dark figure leapt out at her. Before she could draw a breath to scream, the man slammed her against the wall and pressed the cold barrel of a gun to her cheek.

Adam Cortez had been propositioned at the border before.

Every CBP officer had seen more than his share of exposed flesh and sultry smiles. Sometimes it was silly teenagers, coming back from a wild night on Avenida Revolución, Tijuana's underage party central.

A more disturbing trend was for the Mexican cartels to use pretty girls as decoys. While a couple of slack-jawed officers were gaping at young ladies in short skirts and low-cut tops, they smuggled a shipment through another lane. Officers were trained to be aware of these tactics and respond accordingly.

Adam hadn't responded accordingly to Karina Strauss. Yes, she had a knockout body, and her unbuttoned blouse invited a man to take a closer look, but he shouldn't have surrendered to temptation. Of course it had occurred to him that she was acting suspicious, attempting to divert his attention. Especially when the dogs alerted to narcotics down the line. He shouldn't have let her go.

And he definitely shouldn't have used government resources to do a background check on her *after* he clocked out for the day.

Karina Strauss had made quite an impression on him. It wasn't her low neckline or her clumsy attempt at flirting that had captured his interest, although he'd certainly noticed both. What stopped him dead in his tracks was the familiar name—Strauss—and her arresting face.

Her sister, Sasha, was a platinum blonde, and thin to the point of emaciation these days, but the resemblance was striking. They both had the same exotic Eastern European looks, though Sasha was flashier. Karina had a quieter, girl-next-door appeal. With her honey-colored hair and sun-kissed skin, she was a natural beauty.

Sasha had a couple of marks on her record for drug possession and public intoxication, but Karina had never been arrested. That didn't mean she was innocent, just that she hadn't been caught.

Adam wondered if the siblings had similar lifestyles. Sasha was the longtime girlfriend of Carlos Moreno, a Mexican-born drug lord. He'd seen her with the crew leader on numerous occasions, making the rounds at nightclubs, partying like a rock star. As far as Adam knew, Sasha wasn't involved in the smuggling operation.

Was Karina on Moreno's payroll? She made frequent trips across the border, supposedly to buy items for her store. It was a good cover.

He stared at the information on the computer screen in front of him, which included her home address. The next logical step would be to take his suspicions to the investigations unit and let them do their job. Carlos Moreno had a very high profile. The DEA, ATF, and CBP all wanted a piece of him.

Adam wanted a piece of him, too.

A rap at the open door startled him out of his reverie. It was Officer Pettigrew, his superior. "What's up?"

"Nothing much," he said quickly, closing the screen he was viewing. "Just a routine background check."

Pettigrew gave him a bland smile. "See you tomorrow."

Adam logged off the computer and pushed away from the desk, his mind in turmoil. For several years, he'd done unofficial surveillance on Moreno, waiting for an opportunity to get close to him. He'd spent too many nights chasing shadows, seething in solitude. At long last, he'd abandoned the pursuit.

Seeing Karina Strauss had taken him back to a very dark place.

He knew he should file a report on her and walk away. Instead, he decided not to mention their chance meeting to anyone. Pulse pounding, he left the San Ysidro port of entry and headed north, filled with thoughts of a violent retribution.